Air Like Champagne

A Novel of Victoria

Victoria Station, 1880

Photo courtesy of the Kansas State Historical Society

Air Like Champagne

A Novel of Victoria

by Anne Windholz

Aeolian Press, Bartlett, IL

Air Like Champagne

CONTENTS

PART I

Go from me. Yet I feel that I shall stand
Henceforward in thy shadow. Nevermore
Alone upon the threshold of my door
Of individual life, I shall command
The uses of my soul, nor lift my hand
Serenely in the sunshine as before,
Without the sense of that which I forbore –
Thy touch upon the palm. The widest land
Doom takes to part us, leaves thy heart in mine
With pulses that beat double. What I do
And what I dream include thee, as the wine
Must taste of its own grapes. And when I sue
God for myself, He hears that name of thine,
And sees within my eyes the tears of two.

Elizabeth Barrett Browning
Sonnets from the Portuguese

Prologue

Surely the clock made it happen. Her mother's, with gold tracery and ebony hands. Carefully, even tenderly, Beryl wound it each night. Then, returning to her room with a candle, she lay under the blankets and listened.

She listened as its tidy, precise heartbeat punctuated the darkness. Dignified, it ticked from one moment to the next with no doubts, no worrying questions of meaning or utility. It did as it was bid by the winding of a key, measuring life in teaspoons of sound. Outside, the wind wheeled and whispered through streets and trees. Inside and sleepless, Beryl contended against intricate sinews of seconds, minutes, and hours.

She refused to take it with her, despite Marian's protestations. Let an ocean wash away its voice. She would go where she could breathe. Where she could run.

Chapter I

No one in the rail car spoke. The day was Sunday, but this was no sabbath quiet. All the earlier laughing and joking had stopped. Sleeping children sighed. A match flashed as a man lit his pipe. A two-year-old whimpered. Someone cut the pages of a book at regular intervals, but then that discreet tearing also stopped. Everyone was watching. Waiting.

The train headed into a westering sun that made woodwork gleam and curtains glow red as they framed the passing landscape. The view changed constantly but varied little. Still, the men and women gazed at it with strangely alert eyes. Every hill (these were rare), every tree (these were rarer), and every cloud in that unspeakably wide sky was registered and filed away. Certain images compelled immediate attention: a dead and bloated horse, legs sticking up towards the carrion-eaters that circled and descended; a grassy rise startlingly adorned with a yellow door and glass windows; and, leaning against the side of a weathered and solitary shanty, a motionless woman, faceless in a bonnet that extended absurdly beyond the end of her nose.

Beryl looked, her own face still. Unconsciously, her gloved hand touched the delicate construction of net and feathers resting on her head. She never turned her grey eyes from the window. That bonneted mannequin was the only woman she had seen out the window for what felt like hundreds of miles.

After Ellsworth, the land became flatter, the grasses shorter, the shadows longer. The train, despite its elegant passenger compartment and self-important whistle, felt insignificant in the immensity of space. Sparks flew from its wheels, losing themselves in the yellow blossoms that clustered a few feet from the rails. Beryl wished the clatter would cease. Her head ached. They passed over a skeletal trestle that spanned a dry creek bed. The noise crescendoed and then subsided again. In its wake she heard Neil Hunter say to Mr. Grant, "Around here, wasn't it?"

Grant nodded. "Aye."

Douglas Keith turned. "What?"

Hunter answered. "Couple of railroad workers massacred by Indians. Unarmed men. Several others wounded." A rifle rested in his hands. When he had boarded the boat, his people had pressed it on him. "For killing savages, Neil," they had said.

"When was this?"

"Oh, three, four years ago."

Beryl turned to look back at the creek, the shadows falling across it, the lonely trestle. She thought of Mr. Davis, Grant's foreman, and Mr. Staples who was with him. They were alone somewhere on that plain, driving supplies overland to Victoria. Facing around again, her eyes met those of Lydia Randall. Lydia's husband had his arm around her. Under his breath, he swore.

The engine whistled and began to slow. Against the flat horizon, a large station house came into view. Rainwater barrels stood under two windows that flanked a stack of shipping boxes. A small, straw-haired boy with a black dog sat on top of them. The station master, emerging to greet the train, warned him to stay away from the platform's edge. By the door, above another window, a sign proclaimed "RUSSELL." Beryl stood to let in fresh air. She noticed a bay horse tethered on one side of the building, a checkered tea towel blowing out of an open window. The air smelled of dust and soot.

As the car lurched to its stop, she stumbled against her seat. Mr. Cabot, sitting behind her, caught her arm to help steady her. In London such courtesy might have provoked embarrassed blushes and chivalrous attentions; for Cabot, such situations were always charged with potential conquest. In this case, however, both parties were too preoccupied to heed each other. Beryl murmured a distracted "thank you" but her attention was given to what she saw through the windows across the aisle: a few – a very few – frame houses the color of fresh, unpainted wood; a false-fronted grocer's; and a muddy road that ran off into windy prairie.

Cabot spoke to the porter. "Excuse me, my good man, but could you tell me how far we are from Victoria Station?"

"Less than twenty miles now, sir. Next stop, in fact."

A low current of exclamation ran through the car. The few women sat straighter, smoothed rumpled skirts, reached their hands out to rouse children and gather belongings. Men stood, stretched handsomely clad limbs, said things like, "Not far now." "Fine country – look at that sky!" "Damn fine job, lads. We're almost there." James Avery stuck his head out a window and called back, "What a lark, eh Cabot?"

George Grant rose and spoke to his secretary, Edwards, as well as the well-armed Mr. Hunter. At the front of the car, he stood in the doorway and surveyed the small settlement. Broad-shouldered as well as tall, he did not seem bothered by the gritty wind that blew the silver hair from his brow. Nor did he look like what he was: a man come west for his health. The blue eyes, when he turned them back upon his colonists, were alight with pride, pleasure, and determination. He, at least, was certain of his choice.

"So soon now we meet the bride," thought Beryl, "this love of his life."

Will touched her shoulder, handed her a small paper cone of water. Its coolness was soothing to her dry lips, but the taste was mineral, unpleasant. She grimaced.

"Bit rum, isn't it? No worse than Thames sludge, though." Will sat down beside her, took his hat off, put it back on, and rubbed his hands together. His right foot bounced nervously in its boot. Glancing at her, he caught the pensive cast of her mouth. "Almost home, sister," he said, and gave her gloved hand a squeeze.

She acknowledged his gesture with an emphatic nod. But neither smiled.

Closing the house in London had been less difficult than Beryl imagined. She had expected sadness. Instead, when she walked among its sheet-draped furnishings and opened the door to the room where she had nursed her father, she felt only relief. She was glad to close that door for the final time, glad to shut out the green bed curtains, the narrow view of the back garden. She could not regret anything in that house – not the shining breakfast table, not the warm sitting room hearth, not even the blue window seat where she'd often watched passing carriages and strolling people. Not when it meant leaving the hated sickroom. As she helped her eldest brother, Robert, lock the front door, she heard the bells of St. Margaret's peal in the distance. That alone gave her pause. But it was, after all, a celebratory sound. She did not look back as the hansom drove away.

Before leaving England, William and Beryl had traveled with Robert's family to Lindenhurst, a short detour on their way to Glasgow. Across the Midlands the rail ride was dreary — there was little sun and much rain. Birmingham was grim and foggy, black and dark as London. Pedestrians walked, hunched under the skirts of dripping umbrellas. Yorkshire, however, was greening with spring; clouds draped elegantly over mossy hills. This cheering scene did not last. From Skipton station into the dales near Lindenhurst, the carriage ride was long and chill. The children grew querulous. Beryl's nephew, eight-year-old Charlie, insisted he'd rather be a cowboy than master of Lindenhurst; his four-year-old sister screamed when he refused to allow that a girl could be a cowboy too. They had scarcely fallen into a discontented doze when Robert and William began to argue politics, dismaying Robert's wife Marian and driving Beryl to sarcasm.

But on the road from Enderley to Lindenhurst, Beryl found herself aware only of what she had too long taken for granted: the distant blue Pennines; the bud-laced copses; the crumbling burial ground where a medieval chapel once stood. She admired the colors of the wet stones fencing the Newland property; she surely hadn't paid such attention since childhood. When she alighted from the carriage with her sleeping nephew in her arms, she stood for a moment, taking in the tall windows and chimneys of the house. More birds than she thought usual were caroling; the trees seemed lit with their songs. After the cramping ride, she wished she could stay outside with that open-throated music. But Charlie was heavy and the ground wet. She must go in.

A brilliant fire roared in the drawing room hearth that last night in England, defying the shadowy memories that hung, bat-like, just out of the light. Lindenhurst's tall windows looked west into a clearing sky of rose and gold. Beryl sat at the piano, gazing at the grey garden under the glowing clouds. She was part of the picture, her gown's amethyst folds spreading gracefully over the bench while her hands rested on the keyboard. They had lately been caressing the keys into strains of Chopin and Brahms, but she could finish none of the preludes, fantasias, and nocturnes. She could neither read nor remember the music. Some ended abruptly. Others trailed into nothing.

Captain Denton listened with the frustration of continual arousal and constant interruption. He had resigned himself to Beryl's rejection of his proposal, and he had grimly accepted the news of her removal to a place far from where he might ever see her again. But to be balked of these last bits of pleasure was unendurable. He could hardly look at her, but where else was he to look? William opened maps of the anticipated colony in Kansas across the top of the round table, eager to show Denton the spread of his hopes and plans. Denton would have preferred to glare at the dog or frown into the fire. He was, however, a gracious guest and bent his head over the drawings with only the slightest sour turn of lip under his brown mustache.

The Rev. Mr. Seeley and his wife chatted volubly with Marian and Robert. Mr. Seeley had baptized both Beryl and William and assured the group that he felt "most gratified" these young people were "carrying the faith out onto the Great American Desert that God's Word might flower and bloom." His apostolic optimism and soaring rhetoric suffered a significant loss of elevation, however, as he conceded that the settlement would likely be "low church." A Scotsman who "spoke with the growl of Calvinism" was heading the expedition. Mrs. Seeley expressed herself grateful that there was to be any church at all.

Mr. Seeley wagged his head. "Very true, my dear, very true. Darwin and all, a troublesome lot. Pah! But very, very clever. Too clever. Still, we need not fear with Miss Newland and Mr. William. *Train up the child in the way he should go: and when he is old, he will not depart from it.* No, these young people were excellently trained, if I do say so myself. And they will go, well, . . . in the way they should . . . heh?" And he inclined his ear trumpet to Marian, who leaned her sparkling head into its great shell.

"You are a gem, Rev. Seeley," she said, and behind his whiskers the old man puffed with pleasure.

Mrs. Seeley, a small, stout lady who kept her head covered in keeping with the directives of St. Paul and fashion magazines thirty years old, watched William and Captain Denton with her head cocked to one side. "Well, now, I call it a real pity that Miss Newland couldn't see her way to agreeing with Captain Denton."

Alarm leapt into Marian's green eyes. She put her fingers to her lips. "Oh, there's no explaining a young person's heart. But he's quite broken about it, I understand, and we mustn't let him know we still think of it. He has his dignity and wouldn't thank us for noticing his pain, now, would he?"

"Oh, no, I'm sure," agreed Mrs. Seeley, the ribbons of her cap fluttering a little. She sighed and continued, without the least lowering of voice, "In my day, girls were glad when a strong, handsome man offered to marry them. Now they go traipsing off to the colonies without husbands. Most unaccountable, these girls. And Beryl such a pretty woman too, though almost a spinster. I do hope the Indians won't get her, not after she could have had a good man like Captain Denton."

"You're thinking she'll be wedding in a tepee, Mrs. Seeley?" Robert growled.

Marian's alarm increased. Her usually genial husband had, she thought, become spectacularly churlish about his siblings' decision to emigrate. That his younger brother refused to finish at Oxford and pursue a career in the Church of England would have stung sufficiently by itself. But that his sister chose to abandon a comfortable, eminently respectable life in London and invest her marriage portion in "a patch of American dirt" galled him beyond endurance.

Though Robert would not say so, he was hurt that Beryl and Will wanted to leave him and his family. He was public about insisting that their behavior reflected on him badly as a gentleman, a Tory, and head of the Newland clan. As *pater familias* he felt it was his duty to anticipate everything that could, and likely would, go wrong. He complained that he could no longer sleep at night. His consequent loss of the common social graces had Marian close to despair.

Afraid that Mrs. Seeley might go further with the disgraceful subject, Marian picked up a book. "Have you seen this novel by Mr. Dickens? I'm only in the first volume, but it's wonderfully written."

Mrs. Seeley gave Marian a shrewd glance but took the book. "Oh, I'm sure it is, Mrs. Newland. This is quite an old book. And see, Mr. Seeley, how very big it is. So many words in the man."

Robert stared at the old woman's ribbons for a moment, and then continued growling. "Why leave the empire? Why not at least go to India or Australia? She could find her Othello there."

Marian's green eyes suddenly glittered. "Mr. Newland! We are discussing Mr. Dickens."

The honorable M.P. looked at his wife. The chain of gold thread she was crocheting had tensed into tiny knots. "Of course, of course. He wrote *Chuzzlewit*, didn't he? Ever read it, William? A comic genius when it comes to Americans. Always made me laugh." He chomped grimly on his cigar and then said, "A great loss, his passing. Great loss."

"Indeed so," said Mrs. Seeley.

Will, acquainted with the story of Chuzzlewit's imbroglios with treacherous Yankees, ignored Robert, merely observing to Captain Denton that his brother must be getting queer, for he never used to read novels. Beryl, who had only caught the conversation's end, closed her music and joined the group by the fire.

"Which one are you reading, Robert?"

"He's not reading it – I am. But I mean to send it along with you to America. It will pass the time and remind you of home." Marian took the book from Mrs. Seeley and handed it to Beryl.

"I have books for you too, my dear," said Rev. Seeley nodding. "Good reading for long winter nights. You and Mr. William can read to each other while the wind blows and the coyotes howl and whatnot, heh?" The ear trumpet wagged dangerously. Beryl smiled at him.

Captain Denton watched her and turned back to the table. He studied the maps for a moment and then, folding one of them, said to William, "An enviable position, young man."

"What, sitting out there with wind and coyotes?"

"Sitting up nights listening to Scheherazade." Captain Denton tossed the map aside. The remark had been louder than necessary, its point irritatingly evident.

"As I remember," Beryl said lightly and letting her lips smile, "she was trying to save her head from a husband with twisted ideas about matrimony. Neither in a situation to envy."

Marion cringed, wondering where she could find another distraction – a volume of Trollope, perhaps, or even George Eliot? Mrs. Seeley, however, brightened. She so much preferred live drama to three-volume prose.

Will glanced at the captain and his sister. "Beryl's as likely to throw a book at a fellow as read it to him."

"And quite right she'd be, for you're a saucy pup," said Rev. Seeley. "Taking your sister to this Arcady." He pointed to an orange pamphlet that Will had been passing around. "They say here you can grow grapes and peaches. Flowing with milk and honey, heh?"

"Well, rather," said Will. His voice kindled against the gloom. "Mr. Grant insists the air sparkles like champagne."

"Intoxicating," remarked Robert dryly.

Beryl laughed. "Mr. Grant is given to hyperbole."

"But if you don't believe him, my dear, why go? I mean, think of the impropriety for a woman," said Mrs. Seeley, adjusting the ribbons under her chin.

"There's no impropriety," said Marian. "Lord Stannard's daughter, Lydia Randall, is going."

"And you, Mrs. Newland, could you imagine going?" asked Mrs. Seeley.

Marian seemed taken aback. "Me? Why would I want to?"

Beryl knelt down and picked up Marian's work basket. "You might if things were different. If you didn't have your husband, or your home, or your position."

Marian rested her head against the chair back. Tiny, jeweled hairpins sparkled among the sandy coils of her hair. Her garnet gown was edged and ruffled, crossed and crisscrossed, with narrow blue ribbons that ran like rivers over the continent of her skirt. "I don't know. I suppose it might be rather exciting. Mr. Grant seems such a gentleman, so thoughtful of the interests of everyone. But – no. Not to stay. Being a lady traveler, visiting India or Africa or maybe

California, now *that* would be an adventure – and I could come home again and write for the papers and give lectures." Marian laughed, diverted. "But I'd rather just read about those places, sitting in the garden or tucked in one of Robert's great chairs. I don't like dirt, not even for a little while, and I certainly couldn't live with it. I think there must be a lot of dirt out in those wild places."

"Quite right," said Robert, stroking his beard. "A proper, womanly opinion."

"No," said Marian, shrugging crossly. "It's just mine."

Beryl examined the items in Marian's basket. She picked up a small silver embroidery scissors and let her fingers slide back and forth on its short, polished blades. Closing them, she tested the tiny tool's sharp point against the tip of first one finger, and then another. "Mrs. Seeley, I didn't say I don't believe Mr. Grant. I just think he's fallen in love with the place. People in love always exaggerate, don't they?"

"Love?" Robert snorted. "Good god, I hope that's not why you're going. The man got rich on black crepe, gambling that Prince Albert would die. Which he did. Damned convenient. Grant's a Scot, and mind you he doesn't do anything without expecting a profit. Frankly, that's the only reason I have any faith in this enterprise at all."

"We both believe in him then. We just have different reasons." Beryl tossed the scissors back into the basket.

"But is it true that you are leaving on April Fool's Day?" asked Mrs. Seeley.

"I'm sure if Mr. Grant could have arranged things earlier, they'd have embarked on the Ides of March," said Captain Denton.

"Eyes of what?" croaked Rev. Seeley, waving his ear trumpet at Will.

Robert shook his head. "Mother will haunt me nights for consenting to this. I can hear her now: 'Bobby boy, I told you to look after your little brother and sister. Where have they got to? I told you to watch them!'"

The others tittered at his falsetto, even Captain Denton, but Beryl rose abruptly.

"You can tell her that London's wretched fog and three years forced mourning was just like being strangled! I'd go almost anywhere else! Anywhere! But a place that boasts of champagne air? *Champagne?!* Oh, Robert, Mama would perfectly understand." She walked over to the tall windows and stood gazing out, a slender shadow against the purpling sky. With her dark head raised defiantly, she looked very much like that ghostly mother. No one said any more.

Late that night, as the Newlands gathered in the front hall to say goodbye to their guests, Captain Denton gently touched Beryl's arm and drew her aside.

"If you will be taking a library along with you, Miss Newland — and it appears that you will be — then I hope that you will allow me to contribute this slim volume. Some Barrett Browning. I know that you are fond of her verse." He handed her a small, leather-bound book.

She accepted it without looking at the title. "How thoughtful of you. Thank you, Captain Denton." She took a brave breath and went on, "I shall always remember you when I read it."

"You are kind to say so." He watched her small hands play on the binding. She looked up at his face, his brown eyes and thick brows. He was not as old as they all assumed, not nearly the age of Mr. Grant. "I shall not see you again. You depart in a few days, and I return to India. So I want to wish you every good fortune in your new life. You will be careful, I hope."

"I will."

"Yes. And you have courage."

"We'll find out just how much, I guess." She sounded uncertain, a strange shift in tone from her drawing-room declaration.

Denton wondered for the umpteenth time what had happened in London, what drove her from England. He knew her little, though he cared for her much. And now he would never know her better: her motives and ambitions would remain as undiscovered as the taste of her lips, the touch of her hair. It made him weary, the loss of this thing he had never had. His good-bye was brief, his departure hurried, his shoulders stooped as he took her hand. Later, those stooped shoulders were all Beryl could remember of him.

Alone in her room she opened the book he had given her. Inscribed in the front cover, in a carefully controlled script, were the words: *To Beryl Newland, with esteem from Captain Bradley Denton, 1873.* Kind and correct as ever. Tired, she paged idly through the poems until she noticed that one page was folded at the corner. She stopped, frowning. Pushing the volume closer to the lamp, she screened the other pages, but found no more marks. Turning back to the folded one, she began reading:

> *Go from me. Yet I feel that I shall stand*
> *Henceforward in thy shadow . . . .*

She read the sonnet several times. Then, resolutely, she closed the book, blew out the lamp, and crawled under the white coverlet. Her eyes, however, would not close. Lying in the great four-poster bed that had been hers since she'd left the nursery, she saw over and over again those last lines:

> *. . . And when I sue*
> *God for myself, He hears that name of thine*
> *And sees within my eyes, the tears of two.*

She did not open the book again. But the morning she left Lindenhurst, she took it from the small writing desk and placed it in her trunk next to the orange pamphlet that beckoned her to Victoria and the Dicken's novel called *Bleak House*, which was to remind her of home.

Chapter II

The first tremor of trouble came already in Scotland. Despite recruiting promises, Mr. Grant would not or could not cover the costs of the colonists' passage to America. Richard Cabot's blond eyebrows rose considerably when Grant's secretary, Leslie Edwards, announced this to the male colonists gathered in the sitting room of an inn near the Glasgow docks. The jocularity which had preceded Edwards' entrance gave way to silence. Men exchanged glances. Will Newland shifted uncomfortably in his chair at the thought of requesting more money from his brother. James Avery shrugged expensively clad shoulders. For most, this development was an irritation rather than a problem. Sympathy was strong, however, for John Baldwin, a father of five who stood near the mantle shaking his head, and for Daniel MacDonough, a fair young Scot whose careful reckoning had not included the transatlantic fare for himself and his pregnant wife. MacDonough was a likable enthusiast who had spoken of opening a store. He was already economizing by planning to homestead. He simply did not have the capital to purchase land outright like the others. A frown closed his normally open features while he calculated the provisions he would now have to do without. His quiet reckoning made the others more indignant than they might have been on their own behalf. Jack Randall, arms crossed and jet hair standing (as always) on end, demanded to know if the group should plan on any other surprises. Garth Mason, a round-faced naturalist, asked what others wondered: "Why isn't George Grant here?"

"He's at the White Star offices with Mr. Davis and Mr. Keith, checking that all reserved cabins are in order and preparing the stock for loading. We confirmed yesterday that the *Great Republic* will be waiting in New Orleans, and all is arranged with the Pacific railroad for transport from St. Louis to Victoria." Edwards paused, smoothing his grey lapel. "There is merely the cost of the *Alabama* passage, and all is ready."

Randall's arms remained folded. "Maybe, Edwards, but I'm getting concerned. Can you guarantee we'll have an actual roof over our heads when we get to Victoria?"

The secretary repositioned his spectacles. "The building is finished. Sound, handsome construction, from what I've seen of the plans. You need have no worries."

"He knows nothing," Randall muttered to Mason.

Edwards responded with heat. "You forget, Mr. Randall, that I have been to Victoria, and I am going again. I can assure you on my own account that Mr. Grant has chosen an excellent location for the colony, and he has dedicated a great deal of time, money, and energy to this enterprise. You may depend on him."

MacDonough sighed but spoke cheerfully. "Well then, I say let's get these tickets paid for and move on. We have preparations that need finishing, and Jane would like a walk down to see the ship. Who do we pay, Mr. Edwards?"

Buoyed more by MacDonough's optimism than Edwards' assurance, the group paid what was due and broke up. Will and Avery left the inn together, eager to watch the action by the water. Rumbling wheels, hawkers, and gulls competed with their conversation as they navigated the crooked streets along the Clyde. Avery was on the lookout for a pub, but Will diverted him into a small bakery where fresh scones beckoned. "We can eat these instead of stopping for a meal, and I can take some back to Beryl."

Avery watched as a young woman in a crisp apron wrapped their purchase. "Randall's rather a bore sometimes, don't you think? I mean, he was a bit hard on old Edwards."

Will handed a few pence across the counter. "I think Randall was quite right. Why? What have you got against him?"

"His father-in-law is paying for the entire expedition. I don't see what he has to complain about."

"He was sticking up for those who do have something to complain of. Not everyone can toss guineas around the way you do. So Randall married well. So what?" They plunged again into the grimy street.

"She's rather too good for him, don't you think?" Avery poked his nose into the bag, looking for a big scone and wishing he had butter. "I mean, a sweet docile thing and money on top of it. Why Randall?"

"And why not you?" Will laughed. "He's a good enough chap, willing to say what others only think. I say let him enjoy his good fortune."

"Ah, well, I'm doomed to marry some brown squaw who will hound me and make me live in a tepee while she rears my dusky race. Mother will hate that. Which might make it worthwhile. I say, can't we find a pub? This bread is damned dry."

"Beryl says that if Grant keeps Victoria tavern-free, you will waste away for want of liquor."

"Did she really? She's a plucky girl."

"Sometimes I think you quite like her." Will elbowed his friend, almost pushing him into a florid woman pulling two children by the hand. "You know, Denton's done and gone now. He's off to India, she's off to America – with you – and there you are!"

"Are you trying to get rid of her?" Avery evaded the more personal point by digging into the bag of scones again. He found one corpulent with currents and pulled it out, pleased that it was the biggest.

"Not at all. Just want everyone happy. Might leave some for the woman in question, by the way. You'll get even thirstier, eating all of them. I say, Avery, look at that!"

The river came into view, clogged with small boats, wooden-masted sailing ships, and huge steamers, one of them the *Alabama*. Her decks were edged with high bulwarks and bright railings. An intricate mélange of ropes, chains, and cables rose above the narrow deckhouses and giant smokestacks, linking with booms and king posts where sea gulls perched. Polished benches marked a line of stateroom windows running the length of the upper deck. A United States flag whipped at the top of a tall pole. Only ten years before a warship bearing the same name had sailed and sunk under a Confederate banner. For this new vessel a fresh history was being written, a gilded narrative of American commerce, industry, and immigration. William, who had never traveled by sea before, heard her siren call. "What a beauty!" he cried.

"I'll say. A man who can afford to dress his wife like that shouldn't begrudge you the fare to America!"

"What?" Will followed Avery's gaze, which rested on Marian Newland, who stood with Robert and Beryl several hundred feet away. They, too, were taking in the long lines and solid bulk of the steamer. Marian's cheeks were hectic in the March wind and a richly colored cloak blew around her skirts.

"Good God, James, what is this sudden preoccupation with married women? First Lydia Randall and now my sister-in-law? You're in a bad way. We'll have to find you a wench of your own sooner rather than later."

"Wench, indeed. Can't you see that what I need is a real lady?" Avery struck a worldly pose. "Married women are after all the best kind. You can make love to them and never be bothered with commitment. The unmarried ones aren't interested anyway. They want men like you —all passionate earnestness – or Cabot, an Adonis who will throw them away like a toy. Me? Wonderfully witty, well read, incredibly well-dressed, but," and his expression grew melancholy, "pasty-faced." He flicked the crumbs from his fingers. "The married ones, though – well, they're only too glad for some attention."

Will was amused. "Who says you are pasty-faced?"

Avery glowered. "My cousin Phyllis. Vile girl. Nose like a turnip and a body to match. She's one of my reasons for emigrating."

Will laughed. "You just need to find that squaw woman. She will cure your lily complexion for generations to come. But my advice is don't let Robert catch you ogling his wife. And don't hang about so much with Cabot. He's clearly a bad influence." He looked back at the ship. "I meant the ship is a beauty, don't you think?"

"Yes," said Avery distractedly. He was looking at Beryl. Her grey eyes were sparkling and expectant as she faced into the wind and shouted a laughing remark towards her brother. She was less pale and happier than he remembered ever having seen her. He thought she, too, was lovely. He did not, however, say so.

James Avery may have been pasty-faced along the banks of the Clyde, but out on the Atlantic his fine features turned positively green. Three days out of the Firth of Clyde, a storm hit, punishing the *Alabama* with a misery of waves and wind. Avery and Will moaned and moped, taking turns dumping the ill-smelling slop pail. In a foolish moment Avery opened the port hole to get some fresh air, hoping to calm his stomach. Instead, he swamped their small cabin with icy sea water, earning the curses of his roommate and failing to gain sympathy from the steward sent to mop up the mess. Their fellow passengers, two or four legged, fared little better. An anxious deck hand came to Douglas Keith with word that a small black bull was sick. Keith, leaning his long body weakly against the edge of an elegant chair in the saloon, looked at the sailor.

"If he feels as bad as I do," he gasped, "then I feel damned sorry for him."

Beryl's infatuation with the dashing spray and soaring gale deteriorated after only a few hours into something akin to panic. She huddled in her berth. One hand clutched the white coverlet she'd brought from home; the fingers of the other wrapped, tense and aching, around the bars of her bed in a futile attempt to stop the ship's motion and save herself from the swallowing waters. She was little comfort to fourteen-year-old Meg Grant, who shared her cabin and was only a slightly less scared. The two of them suffered more quietly than their male counterparts – they'd been trained to do that – but they were no less miserable. When at last the squall gave way to calmer, bluer seas, the young woman and the girl emerged hand in hand like a pair of limp evening gloves. Only when the ship entered the warm waters of the gulf did Beryl's walk regain its spring and Meg's cheeks their color. By this time they were become friends, not because they had talked for hours or shared secrets like boarding-school sisters, but because they were both young things with imagination enough to believe in their own deaths and, silently, they had shared that terror.

The stormy Atlantic passage was a limited but potent preliminary test of the colonists' fortitude and optimism. Upon the city dwellers in particular it thrust the ugliness that accompanies nature at her most picturesque. As the *Alabama* neared New Orleans, Jason Mayes, tow-headed heir to an estate in Derbyshire, announced that when, if ever, he returned to his hallowed ancestral home, he intended to burn every seascape that hung there. It was a fairly safe proclamation, since the Mayes galleries were largely populated by ugly Elizabethans and pretty men in powdered wigs. There were no sea captains or naval officers among them; an ocean tableau was unlikely. His peers nonetheless applauded his defiance of deluded Romanticism and offered a toast to common sense.

The young men were feeling good. The turquoise waters and the warm sun made their sap rise and their limbs tingle. They strode the decks talking excitedly, letting their plans branch and leaf. New life surged in George Grant as well. He consulted with his foremen and spent hours in the hold examining the livestock; he advised his disciples on what to expect and how to proceed once they got to their destination; he played with the children and reassured the mothers; he spoke of the beauties of the Great Plains before the backdrop of a sparkling sea. The colonists rejected Romanticism, but they listened to George Grant.

Then, just hours before they were due in New Orleans, the *Alabama* stalled on a sandbar, stuck in waters of sixteen feet where eighteen were wanted. Solving the problem was not the colonists' job. They nevertheless paced the deck smoking cigarettes and offering advice to harassed deck hands. The university men gathered in clusters and looked over the railings, debating courses of action much as they'd once argued the merits of classical antiquity versus the Renaissance. Their conclusions were similarly useful. The Wyatt brothers – Nigel, Frederick, and Stanley – got bored and began shooting at gulls. The captain suggested this was not helpful. The women, left in charge of the children and still adjusting to life without nurse or governess, watched them all wearily. Sarah Baldwin and Lydia Randall sat on benches under green parasols, anxiously calling to the small boys and girls who toddled and raced and quarreled on the deck. Jane MacDonough, only a month from confinement, fanned strands of black hair away from her flushed face and gratefully rested her swollen ankles upon the footstool her husband brought her. Thomas Baldwin, four years old, promptly tumbled over it and cried for fifteen minutes.

Beryl listened, chin resting on her hands, squinted at the horizon, and worried her boot against the deck floor. Waves came and went.

Two days were spent in stillness under that uncomfortably warm sun before two barges, each loaded with Black workers, arrived to carry away enough cargo that the ship could free itself and continue on to New Orleans. The lack of progress sobered the colonists again, slowing, though not stunting, their hopes. The group had been clannish for much of the journey, but now some of them sought out the American passengers at dinner, listened to their stories, considered their opinions, and wondered at their speech: the flat, slow, drawl of Southerners, the clipped, nasal rush of Yankees. Beyond the large windows of the saloon where they conversed, a flat marshy delta stretched away from increasingly muddy waters. Humidity took the blue from the sky and left it a hazy white. The cries of herons punctuated a ceaseless hum of insects.

Garth Mason spent hours on deck studying the landscape and sketching birds. Nearby, Grant's nephew Clay took turns looking through opera glasses with Oscar Jones and Andrew Miles, Londoners who hoped to catch sight of an alligator. Douglas Keith stood a few feet away, grinned at their exclamations, and then offered them his field glasses. In her cabin, Lydia Randall covered her son with mosquito netting and let him fall asleep to the crooning of Black boatmen moving up the river. Meg Grant, drawn by their voices, watched these men in fascination from her deck chair, wondering at their shining dark skin, their large, startling eyes, the strange cadence of their songs. She felt she'd walked into a fairy tale, so unlike the pale people she'd grown up with were these men.

Meg was old enough to know her American history and something of the saga of these people; she had read *Uncle Tom's Cabin*; she looked forward to arriving in New Orleans where she might see someone descended from a real Uncle Tom, a real little Eva, maybe even a real Simon Legree. That, as a merchant, her uncle's sympathies had been with the Southern cause during the war did not bother her. She had once heard her father say that his brother "tends to the wrong where his interests are concerned, but for a' that he's a good man," and she chose to believe it. His kindness to her since she'd been orphaned left more room in her heart for fondness than for criticism. When, at last arriving in New Orleans, Grant ridiculed the dark-skinned onlookers who gathered to see "n______ cattle" as his purebred Angus bulls were transferred to the packet, she simply sighed and pretended not to hear.

Beryl Newland did not pretend she hadn't heard. She'd been standing with her brother and his friends, watching the bawling cattle as they were prodded, poked, and cajoled over the gangplank. The smells of the animals, the people, the water made it hard to breathe. She was overwhelmed by a medley of shouting, laughing, commenting, a cacophony of accents and intonations, all different than she had ever heard before; even the French sounded more foreign to her ears than it would have in Britain. The sight, however, was exhilarating: the men, sweaty, some shirtless, urging the animals forward; the bright mass of onlookers decorated in everything from rags to silks; the vessels crowding and crawling along the wharves; the roofs and spires of the city rising behind earthen walls that held back the river. "It's a circus!" she had laughed. "I don't know when I've been so entertained."

Into that excitement, George Grant's derision fell on Beryl's soul like a small, chill drop. Few of her companions noticed the suddenly severe set of her lips. Mr. Cabot, however, saw.

"An abolitionist past time, a lover of the races, Miss Newland?"

Beryl stiffened. Her admiration for Mr. Grant made her loathe to criticize, especially within earshot of Meg. Until that moment Mr. Grant had seemed so much the perfect gentleman — much more so than the man now quizzing her. Worse yet, she knew that though she would never ridicule them, she nonetheless felt strange in the presence of so many people with black and brown skin. She wondered if it showed. Ashamed and unequal to a moral argument on her own behalf, she merely said, "My mother's family were ardent admirers of Mr. Wilberforce. Before she died, my mother wrote letters for the cause of abolitionism in America."

"Ah," said Cabot.

Jack Randall had heard both Grant's remarks and the brief exchange between Beryl and Cabot. He wiped his brow with a small square of fine, white linen and then observed, "Slavery was damned wrong. But those Black folks need to be guided, just like children. Can't understand higher thinking. Grant should watch his mouth, but don't worry too much about them getting their feelings hurt, Miss Newland. A pretty dense lot, I should think." He tucked the linen into his pocket.

Beryl thought she would suffocate; all joy was gone from the spectacle. She touched William's arm and turned.

Behind Beryl stood a respectable, well-dressed man; a simple gold pin adorned his tie. Beside him stood a pretty woman in a gown of pale lavender; the ruffles along its bodice and sleeves lay delicately against the smooth ebony of her skin. It created, William noted with a start, a gorgeous contrast. The lady lowered her eyes, but the gentleman looked directly into Beryl's agitated face, then into that of her brother. He looked longer at Mr. Cabot, and longest of all at Mr. Randall.

"*Better fifty years of Europe than a cycle of Cathay*, hmmm? Always so honored when Queen Victoria's subjects cross the sea to spread their enlightened understanding. Welcome." He tipped his hat to Beryl – handsome, slightly mocking. He then walked away with the young woman, who never raised her eyes. Her skirt synchronized, nervously graceful, with his angry stride. After only a moment, they were lost in the crowd.

Randall said under his breath, "God-damned n_______!" He moved to pursue him, but Will stood in his way.

"No – don't, Mr. Randall. That gentleman was right to be offended." Beryl's protest was firm. "Please, let's go to the hotel. I feel ill."

Avery, engrossed in watching the animals, had missed the encounter altogether and only heard her last words. "What's the matter? A touch of voodoo? I say, let's go questing some Creole cuisine. There's a charm will perk you up, Miss Newland! We'll have to eat buffalo and nothing but buffalo soon enough, I expect." Seeing her agitated expression, he said with greater concern, "Why, are you really sick?"

"She's been insulted!" said Randall.

"I have not." Disgusted, Beryl shook off the support of her brother and Mr. Randall. "I'll be fine. I just need to rest. The hotel will have a dining room, won't it? We can eat there – let's call Miss Grant and Mrs. Randall. Perhaps the others will join us later. I'm sure a carriage ride is just the thing."

Mr. Grant, perceiving their departure from the docks where he was overseeing the unloading, shouted after them, "Off so soon? Well, you might as well play while you can; there's work enough ahead with these bonny brutes!" He looked cheerfully at Ian Duncan, a brawny, curly-haired Scot who slapped the backside of a recalcitrant beast and shouted there was work enough already.

Randall glanced toward Beryl. "We've seen enough black bulls for one day, Mr. Grant." She stared back at him coldly, then turned her shoulder.

Randall declined to join the group heading to the hotel, saying that his wife and boy would not be ready to disembark until evening. Meg, however, eagerly climbed into an open carriage with the Newlands, Mr. Avery, and Mr. Cabot. While she and Beryl settled their skirts, William murmured to Avery, "Perhaps you were right, James."

"About what?"

"Randall doesn't know when to shut his bloody trap."

Avery nodded and then shrugged as the driver clucked to the horses.

For several minutes the group was subdued, but they were soon drawn out of their brooding by Meg's excitement. She asked to see some of the city; Beryl was willing and the driver obliging. Miss Grant rode with clasped hands, enraptured at the lovely homes, the long galleries laced with wrought iron, the arched gateways beckoning to cool, secluded gardens. They stopped in a market, where Mr. Cabot presented her and Beryl each with a nosegay of bright blossoms while Avery berated Will, who refused to support him in his plan for carrying a large basket of crabs to Kansas. Riding along a wide, tree-lined avenue toward the hotel, Beryl felt revived. She thought the air was purer in the city than down by the river and said so.

Cabot made a noncommittal sound. "Perhaps. It wasn't always so good. The epidemic in the fifties almost destroyed New Orleans."

"What epidemic?"

"Oh, bad sanitation led to Yellow Fever. Bleeding from the mouth and ears, bodies piled up in the streets, a real horror. From what I've heard, the Black Death could hardly have been worse. Whole families – servants, masters – all dead within days, even hours." He considered the gold pocket watch which he dandled idly from its chain. The crystal face flashed and winked whenever the sun penetrated the weaving branches over their heads. "Of course, it prompted the usual superstitious hogwash. The ignorant spoke of voodoo. And those who should have known better said it was the judgment of God on this decadent city. Mostly northern abolitionists, I'd bet."

"I say, Cabot – Miss Grant, you know."

Cabot looked, amused, at Meg's wide eyes. "Oh, now, it's just a bogey story. Nothing to fear, child. The bad old times are over. And see how beautiful New Orleans is today."

Meg smiled at him a little; she was willing to be both scared and reassured by this handsome man.

Heavy-eyed, Beryl gazed at the elegant buildings. "Are they over?" she whispered to herself. She looked at Will and, involuntarily, sighed. "I wish we were home."

Meg raised her freckled face to Beryl. "You don't mean *home* home, do you, Miss Newland? You don't mean you want to go back to England again?"

Beryl's eyes threw off their sleepy sadness. She brushed back the girl's red bangs with softly gloved fingers. "No, Meg. When I say 'home,' I mean Victoria, of course."

"Of course," echoed Cabot to himself. He studied them. "Home." And he clicked the watch shut.

Near dusk the cars again slowed, the whistle called. At first there seemed nothing but vast plain, running dark and desolate to an empty horizon. By the time the train stopped, however, the emigrants could see, up a small rise some two-hundred feet from the tracks, a large, gabled stone building silhouetted against the sky. Perhaps the conductor announced Victoria Station; no one could say for sure. None were listening. They knew.

Mr. Grant disembarked first, moving quickly back to the freight cars with Duncan and Keith to unload the cattle and horses. Then Neil Hunter went down the narrow steps of the passenger car, firmly holding his rifle. At the bottom, he stood for a moment. Beyond the wooden depot platform, there seemed to be nothing but wind, wind that blew the short grass into black shadows. Never had he seen such darkness – and this despite the continuing afterglow of the sun in the west. He found his eyes straining to see the lights of farms and villages that were not there. The moon was new, invisible. Perhaps, he thought, that was the evening star shining serenely in the eastern sky. It reminded him of the woman back in Scotland, waiting to join him. Both seemed impossibly distant. He turned his back on it to help the other passengers disembark.

While Grant was busy with the animals, the colonists remained standing awkwardly on the platform with their bags and trunks rather than moving up toward the hotel depot. They stood there still as the engineer gave a departing whistle. There was a clatter of rails. The line of glowing windows passed fast and then faster; the faces looking out at them blurred. The Kansas Pacific moved away into the disappearing western light, leaving them alone with the wind and that growing blackness. The Baldwin children huddled around their parents. They had no inclination to run in that great space even though they had been confined to the narrow aisles of the train for several days. Jane MacDonough sat on a trunk, cradling the swelling belly under her skirt, and cried. While Daniel tried to comfort her, the other young men looked away, uncertain what to do.

Lydia Randall knelt beside the distraught woman and, lifting her blue eyes to the sweeping land, breathed, "Why, it's like the Fens, Jane. It's quite beautiful, don't you think? Just like East Anglia. And look how many stars there are." She rested Jane's damp face against her shoulder.

Beryl drew her grey cloak more closely around her shoulders and pulled its wide hood over her head, hiding the fashionable hat that now seemed too feathered and frivolous. The air was not cold; it was quite pleasant, in fact, after the stuffy cars. But she felt the need to wrap herself in something, to create a haven against the sprawling country. *I lift up mine eyes to the mountains, from whence cometh my help.* The words ran unaccountably through her mind, an antiphon to Lydia's soothing murmur. She whispered to Will, "It's so flat. Like a cloth stretched over a table. Are there no hills here? None?" She looked up at him.

William did not answer. At the behest of Mr. Edwards, he and the other gentleman began carrying trunks and bags toward Victoria Manor. The relief they found in action was palpable. Hauling luggage, lifting crates, calling to animals and making decisions about what should go where, the young men became animated, argued, and even joked in the darkness. This was, at last, the real beginning of their adventure. Doing was all that mattered; it filled the empty immensity. Thus, though the five women were not exactly forgotten, they were largely left to answer their own questions, to make their own sense of what was happening. Their male companions neither had nor wanted the leisure to ponder, worry about, or wonder at this place where they found themselves.

So the women gathered their children, said a silent prayer, and turned their eyes to the manor house where lamps were beginning to shine in the windows, sending squares of light and shadow onto ground that had for centuries known only the illumination of fire and sun and moon. They followed those squares of light like a road into known territory, like a map guiding them to a place marked "home," whether or not they could ever call it by that name. They studied the stairs on either end of the stone building, leading up to rooms where they would find walls on which to hang their portraits, hearth mantles on which to put their clocks, small tables on which to set their silver, and newly laid floors on which to spread their babies' blankets. Consciously or not, they yearned for this shelter that would not move, this shelter that would shut out that constant wind, that too imposing sky, that great wilderness of grass. It gave them courage, reminded them that even here, in this alien place, they would be able to find or create the familiar.

The women stepped onto the long veranda which encircled the building. Beryl took Meg Grant's hand. The girl was trembling. When Beryl asked her if she was all right, she said simply, "I never knew there was this much of – of anything – in the whole world." She gestured out at the night. Beryl, gazing into the vastness with her, understood.

Chapter III

There was no trail. They left the hotel, its stone gables sandy gold against a blue sky, and crossed the tracks into a sea of grasses. Out of those subtle swells eddies of gnats rose, accompanied every now and again by the brief, sweet solo of a lark. The riders, following a dry ravine to a distant rim of trees, stopped and listened. The morning sun shone on them: placid, indifferent.

They rode on. Alone, the two men might have traveled more quickly, but Beryl had never been an equestrian, and the years in London had taken away what ease she felt on horseback. As they descended toward a small stream, she leaned awkwardly against the saddle horn and brushed at flies with her right hand. The shuddering of the pony's dusty hide whenever one of the insects landed on its neck repulsed her. William watched, frowning. Mr. Keith at last said:

"You know, Miss Newland, this is no country for riding side saddle. You'd feel more comfortable riding – " he wanted to say, "like a man," but reconsidered and merely concluded "the way we do."

She had been concentrating on where her pony was stepping, on the chalky stones and sandy ground that grew arid only inches from the trickling water. Self-conscious, she straightened up in the saddle. "I'm fine. I just need more practice. I don't see how hitching up my skirts and straddling this animal will much help."

"It would be more sensible," remarked William. "That's not the right saddle for girl riding, and after all, there's no one to see. Marian would be shocked, but I shan't tell her."

"I'd just as soon take up smoking, thank you."

"My grandmother used to smoke a pipe," said Keith, quietly running his reins through gloved fingers. "A fine Highland lady. None finer." He studied the clouds drifting along the western horizon, then turned his mild eyes on Beryl. "But o' course there were some as said she was a witch. She had an uncommon gift of healing. Knew which plants closed wounds, which herbs gentled the spirit. She claimed tobacco helped her think. My mother was a good English Christian, though, and said it merely made her smell like a chimney." He looked back at the clouds.

Beryl stared.

Will remained quiet, but his lips were suspiciously crooked. He struck the grass along the bank with his whip. The wind whispered through the broad leaves of a cottonwood. Birds trilled.

Beryl turned her eyes to the open sky that stretched far away behind him. "Indeed." Her mouth set itself into an obstinate line. She clucked to her pony. The duo picked its way forward.

William sighed. "Shouldn't we be getting to our section soon? Though it all looks rather the same to me." He squinted to see the edges of the plain.

"You'll start recognizing landmarks soon enough. It's surprising, how quickly a man learns to read the face of the land. But still, I wouldn't stray far from dependable trails. Can't lose yourself that way. We'll cross the Old Denver Stage Road just ahead, and Victoria Creek lies not far beyond that. This stream feeds right into it, near where it turns to the west. Now I'd suggest – "

Beryl's pony stumbled. Beryl cried out, righted herself, and then stopped the animal. The line of her lips was stretched so tight now, it seemed ready to snap. She slid – almost slipped – from her mount and gathered up her long brown train. The bundle was clumsy. Stockings and boots public, she glared at the pony. It gave her a nonchalant glance and bent to bite the head off a dandelion. Gripping the saddle tightly with her left hand, Beryl put her foot in the right stirrup. Mr. Keith was quickly beside her, supporting her, making it possible to swing her left leg over the animal.

Ponies are not big: convention was toppled with startling efficiency. Beryl shifted; her legs instinctively tightened around the pony's body; and there she sat, with a wealth of skirt gathered in her lap. She felt embarrassed, exposed, and oddly secure.

Keith studied the way she was seated and then walked back to his horse. "As I said, a fine Highland lady. None finer."

Will admired common sense, but the sight of his sister's calves elicited a resurgent respect for feminine modesty. He rode over.

"You've proven you can take a dare, Beryl, but I'm not sure this is proper."

"You're not very steady in your opinions, are you? After all, who's to see?" She settled herself a bit more comfortably. "You know, William, you look and talk exactly like Robert sometimes." She gave her pony a spirited kick. William decided it served her right that she appeared utterly graceless as she rode after Mr. Keith.

The land the Newlands had invested in ran on two sides of Victoria Creek at a point where it twisted and turned not once but twice, looping south, then north, then south, then north again before heading straight west onto Mr. Grant's property. The proximity of the creek ensured the presence of trees, elms and cottonwoods with leaves still wearing the bright green of spring. The water, which swept shallow and quick in some places, ran slow, deep, and almost stagnant in others. Mosquitos hovered. Beryl dismounted in a shady thicket of reeds and saplings, glad to let the skirts fall again around her ankles. She wrapped a veil over her face and listened to the insects whine, frustrated, outside its netting.

"What a relief to see trees! But we won't want the house close to the water. So many bugs!"

"Not safe anyway. This is dry country, but floods come with the heavy spring rains. I'd recommend a house and outbuildings up that hill to the north." They walked with their animals to the spot where Mr. Keith pointed. There, the midday sun was merciless. The ground seemed rocky.

"Will this be hard to clear?" Beryl asked.

Keith kicked some stones with his foot. "First year'll be tough, breaking the sod. But rocks shouldn't be that much of a problem the further you get from water. Be glad for all this stone. It's the best material for a solid house and barn."

William took his jacket off and looked down at the whitish earth. "Won't be fun quarrying that stuff."

"No," acknowledged Keith, "but limestone is easy to work with, easy to shape when it's freshly mined. Exposed to the elements a while, it becomes hard. Perhaps you'll want to start with a wood frame house, but stone buildings stand up better in the heat and the cold. They'd be cool on a day like today." He wiped his brow. "Have to see how deep this shale is – you want to be able to dig a cellar and a well. But this is a bonny spot."

Will paced out some lengths. "I think just a cottage at first – parlor, kitchen, a couple bedrooms. Windows here, maybe, to watch the sunsets, and a door facing to town."

Keith shook his head. "Not good to face north. Hill folk say it's bad luck. The sun never shines on the entrance to your home."

"Let it face east," said Beryl, "with a parlor on the south side where the windows will be full of light. But let the house look east. I'd like a wide veranda, where we can sit in the mornings and watch the sun come up."

"Farmers don't have the leisure to sit in the morning, Beryl. Why not face west, so we can watch the sun go down?"

"I want to be able to see the sun rising, coming from England."

Beryl climbed a bit further up the rise. It was, she realized, a rather substantial hill. Looking north, one could see for miles. She wondered if the lights from Victoria Manor would be visible at night. Looking south, she saw the trees running along the creek and, far beyond them, bluish bluffs marking the Smoky Hill River. Then she looked east.

"What is that – out there – those animals?"

Mr. Keith looked where she pointed, then got out his field-glasses. William shaded his eyes. "Is it bison?"

"No – antelope"

"Antelope!"

Keith kept his eyes to the glasses. "Not far, actually."

There was a moment's silence. The two men were still, watching those dark shapes. Beryl was fascinated. Back in London she'd seen her cat freeze just like these men when he had spotted a mouse in the pantry. She wondered how long before the men sprang.

Will spoke. "Close enough to make it worth a try?"

"Are you up for it, lad?" The Scotsman lowered his glasses, measured his companion.

Will almost whooped.

"But do you know how to shoot?"

Will was surprisingly humble. "I've been fox hunting, but those conditions are rather different. If you take the lead, I'll follow."

Keith nodded, then hesitated. "Miss Newland?"

"Oh, go on!"

They moved quickly. The Scotsman loaded his rifle while William ran to his mount. The horses had been lazily grazing among a thicket of scrubby trees, but they responded rapidly to the hunters' excitement. Both men were tall and sat well on their mounts. Will was compelled to clutch at his bowler as they galloped away, but the russet-haired Scotsman was a graceful, romantic figure on his white steed. Out of a Waverley novel, thought Beryl with amusement.

The riders crossed into the distance in very little time. Beryl watched them intently, watched their far-away quarry, watched the startled birds that rose from the grasses as the horses raced.

It took her a few minutes to realize she was alone.

She heard the wind running against the ground and sorting the leaves of the trees near the creek. Crows cawed in the creek bottom. Her pony raised his head and gazed disinterestedly toward the water. He cared neither to join his brothers in the hunt nor to keep company with the woman who had perched so uneasily on his back. He chewed contentedly at the prairie, lowering his nose into the buffalo grass and whipping at flies with his tail. Insects ticked. Beryl's veil blew, warm against her face. She was glad the brim of her hat created some shade.

Her eyes narrowed, struggling to keep the shrinking figures of her companions in sight. She grew dizzy staring into the brightness. The wind pushed ineffectually against the heavy drapery of her skirt. Her ears were used to the background bustle of a London street. She found this vast silence uncanny.

Surely she was being watched.

She whirled and faced a blank horizon. The need to urinate, urgent and sharp, came on her. Nervous desperation made her hands clammy. She tore off her gloves.

Beryl forced herself to look away from the far away men and let her eyes fall instead on the carpet of short, wide-bladed grass beneath her feet. Red insects crawled with unthinking industry up and down a small city of anthills. They did not know why they did what they did, an ignorance that seemed to add to, rather than detract from, the energy they expended in service to the colony. Beryl kicked one of the sandy piles, taking a certain mean pleasure in watching the ants scurry amid the destruction. Then she felt sorry. She tried to help the creatures set things to right again, lifting the hem of her skirt and using her boot to push the scattered dirt back into a sort of pile. This only created greater agitation. "I shouldn't have done that," she thought.

She looked out again over the grasses to the small dark spots on the horizon, and to the cloud of dust that marked her companions' progress. She shivered in the warm sun, felt again the painful urge to urinate.

Walking helped. She walked to the area Will had paced off for their home; walked through walls and cupboards as freely as a ghost; walked back and forth over the hearth which now burned with sprouting sunflowers. She crushed the weeds growing where thresholds would stand, imagined views from windows framed and curtained only by her mind, saw a table and chair in a room now papered in blue sky. She fussed around the sitting room, placing an etagere against a spindly young tree, a sofa over a bed of small blue flowers, and a piano against a wall of sun and near a window of wind so that she could look out as she played. She could hear the music in her mind; her fingers played it against her skirt, something she'd heard in an opera by Grieg. *Solveig's Song.* She waltzed over the bare dirt until the words of the aria became too haunting and drew her eyes in dread to the window. She thought she almost discerned the ticking of her mother's clock on the mantle before the music stopped and the walls of the house fell down.

She must relieve herself. She did not want to lose sight of William and Mr. Keith – they were still visible, though very far away – but she resigned herself to taking care of her needs while she had some measure of privacy. Walking down from that small eminence where the Newland place would stand, Beryl found a cluster of bushes. Glancing around uneasily, she crouched, cramped by her corsets, with her back to thorny branches. Uncertain about the best way to proceed (she'd always had the benefit of a water closet, a privy, or at least the privacy of a bed pot before), she knelt down with her knees apart and spread the bulk of her brown skirt and petticoats wide before her, carefully lifting and pushing the rest away from the back of her body. The grass scratched at her knees. She looked like she was praying, posing for an inspirational painting –

"Miriam in the Wilderness" – with her dress encircling her picturesquely. Such clothes had advantages she decided – though it would be hard for anyone to maintain modesty for long on this open plain.

A sudden thought of Indians crossed her mind. She froze for a moment in an agony of apprehension, then quickly reached under the back of her skirts (a decidedly unprayerful pose, though now she really was praying), awkwardly shifted her undergarments out of the way, and urinated.

Done, she stood, trying to smooth her skirt back into modest lines and make her flushed face conform to the calm of the sky. Her bustle seemed out of line; she pushed at it and then saw the urine trickling along the dry ground from under her skirt, pooling along a small tuft of grass before the earth sucked it away. Hastily, Beryl swept her dress from the path of the rivulet and kicked dirt over the wetness. She abandoned the small, ugly grove of bushes, hugging her arms to herself as though cold – a ridiculous posture in the heavy May warmth – and stood listening. She heard the ticking of insects, the pedaling of wind, but nothing else. She let out a deep breath.

Resolute, she went to the pony and led him up the rise. She ignored his baleful whinny and told him in a tart whisper that there was grass away from the creek as well as beside it. She wanted company and she wanted shade. A low cluster of white rocks, only a few feet from where she'd told Will she wanted their veranda, beckoned. It seemed like a landmark; it broke the sameness of the ground; it was a place to sit and rest and watch. She offered the pony some purple-fringed flowers, and, while he munched, searched the saddle bag until she found a large knife. She felt reassured by its weight, by the lethal glint of its blade. It empowered her after her loneliness, allowed her to defy and in some measure defeat the humiliation of the last half hour. Gripping it firmly, she sat on the biggest of the stones. She put her gloves back on, smoothed her hair, and readjusted her veil. And there she sat, looking east toward the dark running lines of antelope with the expression of a monarch watching the battle that would determine her fate. The men were gone, hidden, perhaps, in a hollow not immediately apparent on that plain. She watched and she waited, facing England.

Grant's eyes snapped sparks, belying the quiet, almost conversational tone with which he addressed his agricultural manager.

"That you abandoned the hunt and came back doesn't excuse the fact that you left a woman alone and defenseless in the first place." He leaned over the desk, driving the forefinger of his right hand against its polished grain. A jewel glinted, deep red, on that hand. "What were you thinking, Keith? What were you thinking? There are the butchered bodies of men buried just 500 yards from where we lay our heads at night; there's the skin of two rattlesnakes that Fletcher killed in the privy yesterday – yesterday, man! – slung over the front railings for all to see. And yet you leave her alone on a pile of rocks with nothing but a bowie knife for protection. Exposed like a motherless lamb!" He pushed back into his chair, closing his hand into a frustrated fist.

"I have no excuse. It was foolish, thoughtless."

"Damn you, man, it was worse than that! It was unchivalrous!"

Keith looked at his employer with an unhappy expression, but the image flashed into his mind of Miss Newland sitting, straight and stern, against the white stones, the long knife resting in her hands like a scepter. When Keith had inquired after her welfare she ignored his question, merely saying "But Will, where are the antelope?" Douglas Keith doubted that Beryl Newland wanted chivalry.

"And as for you, William Newland, abandoning your sister like that – well, it doesn't speak well for your responsibility. This isn't a game, young man. We're not playing skittles at Oxford anymore."

A painful red stained Will's cheeks. He lifted his chin in some defiance – a characteristic movement that Keith had observed more than once in his sister – but he was ever conscious of being the gentleman.

"I didn't realize the danger, sir. Excitement got the better of me. And Beryl is quite independent. I'm not used to thinking of her as needing protection. I should, of course, have been more aware."

"More aware, he says. Exactly how much more aware does a man need to be? I'll be sorely disappointed in you, William, if you behave with no more care than your friends."

His reference was to Avery, who had saved a bottle of French wine to celebrate the colonists' arrival at Victoria. After most of the others retired their first night at Victoria, he, Cabot, and the Wyatt boys had gathered on the veranda for a small celebration. In plundering his trunk, the Wyatts found that Avery had more than one bottle in reserve and, having thoroughly enjoyed the first, assured Avery, Cabot, and each other that the occasion demanded opening another. In the morning Mr. and Mrs. Baldwin entered the station waiting room to find it fragrant with the odor of fermented grapes and littered with five empty bottles of impressive vintage. Sprawled on the iron benches which lined the walls were the snoring and inelegant forms of young men. Mrs. Baldwin hastily retreated. Mr. Baldwin then kicked them from their stuporous slumbers.

Will was amused as well as disgusted, but it was the former which sauced his story with relish when he narrated the incident to Mr. Keith and Beryl during their ride. His humor had been checked by Beryl's reaction. Frigid disapproval he might have ignored, but the combination of sorrow and anxiety in her face gave him pause. After over a month of travelling together, his sister now knew these men personally; they were no longer just names and faces in the distance of her brother's life. What is more, when they had gotten drunk that night, they had done so just downstairs from where she was sleeping, from where Mrs. MacDonough was crying, from where children were lying in small dark bundles. The prairie knew no privacy; the colonial life offered no sacred domestic space. The life of the one was, in some measure, the life of the many. Will was used to being entertained by his friends' escapades; he was not used to seeing their broken bottles litter his sister's path. The story grew sour in his mouth; he swallowed unsaid the final funny tidbits.

Keith had listened quietly, fixing his brown eyes on William with that same disconcerting stare he gave to plants and animals he wanted to understand. "Wandering drunk in the dark is plain foolishness out here, and nothing to laugh at, lad. Like as not, one of your friends will end up burying his boot in a rattlesnake's nest. You might be telling them that."

William had not appreciated being chastised by Mr. Keith then, and he was galled to find Mr. Grant linking him with Avery and Cabot's behavior now. Surely the desire to bag an antelope did not deserve to be associated with those others' bacchanalian revels.

"I hope you believe I would never behave in such a manner, sir," he said stiffly.

Grant softened just slightly. He liked William Newland, liked his ambition, his earnestness, his youth. "I trust not. And in the matter of the hunt, Keith is more culpable than you; he hasn't the excuse of ignorance. But you both need to remember we're not in England or Scotland now; this land is a wilderness. Its people are wild, its animals are wild, its weather is wild. Would you let Miss Newland walk alone at night in London? Well, I'm telling you, lad, think of it as night here all the time. A man needs always to be vigilant, and a gentlewoman must never be left alone. We're the ones bringing civilization and the light that comes along with it. It's not day yet." He studied Will for a moment. "Your sister – can she shoot a gun?"

"I think not, sir."

He turned to Keith. "Do you think any of the other ladies can?"

"Randall told me his wife used to take part in the hunts on her father's estate, but I don't know that any of the other women can handle firearms."

"They need to learn; even Meg is not too young. Your penance, Keith: to teach the women to defend themselves – from snakes and men. The sooner the better." He turned to the window and gazed out. "The place is glorious, but it's crawling with rattlers. They'll play the devil with our livestock."

Keith followed his gaze. He was quiet a moment and then asked, "Still no word from Davis or Staples?"

"No." Grant pulled at his beard. "No."

The streets of Hays City left the impression, primarily, of dust. Storms during the week had beaten the dust and manure into pulverized muck, but the impression of dust remained. Perhaps it was the baked color, or the gritty, soft texture. Dust ground itself into the boards of the sidewalks, nestled in the curtains of the houses, scratched itself into the eyes. Transients and ne'er-do-wells seeking small jobs for the cost of a dinner or drink could depend upon being wanted to wash away the film that accumulated on the windows of merchants and saloon owners. Tommy Drumm was reputedly so soft-hearted that he would give a man work wiping already clean glass. But usually a soft heart wasn't necessary, because the battle against the dust was perpetual. Dust filled the creases of boots and the lines on faces. It dimmed the shimmer of satin gowns and made the dull bombazine of mourning even duller. The sky above Hays City might be clear, even brilliantly so, but dust clung to the body of the town like a stifling skin, making the inhabitants thirsty – thirsty for water against the face and hands, and, too often, thirsty for something stronger than water on the throat.

It might be dust, then, that accounted for the thirst of the dozen British colonists strolling the wooden walkways of Hays City on Thursday afternoon. After four days there was still no sign of the supply wagon from Salina, so Duncan, Randall, and a few others persuaded Grant that certain goods had become necessary enough that a trip to Hays City was warranted. Grant himself had business there, but he was unwilling to leave the manor before the livestock and the colonists were well and confidently settled. Edwards had been to Hays before, however, and could be trusted to guide the colonists who wanted to make the trip. They rode into town on horseback, with Duncan and MacDonough driving a team and wagon.

In a place where "respectability" was only beginning to gain the upper hand, the Britons' polished manners, rich accents, assumption of superiority, and, not least, their clean clothes, were necessarily noticed. They drew stares in the general store, where their fashionable bowlers and delicate gloves left women in calico feeling dowdy as well as dusty. In Ryan's Outfitting, Avery was irresistibly drawn to an intricately embroidered leather vest – it must have originated in Mexico – and insisted on donning it immediately along with an expensive cowboy hat and some stiff boots that pinched his toes. (He swore that he had dainty feet and therefore the larger size the clerk tried to sell him could not possibly be right). He limped after his compatriots carrying a sack of cornmeal and his discarded London finery, proudly ignoring the guffaws that followed him down the sidewalk like a faithful dog. William was annoyed at the attention his friend drew, and Randall was inclined to be truculent, but Cabot was merely amused. Conscious that the looks he attracted were admiring rather than derisive, and quite often originated from under the few delicate veils and pretty bonnets the town offered, Cabot was inclined to be indulgent towards Avery. The clown, after all, only underscores the dignity of the hero.

Flour, coffee, and tea (they had not yet discovered how bad American tea was); biscuits and buffalo meat; coal and seed; kerosene and nails; crates of canned peaches and two bushels of potatoes; oilcloth and newspapers from Denver and Kansas City were loaded into the wagon. Randall arranged for an order of lumber from the sawmill, where he also purchased a small, cunningly made wagon for his little boy. Edwards did some work for Mr. Grant in the land and deeds office and helped MacDonough seek a midwife for advice about Jane's condition. But as yet most of the men had little serious business in Hays City. They were satisfying their curiosity, checking out the amenities this prairie metropolis of five hundred souls had to offer: a new and respectable-looking school, a few stores, a pretentious hotel, some humble boarding houses, and a long line of brothels and saloons. Their interest in the latter was perhaps disproportionate, given the faith their mothers had in them as Christian gentlemen. Of course, their mothers had never experienced such dust.

"It's time to be getting home, isn't it?" MacDonough noticeably lagged behind his companions, who did not seem inclined to leave Hays even though the wagon was full. His face was drawn. Perhaps the dusty air did not agree with him, but more likely worry was the poison in his system, worry that would not be purged until Jane was safely delivered of her baby and freed from a despair she seemed unable to cry away.

Keith and Edwards looked at him sympathetically, and the former opened his mouth to concur, but big Ian Duncan – friendly, well-meaning, and better able to discern the mood of a steer than the feelings of a fellow human – broke in. "May as well test the hospitality of our neighbors and enjoy a drink before returning to Victoria, eh, lads? It's a long drive back, what with the load in the wagon and the boggy road."

Michael Fletcher scratched his blond mustache and scowled at Avery with an animosity only half genuine. "They'll be many a dry day in Victoria thanks to Cowboy Jim's inaugural fête. Better drink while we can."

Avery was unperturbed. "You, sir, are just sorry you were not invited to the party."

"Damn fine party it was, too," commented Cabot, consulting his watch.

William felt compelled to break in. "You weren't in a London club, you know. There were women and children upstairs."

Nigel Wyatt was snide. "William Newland Grundy, protector of youth and innocence. You really ought to have stayed in England and written sermons for the edification of old ladies and vicars."

William ignored him. It was well known that the youngest Wyatt brother had been expelled from public school, and his family had not even been able to buy him a commission. Nigel didn't much care; even as the third son he could count on a substantial allowance from his family. He needed no profession. He could devote his days to polishing his natural gifts: pride, presumption, and a mean pugnaciousness. They gave bold, dark outline to a man whose slight build, almost albino hair and complexion, and rabbity pink eyes made him seem otherwise in constant danger not simply of fading into the more dramatic background of a window, a tree, or a shelf of books, but of actually disappearing altogether. His brothers, equally pale but defined by a more genial energy, were decent enough chaps, but Will considered Nigel less than contemptible, a nonentity. For that, Nigel hated him.

Keith, near the front of the group, stopped. "A brief drink won't be hurting anyone, but it needs to be brief. We'll want to be back before sundown."

"Well, gentlemen, to whom should we give our custom? The number of choices these Americans provide is positively dizzying." Cabot scanned the establishments lining North Main Street with an expression not entirely complimentary to their diversity.

Randall, also impatient to return to his family and eager to avoid the possibility of a new and even more acrimonious debate, proposed in a deliberately commanding tone, "We're just doors from the Dalton place. Looks decent from the outside. I say let's stop there. Edwards, Duncan?"

The men entered the low-roofed structure and then stood blinking for a few minutes, trying to adjust their eyes to the darkness. The natural light in Dalton's was minimal: dusty sunbeams struggled through a pair of large but well-shuttered windows. Two men in clean white aprons – one middle-aged and stocky, the other no more than sixteen but with an old sort of face – stood beside a long wooden counter, wiping glasses. Behind them, on roughly finished shelves, a legion of liquors, wines, beers, and whiskeys crowded – mostly whiskeys. The bottles and decanters were brown, green, or clear glass; some were unopened, but most seemed to be in use, loosely corked or capped. The patrons were what the Englishmen would call American-looking: lanky, brown, dressed in the flannel of teamsters or the blue of soldiers. Their dusty and shapeless hats, their well-worn boots, emphasized the artificiality of Avery's costume. Even he felt it. A black man, sweeping some broken glass into a pan, raised his eyes and stared at the newcomers. The sound of talk subsided. Will looked uneasily at Keith, who'd removed his hat and was studying the situation with those thoughtful brown eyes.

Randall went up to the counter, closely followed by Fletcher, Edwards, Duncan, and Mayes. The Wyatt brothers hung together, considering things, and then sat at an empty table near the door. Cabot and Avery sat with them. MacDonough sighed heavily and then said to William with forced cheer, "Well, Newland, let's have a drink." The two of them joined Duncan and the others.

Inertia is a powerful force. Though the men drinking in Dalton's saloon distrusted strangers, especially foreigners sporting fashion that represented more than a year's worth of their own hard-earned income, their tendency was to exchange contemptuous glances and then mind their own business. One or two of the less wholesome customers could be counted on to stare belligerently in hopes of igniting some sign of cowardice or challenge, but on the whole the men just wanted to be left to wallow or whine in their glasses as their case demanded.

The taciturn Scotsmen understood and respected this reaction, but the English, representatives of that empire on which the sun never set, could not comprehend the lack of hospitality. Where they were not made welcome, they would make themselves appreciated. Leslie Edwards, after a genteel sip of some startlingly strong whiskey, clapped Duncan on his broad back and, fortified by the prodigality of his employer, addressed the room with complacent cordiality. "I say, drinks for all our American cousins, compliments of George Grant, founder of the Victoria Colony!"

One young farmer with green eyes and yellow hair noticeably brightened at the possibility of a free drink, but any illusions he or the Englishmen had regarding Anglo-American friendship were quickly and crudely dispelled.

"Don't drink with no god-damned Brits." The low growl issued from somewhere in the more shadowy part of the shadowy room.

"I beg your pardon?" Edwards was still smiling.

"I said, we don't drink with no god-damned Brits. And certainly not with them that think they can come in, buy up American land, and populate it with puppets like that." The man, a handsome specimen with thick brown hair and the dusty blue uniform of an army corporal, stood up as he spoke, looked pointedly at Avery, and spat. Laughter circulated like a foul odor from table to table.

Avery took off his fine new hat and stood up. "My good man, I take great exception to that." Cabot stood up next to him.

"Take what the hell you will, but git out of our saloon. Better yet, git out of our state."

"Shit – vacate the country!" chimed in another soldier. The odor spread, grew more intense.

"Gentlemen, you're a low-class brand of Yankee or you wouldn't settle for vinegar like this." Nigel Wyatt put his glass down on the table and pushed back his chair, a specter speaking out of the artificial dusk. "But then it's always been my feeling that the lower classes need a good beating every now and then. A purgation if you will. And if your betters in these United States won't administer it, well then those of us committed to the civilizing of the world had better do our duty. That being said – " Before his brothers could stop him, before any of those around him even realized his intention, Wyatt stood, picked up the glass and shot it swiftly at the temple of the man who had begun the altercation.

Edwards's face became ashen. The secretary's spectacles were blank circles of shock as he turned toward Will. Will's hazel eyes widened for a second in answering dismay – the glass missed its mark and shattered against the wall – but then grew grim. After all, he too was John Bull's son, and a tension that had been growing in him for days made him suddenly grateful for the opportunity to hit someone.

It was like a scene out of the dime westerns and penny dreadfuls these young men had devoured as schoolboys. Tables were overturned, bottles flew, men threw themselves at each other. The Wyatt brothers sank under a sea of blue. Cabot took off his jacket with a studied grace, proud of his finely formed shoulders and muscular chest, and struck a fine, pugilistic pose – a pose prematurely ruined by a blow to the abdomen coming from a man who was snaking around the floor on his knees, striking, tripping, even pinching. A howl of rage broke from the proprietor behind the counter as a missile crashed into a line of glasses. The sixteen-year-old pulled a rifle out from somewhere in the darkness, cocked it, and shouted out, "No shooting! No shooting! I'll kill any man who pulls a gun!" His voice cracked down the middle as he spoke, from the stress of excitement or, perhaps, adolescence. The black man, Joseph Carter, watched in amazement as Randall first threw against the wall a small person in red flannel who'd been scaling his back like a rock face and then, by accident, sent a powerful punch into the open jaw of Jason Mayes. Contempt set Carter's mouth in a firm line and, signaling Dalton with a jerk of his head, he disappeared into the back room and out the back door.

Keith, seeing this and sensing the inevitable, moved quickly from where he'd felled a stripling teamster by the front door, grabbed MacDonough's beer-drenched arm and roughly shoved him away from the counter, out of the saloon, off the sidewalk, and into the street. Anyone watching – and there were already gawkers congregating safely out of firing range – might have justifiably thought that Keith was the young man's antagonist. But the words of the aggressor were gently spoken. "Jane needs you, Danny boy. And someone'll have to cart home all our broken heads." Before MacDonough could respond or protest, his companion disappeared back into the low building, leaving him ankle-deep in the choking epidermis of Hays City.

The storm was just breaking when Meg came up to the room with a lamp. The thunder, distant for more than an hour, suddenly fell upon them with a fury that seemed to crack the sky from one end to another. Electricity shattered its face, breaking it apart first this way and then that. Meg came running down the hall and into the room with dazzled eyes and soaked shoulders.

"Beastly storm! Another one! Every afternoon it seems! We had bad storms at home when I was growing up, but I've never seen the like of this." She caught her breath and peered into the gloom of the room. "Whatever are you doing? Everything is turned upside down!"

Beryl looked up from a small thick book she'd been reading and said rather dryly, "No, it's merely taken out. I've been unpacking my trunks, looking for something useful."

"Useful? Really? What can these be good for – but they're ever so pretty!" Meg lowered the lamp to examine some cutglass candlesticks. Beryl sighed and nodded. She had spent the afternoon making similar observations herself.

Beryl should never have allowed her sister-in-law to pack the trunk of domestic goods. Marian had no conception of life on the plains, no sense that three boxes of beeswax candles might be worth more than the two empty cut glass candle sticks that created resplendent prisms on the bare floor of Beryl's room. Five embroidered doilies, two ridiculously fussy antimacassars (which Beryl was certain she'd seen Marian working on during holiday visits for at least half a decade), four fine linen table cloths – one edged with Irish lace – with twelve napkins to match; a set of china delicately decorated with sprigs of English rose, including a tea service and a platter big enough to hold a roast pig; thirty shining silver spoons, knives and forks; eight etched-glass goblets, paired with seven etched-glass champagne glasses (the eighth lay with its stem broken against the edge of the trunk); a vase of sky-blue glass; and two small white cotton towels – something practical at last! – where Beryl could have wanted twenty. Such was Marian's conception of housekeeping. For a good thirty minutes earlier in the afternoon, while the sun still shone and the sky was still blue, Beryl had sat on the floor of her room with a small, gilt-edged wall mirror in her lap and looked back and forth between the plain white chamber pot which sat, fat and obscene, under the end of the bed and the doleful but elegantly framed reflection that gazed back from against her knees.

"I shall go mad if I must use a lace napkin to wipe out the pot," she said to herself.

She placed the mirror up on the bed and reached to the bottom of the trunk for some flat, square packages, grimly confident that she would find no brushes here either. Pulling off the brown wrapping, she was stopped in her complaints. "Oh," she breathed, "Oh, Marian."

What she found were two framed portraits. One, in a heavy walnut frame, was a painting of her mother and father in the early days of their marriage. It was a good if not a perfect likeness. The furious wealth of curls clustered on either side of her mother's round face was nothing Beryl could recognize, but the amiable grey eyes were there, though brighter than she remembered. Warren Newland stood beside her, a man with a firm, clean-shaven jaw and a soft wave of light brown hair combed away from a high brow. When he died, he was bald, his strong jaw grown slack with suffering and rough from the stubble of a beard that grew in ugly patches. It was good for Beryl to be reminded of how he had been in her childhood, of how he had once been like William. She marveled that Marian had sent along this portrait. As far as she knew, it was the only representation of her parents that existed. But then Robert, situated at Lindenhurst, had many constant if less literal reminders of his parents while his siblings had only the sense of absence to refer to in a strange land.

In the other frame – a small gold one with ornate William Morris carvings of birds and flowers – was a daguerreotype of Marian herself, with her husband and two children. It must have been recently made; Beryl recognized the collar that Beatrice wore tied around her neck as one she had given the child only last Christmas. The little girl's hands and face were fuzzy; getting her to stand still for as long as the camera plate demanded had clearly been impossible. Charlie did better. He looked solemnly back at Beryl with the same serious expression that had, with little more substantial effort, earned his father public esteem as a respectable man. That the boy might himself be a man before Beryl saw him again made her feel slightly sick. She had been with the child and his family only a little over a month ago, but already their images, like those of her dead parents, came to her shaded in sepia. When she looked at Marian's kind eyes – even the strain of remaining motionless for many minutes had not drained the kindness from them – she forgave all the silly, useless, beautiful household items her sister-in-law had sent along. They were, after all, redolent of that woman's taste and grace, reminders of the pretty ribbons on her dresses and the sparkling pins in her hair.

Of course, there was still the chamber pot to deal with. It sat there as odious (and odorous) as ever: complacent, sure of its indispensability and brutally unsentimental. Beryl had come to the United States with few illusions, but she had not reckoned on all the realities of being without a housemaid. Even on the miserable trip across the Atlantic there had been stewards to save her the trouble of disagreeable tasks. She sighed, gently laid the portraits on the bed next to the mirror and rolled up her sleeves. She got on her knees and opened another smaller trunk, seeking something ugly and practical.

Robert's housekeeper, God bless her, had sent the ugly and practical.

So when Meg Grant came into the room later with a lamp to dispel the unnatural dusk that had fallen with the storm, she found Miss Newland seated among an odd assortment of brushes and dusters, aprons and rags, soaps and polishes. Beryl was gloating over a fat, unwieldy tome entitled *Guide to Household Management, by Mrs. Isabella Beeton.*

"How can you read without light?" Meg looked about and then cautiously closed the lid of a trunk and set the lamp upon it. "And why are you here alone? The storm is dreadful. Uncle George says we should all come downstairs in case a cyclone comes. Of course, it looks as though it's already hit here."

"You are getting cheeky, Meg. You used to be such a sweet girl."

"I used to have a bed to sleep on. Now you've covered it with – forks? That won't be very comfortable."

"I'll clean it up. I intend to clean many things up. Which is the point of this mess."

"You do have the prettiest stuff. My mama once - "

Cut off by a deafening clap of thunder, Meg flinched. "You must come *now.*" She bent over and scowled into Beryl's face.

Beryl took in the girl's pleading eyes, fierce mouth, and long red braid which fell over her shoulder and almost into Beryl's own lap. Rain hammered the window, its violence occasionally accentuated by gusting wind. A cold sound, the sound of England. But the room was sticky and hot, charged by a foreign ferocity. Perspiration beaded on Meg's brow, curling the hair around her face. Beryl wiped her own forehead. "Of course I'll come. Mrs. Beeton is not so terribly riveting. Is everyone else down in the waiting room?"

Meg reached for the lamp and pulled a hood over her head. "Those who are here of course. The others – no."

Beryl stood and wrapped herself in a shawl beneath which she clutched the invincible *Mrs. Beeton*. She stretched her free hand out to Meg and together they went down the dark hall through a common sitting room and out into the storm.

The steps leading from the first-floor lodging rooms to the ground-floor station rooms were outside. In the storm, they were slippery. Sheets of rain slung themselves at the building and at the two women groping their way down the stairs. If not for the constant lightning, it would have been impossible to see. Under the veranda roof which circled the building, they found shelter enough that, looking toward the east, they could see the brightness of late afternoon still gleaming beneath the clouds. To the west, all was black.

They pushed through the screened door and stood dripping and gasping. Lamps were lit all along the walls of the station room. Their flames danced when the building shuddered against the storm. Under one window, water was creeping between the sill and the glass. Someone had rolled an old blanket beneath it to stop the pooling. Otherwise, the room was tight, snug, and oppressively warm.

Mr. Grant sat in the station office, talking to Neil Hunter and Garth Mason. Mrs. Baldwin bent over a kettle on the great black stove in the middle of the room. The aroma of coffee hung in the air. Beryl was disappointed; she longed for tea. The Baldwin children huddled in a circle on the floor near their mother; their father sat with them, telling stories with great drama. Between storm and fairy tales, the children's eyes were wide. Lydia Randall sat with her child in her lap on a bench against the east wall. Her face was composed, and she talked soothingly, not to the child, but to Jane Mac-Donough, who sat next to her and looked fixedly at the door leading into the station. Both women's eyes grew eager when the door opened; both looked down, one with a shuddering breath, upon seeing it was only Meg and Beryl who came in.

Beryl peeled the dripping shawl away from her hair and skirt and threw it, along with Meg's cloak, onto the iron bench by the door. "The Kansas Pacific has given us a hotel when what we need is an ark," she commented. She meant it as a pleasantry, but immediately saw by Jane's face that it was the wrong thing to say. Perplexed, she looked around at the small group. "But where are Will and Mr. Avery? And the others?"

"I told you they weren't here," whispered Meg.

"But surely they should be back from Hays City by now. I thought you meant Mr. Davis and Mr. Staples still hadn't arrived."

"They haven't." Meg's pupils were large and black. "None of them are here."

Beryl felt an odd clutch at her heart. She reacted to it with anger. "William hasn't the sense of a cat," she snapped.

Mrs. Baldwin looked up at Beryl with tired eyes, and said, "Oh now, Miss Newland, they'll know how to take care of themselves."

Her husband broke his storytelling to add in a confident voice, "Truth be known, they're probably safer out there in a low ditch than we are in here. Though this is a fine strong building, isn't it my bairns?"

The little Baldwins looked at him solemnly and assured him it was like a fort. The oldest children had been clamoring to visit Fort Hays for days now. They had not gotten their wish, but this did not stop them from imagining all manner of wonderful things about what a fort might be like. They were comforted by the presence of their father and could therefore turn the rough storm into an adventure. It reminded them of being at sea, except better, for here there were no waves, they did not feel sick, and they could not drown. They chattered and laughed and cried a little when the breaking thunder seemed too powerful even for their father. They noticed, in their childish way, that the adults looked orphaned and anxious. Mr. Grant alone seemed to be in full command. He stood with his arms crossed, glaring out the window. The children considered him their captain and hero. They trusted him to go down with the ship.

As the time neared five o'clock, Meg and Beryl consulted with Mrs. Baldwin. Pulling a long table away from one wall and opening a locked cupboard of supplies, they began laying the table for tea. Their numbers were so diminished that when at last the colonists sat down to eat the salty cured ham, bread and butter, coffee and tea (Beryl had prevailed upon Mrs. Baldwin to use some of their precious store), the table seemed far too big, seemed to make them impossibly distant from each other. The lightning had lessened; fewer brutal crashes interrupted their halting conversation. Mr. Grant offered a blessing in thanksgiving for their shelter and a petition on behalf of their absent comrades. Jane worried the tablecloth with her thin hands. Lydia insisted she drink some milk and eat for the sake of the baby. Lydia was the only person, other than her husband, to whom Jane would listen. On the other side of Jane, the little Randall boy and the Baldwin children ate well. The Grant cousins were hungry: Clay bolted his food unpleasantly, much to Meg's embarrassment. Across the table Beryl took ferocious bites of her bread and butter while she berated William over and over in her head. Mr. Hunter bent his own dark head studiously over the ham and thought of his lover back in Scotland. Garth Mason spent only five minutes at the table before going to check on the livestock. Mr. Grant ate little, but smoked and drank coffee, and swore every now and again at the thunder with a wink of such comedic force that the children giggled.

Toward the end of the meal, the rain again fell violently. The sky again shattered with light and sound. The eldest Baldwin boy, Neville, went to the window and stared out at the ground until Mr. Grant insisted he move back from the glass. The rain striking the building grew louder, harder, like the throwing of stones. The Baldwin boy sidled a little closer to the window again and exclaimed in wonder, "Father, it is snowing marbles!"

The hail went on for ten minutes. When it stopped, the storm was finished. Wind blew the clouds east; the western sky threw gold and red onto their retreating forms. When Meg opened the station door, a cold ghost of air crept along the floor of the hot room. The children clustered around her, wondering at the pebbles of ice which sheeted the grass like a freak snowstorm. Given permission to go out and play, they waded across the porch the way they would a slippery stream. Meg and her cousin Clay were soon attacking each other with snowballs of hail, while the small children gathered the hail in great handfuls, sucking on it and crying when it melted and burned their hands with cold.

Beryl swept the icy piles from the porch and watched the children play. She gratefully breathed in the brisk air. It smelled sweet, like rain and blossoms and grass: the perfume of torn meadows and stripped trees. Mr. Grant, standing next to Mr. Hunter and Mr. Baldwin, admired her as she faced the setting sun whose gold suffused her features and heightened the blue lights in her tightly coiled black hair.

"Invigorating, isn't it, lass?"

Beryl leaned on her broom and looked at him. "Yes. Yes, it is."

"You might even call it champagne air?"

"You might," conceded Beryl, smiling.

Neil Hunter gazed out into that same sun and suddenly nudged Mr. Grant. "There they are. By Jove, Grant, there they are."

"What, the boys? That'll be good news for Mrs. MacDonough and Mrs. Randall."

"Noo," said Neil slowly, "I think it's – "

Little John Baldwin broke in with a yell. "The army! The army is coming!"

The small dark shape that had been moving over the white plain had become a man on a horse followed by a very big wagon. The man did indeed wear the blue of the United States calvary. The wagon, loaded with goods and covered with a battered tarp, was driven, however, by two Britons: the missing Ben Davis and Gerard Staples. The children shrieked with delight, and the other women rushed outside. In the excitement Beryl was perhaps the only one who noticed Mr. Grant's face. Relief washed over it like glory over a sinner reclaimed. You might not realize sin's stain until it was gone, she thought, and you certainly would not suspect the anxiety dogging this man until you saw it disappear.

"By God, Davis, where have you been? We've been waiting and expecting you over a week!"

Ben Davis jumped down from the wagon. His clothes were muddy. The left side of his boyish face was bruised, the skin scabbed. But his voice was glad and hearty as he called out, "Victoria at last! How are you all? Mr. Grant? Ladies? And yes, we have some cakes for you," he laughed to the hoard of small heads circling his knees. "This is Captain Weeks, from Fort Hays. Capt. Weeks, Mr. Grant, founder of Victoria. We have the gentlemen at Fort Hays to thank for getting us here safe."

Captain Weeks shook hands with Grant and tipped his hat to the women. "Our pleasure. Had to make sure you got your supplies. Way these fellows were headed, Denver was their bunk."

"What happened?"

Staples, short and stocky, limped over from the wagon with a bedraggled parcel for the children. He shook his sunburned head. "I've never seen storms like out here. Barely get going and it rains, or hails, or blows. The creeks were flooded. The trails indecipherable. Altogether a contrary country, Mr. Grant." His tone was not friendly.

Ben took up the refrain more cheerfully. "Got lost more times than I care to remember. But arrived at Fort Hays almost by accident, and there we found the help we needed to get us here." Ben scanned the hail-strewn hotel, its stones a wet, glistening yellow in the evening light. "Fine looking building, even if it is the only one like it for half-a-day's ride! But where are the others? Staples and I can't unload without some of Duncan's brawn and Cabot's brain."

"No, you boys are about whipped, sure enough." The captain remounted his horse. "Sorry I can't stay to help, but if you folks need anything, just send over to the Fort. Always glad to see civilized people coming into the country. Not to mention cultured people. Mr. Grant." Captain Weeks gave a snappy salute, to the delight of the children, and turned back to the west just in time to see another wagon coming along the rails from the north.

"Daniel!" cried Jane joyfully. For the first time since they had arrived in Kansas, her expression brightened. She eagerly set off, moving heavily but quickly over the slushing hail and broken grass. The older Baldwin children ran after. She was not far from the rumbling wagon when she stopped, her voice changed. "Daniel. Daniel?"

Her husband jumped off the wagon and threw the reins to Keith, who kept his face steadily turned away from the crowd awaiting them on the platform. He went to her and hugged her hard. "I'm fine, Jane, just fine. But as for them – ." Disgust graveled his voice. He shook his head at Mr. Grant, then caught sight of Captain Weeks. "Yankees causing trouble here too, Janie?"

"That's Captain Weeks. He brought Mr. Davis and Mr. Staples from Fort Hays. Were you attacked by Indians?"

Grant was now at Jane's shoulder, ordering the Baldwin children back to their mother. "Keith? Edwards?" His query was loud and hard.

Leslie Edwards looked vaguely towards the manor. He had a black eye. His spectacles were gone. "Sorry, Mr. Grant. Had a bit of trouble."

"Where?"

"Not all American soldiers are as interested in helping us as Captain Weeks."

"I asked you once and I'll ask you again. Where?"

"Dalton's public house." Keith answered, turning toward the manor. His lip was split, swollen; it still bled a bit, but his words were calm and matter of fact. "Not the fault of these lads, Mr. Grant. They were just upholding the honor of the mother country."

"By drinking when there's work to be done?"

"I say, Grant," came Cabot's languid voice from the back of the wagon, "we didn't even have time to drink. Insult upon injury don't you know. We fought dead sober. And a gallant battle it was. But you know, I do rather think Fletcher's head is broken, and the doctor said he should have rest and quiet. That storm was not helpful. Randall and Duncan, do help me get him in. He's quite ruined my pants with his blood."

"Not to mention my vest." Avery was regretful, looking down at the dark stain inking across the bright embroidery, unaware that an equally ugly stain had spread from his temple and caked the inside of his new hat with clotted hair. "Boots are in jolly good shape though. What a lark, eh lads? Just like school days."

Those on the veranda and on the depot platform said nothing. Even the smallest children said nothing. Fletcher was carried in. Captain Weeks watched the proceedings; watched the bruised sons of Britain, watched their silent, waiting women, and watched George Grant, the man who had bought up half of Kansas and whose reputation had preceded him, legend-like, onto these western plains. The silk merchant's face was stony. The ring on his right hand reflected back the red of the sky like an angry eye. He barely nodded to acknowledge Weeks' departure and said nothing as he turned around to face the darkening stones of Victoria Manor.

Chapter IV

The June beetles were in their death throes the week that Jane Innes MacDonough came to childbed. Legions of them. They were big, black, and ugly. They fell from the ceilings onto the tables and into the beds where, momentarily, they upstaged the flies and the bedbugs. They whirred into lamps, threw themselves blindly against walls, and lay on their backs wiggling their legs, inching over the floors on hard shells by sheer force of that frantic clawing of the air. The dead ones lay with limbs folded reverently over exposed bellies. The children kicked them about the depot like shuttlecocks.

One of these bugs, trapped in an extra fold of the mosquito netting Sarah Baldwin had tacked around the open window, captured Jane's attention. The other women, looking at her, could not understand what so fascinated her; when Lydia spoke, she did not seem to hear. Following her gaze, Lydia thought perhaps it was the high, thin clouds combing themselves out beyond the window frame. The morning was still and bright. The day promised to be hot once again. Sarah, sitting on a worn trunk, sighed. She too watched, perplexed at the odd, probing expression that took over Jane's face between the desperate, open-eyed agony of each contraction. Like Lydia, Sarah glanced, wondering, toward the window. She would have been able to understand sleepiness or nervous chatter, a whimpering for mother or husband, an angry complaining, or a quiet supplication – she had experienced all of these. But this strange, absorbed abstraction that seemed to leave behind the room, the people, even Jane's own laboring body, left her uneasy and anxious.

"How long has it been?"

Lydia pushed back a limp cuff. "I don't know. Perhaps an hour."

"They should be back. She hasn't had many spells. Maybe she can wait longer. But she seems so far away between times."

"Too far."

"Was it at all like this for you?"

"Oh, I suppose I was even further away. I know nothing that went on. They used chloroform."

"Did they? Like the Queen?" The elder woman's low, weary voice brightened with interest. "What was that like?"

"Mr. Randall was upset by my pain, little though it was at that point. He insisted that Mama persuade our family doctor – a kind, old gentleman – to do something. So he did. He assured me that I need not be afraid: he would give me a drug to breathe from a cloth and then I would sleep, and they could do the rest. And so they did." Lydia paused, glanced at Jane, and then whispered, "But of course, I did not hear my baby's first cry, and the instruments bruised his head. I've often felt guilty at not being awake to protect him."

Sarah wanted to tell Lydia that she hadn't heard the first cries of all of her children either, not because they had been obliterated by peaceful oblivion, but because some of them had been drowned by her own screaming. She was stopped, however, by Jane's quickened breathing, her suddenly wandering eyes, and her bare arms bracing themselves against the sheets. Sarah crossed to the other side of the bed. She took up one of the girl's tense hands and Lydia took the other. Together, they faced the rising wave.

In the netting by the window, the beetle struggled.

"It was a mistake not to send him."

"But he wanted to be near her. He can't be both here and there."

"Even so. The waiting is tearing him up. Poor chap."

Cabot's eyes followed MacDonough as he paced up and down, over and across the depot platform. The cheerful Scot whom Cabot had first met in Glasgow, boyish in his enthusiasm, his optimism, and his self-confidence, was gone, defeated after only two months by things he could not understand and that he didn't know how to fight: his wife's depression, her impending motherhood, and his own great love for her. A brutal, blistering sunburn seemed to be peeling away the last vestiges of an old happiness from his face even as Cabot watched, and yet the distracted young man continued hatless beneath the midday sun. Cabot shook his head. Women ought not be allowed to ruin a man like that; it was what came of taking any one of them too seriously. He took the cigar from his mouth, examined it for a minute, and then crushed it out against the leg of the bench. Thomas Baldwin, aged four, watched. When Mr. Cabot and Mr. Avery got up and walked away, he crawled under the bench and carefully retrieved the half-consumed cigar. It would, he knew, be an excellent instrument to plague beetles with.

Mesmerized by its twisting legs and helpless turning, Jane did not realize that what she looked at was merely one of the beetles she had long since added to her list of Kansas horrors. Gazing at it in the gauzy netting, she believed herself back in the garden behind the house in Elgin where she had grown up, back in a garden of hardy pink roses, daisies, and four-o'clocks, whose fuscia blooms always delighted her by truly opening every day in time for tea. Patches of heather stolen from the hills grew along and between the stones. Sprays of lavender bent across the path. A pretty, raven-haired, solitary child – her older brother and sister had died of whooping cough when she was still small – she made each rock, plant, and creature in the garden into a playmate. She gave each a name and a history. She followed their stories through the changing seasons, commencing their dramas with the first buds of spring and narrating them well past winter's first snow. She was imaginative rather than sentimental, and she fully believed that the garden was enchanted, just as enchanted as the fabled garden of Eden – which was, of course, a fable, as her agnostic Uncle Charles assured her when she was only eight years old.

Jane did not like spiders. The day she discovered a yellow and brown spider hanging in a dew-bejeweled web against the northwest garden wall, however, she was certain that she had discovered the garden's queen and, accordingly, christened the creature Victoria. She admired the long, delicate legs that fanned out from the creature's body and extended over the silken threads like the silhouette of a skirt; she appreciated the full, strikingly patterned abdomen which provided the seductive curve of a bustle even in the days before the child – or anyone else – knew what such a thing was.

The spider was beautiful – and scary. When the regent quit her throne in the middle of the web, she left with frightening speed and ruthless purpose. The graceful limbs became slender, articulated needles that could move faster than a child could run and could clutch, spin, and mummify without mercy. Jane respected this power and was careful. She stood well away from the web and its fiercely beautiful monarch. She understood that both reverence and fear are due a sovereign.

Now, twenty years old, she watched the crooked, stunted legs of this panicked insect and wondered at the metamorphosis of her lovely queen into such an ugly fat thing. She watched those legs ineffectually weave the air and wondered how they had managed to create the odd, gauzy sheet of white, wondered even more how they could be satisfied to navigate such a plain, uninteresting web after the beautiful ladders and latticing of their garden palace. She was concerned at this turn in her sovereign's fortune, concerned that the delicate body had become big and black and squat. She would like to have expressed her concern, but she was afraid that the spider might turn on her, offended by presumption and pity; might come after her with those sharp crooked legs; might crawl over her and wrap her in a stifling, silky shroud so that she could not breathe. Jane wished to live, so she remained quiet and watched.

But some say queens can read minds. Victoria was, after all, a bewitching creature, and Jane suspected she herself was the object of a cold stare across that strangely bright space. Certainly those legs grew ever busier and more horrid, weaving, weaving. Anxiety spread cold tentacles across Jane's frame. Her eyes became searching, frantic. She must escape those legs, must get away – but there were too many of them; she had only two and there was nowhere to run. The stone bench which had shielded her from storms was gone; the great oak whose branches had once saved her from a rabid sheepdog was gone; the garden was gone; Scotland itself was gone. There was only this small, stifling room and the emptiness which surrounded it and exposed her.

The queen did not leave her seat, but nonetheless silken strands began to wrap themselves around Jane's own great and swollen abdomen. The weaving of those legs was cruel and purposeful. Jane felt her breathing grow quick and shallow; she couldn't get air. Terrified, she struggled. The webbing not only held fast, but pulled tighter and tighter, squeezing her ribs, her back, her hips, squeezing the life from her body, squeezing it into one huge, burning, slow-surging fury that bored against her insides and would break her into pieces. From across a static of pain, someone tried to talk to her. Jane could not understand the words. She understood only that she must explode and die; that she, like the beautiful, monstrously metamorphosed queen who was killing her, was doomed to become nothing more than a small, dried husk blowing on a cold wind, and then away.

Elizabeth Sullivan had taken up midwifery in 1858, at the age of twenty-three. A refugee from the Irish potato famine, she emigrated to New York, then Massachusetts, and later Illinois where she buried her mother and father, married a railroad man named Joey Cavendar, lived with him for six years and, after two lonely years without him, received a telegram informing her that he was among the dead at Gettysburg. She bent low under the weight of that blow, a widow left to raise a seven-year-old daughter on a street of poor Chicago row houses. Her sister, recently married to an industrious fellow determined to make his way upward in the slaughterhouses west of the city, invited Elizabeth to move in with them, but she declined. She did not wish to lose her independence buried in a small place where the dirty laundry smelled of blood.

She gradually realized that all of great noisy Chicago had become such a place for her. She had many friends, a supportive church, and a loyal clientele among her Irish neighbors, who preferred and trusted her wisdom in birthing children over that of an expensive doctor who could do no more – and who sometimes did a good deal less – than she. Elizabeth was nonetheless dissatisfied. As her grief lessened, she became determined to emigrate yet again. When, after the war, one of her closest friends set out to join her army husband at a fort on the great plains, Elizabeth, her daughter Rachel, and her five dogs went along. She told her weeping sister that there were women who needed help delivering babies on that frontier, and sure she wasn't going to sit and rot in Chicago all her life.

She still had five dogs the summer of 1873. Two were bulldogs that had originally come with her from Illinois; the rest were replacements for the dogs she had lost: one to drowning when the great flood destroyed the original Fort Hays site, one to the poison of a frightened rattlesnake, and one to a goodly old age. All five were in the yard as Neil Hunter and George Grant rode up to the house on Peachtree Street; all five set up a roaring that would have done justice to a dozen caged bears; and all five took distinct pleasure in flaunting their fangs for the edification of the intruders. A lace curtain pulled back from an open window and a pair of black eyes peered out. After a moment the curtain fell, and the front door opened.

"Give over with the palaver, Skip. Shut your mouths, all of ye, and let the gentlemen talk. Shut 'em, I say. That *will* be enough, Blair. Get *down*!"

A small woman gave the brown sheepdog a mild kick with her foot. He looked at her reproachfully and then sat in the dust next to the step, glaring at the riders. The unfriendliness of that welcome was not mitigated by a rifle which rested, baby-like but cocked, in the woman's arms. The brown hair pulled achingly tight over her scalp, the deep hollows of her eyes and cheeks, and the sharp edge of her jaw, all gave her something of the aspect of a death's-head. When she spoke, however, life, strong and vigorous, sang out in a richly modulated brogue.

"And now what would you men be wanting?" Two teeth were missing from the left side of her unsmiling mouth, but their absence did not interfere with the singing quality of her speech.

Mr. Grant dismounted and strode toward her, removing his hat. One of the bulldogs shifted his paws threateningly. Grant eyed him and proceeded no further. "Thank you for calling off your dogs, madame. Mrs. Cavendar, yes? I'm George Grant from the Victoria settlement, and this is Mr. Hunter. We've come from Daniel Mac-Donough, who said he spoke with you a few weeks ago about his wife's confinement. The child is on the way, Mrs. Cavendar, and Mr. MacDonough wanted us to fetch you along to help. So if you could gather your things. . ." He was already turning back to his horse.

Mrs. Cavendar let the rifle rest more easy, but her words were sharp. "Why didn't he come?"

Grant turned around, surprised. "He couldn't bear to leave his wife. Surely that's not uncommon."

"Humph. And why should I believe you're come from him and not come to carry me off into the grass and kill me?"

Mr. Grant looked at her, stupefied. "Surely, madame, you can see that we are gentlemen."

"I see that you wear mighty fine clothes, but all that shows is that you haven't enough work to wear them out. Sir, not your outfitten nor your fancy ring – " (she cocked her pointy chin at the red jewel flashing in the sun) " – are guarantees of anything."

Grant bristled. "My good woman – "

Neil Hunter interrupted. "Please, Mrs. Cavendar, Mr. Mac-Donough is desperate for help. His wife has been down since before midnight and isn't getting along very well."

"Midnight!" Professional anger broke through her suspicion. "Mother of God, it's past noon. Why did you wait so long? Is there anyone with her but him?"

"One of our horses got his leg caught in a hole. We had to shoot him, and then use the spare we'd brought for you . . . "

The woman turned back into the house, not waiting for the explanation. The men heard her calling to someone. A very few minutes passed, and she was out again on the porch with a carpet bag and a lilac-colored bonnet on her head. She pulled a short grey jacket on over her calico. "You haven't told me yet – is the young man the only one with her?"

"No," said Grant, moving toward his horse. "The women are taking a hand."

"What women?"

Hunter answered. "From the colony. One has five children herself. But they'd be glad for the help of someone who knew the business from the outside in, not just the inside out." Hunter looked confused for a moment. "If you know what I mean."

Deep in the tunnel of her bonnet, Mrs. Cavendar's eyes lit up; they were in fact not black but deep blue. "You're a comely fellow and an earnest one too. I'm betting there's a pretty lassie you're thinking of when you plead so lovely-like. Eh? I thought so! Well for your sake and for the sake of the young MacDonough, we shall go like the wind. Rachel! Where is Brownie? Hurry up, child!"

A slender girl about the age of his niece ran before Grant leading a chestnut pony. "Sorry, mum. He would be balky."

"Him and some others," muttered Grant.

Elizabeth pulled up onto the pony. At Grant's words she turned to look back at the silk merchant. "Call yourself a gentleman, do you? There's presumption. Nothing but an Englished-up Scot you are. Coming in and planting 'colonies' in a free country. Pshhh. That's the way of the Saxon. No self-respecting Celt would consider intruding on another people in such a manner. But then, from what I hear, we Americans needn't fear your invasion too much. Such a mess at Mr. Dalton's. Such a mess!" She chuckled, clucked to herself and her pony, then gave a brisk whistle. "There now, that's enough chatter. Come on, Blair me boy, you be my guardian angel. Rachel, I'll send word if I must be away overnight. Should anyone else need me, tell them I'm gone to Victoria."

Will Newland studied the stunted tree. It was pathetic and spindly, cowering like an abused child before the whipping wind. Half its leaves had been chewed away. Near its roots, the ground was pocked by gopher holes. He shook his head at it, and at the equally frail line of saplings behind it.

"That's the best you can show for three years' work?"

Lewis Watson was a mild man, but the imputation that some failure on his part accounted for the weak exhibition riled him. "Damn fine showing considering what I've been up against."

Garth Mason took in the carefully fenced plots, the scientifically spaced plantings, the meticulously constructed supports of sticks, strings, and twine to which grapes and tomatoes, beans and cucumber clung tenuously. "You've put an admirable effort into it, I'd say."

"A labor of love, sir. Not that I couldn't achieve more with more resources. A real shame that the corporation back in Illinois won't put forth more. What I wouldn't do." Watson, visionary or fool (he was called both by his neighbors), combed bony fingers through hair that might have once been golden but was now bleached and parched into a fine, dry straw. "You of course know about the great fire in Chicago? Well, that was the end of my hopes. No one would invest any more after that. Since then, seems it's been me against the whole of Kansas. And Kansas ain't no easy bitch to please, you'll soon find." He looked meaningly at Will Newland.

Ben Davis was letting the powdery soil run through his fingers. "Been an unusually dry year?"

Watson put his hat back on and measured the question. "No. I wouldn't say so."

"No?" Davis glanced at Keith." But surely you've had better crops than this."

"Haven't made any money yet if that's what you mean. Not even when the folks back east were still supporting me. Water's always a problem. Had a plan to dam Big Creek, set up some system of irrigation, but can't do that now. I haul water as best I can."

"Big Creek?" Will looked puzzled.

"The Victoria," said Keith.

Wry amusement wrinkled Watson's face and drew his wilting mustache away from a surprisingly handsome set of teeth. "You mean to say you've renamed the crik Victoria? Well, ain't you Brits a wonder. Locals will be surprised, that they will." He chuckled.

Keith shrugged. "Kansas Pacific was willing to have Mr. Grant rename everything so long as he'd come. Such christenings have less to do with what Brits'll do than with what railroads will do."

Watson wiped his brow and started back toward a small, porched shanty. "Oh, the KP is generous after a fashion. They've chipped in since the Illinois folks pulled out. Helps a bit. They'd like a pretty bit of farmland to show off around the Ellis station, that's a fact."

"But they were sponsoring their own experimental farm, weren't they?" asked Garth Mason.

"Oh yeah, fellow named Elliot headed it up. Seen his *Climate of the Plains?* Circulated a few years back; don't know if it got across the Atlantic though. Anyway, he claims that if you plow the land deep enough, the air will be re-hydrated; there'll be more rain, more plants will grow, making for even more moisture, and eventually the whole climate will change. Then you'll have rain and rich soil both, better farmland. Gents, a professor from Harvard visited a few years back and pronounced that someday this land will be producing wheat for all the United States, and Europe as well."

"I don't doubt it. It merely takes good planning and management," said Will, clearly of the opinion that up to this point those assets had been lacking. "Where is Dr. Elliot? He's the man I'd like to consult." The implied insult to Mr. Watson never occurred to him.

"Oh, he's been gone a few years already. The garden didn't bloom quite like he thought. He went for greener territory."

"He gave up?"

"Don't look amazed, Mr. Newland. Sure, there might be something to Elliot's claims," said Watson, "though it seems to me that a land already so rich in plant and animal life doesn't need changing. You're skeptical, Mr. Mason? Why you only need to have eyes to see – plenty of indigenous growth around here – grasses and trees and animals."

Mason, a gentle, pacific sort of man, smiled at Mr. Watson. "I'm willing to have my eyes trained. I must say, however, that they are rather overwhelmed at present by the vision of poultry – everywhere." He watched a rooster emerge from the privy. "Positively everywhere. Now that turkey, for instance, is certainly a transplant, yes?" He pointed to a big tom, stretching its neck out in an ungainly chase down the row of wilting tomato vines.

"All of 'em are. Friend from Quincy – Illinois, you know – brought them in to fight the bugs. Don't know whether it helps the plants, but they eat well, and me and the other fellows get eggs and an occasional chicken stew. Course I lose a number to snakes and coyotes, but I have to expect to share. And the birds, well, they're company." He gazed almost fondly at a scrawny red hen scratching in the dust and at the brood of yellow chicks that followed her with bright black eyes.

"Give me a good dog," grinned Davis, but Watson went on:

"It's a question of figuring out how the country works, I think, and adapting. But say you go in for Elliot's theories, and lots of folks out here do, well I'm not sure it's fair to fault him for not living them out. There's the thinkers and there's the doers, as I see it, and you need to understand that breaking ground out here can break a person too, sometimes darn quick. It's sure as heck broken more than one plow. I myself lost two the first year."

"We won't have that problem," said Will. "Grant is supplying both good backing and modern technology. This prairie won't defeat a steam plow. And you must pardon me, Mr. Watson, but it seems to me to show a lack of pluck in Elliot, giving up after only a few years." Will crossed his arms and looked out over the struggling fields. "Can't expect to change the climate of an entire country in one or two seasons."

"Elliot was brilliant, maybe, but he wasn't patient." Watson paused a moment, studying Newland's wavy hair, hazel eyes, and well-clad limbs. He observed how one foot continually tapped the ground. As an afterthought, he added, "And he wasn't young." He approached the single step that comprised his stoop, looking warily into the shadowed dust beneath it. He'd discovered a bull snake curled there the week before. "Sticking it out is a long, lonely business for most folks. Of course, you've got your countrymen to keep you chipper. And you'll want them. Lord knows Kansans ain't a welcoming or helpful lot. Never seen such skinflints." He shook his head and grabbed a rough porch post as he swung up the step. A sliver jagged into his hand. Cursing, he reached into the open door of the shanty and pulled out a black bag.

"You're a doctor then, sir?" asked Davis.

Watson squinted at his hand. "Trained for it, but studied to be a botanist, not a medical man. That's why I came out here. Could justify spending my days studying twigs, I guess. And I was certain – still am – that this land can be made to work. I sure would like to give all my time to nursing the co-op farms, sure would. But – " and he gazed grimly over the garden and the stunted stand of trees he optimistically called a fruit orchard, " – the land sucks money like a snake sucks eggs. Gone back to doctoring just so I can afford to keep a horse. Tough place for a man without a horse, that's sure." He pulled the sliver from his hand; the small silver instrument he removed it with glinted.

"A lot of call for a doctor out here, I suppose," commented Mason.

"Lotta call for someone to treat all the sickness. That's one thing, anyway, that grows out here with very little tendin'. Lotta call for someone who can dig out bullets. Lotta call for someone who can amputate. Lotta call for someone who can sign death certificates. Hell of a lotta call for that."

The listeners were silent. Wind rushed over plowed ground. Dust devils wove among the tiny trees.

"Not meaning to be morbid, gentlemen." Watson grinned. He shut the medical bag. "I'm due for a trip back East for some of my ma's good cooking. Canned beans and salt pork for a year will sour a fellow, you bet. You're not reduced to canned beans yet, are you? Well, not to worry. The Smoky Hill country is more hospitable than the dirt here in Ellis. Thirty miles makes a considerable difference somehow. And seeing as how you're settling along the Big Creek — oh, beg pardon, the Victoria — well, so much the better. Though I'm a bit surprised at your interest in agriculture. I'd heard Lord Grant was going in for ranching."

"Lord *who*?"

"Lord Grant. Don't I have the name right?"

"Mr. Grant is a very rich man and a worthy man, but a peer? No — anyway not yet." Will paused. "He's certainly capable of anything."

"Well, I'll be." Watson went into the shanty and retrieved a bottle of whiskey along with two glasses and a tin cup. He lined them up on the rough railing. "We'll have to share," he said, "High tea it ain't, but I hope it'll pass muster." He poured the drink. "So tell me, how did Grant make his fortune?"

Mason reached for the tin cup. "Silks. He's co-owner — or was before he retired — of a highly respectable establishment in London."

"You don't say. Got rich on top hats and ball gowns, I'll bet, eh? Well, it ain't as manly as oil or railroads, but it'll do in the U.S. of A. Money makes aristocrats here. Maybe his lordship knew that?"

Will and Davis seemed amused by the turn of conversation, but Keith quietly redirected it. "You must come out to Victoria and see the livestock, Dr. Watson. Aberdeen sheep and Angus cattle, first and finest in the country. I think you'd enjoy looking over the animals, and we could take you out to some of the estates where we're breaking ground. Mr. Newland here is perhaps our most enthusiastic farmer. Could look over his place, see what you think, give him some advice. And of course you could meet Mr. Grant."

Watson sighed. "Can't afford to get away much, but I thank you for your offer. Be an honor to make Mr. Grant's acquaintance. He's become a fair legend out here, you know."

Watson walked with the men back across hot fields and still-virgin prairie to Ellis. Insects buzzed and ticked, jumping and flying against their trouser legs. The air shimmered along the edges of the earth. In town, barefoot children gathered around a large rain barrel outside the grocer's, taking turns at dunking their sweaty heads. Ben Davis watched, delighted. "Now there's just the thing, lads." He made a move to join the urchins when a tall blond woman in a brown stuff dress pushed open a screened door and hollered at them to dirty someone else's water. They scattered, dripping and giggling. One or two yelled taunts back at her as they ran. She shook her head and turned a frowning eye on the boyish, sandy-haired Scotsman. Davis blushed, tipped his hat, and slunk back to his companions.

Watson gave him a sidelong look. "Susannah Larson. Pretty lady but takes her water very seriously. They say last summer she near scalped an Indian for daring to drink a dipperful." The doctor saluted her. After a moment, she raised her hand and turned back into the store.

The men's relief at reaching the shade of the depot was palpable. They collapsed on a bench, displacing a sprawling grey cat. "I congratulate you on your decision to build a porch on your claim shanty, Dr. Watson," said Garth Mason. His round, thoughtful face glowed red in the heat. He ran his sleeve across his brow and fanned himself with a limp hat. "Shade's a blessing after that sun. And only June! I shall follow your lead and construct a porch, without doubt." The others grunted agreement.

"One of my small luxuries, well worth the lumber," nodded the doctor, pleased. "I like to think I defeat the heat and the wind with that porch. Don't of course – just cheat 'em a bit. But it's soul-satisfying all the same. That it is." And when his visitors left on the train – it was a wonder to him that these men were rich and foolish enough to ride the train just for a trip from Ellis to Victoria – Watson looked out at the hot plain beyond the tracks with a satisfied expression. He sat for a while, watching the cat worry a dead beetle, and then, disturbed by her toying, kicked the insect over into the grass. The cat glared, indignant at his intrusion into her private business, but he was oblivious to her displeasure. The thought that his porch had earned a compliment cheered him for days; it was almost as though the British gentlemen had applauded his entire operation. It gave him the confidence to persevere. His effort, his ingenuity, had been acknowledged. He felt as if he had come up against a long-time adversary and, for the first time, won.

"You must get those brats out of here. That's the first thing. They're too little to keep quiet and may be frightened when the girl cries out. Where's their father?" Elizabeth Cavendar marched into the station room as though she owned it. "And what're you great lunks doing to help? Sitting here admiring your fingernails, I see. Not even as much use as a pair of doorknobs. Get yourselves up and help that young thing with the children. Can't you see she's worn to a wisp? Call yourselves gentlemen. Psshh."

Avery looked up, amazed at the tongue-lashing that had blown in with a hot wind, and then stumbled to his feet. Cabot stumbled up too and, under the scorn of that charming Irish voice, for a moment actually suffered a lapse in his customary elegance. The skull-faced little woman seemed utterly indifferent to his beauty; she hardly looked at him but sent a contemptuous glance toward Grant as though she held him personally responsible for a thoroughly bad lot. Meg picked up Elijah Baldwin and gazed, half amazed and half admiring, at the tiny person who came in and mowed down the men like clover.

"Now where is Mr. MacDonough and his wife?"

A young, grey-eyed woman pushed through the screened door bearing a bucket of well water. It sloshed onto the hem of her muslin dress, leaving a brown stain. "Are you Mrs. Cavendar? At last! They are upstairs. Let me take you." She handed the bucket to Avery, who looked grateful for gainful employment and smiled hopefully toward Mrs. Cavendar, as though waiting for approval.

She paid no attention to him. "And you are?"

"Beryl Newland, ma'am."

The upper hall of the manor was stifling and dark since most of the colonists kept the doors to their rooms closed. Beryl passed them all to go to the last. She knocked gently and then went in.

Mrs. Cavendar followed her into a corner room with windows facing west and north. Both were open, both draped with mosquito netting that struggled against gusts of hot, unrefreshing wind. A gaudy splash of sunlight fell on the floor of the room; as the minutes passed, it slowly stalked the woman who lay staring in the iron bed and the man who bent shudderingly over her hand. Mrs. Cavendar recognized the man but focused on the woman. Only once before had Elizabeth Cavendar seen such eyes; they looked blindly into the glare. She set her lips.

"Cover that window," she snapped to a pale, thin woman who watched at the other side of the bed. "Who could be at peace in such a light? This poor lass wants something more soothing." The pale woman quickly rose and fetching an embroidered coverlet from off a trunk, began to hang it from the row of nails that did service for a rod above the window.

"God, no!"

The woman on the bed, who'd been staring as if dead, sat up, screaming. "I won't be able to see! I won't know where she is! I won't know where she is! She will kill me, kill me. Don't cover her! I must see her! I must know!"

Daniel was anguished. "Help her! Help her!" He clutched at his frantic wife.

"Go, Miss Newland. You're not needed here," said Mrs. Cavendar to Beryl, who was watching the outburst in horror. After the door closed. she said, "Hush yourself, Mr. MacDonough." Still wearing the lilac-colored bonnet, she dropped her bag and put her hand on Daniel's shoulder. The small grip was painful. He leaned on that pain for support. "Hold onto yourself, lad. You can't help her by adding to the din. Hold *her* hand and hold *your* tongue." He swallowed and nodded.

Mrs. Cavendar let go of the husband and turned toward the wife, cupping the contorted face in her hands. She whispered then as one whispers to children to hold their attention.

"Calm yourself. Calm yourself. No one shall hurt you. No one shall hurt my child. No one." The wide, panicked eyes searched for the crooning voice, then set themselves on the deep blue eyes buried in the tunnel of the bonnet. The screams quieted to a feverish whimper. "Now tell me, lassie, who is it that you think is trying to kill you? You may trust me to protect you, but you must first tell me who is after you."

For a time, it seemed that Jane could not speak. Then she said hoarsely, "'Tis the queen." The words came out strangled with fear. Spittle patched her lips. "The Queen."

Elizabeth looked at Daniel. He shook his head, despairing. She felt Jane's abdomen; it was not yet hardening for a contraction. There was some time. She took a small rag, moistened it in the basin near the bed, and wiped Jane's lips gently. Then she whispered again. "The queen. What queen? Where is she, my dear? Can you tell me?"

Jane glanced fearfully at the half-covered window where Lydia stood, uncertain and upset. Elizabeth looked with her and whispered, "In the window?"

"Not in the window. She's in the web, the web!" Jane's watching eyes grew wider, the pupils dilating wildly. "And she's coming!"

Elizabeth felt the contraction rising in the girl's body. She pulled the bonnet from her head, breaking the knotted strings. Her eyes grew fierce, forcing the girl's agonized gaze back to her face. Over Jane's terrified cries she called to the older woman who came rushing to the bed, "How quick are they? How quick are the pains?"

Mrs. Baldwin's face was ashen, but her answer was steady. "Only two or three minutes. Getting closer and longer."

"Very well, then. Let's get her through this one and then we'll see what we can do." She called to Lydia to check the window. "There's something there. Find it!" Then she turned her attention back to Jane. She never looked away from Jane's face. She kept both hands tightly, lovingly, around the girl's cheeks. She braced her knee against the bed to keep from being thrown off by the writhing body and kept whispering, low and soothing. When the contraction ebbed, she was still whispering, a low musical murmur that compelled Jane as surely as the firm fingers and blue eyes. Jane grew quiet: panting, exhausted.

Mrs. Baldwin watched her and let out a quivering breath. "I don't know what's wrong, ma'am. She seems to be well in body, but this terror . . . I don't know how to help her. I've borne five children and know nothing about it." Her eyes filled with tears. She bit her lip hard and turned abruptly to gather up the soiled rags on the floor.

Mrs. Cavendar was quiet a moment, stroking Jane's long hair away from her brow and studying Mrs. Baldwin's tired face.

"Are those your children downstairs, ma'am? I'm betting you've been up here since dawn. Well now, that's just enough. You go down to those children and rest a spell. Sure those little ones will be more'n glad to see you, seeing as how their only entertainment has been the idling of those fops." Mrs. Baldwin began shaking her head, but Mrs. Cavendar went on, "Do you take Mr. MacDonough down too. It'll be a help to him to get some fresh air, and he's more like to go if you go too. Get him some tea, try to perk him up a bit. The lad's wearing down."

Daniel heard and protested. "I won't go, Mrs. Cavendar. Janie needs me."

"No she doesn't, much as you'd like to think so. Certain it is she hasn't been crying for you the way you've been crying for her. Now you remember, Mr. MacDonough, that women have babies all the time. It's a natural thing. It's not pleasant in the doing, but it's perfectly natural. We need to make it easy for her, lad. She's frightened and wandering in her mind, and your worry is just another distraction from what she needs to be thinking about. This lady here can tell you 'tis true, for she's had many children herself."

Mrs. Baldwin nodded and tried to smile.

"But what can I do? I'll go mad – and if she dies – "

"Well there now, just see how helpful you are." Mrs. Cavendar could scarcely hide her glee at winning her point. "Talking of death. Very helpful. Very helpful indeed. Perhaps you'd be liking to bring up hell next? Pshh. Trust me, young man, you won't go mad, and she won't die. But I have work to do and I can't do it if you make me keep arguing with you."

"But what can I do?"

Mrs. Cavendar was easing Jane into a sitting position, gently spreading her legs. She brushed impatiently at the flies that circled and settled on the basin, rubbing their forelimbs together in greedy anticipation. "My dear Mr. MacDonough, weren't you raised a Christian? You can pray? Well then, in the name of the saints and the Virgin and Jesus Christ, do so! And have pity on someone other than yourself. This lady has been breaking her back for your Janie all day. I'd think you might like to do something for her. Now go! And send back Miss Newland to help. She looks fresh and strong."

Lydia, who had settled herself back on the bed with Jane, raised an alarmed face.

"Oh, but Miss Newland couldn't."

Daniel, after a wrenching embrace, was already on his way out with Mrs. Baldwin. Elizabeth was rolling up her sleeves, preparing for a closer examination of the laboring woman. Her eyes were fixed on Jane's face, watching for signs of the next contraction, but she turned them sharply upon Lydia.

"Why not? Is she ill? Consumptive?"

"Oh no. But – " Lydia struggled to articulate an objection that seemed to her so obvious that it shouldn't need to be mentioned. "She is unmarried."

Mrs. Cavendar's narrow eyebrows slowly crept up the front of her skull. "Well now, you don't say. That is surprising, her such a pretty woman." She shut the door firmly. "Is that all?" She turned, folded her arms, and stood measuring Lydia up and down. In the strange half-light of the room, Lydia looked like a pale angel caught off guard by a small mocking demon. "Ignorance – for sure that's what you're talking about – is no excuse for not helping when a hand is needed. I delivered more than a dozen babies before I was wed, and it didn't compromise my good name one bit. And I was glad to know what I was getting into, I assure you. So save your delicacies, my lady. We haven't time for them." She shook her head, exasperated, and went back to her business.

Lydia, naturally self-deprecating and unnaturally willing to be at fault, was crushed. She nodded. "Of course. I'm sorry."

"Never mind. She's coming on with another contraction. Help me with her."

Jane's terror was not lessened. Her cries crawled along the walls, through the doors, and out into the heavy air. In the station room, everyone was stilled by the sound. Mr. Baldwin, just in from the homestead, looked at his wife's anguished face and then whispered to the children that they must go with him for a ride until Mrs. Mac-Donough felt better. Beryl, upstairs in the dark hall where she'd been seeking the courage to enter yet another sickroom, quailed. She felt the urge to run. Then she clutched the door and forced herself inside.

The contraction had passed by the time she entered. Mrs. Cavendar was muttering to Lydia, "She's fighting it, fighting it too much. We have to calm her. What is there by that window?" She followed Jane's stuporous gaze.

"I don't know." Lydia's brow puckered miserably. "Nothing unusual. The sky, the mosquito netting" She paused. "Dirt."

Elizabeth shook her head and frowned. "Well, finish covering it. Let's get rid of that awful sun." She turned back to Jane, who immediately stiffened and stared as Lydia shut the light out.

"I can't see her! She'll come for me! I can't see her!"

"Who, dear child?"

"I told you – the Queen."

"Not at all." Elizabeth's voice was firm. "She's quite gone. How could she hurt you?"

"I don't know," said Jane vaguely. "She's magic."

"Indeed?" Elizabeth was conversational, interested. "Well, I have my own magic, lassie. And I shall work it now. Do you trust me?"

Jane just looked at her, the odd animated skull with the lovely voice.

Elizabeth went to her bag, searched a bit, and took out a small vial of clear liquid. Crossing herself, she went over to the western window and began deliberately sprinkling the frame, the coverlet, the glass, and the netting. She turned and sprinkled the bed where the laboring woman cowered, and then she crossed herself a second time. As she did so she saw Beryl standing, appalled, by the door. She capped the vial with a snap. "Don't be afraid, miss. For unbelievers my sprinkling does not harm. For me and for her, it gives courage." She went to Jane. "Now, Jane MacDonough, you are completely safe. You may hurt – indeed you will – but *you cannot be killed.* Do you understand? All the angels in heaven stand guard around you. There are no queens in the room but you. None but you." She began speaking as if to a child but then, feeling her way carefully, her tone changed. She spoke as one adult to another, reasoning in a firm, kind voice. "You are the only queen here, and why? Because you are having a baby. 'Tis no evil outside you that you're feeling; it's just your own child trying to get out after months and months. No, look at me," she insisted as Jane began to tense against another contraction. "Your body was made to do this. God made it so, my dear, and he made nothing that isn't good. So let your body do its work. Let it go. No evil can come to you. None at all."

Jane's face was crumpling; her eyes were unconvinced. Elizabeth exchanged a grim glance with Lydia, and then confronted Jane more firmly, cupping the girl's face once again in her hands. "Trust the good magic, my darling, mine and yours. Ride on it. And let your baby come."

The contraction came in its full fury. Jane stared into the midnight eyes. Why fight it? If this is death, why fight it? Better to drown, to slide away on the spell and die. Her fingers reached up, crushing themselves into the small wrists which framed her chin. She whimpered, but she did not wrestle the wave; she moved on it. Then, unexpectedly, she felt herself become part of it: terrible, inexorable, powerful. She yelled, leaning with the surging of her body, but did not scream. The terror was gone. For a brief instant she gazed upon flaming branches; tried to cover her face; and, from a blazing crest of power and pain, cried out before life.

When it passed, Elizabeth, well satisfied, looked at the women sharing the watch and broke into a transfiguring smile. The girl would ride it out, and the wait would not be long.

"Beryl said that the midwife didn't approve of the name at all."

Cabot gazed with distaste at the rim of grime forming under his nails. "That woman, Newland, would have something to say about the way the sun came up. And it wouldn't be good."

Avery looked up from his biscuit. It was a dry thing, spread with grease – there was no butter – and it made him thirsty. "Whatever could she find wrong with it? I think it a fine name. Patriotic and all."

"Well, for one thing she hates Grant."

Newland shook his head and scratched the back of his neck where the mosquitos had been biting. "What can she have against Mr. Grant? He's the perfect gentleman."

"She's an American, Newland. She doesn't give a damn about being a gentleman. And she's Irish, so she cares even less. Which of course explains her disdain for the name Victoria. Doubtless she drank in Fenian fury with her mother's milk."

"But one could argue the baby is named for the colony, not the Queen."

"I don't know about that, but Beryl told me that Mrs. Cavendar looked very queer when she heard the name and said something like, 'The "queen," lass? Are you sure?' and Jane said she was, quite. And Mrs. Cavendar shook her head and said, 'Poor little colleen.' Beryl wasn't sure whether she meant Mrs. MacDonough or the baby. Curious story. Wish I'd seen this woman. Beryl said she was a tartar."

"No you don't, Newland. She'd have stripped you to the bone with that tongue of hers. You're exactly the type of fellow she'd enjoy chomping to bits. Without doubt, *'The nightmare life in death was she.'* The only one she spoke decently to was Neil Hunter, and of course MacDonough. She felt sorry for him, no doubt."

"What 'type' do you mean?"

"Conceited."

"Conceited?" Will was indignant. "I'm not the least conceited. I just recognize my talents and make use of them. Which is more than some of us. Quit drinking all my water, Avery. And what is so precious special about Neil Hunter?"

Avery spit a mouthful of water at William. "I do think Mr. Newland is jealous of the affections of this lady; what do you say, Cabot? A bit old for him, perhaps; a bit spiny and tart tongued, but then that's how he describes his sister to us every day. 'Twould be a match in heaven: a fair Irish lass wedded to an exemplary specimen of English manhood, our own 'heir to all the ages.' And she could birth her own babies, which would doubtless be a savings, would it not, Mr. Newland? For I'm sure with such a talented father there would be quite a litter of them."

Cabot studied the pile of lumber. "We might have enough for a nursery."

"May you both find rattlesnakes in your stew."

"Well there now: the man will be as tart as his shrew-wife. A cruel cut, Newland, a cruel cut indeed. Thank God there is no stew."

"It's too damn hot, anyway."

The men were quiet for a few minutes. Cabot laid back and covered his face with his hat. Avery watched him and then asked Will, "How did Beryl find it?"

"Find what?" Newland sounded irritated.

"Helping with the birth. A bit rough?"

"Oh, not for her. She's nursed a lot. It's what women do."

Avery looked at him. Avery had seen her out by the pump the evening the MacDonough's baby was born. The stars stretched away, impossibly beautiful, while Beryl Newland clutched the side of the building and vomited into the dark, soiling the front of her dress. He had not revealed himself to her then, and he did not reveal what he had seen now, only observing, "She doesn't seem to eat any more."

"Of course she eats. It's just that the weather's too hot."

"Oh."

Cabot turned over on his stomach, bored. "Well, you may marry the old Irish midwife, Newland, but I shall wed young Victoria Grant MacDonough. I shall be just about ready when she grows ripe. Yes, I should think forty a quite tolerable age to settle at last." He searched in his pockets for a smoke. "She will be a handsome woman, I think, given her parentage, and after what Grant has settled on her, she will be a suitably equal match financially."

His companions burst into protests. "As if Danny MacDonough would ever let his daughter marry a cad like you! Go on!"

"Especially after that christening present. I mean really, Cabot, it was worthy of Avery."

Avery began sorting nails into piles. "I have exquisite taste in gifts which you cannot appreciate, Newland. And as it happens, I DO think Cabot's gift was inspired."

"A pet prairie dog? I'm surprised Mrs. MacDonough will have the thing in the house. And how long do the creatures live? Victoria will never even have it to play with – if one plays with those animals."

Cabot shrugged. "The point is not the prairie dog as plaything; the point is that it is memorable. I imagine the creature will last no longer than Grant's preposterous promise to support the increase of that black cow he gave the baby until she comes of age. The entire state of Kansas would not be big enough. But his gift is handsome all the same, and to compete, mine must be memorable. And so it shall be. People will tell young Victoria stories about the prairie dog. She will be charmed and wonder who presented her with so quaint a gift. She will meet handsome old Mr. Cabot, be captivated, and of course come to love him. She shall marry him and be a comfort to him in his old age."

"And he shall give her the clap for her pains," concluded Newland. "That is, if she doesn't catch something from the prairie dog first."

"You really are nasty, Newland. I thought it a charming story. Only throw in some parental disapproval and a seduction, both of which one can count on with you as the hero, Cabot, and you've got a plot worthy of Rhoda Broughton."

Cabot did not take offense. He merely laughed. His reputation was a matter of some pride. He enjoyed the role of *roué*; it did not interfere at all with his sense of himself as a gentleman. He stood and stretched. "Why we are out here helping you put up your place when you are so insufferably irritable is beyond me, Newland. I'm not at all sure farming agrees with you."

Will stood as well and pulled leather gloves gingerly over his hands. They were raw and sore from unaccustomed labor. "You do it because you are secretly in love with my sister. But you won't get her, either of you. What the – " He looked oddly at his left hand, and suddenly let out a yell. He pulled the glove off and threw it from him. An insect had become caught in one of the fingers; a small angry red welt was rising on the tip of Will's fourth finger. He swore.

Avery moved to examine the wound while Cabot warily approached the glove. "Did you kill it, old man?"

"I don't know." He swore some more. "I think it was a bee."

"There's no stinger in his hand," remarked Avery. "Better be careful."

Cabot lifted the glove and, holding it far from his body, shook it. Out of it fell a small yellow and black wasp, its wings and legs broken. It was still alive; its speared abdomen wiggled up and down to an evil beat. "Not a lethal specimen I think, Newland. You'll live to strike another nail."

Will came over. "More bloody bugs than I've ever seen in my life. Can't work, can't eat, can't sleep for them." He crushed the insect with an angry boot and walked away. Cabot followed, but Avery bent down and examined the broken body in the grass.

"Poor little drone," he said. "No more flowers for you."

It was as philosophic as he ever got.

Chapter V

At first, the flame merely toyed with the straw and the milk-weed. It licked the stems of the sunflowers and tickled the swaying grass. It danced against the side of the shed and seemed content to philander in its shade. But five minutes had not passed before the wind provoked it into a passion that fed and spread up the side of the shed, over the field, and across the plain. By the time Hubert Render spotted the fire from the Hays grain store, people could hear its roaring, and the smoke, which might have been mistaken for just another dust devil, made the eastern sky black. The wind blew from the northwest; the town would be spared. But the homesteads and settlements to the south and east lay helpless. As dusk fell, the wind pushed the fire harder, then harder yet. Behind it, the ravaged land quivered, black and smoking, from the force of the attack. The charred remains of small animals – and some bigger creatures – shivered, stripped and staring, under a choking sky. Night fell, and flames screamed across the earth.

In Victoria the women stood on the porch of the hotel clasping hands, looking at the backwards dawn rising in the west. They watched as it slowly reached hungry arms toward them, coming to them like an unwelcome lover. Then one of them broke away and flew toward it.

"Beryl!"

The cry was lost in the rising roar.

The telegram arrived on July 10, three weeks after the birth of Victoria Grant MacDonough. Despite Hunter's face when he gave it to him, Mr. Grant did not immediately read it. He was taken up with welcoming the distinguished group of emigrants just arrived that morning: Captain Charles Prescott, son of the late Sir George Prescott of Kent; Major Tilson of Her Majesty's Forty-Second Highlanders; and the honorable Vincent Spenser, son of Lord Herries of Everingham, Yorkshire, with his manservant Richard Manley and his French cook Oscar Tabermann. Avery was excited. "Soufflés, my dear Newland. Soufflés!"

The number of colonists had been growing steadily since the original group arrived on May 10th. By July there were already sixty people come to Victoria, most young single men from England and Scotland, although a few Americans, lured by Grant's expansive invitation in New York and Chicago newspapers, had also decided to cast their lot with the Britons. Wood-frame houses and a few stone ones began taking shape on the "estates"; some of the earliest colonists – Baldwin, Miles, and the Wyatt brothers among them – had begun the arduous task of breaking the land, gouging foot-wide furrows into the ground and burying germs of corn in the affronted earth. Steam plow there was none – or at least not yet. Will Newland announced that he would not begin farming at all if he could not start off right. This was in part a not-so-politic attempt to hold Mr. Grant to his original promise to provide the machinery; in part a humble acknowledgment that, all his athletic prowess on the cricket field notwithstanding, Will was not yet ready physically to engage in a direct wrestling match with the land; and, in large part, a stubborn declaration of his belief that he knew best how to do things, and the best way to do agriculture was the most modern, scientific way. If the Wyatt brothers were able to boast sixty acres of knee-high corn not long after the summer solstice, he shrugged. Let them brag about their brutish accomplishments. With a steam plow and the latest agricultural innovations, next year he would produce double their yield, and do it like a gentleman. In the meantime, he had a sister to make a home for, and he wasn't going to let her stay in some bloody sod hut.

Beryl raised her eyebrows the first time she heard him make this solicitous comment in her presence, but she acknowledged she was pleased with the small house that quickly grew on their land. It was wood, not the more durable limestone – Will was impatient with the prospect of playing miner and stone mason, and only used the native rock to construct a hearth and chimney – but it evinced some creditable craftsmanship. When she exclaimed over the pretty molding around the parlor door, the handsome bookshelves flanking the fireplace, and the small but cunning cabinet built into the kitchen, Will looked pleased.

"You know," he said, "Avery did all that. Learned it as a child from a carpenter in his father's employ. His father encouraged him to watch the old fellow – said a highborn man should be ready to learn from those who were his inferiors in class but his superiors in skill. You've been thinking him a fop, but all this time he's been making our place as pretty as a parson's cottage. He's quite a crafts-man. Between the two of us, we've hardly had to hire out for help at all."

"And Mr. Cabot?"

"Spirit willing, flesh weak. He can't bear to dirty his nails. But he's first-rate at giving advice. Has an opinion about everything. He says the parlor won't be a proper parlor at all without roses on the wall-paper – so you shall have roses, of course."

Beryl looked at the bare yellow boards. "Did you put up tar pa-per? Aren't you supposed to do that to keep out the wind?"

"Between the inner and outer walls, of course. You don't trust us, do you?"

Beryl didn't say anything, merely ran her fingers over the new-smelling lumber. "Where does the wood come from?" she asked. Her eyes strayed to the glassless window and the sweeping flatness it framed.

"Oh, Denver, I suppose. Lots of pine forests in the mountains west of there. Comes in on freight. Do you recall the new man from Devonshire – Pettimore? He plans to go into the lumbering busi-ness right in Victoria. Once that happens, we'll be saved many hot trips to Hays City. I'll be glad for it. And the building will give the town a fortress against any – trouble."

Trouble, of course, meant Indians. After two months Beryl had yet to see any of the indigenous peoples who regularly tracked over this vast plain; her knowledge of the American Indian remained lim-ited to poetic panegyrics on the noble savage and sensationalized accounts of massacres. She had not looked into the eyes, heard the voice, or touched the hand of a single person of native blood; she had no human reality to set up against the mythic picture in her head. But with fear she had formed an intimate acquaintance. Several times already she had crouched on the floor of Victoria Manor with the other colonists, breathless, straining to shape footfalls from the soughing in the grass and human contours from the quiet grey shadows. She always bore in her hand the long-bladed bowie knife; she would not be dependent on Mr. Hunter's rifle, Mr. Keith's pistol, or even Mr. Grant's pearl handled revolver, handsome though it was setting off his finely formed hand. On one occasion the warning had come from Jason Mayes, galloping madly back to Victoria early on a bright June morning. The colonists collected children and shuttered windows, burying themselves in the manor house with the dark and the fear while outside a lark sang. Another time, the scare had occurred on an opaque, starless night. In the station room Meg leaned against her cousin Clay, shivering at the lonesome call of crickets, while Beryl watched her brother peer into blackness and listened to Jack Randall's angry whisper that one could hardly trust the outcry of a drunkard. True, not long after his hysterical yells had driven everyone else from sleep, Mayes fell snoring into a corner, almost as content with his head (still bandaged from the assault in Hays) cradled on his arm as the MacDonough baby who snuffled and sighed nearby at her mother's breast.

Uncertainty heightened the fear. Crowded together on these occasions, with all the odors and sounds of humanity unpleasantly near, the colonists discovered that the annoyances, jealousies, and desires which they kept carefully tucked under their cravats and lace collars during the normal intercourse of the day did not dissolve into an uplifting unity when they faced a common enemy. Rather, these too-human irritations were magnified, became of a piece with the oppressive anxiety that cramped the limbs and caused the brow to drip; they became choking; they became proof that the neighbor who slurped his soup was almost certainly the weak link in the chain that would break and cause them all to perish. A young man from Lancashire, biting his pale lip and thinking longingly of home, was determined to rip the head off the youngest Baldwin boy the next time he began whining for a dipper of water.

The waiting oppressed Beryl. It oppressed them all. But Beryl had thought she knew about waiting, had considered herself expert in the ways of anxious longing, dreary impatience, and dread. She knew the ticking of clocks in dark hours, the dull certainty that tomorrow would come the same as today but with less hope. She knew waiting in England. Here, though, she found herself waiting without the regular passing of the pendulum and the comforting sense of being alone and set apart in her suffering. She heard the short anxious breathing of her companions and the shifting of their bodies. The rooms where they cowered smelled of sweat – not all the potpourri in Kensington could disguise it – and tobacco smoke. She found herself longing for certainty even if it was cruel, longing for light even if it brought horror, and waiting for relief from a lonely, because unique, sense of guilt. No one, she thought, would understand this, would understand that she felt like a trespasser on this land, and it made her more afraid. She deserved to be hacked to death. The recognition did not make her more just. It only made her pray for thicker walls, for more weapons, for an armor of steel.

So when Will told her about Pettimore's lumber store, she was glad.

There was, of course, no talk of Indians or missing steam plows or ripping off of children's heads the morning Vincent Spenser disembarked at Victoria Station. He got off in a cool, bright sunshine that made the air effervescent, that gave every blade of grass exquisite definition and made the sable coats of Grant's cattle shine. Not everyone could be at the depot to welcome these newcomers, though everyone was aware of their coming. Work was plentiful even for those with well-padded pockets, and on such a day most people were out on the land with their livestock, their plows, or their water witches. Yet the position of Spenser and Prescott and Tilson was notable enough even in this company of colonial aristocrats that Grant felt they deserved some little fanfare. He did not even see the grim expression on Neil Hunter's face when the telegram was delivered to his hand. He tucked it into his waistcoat pocket, saying genially, "Later, my lad," and strode out onto the platform with his foremen, Duncan, Davis, and Keith, and Edwards, his secretary – the official administration of the Victoria Colony.

Beryl sat on the veranda with Lydia Randall and Meg Grant, shelling peas from the communal garden behind the manor. They were unusually successful specimens for that time and place; Meg had hand-watered them, and the grateful vines had put forth a profusion of blossoms that became satisfyingly fat pods by midsummer. Beryl reveled in the crisp green pockets of sweetness that burst open beneath her fingers, and she and Meg munched the fresh peas until Lydia admonished them.

"What will we have to brighten our table if you keep eating like that? Cornbread and sowbelly alone will not make for much of a feast."

It must have cost Lydia something to reprove them, even gently. Mrs. Randall had become ever quieter and more self-effacing since they had arrived in Victoria, pale as moonlight and about as thin. The bodice of her white gown hung loosely over her breasts, and the bracelets encircling her slender wrists showed them to be less graceful than bony. Beryl might have wondered at this, but she knew her own cheeks were growing hollow and that now she was able to pull her own stays unnaturally tight. Meg alone seemed to be flourishing. Her cheeks were ruddy with health, not sunburn, and her eyes were bright, interested, and young – like those of her uncle. Beside her Lydia looked brittle, exquisitely fragile. But she laughed when Meg crept behind her and pushed a palmful of the fresh peas against her lips.

"There now, I didn't say they weren't delicious." She looked down at the bowl on the porch and fretted. "I'm afraid one of these new gentlemen will be able to devour the entire morning's work in one swallow."

"If they eat everything, then they can hardly be real gentlemen."

"Oh, they're real enough." Lydia nodded her head. "Quite manly specimens."

Beryl wrinkled her nose. "Indeed."

"Whyever do you say it like that?"

"Manliness means a self-absorbed boy with muscles and a magnified sense of his importance in the world."

Meg's mouth fell open, and then she burst into a laugh. "Why, you are a manhater, Beryl Newland. I'd never have thought it! Who soured you so?"

"I am not a manhater. I just don't like 'manliness' – if you'll forgive me, Lydia. I'd rather have better reasons for admiring a person."

Meg looked wise. "It's her brother. 'Tis that handsome, cocksure brother that's done it to her."

Lydia smiled and pushed back a strand of wavy hair. "Oh, there's nothing of the boy in these men, Beryl. All three of them are soldiers of the bravest sort. Mr. Spenser, you know, was a prisoner of war."

"What – for England!"

"Well, no." Lydia hesitated, remembering Beryl's reaction to Mrs. Cavendar. "He was a Papal zuoave. Suffered a great deal for his faith. I believe he's coming here in part to escape some bad memories. To heal."

Meg looked puzzled. "What's a zuoave? Mr. Cabot said it was because he'd gotten a barmaid in trouble and his father wanted to keep him from marrying her."

"Meg!" Lydia could not keep the shock and severity from her voice. "Shame on Mr. Cabot. And shame on you for speaking of such things. A well-bred girl ought not to pass on gossip or slander a gentleman." She shook her head and frowned. "Richard Cabot needs a tongue-lashing."

Meg flashed a sidelong scowl at Beryl. "Well bred," she muttered into the bowl of peas.

Beryl studied the color which inflamed Mrs. Randall's face for a moment and then stood up with a wide smile. "Well, ladies, I rest *my* case. Vincent Spenser and his companions will have to prove to me they are something better than a Mr. Cabot."

At the luncheon where peas played a prominent part and where nobody – man, woman, or child – ate more than their fair share, the honorable Vincent Spenser seemed well on his way to placing golden-haired Mr. Cabot in the shadows. He was of medium height where Richard Cabot was tall; he was dark where Mr. Cabot was fair; he was of rugged countenance where Mr. Cabot was of a classic profile. But he was also soft-spoken, courteous without being either self-conscious or vain, and pleased to speak of his adventures without wanting to brag about them. Once or twice, at an ironic comment from Nigel Wyatt, Beryl thought she saw a lethal light kindle in his black eyes. So quickly was the flame doused, however, that she wondered whether she'd really seen anything at all. He joked with Mr. Prescott and Mr. Tilson about being seasick on the passage to America and seemed ready enough to laugh at himself and at the absurdities of the world. Mr. Cabot was probably the more intelligent man, but to Beryl he was hardly the more attractive. When

Spenser made the Sign of the Cross before the meal as Mr. Grant said grace, she discovered Cabot watching her. She felt furious, caught as she'd been caught in New Orleans. She hated Catholicism. Mr. Cabot was constantly cornering her. He was, as Lydia contended, no gentleman.

Major Tilson was a warm-hearted fellow who made much of the children and delighted them with a toot and a wheeze of the bagpipes. Captain Prescott was his contemporary but seemed much older and more serious; he asked many questions about the land, the climate, the number of settlers and the prospects for success. Since he had purchased more land than any of the other colonists to date, his earnestness about the endeavor was not surprising. Beryl found him a charming dinner partner. He talked about the concerts in London that season when he discovered this interested her and seemed eager to please. After they had been visiting together for several minutes, she mentioned that her brother, William Newland, was out working on their house near Victoria Creek. On hearing William's name, Prescott gave a sudden, surprised turn.

"Your brother is William Newland? Do you have another brother — in Parliament? You're from Yorkshire?"

"Why, yes," cried Beryl, delighted. "You know my brother Robert? I grew up at Lindenhurst, near Enderley."

Prescott's eyes lit up. "I know of him — well-respected man. But I also know of your brother, and you, in fact, through a mutual acquaintance. Captain Denton, I believe?"

Startled, her smile froze. Of course, she should have anticipated the possible connection; the Newlands did not have a large number of military acquaintances. Still, when Prescott surprised her with Denton's name she felt as though her rejected lover had suddenly walked into the room. She saw him as vividly as if he were seated beside her at this long table where the flies hovered and the grease that substituted for butter ran in the midday heat. Saw his brown eyes and the painful stoop of his shoulders as he turned from her. *Go from me . . .*

She answered with a still expression, her voice not quite natural. "Captain Denton was a good friend."

Captain Prescott said, "Yes. A good man. He spoke of you – of your family – often. To think that I should meet Miss Newland here!"

A long pause.

"He's gone to India now, I think?"

"Yes. Nothing for him in England anymore." There was regret in the captain's answer. He briefly glanced at her. Then he swirled the tea in his cup and took a sip.

She was sure he knew. She turned her attention to her fork and spoon, to the careful alignment of that polished silver on the fine linen cloth. When she was able to raise her eyes, she saw Vincent Spenser studying her. He did not immediately look away when she met his gaze. His expression under the black brows and mustache was thoughtful. She gave a compressed smile and turned her attention back to the silverware. He lit a cigarette. The smoke sidled around his head.

Prescott knew, and Spenser guessed. She had never met these men before today and here they were, digging around in her soul. It shouldn't matter. Girls turned down offers all the time. But still . . . She curled her fingers tightly into her lap and stared out the window at the plain where grasses dipped and bowed and insects hummed. She wondered if the meal would ever end.

George Grant stared out that same window two hours later, stared out at the late-afternoon sun with the open telegram in his hand. He watched the grasses dip and bow, watched their shadows reach like thin hands toward the manor house and listened to the dirge of the crickets.

"What will we do for them, sir? What can we do?" Neil Hunter's face was drawn.

"There's nothing we can do. She's gone." He seemed unable to say more.

Hunter took a breath and persisted.

"But when they come. What will we do?"

A sudden fury flamed over Grant. "Pray we are spared, damn it! Pray we are spared!"

The manor shuddered at the slamming of his office door. Upstairs, the infant Victoria cried and would not be comforted.

A person trying to outrace a prairie fire on horseback is almost certainly doomed once a strong wind helps force-feed the flames, but as long as the wires aren't cut, telegraph can send a warning faster than the wind. The inhabitants of Victoria therefore knew they were in trouble even before a dark haze began smearing the western horizon.

It was late evening. Most of the men were come in from the fields and building sites where they spent their days, so there were many hands to mount a defense. Grant and his foremen set to work immediately, trying to corral the agitated animals who, though they could not yet see the flames, nonetheless bawled and balked in fear. A frenzied ram ran against a fence rail and broke it; for a moment the beast struggled, and then it ran across the railroad tracks, down a ravine, and, unwittingly, in the direction of the advancing fire. The other sheep surged to follow; complete disaster was averted only when Garth Mason maneuvered a heavy wagon against the opening, tipping it to block the way of the frantic multitude. Dogs barked excitedly; unnerved thoroughbreds were hustled into the livery barn, where they screamed and stamped.

Several young Englishmen were filling barrels and buckets with well water. When he ran out of larger containers, a wild-eyed young man named Carrigan began filling coffee cups with water. Randall hollered at him in disbelief. Keith pulled Carrigan aside, shook him, gave him a shovel, and redirected him to dig a trench around the chicken house. His was a minor contribution to the great plowing effort already begun around the perimeter of the town's main buildings: the manor, the stable, the embryo lumber yard, the skeleton of Neil Hunter's store, and a couple of new houses lucky enough to be near the station. More than two dozen men were plowing, sweating behind dogged teams of horses, attempting to tear open a strip of earth wide enough to separate them from the conflagration that seemed to roll toward them. William Newland found himself behind a tired pony, guiding an unwieldy, old-fashioned blade that wrenched the sod like a dull scissors. He did not complain.

From outside the slowly widening ring of freshly turned ground, from the tents and few houses that had already given some definition to the outskirts of the Victoria settlement, people ran to the manor clutching blankets, pictures, clothing, and seed. At the manor itself women were slamming shutters, pulling children, laundry, and animals into the stuffy darkness. A rooster crowed in fury as Thomas Baldwin pulled it by a claw into the station room; his little sister followed, cradling an apron full of baby chicks. Jane MacDonough held her own baby tightly in one arm, and in the other carried a cage from the back porch up onto the stair landing. The prairie dog, Cabot's christening gift, would not perish by fire. Jane's eyes were fierce.

Downstairs, Neil Hunter barked orders. He told Beryl to gather rags, gunny sacks, and sheets. She and James Avery soaked them in water and lifted them in a dripping, sodden mass onto the back of Daniel MacDonough's wagon. She watched the men drive off toward the plow line, not far beyond which a roiling blackness surged forward with the natural dusk. She wiped burning eyes, turned anxiously trying to catch sight of her brother, and then saw, to her south, a snaking line of blue stirring up a cloud over the land almost as ominous as that roiling in the north. The flames descended with the night upon Victoria, but not before the soldiers from Fort Hays had come to join Johnny Bull in the battle.

Word that Rowena Seth had died somewhere along the banks of the Mississippi traveling to Victoria spread slowly at first. Neil Hunter felt it was not his place to tell anyone, and Mr. Grant did not seem inclined. But the orphaned children and the widower would be arriving soon, and some provision must be made for them. Sunday the 17th of July, Grant received another telegram from Mr. Seth, this one from Kansas City. He and his family would be arriving on Tuesday. They were sick. Very sick.

Randall was almost immediately belligerent when he heard of it.

"Don't misunderstand me, Grant, I want to help these people, but coming in here with some kind of plague? Well, I say send them elsewhere. They can hardly expect us to welcome them. Send them elsewhere."

Mrs. Randall shook her head. "We must take them in. Where else can they go? The children have no mother."

"Lydia, you don't know what you're saying. You and Mrs. Mac-Donough should be the last ones arguing for taking in disease. What about your own children? Your own children need mothers." Randall became increasingly worked up. "Send them along, I say! Wire them money and send them along!"

"Good lord, man, you'd send Jesus Christ himself to the devil. Have a little pity."

Randall was sarcastic. "I suppose you, Mr. Avery, are volunteering to take them into your bachelor's quarters upstairs?"

Daniel MacDonough looked uneasy and unhappy. "We have infants and women to protect – and yet turn these people away? Impossible!"

Mr. Baldwin stood with folded arms, shaking his head. "Of course we must do something for them. The question is what. Where do we put them? Precisely how sick are they? If the disease is infectious, we can hardly have them in the manor."

"What killed Mrs. Seth?" Mason's query came quietly from the back of the room.

"Yellow Fever, I'm betting," said Cabot. "They had another outbreak in New Orleans just last month. It's the scourge of the place. Happens almost every summer." Meg looked anxiously toward her uncle. She had not forgotten the ugly descriptions Cabot had given of the sickness.

"'Tis nothing like Yellow Fever, Mr. Cabot, and I'll thank you for not making things worse than they are." Grant raised a cold, contained face to the young heir; his blue eyes were calm but also hard. Beryl had never seen him look so unapproachable.

"The telegram says very little," Grant continued. "Mr. Seth's funds have been spent on the illness and he cannot be sparing extra coppers for words. But" – Grant took a heavy breath – "it would appear to be typhoid."

A cricket called. It was, for an instant, the only sound. Cold crept into the corners of Beryl's being and crouched there.

Keith spoke first.

"We can't have them in the manor – they'll understand that – but we must make a place for them. We can put up a decent shelter for them in the time we've got. Pettimore has plenty of lumber and we have plenty of hands. Should get someone to Hays City for a doctor – or maybe out to Ellis to bring back Lewis Watson."

Mrs. Baldwin, who had been listening intently, broke in. "I have extra bedding and some small things for the children. I'm sure my bairns won't mind sharing a bit with little ones who've lost their mama." She hugged her eldest to her. The child struggled, unhappily wondering what he was going to be asked to sacrifice. "And we'll want to kill some chickens. They'll be needing a good, healthful broth. I suspect they won't be up to regular food."

"Thank you, Mrs. Baldwin. You see what you can do." The granite cold of Grant's face thawed slightly. "Keith, get a crew of lads to work on a shanty. Now is not too late to start. Hunter, you and Edwards go for a doctor. We're going to be needing advice on how to handle this situation. But we will not be sending anyone away, Mr. Randall." Contempt edged Grant's words. "We do not send away our own in Scotland."

"Mr. Randall never meant to suggest that these people be left out to die on the prairie. His desire to protect his wife and child, and the women and children of this community, exhibits a manliness that I, for one, could never wish him to shed in favor of a mere clan loyalty. I will thank you, sir, not to address my husband in such a tone again." Lydia was like a beam of white-hot light. Her slight frame, her deference, suddenly seemed a feint; she was the daughter of Lord Stannard, daughter of a noble house that extended back in history to a time when Mr. Grant's forbears were mere grubbers in the mud. The blood flamed up when the pride was struck. She was pale and beautiful and utterly wrong.

Or so Avery thought. He whispered to Will, "God, what a waste of a woman. And the cad lets her defend him. Grant's too much of a gentleman to contradict her."

Mr. Grant did not. "My apologies, madame." He did, however, deliberately turn to Hunter and Keith.

Randall did not seem embarrassed; he put his arm around his wife. They presented a united front of offended dignity. As they turned to leave, however, his wife went up to Mr. Pettimore, a small, intense, bald-headed man, and quietly handed him several gold pieces.

"You must provide the very best materials, Mr. Pettimore," she said. "The very best."

Mr. Pettimore nodded up at her. "To be sure, my lady. Not that I need your money to do that. But of course. The very best."

She smiled. Avery ground his teeth. "A waste, Newland. A total waste. Randall won't like her moving money from his pocket and into Pettimore's."

Newland shook his head a little at Avery. "You're getting rabid, old man. Let's go to work." He turned to Beryl. "I'll see what I can do to help out Keith."

She nodded. He went on, "I say, Beryl, you are such a good nurse, you have so much experience, why don't you offer your services?"

Beryl's head whipped up in alarm. "Oh no. I couldn't possibly do that. No." And before he could say more, she slipped between the men to join Mrs. Baldwin. He looked after her, puzzled and frowning. Then he shrugged and followed his friends out into the glaring sun.

The Seths arrived at Victoria, Kansas, on July 27th, 1873. They came on a hot evening, emerging from a quarantined passenger car that the Kansas Pacific afterwards had stripped in Denver. There was no jovial welcoming committee – only Mr. Grant, Mr. Keith, and, from Ellis, Dr. Watson, who watched the approaching train with squinting eyes and a grim, downturned mouth. The depot platform was otherwise empty; a lonely spaniel panted in the shade of a water barrel. William Newland stood with James Avery on the porch of Victoria Manor, still holding the remnants of tar paper he'd helped nail on the roof of the waiting shanty. Up in the northwest window of the hotel, a woman's form could be dimly seen behind a loose screen of mosquito netting that sucked in and out with the wind. Two bay horses, hitched to a wagon lined with blankets and a pillow made plump from the feathers of Derbyshire ducks, shifted their hooves nervously.

There was no welcome feast either: no linens and silver, no fresh garden peas, not even humble cornbread and sowbelly. Only Sarah Baldwin's pot of broth and a pan of gruel which simmered on the stove in readiness to deliver when Mr. Grant gave the word.

They took some time to disembark. A porter came from another car and opened the door; then, after calling in to the occupants, quickly moved away. A tall, sixteen-year-old youth came first, looking with hollow eyes at the hot, barren landscape. He gripped the railing to steady weak legs. Behind him came a small girl, about eight years old, with pretty auburn curls. She seemed more energetic than her brother, but her face was grey. She clutched to her chest a carpetbag that was almost as big as she was. Mr. Keith reached up to take it from her and led her by the hand to the waiting wagon.

For a moment, no one followed. Mr. Grant moved toward the steps of the car and was met by a big man – or a man who had once been big, for his clothes and the skin around his jaws hung in ample folds – who extended his right hand and said with a low, heavy Scotch accent, "Mr. Grant? I'm glad to meet you, sir, but I must beg help for the other bairns. They canna' walk."

Mr. Grant entered the rail car without hesitating, and Dr. Watson put down his bag and quickly followed. In a couple of moments they came out again, each of them carrying bundles made up of matted hair, sweaty flesh, and dank sheets. The children were not small; Will thought that the girl Mr. Grant lifted slowly into the wagon must be almost a woman. Her boots – coquettish in their styling and evidently new – hung awkwardly at the end of long limp legs. "My God," Will whispered to Avery. "There's blood."

Avery stared for a minute. "Nosebleed," he said. "The other boy has one as well." They watched Dr. Watson wipe the face of the redheaded youth who moaned and shivered in his arms. Keith helped Watson lift the boy into the wagon, and then they both lent a hand to Mr. Seth, who carried a blond-haired child against one shoulder and a bigger, dark-haired child against the other. Seth refused to put either child down; he murmured to each in turn as he got into the wagon. The child nestled against his left cheek whimpered a reply, but the blond child on the right remained motionless.

Watson saw Mr. Seth settled and then ran for his bag. He jumped into the wagonload of sick people, calling to the young men on the veranda: "Tell Mrs. Baldwin to send the food along now – and I'll be needing a nurse."

Grant and Keith hurriedly carried down two trunks and some loose clothes from the car; the engine huffed impatiently, spitting sparks. When Watson looked back and saw Keith bringing a bundle of the children's blankets and a woolen cloak, he called back, "Don't bring that. Leave it. Burn it."

"But surely the cloak – 'twas my wife's – " Mr. Seth's words trailed away. Watson's mouth twisted unhappily under the long mustache. He shook his head. Mr. Seth's heavy forehead crumpled, but only for a moment. Then he lowered his weary face into the dirty, tousled hair of his children.

Beryl came out of the station as the wagon slowly rattled toward the tiny shanty and the train pushed off to the west. She carried a steaming kettle wrapped securely in a bright blue towel. Grant, now mounted on his horse, rode up to the side of the veranda and reached for the gruel. Beryl handed it to him.

Will turned to her. "Beryl, they're needing a nurse. Why don't you go along and help?"

Her back stiffened. She said nothing.

Grant settled the pot against the horn of his saddle. "Is this tureen full – is it likely to spill?"

"I don't think so. It's a short ride; you should be all right, sir."

Will persisted. "Dr. Watson wants a nurse, Mr. Grant. Beryl's done a good deal of nursing. Would you like her to come along with you?"

Beryl turned around and looked Will full in the face. Her usually calm grey eyes were angry, like those of a trapped animal. Still, she said nothing. Grant, sensing her feeling, responded uncertainly, "I don't know. Is that something you'd be wanting to do, Miss Newland? I'm sure a woman's hand would be a dear welcome to those children, but . . . "

Will interrupted as Keith came up beside Grant. "Beryl, you're the only woman who can do it. The others all have children – and Meg is nothing but a child herself yet."

Will's assumption that his sister would nurse the family of sick emigrants was, to him, perfectly natural. He believed that the woman of good and gentle breeding, the truly womanly woman, had an innate sense of noblesse oblige that ensured her dedication to helping the poor and sick, no matter what the cost to herself. And, indeed, Mrs. Baldwin and Mrs. Randall had already needed to be dissuaded from having any more direct contact with the suffering Seth family than the making of broths, the gathering of blankets, and the giving of money. William knew little of the terrors Beryl had suffered caring for their dying father. Of course she wanted to help. She was a good woman. It was what she was called to; it was her Christian duty. It was the duty she owed the Newland name. He waited.

Beryl struggled for a moment and almost gave in before Mr. Grant's sad, compelling eyes. She felt the nudge of her own compassion. That still, golden-haired child and the father with a sick, sagging face sick appealed to her, both for themselves and because they were emblems of that sweet melancholy assurance: *Whatsoever you do to the least of my brothers, that you do unto me.* And yet in almost the same instant she could smell the vomit; she could see the bloody puss as she washed it into a bowl; she could hear the rasping, rattling groans that made her own breathing hurt. She quailed at the panic of being trapped behind a closed door with the dead. She hated waiting by a sick bed; she hated it. It was unfair that she should always be the one locked away from the sun, facing the grave. Hot rebellion burst from her throat.

"And you're not capable, I suppose? Only spinster women are expendable? If they need a nurse, I say you go and nurse them, Will Newland. I'm not able." As soon as the words were out, she felt how they burned. She could not even look at Mr. Grant. Tears of frustration, anger, and remorse clouded her vision.

"It's a hard job, that's sure, my lass," said Mr. Grant. "And I'm not convinced I want you or any of the women doing it. The fewer of us exposed to the contagion, the better. Do you stay here. But if Mr. Newland wants to come along and help, well he's welcome. What say you, Will?"

Will was taken aback. He hesitated. Before he could reply, James Avery said:

"I'd be happy to do what I can, Mr. Grant. I don't know much about tending the sick, but I'm sure I could learn from Dr. Watson. It'd be a jolly good day's work to play Florence Nightingale. And maybe Will can a take a turn when I get too tired. No need for Miss Newland or any of the ladies to risk themselves. They've all done enough already."

Everyone looked at Avery in some astonishment. There he stood, the same pasty-faced young man with wide blue eyes and wispy brown hair who insisted on wearing an embroidered waistcoat even to erect a shanty. And yet there was no joke in his expression, no laughter in his voice. He looked as sober and sincere as a puritan.

Will's natural compassion was submerged in a wash of humiliation. Beryl and Avery both made him look like a bloody fool. He crumpled the tar paper in his left hand, smudging the fingers black. "Of course, Avery. Just send word."

Beryl found she could not speak, but as the men turned to follow the forlorn wagon, she touched Avery's arm. When he looked down at her, she mouthed the words "thank you" with trembling lips.

Avery felt a sudden buoyance at the sight of her shining grey eyes. "By God," he thought as he rode away, "this doctoring stuff is quite agreeable. I shall have to become a surgeon!" And, for a moment, the sad picture of the Seth family, beaten down like saplings under a brutal hail, disappeared from his sight, replaced by a beatific vision of himself, nobly bending over a sick bed (without anyone in it, oddly enough) and approved by a charming angel with lovely eyes and a rich cascade of black, Pre-Raphaelite tresses.

Not that Beryl had Pre-Raphaelite tresses. Indeed, the next time he saw her two nights later, when he emerged exhausted from the small shanty, he was startled to see a slender shadow move toward him: Beryl in the starlight, with dreary eyes and a pinched face, her black hair lank and pulled unbecomingly back from her brow. She reached out her hand but did not touch him.

"How do they fare, Mr. Avery?"

He could not talk for a minute. He cleared his throat, and then said, "The two very sick boys are dead. And the others – the girls -" He stopped again. "I don't know. The poor chap. The poor chap."

They stood still in the darkness. Above them, the freezing stars arced. Around them, the air of that flat land hung hot and humid. Mosquitos swarmed, pricking flesh and whining to themselves irritably.

"I wanted to come," she began. "I tried . . . "

She broke down and sobbed, bending double as though she were ill. He bent over her. Then they both fell to their knees, and there in the dirt they knelt for some time, grieving the dead.

Chapter VI

Where is Will?" Beryl's throat was parched and choking from smoke and ash. Her words came out a mere croak. Ben Davis splashed his grimy face, causing black rivers of water to stream down his cheeks and neck. The fire sent macabre shadows dancing along his features, and Beryl felt them playing on her own as well. It was near midnight and the blaze had only just reached the edge of the plow line encircling Victoria's corrals and primary buildings. Beryl nonetheless felt as though she were already being singed by the inferno, burned and bruised in some forgotten circle of hell. And she could not find her brother.

It was madness to try and do so. Davis shook his head. "There's no telling, Miss Newland. I've been watching the livestock. No doubt he's out among the soldiers. They've got guts, those Yankees. Rush right into the flames with a hoot and a holler. Utterly fearless. They must've learned it in the war."

Beryl struggled to keep her hoarse voice steady. "Are you telling me he's out there in the fire?"

"No," said Davis, realizing he'd blundered. "Not likely. No one is in the actual fire. At least I hope not. But the fire keeps threatening to jump the break, and it needs to be beaten down every time that happens. Probably he's too busy to come find you. And I need to get back myself. But try not to worry. If I find where he is, or someone who knows, I'll send you word."

Beryl watched him head back toward the corrals, where the cattle and sheep were bawling and moaning like lost souls. She shuddered at the sound, and at the crawling ground beneath her feet. Wild animals – rabbits, gophers, snakes, occasionally deer – crossed the unburned safety zone the humans had created, fleeing the fire that licked the earth behind them with a branding tongue. They became monstrous in the uncanny light, a nightmare of rodents and serpents, coming straight at her but then shooting around her, almost shooting right through her, as though she were a wisp of smoke.

Their fear, however, touched her like tentacles of electricity, shocking her, reminding her of her physical danger, urging her to run. Instead, she walked to the manor, climbing the east steps to where she could see the edges of the fire and escape that creeping ground. She found the two eldest Baldwin boys, Neville and John, on the landing, each hoarding a bucket of water. They coughed at the smoke, but their eyes were eager.

"Shouldn't you boys be inside with your mother?"

"We're protecting the manor, Miss Newland," said John importantly. "We're old enough to help. And father told us to stay here and look out for him. He said as our looking after him so would give him good luck."

"Can I join you? I'd like to look out for my brother and his friends."

"Why of course," said Neville. "Though I'm surprised you're not huddling inside like a shiv'ring lassie."

John nodded. "Mother said you're not very brave."

Beryl sat down beside them, pulling the damp and filthy skirt away from her aching ankles. At John's comment, she paused in her motion. "Why does your mother say that?"

"Why, cuz you wouldna' help nurse them sick bairns. She said as you was right not to do it, but tweren't brave all the same." He delivered his information matter of factly.

Neville scowled. He was old enough to know that some things should not be repeated. "You're a blithering idiot," he said, cuffing his younger brother and causing some of the water to spill.

"Am not! Anyhow," said John in a comradely fashion to Beryl, "I'm glad you're here. I should hate to be dead. Can you feel in a coffin? For it must be very hot tonight." He coughed and tried to rub a speck of ash out of his eye.

Beryl stared at the boy. "What do you mean?"

"Why of course they must be all burning up, don't you think?" He looked north and pointed to where the flames were ripping the horizon. "It's where they are, isn't it?"

Beryl followed his gaze, stricken. "Oh God," she whispered. "Oh God." She sat for a minute and then, without saying anything more, rose and hurried down the steps, back into the blackness. The boys watched her, surprised. Then John turned to Neville with a troubled expression.

"Oh," he said, all his bravado gone. "Nev, they must be able to feel it, or she wouldna' ha' rushed away so. Oh, Nev, do ye think it's true?"

Neville frowned, worried, and put his arm around his brother. "I dunna know. Not if they're in heaven, I guess."

"But what if they're in hell?" The game was over. John suddenly seemed awake to the fire's roar, to the frenzied shadows where animals screamed and men shouted. "Oh, what if hell's like this? What if we're in hell?" He burst into tears. "I want to go home. What if we're all in hell?"

"There now don't be a baby," said Neville gruffly. "We'll go find mother, and she'll tell us it's all right. That other, why she's just a shiv'ring lassie." He uttered his contempt with a twitching lip and stood up, pulling John up with him. But John shook his head, tugging at Neville's shirt.

"We canna' go, Neville. We have to stay here for father."

The two boys looked at each other for a black minute and then silently crouched back down against the stone wall of the manor. Their buckets stood before them like fonts of Mrs. Cavendar's magic water: murky talismans for keeping all evil away.

Warren Newland was already ill when his wife died of pneumonia during the winter of 1867. He complained to her throughout the autumn of fatigue and dyspepsia; he lost his enthusiasm for hunting and fishing, left his fossils — he was an avid collector of worms and larvae that coiled eternally in fragments of stone — to collect dust on a shelf, and pushed away his plate unfinished long before grief at the loss of Eleanor crippled his will to live.

Eleanor Newland listened to his complaints only half-seriously because he refused to see a physician. If he thought he was truly ill, he should consult Hill about it; since he did not, she considered his aches and pains an excuse to regain her sympathy. He had displeased her mightily by sending away Beryl's governess. Mr. Newland was short-tempered, a brilliant man who had little patience with those denied the quick insight that he took for granted. Mrs. Newland saw only frustration and heartache in his plan to teach the girl himself. He had tutored Robert several years before, and the experience had been miserable for both of them, not because Robert was not a smart boy, but because he was not as smart as his father.

Robert endured the lessons for his mother's sake. He became adept at surreptitiously watching the clock; he proved somewhat less skilled at conjugating verbs or explaining the positions of Malthus and Macaulay. Robert was dutiful, but he also had a keen sense of justice. When one day Mr. Newland called him a blockhead in mathematics and a disgrace in Latin, he quietly said, "I'm sorry, sir," walked out of the library, and refused to return. His performance at school had been consistently satisfactory, and he simply would not brook being called names by his father.

Mr. Newland, disgusted, abused him at the dinner table for a week and then sent him back to Eton, convinced that he would only distinguish himself by his outstanding mediocrity. But, after all, mediocrity was hardly a liability for a gentleman's son; at Oxford Robert's academic performance was in fact slightly above average. Ultimately his personal virtues – methodical earnestness, unquestioning patriotism, and a Christian affection for dogs and claret – carried him farther than a scintillating intellect might have. His father held him in some contempt but treated him with courtesy and acknowledged that his heir turned out a decent man.

Mr. Newland was convinced that Beryl would be easier to deal with: she was clearly very bright and, since she was a girl, would be more malleable. She had a sweet temper, he thought, and was like him in many ways. Mrs. Newland concurred that she was like her father, but not necessarily in ways flattering to either of them. Beryl at sixteen was pretty, affectionate, and talented; she was also extremely sensitive, sharp-tongued, and, her mother thought, rather spoiled.

"You'll find she's not quite what you imagine when you begin to work with her," said Mrs. Newland shaking her head. "You see her sit nicely at the table and hear her play piano in the drawing room and decide she's a docile young lady. You'd do better to think on her quarrels with William, for he's more like you than she is."

"She'll respect her father; if she doesn't, well then that's the first lesson she shall learn. If the governess hasn't got her under any better control than that, then it's well we're rid of her." He shifted in his chair and winced.

"Miss Broome has been an excellent teacher. I think it a disservice to both her and Beryl to dismiss her. She's a superior musician and you'll not be able to provide our Beryl with any such instruction."

"Beryl knows more than enough of music to please herself and to make her agreeable in company. She's never going to be a Liszt, Ellie. And Miss Broome's salary will be happy at home in my pocket. Give the woman good references, and you'll find she won't much regret losing her pupil. None of these governesses are much attached to their charges. Why should they be?"

Mrs. Newland pursed her lips and smoothed the lap of her brown gown with a firm palm. "You do her an injustice." She waited a moment and then said, "I am asking you please to keep her on and to allow Beryl to continue her study as she has been. She's doing well, and she's happy."

"And why the hell can't she be happy working with me and saving us some money?" The explosion was sudden. "Why are you always questioning my decisions? Why are you always implying that I'm not fit to work with my own children?" His voice rang, a rough clapper inside an angry bell. A maid dusting in the hall cringed. "If you were a real wife to me, you'd support my decisions, not continually oppose them. Who are you, Mrs. Newland, to set yourself against me?"

Mrs. Newland stood up. She lifted her chin and looked at him with cool grey eyes. "I'm not setting myself against you—"

"By God, you are! You constantly stand in the way of what I consider best. Every time I make a decision, you dissent. I am tired of it, madam. Damned tired of it. Get rid of that governess. I'll call in the rector if you cannot obey as a wife should." He rose, shaking with rage.

She stood before him, unmoved. Her expression was more pitying than anything else, though a keen observer might have seen lines of exasperation and weariness etched along the edges of her eyes. "You will find it's a mistake, Mr. Newland. I'd not be doing my duty as either a wife or a mother if I didn't tell you that. I hope you will reconsider." She moved quietly toward the door, then stopped and said without turning around, "I shall of course always be glad to speak with the rector about my deficiencies." There was just the slightest touch of amusement in her voice. She knew that Mr. Newland was rather jealous of her friendship with Reverend Seeley; she took the old gentleman's earnest non sequiturs so much more seriously than his own impassioned declarations.

It was her husband's great complaint against her: that she did not take him seriously. Early in their marriage she had been quite shattered by his rages – until she came to the conclusion that they were more sound than fury. On one occasion, pushed beyond endurance by his ranting, her anger upstaged her tears and she simply marched out on him, giving him nothing but freezing silence for a period of some days. She was secretly amazed to realize that as long as she cowered, he bullied, but that when she dismissed his behavior as beneath her notice, he was miserable and lost. He obviously needed to hear himself shouting at the world every now and then; it gave him confidence. Without her to validate the justice of his wrath, to play the target, he was defeated. Once she realized her power, his dominance was at an end. She loved him, firm in her conviction that he was a man of integrity and honor; she appreciated his intellect and enjoyed his geniality as a host. His less amiable attributes she dismissed as childish. When he was unreasonable or unjust, she ignored him as she would a toddler having a tantrum. He frequently won the immediate battle, but, since he could not bear to be ignored, she always won the war.

Miss Broome was dismissed. The fond father never tutored his daughter, however. Shortly after the governess bade Beryl an unhappy farewell, a cold infected everyone in the house. For two weeks in November, the sniffling, wheezing, and hacking was general among family and servants alike. Mrs. Newland suffered from a wretched cough in the later stages of the infection that, to the surprise and horror of all Lindenhurst, quickly developed into pneumonia. Her insides tore apart with the spasms that left her purple and gasping. She could not breathe and cried weakly. Her children watched her face fade into the pillow and listened as she pled with her husband to take care of himself, to see a doctor if he felt poorly;

never mind that she hadn't taken him seriously before. When she could no longer speak, she regarded him with glittering eyes, eyes continually made more brilliant by the welling of tears. Then she hadn't the strength to hold her eyes open anymore; she held the hands of her children, listened to the ticking of the clock, and tried to comprehend the low mutterings of Rev. Seeley: *O Almighty God, with whom do live the spirits of just men made perfect, after they are delivered from their earthly prisons; We humbly commend the soul of this thy servant, our dear sister, into thy hands, as into the hands of a faithful Creator . . . .*

A week after she first fell ill, Eleanor Newland died.

It was in keeping his final promise to his wife that Mr. Newland's cancer was revealed.

At first, he seemed to care very little. The pressure in his belly was nothing compared to the pain in his breast, and the thought of dying and joining his wife was a relief. But when the first violence of grief passed, a profound fear of death asserted itself. He spent hours discoursing with Hill on possible changes in habit and diet that might prolong his life. He tracked down folk remedies, riding around the moors seeking out cottagers and gypsies, and at night he drank odd concoctions in the privacy of his room. He harangued his daughter on the stupidity of death until she, who needed no convincing that it was a very bad thing indeed, almost wished she could die so that the ringing in her ears might stop. The nervous, girlish shuffling of her feet matured into an exasperated grinding under her black skirts. "I *must* go and see about the dinner, Papa," she would burst out at last and flee. Then he would retreat into his library, where he pulled the fossils of weirdly coiled creatures out of their drawers and worried over them, engrossed sometimes by philosophic conundrums on the transience of mortals but more often plagued by images of worms crawling in corpses, worms curling up to die in skulls, worms becoming calcified in stone.

The disease did not finally fell him until a month after Beryl's seventeenth birthday. Her birthday would have been a grim affair, except that William and Robert, with his new wife Marian, came to Lindenhurst bearing the vigor and freshness of outside society. Robert and his friend Captain Denton talked politics with her father for hours; their talk cheered Mr. Newland, reminded him that he was still part of the world, though his sickness kept him home more and more. His cheerfulness liberated Beryl, allowing her to wander around Lindenhurst with Will and Marian for an afternoon without the worry that she was needed or the guilt that she could not bear to be found. Will told her stories about his chums from school – some of which she found scandalous and made her laugh – and teased her endlessly about her hair, newly pulled back and piled in plaits on her head. "Tis a black crown, Beryl. I say, you do look like the queen of spades."

"Nonsense," said Marian. "It looks very becoming; you are lucky not to have to wear a hairpiece. You've inherited your mother's lovely masses of hair." Marian was gentle but matter of fact in the mention of her mother. Beryl was grateful. The maudlin references of her father made her uncomfortable; worse yet were the times when he expressed bitterness over her mother's failings and commenced upon tirades that confused her because she knew that, somehow, they were not about Mrs. Newland at all. Marian seemed to know Mrs. Newland better than her own father did – and she had never met her.

"Oh, it's your hair that is beautiful." Beryl admired the way the pins sparkled in her sister-in-law's immaculately sculpted chignon. "Mine's heavy and black. And my clothes are heavy and black. Everything around here is heavy and black. You can't think how dismal it is, Marian, with father sick and mother gone. I wish I could go to school like Will, but I suppose I'm quite done. Papa says there's nothing left for me to learn." Beryl threw herself onto the turf in discontent.

"Sounds beastly, sis," said Will, sitting down next to her. He pulled her skirt out from under his boot. "Father has become an old bear. But of course you must take care of him. There's no one else to do it. And you can always read my books when I'm done with them. I have one or two good ones I can leave with you this time, in fact."

Marian looked at the blue September sky shining above the Pennines. "He'd do better in London. Robert is going to talk with him about it. No doubt Mr. Hill is a competent physician, but he did not do much for your mother and in London there are specialists with experience in your father's condition. And it would certainly be better for you to be among people. It's very beautiful here, though."

"It doesn't matter where you are, if you're kept in prison all day," said Beryl scowling. "I would like to go to London again. That would be better – much."

At first it was. Mr. Newland was buoyed by hopes of recovery and became a better companion than he'd been since his wife's death. They rode the carriage around Hyde Park and admired fashions and flowers; they attended services at the Abbey where Beryl was transported by the music. He watched her affectionately. "The music turns you into a kind of angel, doesn't it, lass?" Captain Denton visited him often, bringing archaeological journals and good conversation, and then received permission to escort Beryl to an art exhibition – where for the first time she felt like a grown-up lady. The paintings helped her forget herself for a few hours, and if Captain Denton did sometimes look rather too long into her face, she nonetheless thought it worth the trouble to be accompanied by such a handsome uniform.

Beryl had even more fun with William when he came up from school. Her father gave them a day, and they took an excursion to the Tower of London where Will regaled her with history she already knew. She soberly studied the block where Ann Boleyn lost her head. Will told her she should learn a lesson from it, and she replied that with his radical politics he'd be locked in the Tower decades before the Queen ever realized she existed. Afterwards they strolled the Strand, eating pasties they bought from a vendor and laughing at a Punch and Judy. It all seemed a holiday. Beryl even liked the house in London: the pretty blue room that looked out on the street of passing people; the cozy parlor; the narrow garden behind the house. She almost forgot why they'd come.

But stifling fogs accompanied the assessment of physicians whose competence could not be questioned, men who nodded knowingly as Mr. Newland described symptoms, shook their heads as they explored his body, and became grave behind their spectacles when offering their prognosis. With hope gone, Mr. Newland sank into a dark and angry depression. The disease gripped him in gory earnest. The cramping increased. Mr. Newland moaned, whimpered, and swore, alternately clutching his daughter's hand while demanding her sympathy and love, and then throwing it away in angry envy of her youth and health. He complained continually about the food which he could not keep down, about the street noise which he could not stop, about the tenor of Beryl's voice when she read to him. She sat beside him, fighting the ache in her throat and sliding her heel in a grim rhythm along the floor. Once he heard her boot scraping and yelled at her to stop fidgeting. She learned to grind silently. Her sole wore itself out in an oddly crooked way.

Mr. Newland kept Beryl chained to the sick room as he grew more and more ill. He complained that the nurse they had hired to help Beryl was cold and unfeeling. When his incontinence grew and he smeared his sheets with bloody, soft, foul-smelling feces, he horrified his daughter by insisting not only that she clean up the mess he left, but that she clean him as well.

She could hardly speak. "I cannot, Papa. Do not ask me – it would be indecent. I'm sorry – but I would be sick."

Her father pulled himself up onto his elbow, his blue eyes wild. "Indecent? Indecent? I'm not asking you to lay with me, I'm asking you to wipe me up so that I'm not left with some stranger cleaning the crap off of me like a bloody beggar in a poor house. You're a grown woman now; your mother would do it. How did you become such an unnatural slut?"

Beryl recoiled but retorted, "I'm not unnatural or a slut. But it wouldn't be right to see you that way. I can't." She backed away from the bed and began to cry.

The nurse, a big, red-haired woman who had been stolidly standing by, took the girl's part. "You let me clean yer up, sir. Means nothin' ter me, I'm paid to do it and I does it well."

A series of expletives spewed from the sick man's mouth, ugly as the matter which leaked from his anus and made the air of the room putrid. Beryl covered her ears with her hands and began shaking and screaming; she seemed unable to stop. Her screams drowned out her father's curses. The nurse ran to her, restraining her in her large arms.

"There now, stop do yer," she said in a strong, gruff voice. " 'e don't mean it, 'e's a dying man. Don't take on, lass, don't take on. Tain't you, e's mad from the sickness, 'e is." She led the hysterical girl from the room, leaving Mr. Newland panting from the exertion of his rage and lying in his own excrement.

When the nurse returned, she found him sobbing, crying over and over, "I'm sorry, I'm sorry, tell her I'm sorry." She said nothing, but proceeded to clean his soiled, naked body with business-like proficiency. She shrank neither from the task nor from the odor. She wiped the dying man's emaciated buttocks and swollen belly as calmly and gently as if he were a pretty baby of six months. Then she lifted him, again like a baby, onto a clean blanket, wrapped him up, and set him in a chair. She put a book into his trembling hands and dexterously gathered up the stinking sheets. She did not turn around as she left the room, although she heard her patient weeping and pleading.

"Tell her I'm sorry. I'm sorry. Oh, Ellie, I'm sorry."

In mid-August, the last of the doomed Seth children died, leaving only the broken father and the sixteen-year-old son remaining from the family of eight that had left Scotland in early June. Disposing of the bodies was a vexing question, as everyone felt it demanded both reverence and speed. The only formal cemetery in the area, if one could call it that, was Boot Hill in Hays City, and none of the Britons could stomach the thought of burying these children in soil where drunkards, suicides, whores, and criminals lay rotting. Only half a month before, Cabot pointed out, the notorious Kate Coffee, owner of a Hays dance hall and brothel, had been laid to rest there after having been murdered by a man known to have raped a fourteen-year-old farm girl. Cabot sympathized with Katie on her unhappy end, but he did not want any of the Seth family sharing her unhallowed ground. The Wyatt brothers, who had themselves made numerous forays into Hays' red-light district, were contemptuous of Cabot for publicly acknowledging his intimacy with the ways of the fair fallen, but they concurred with his conclusion.

Mr. Grant brooded, riding his handsome stallion for hours the day after the first two Seths, Jerad (the fair, still child) and Robert (the dark-haired, whimpering one), died. He had made no plans in his community for a cemetery (the pardonable oversight of an optimist), and given the nature of their illness, these dead should probably not be buried in the village of Victoria anyway. So he rode and rode until he found a pretty bluff about four miles north of the manor house where yellow flowers bloomed. and bees hummed. His choice was sentimental; he hoped that, as the bluff overlooked a valley to the east (or such as existed in that part of Kansas), the children's bodies might rest peacefully, facing the Mississippi River where their mother lay. He did not share this thought with anyone else, however. He merely informed Keith that he'd found a site and that coffins should be built as soon as possible for the emaciated bodies.

There was no preacher to give a blessing to the dead. So on that morning in August when the last Seth child to die – the auburn-curled, eight-year-old Emily – was laid next to her sister with the coquettish boots, Will Newland took up the office – or at least the book – he had spurned in England. Nervously, though with a dramatically fine intonation, Will led the burial service of the Church of England. One after another, the small boxes were lowered into the ground.

"I am the resurrection and the life, saith the Lord: he that believeth in me, though he were dead, yet shall he live: and whosoever liveth and believeth in me, shall never die. Jesus called them unto him and said, Suffer the little children to come unto me . . ."

Though few had been present to welcome these ill-fated children, each time another one died the entire colony of young British men came to bid them farewell. Each time William Newland officiated. Each time his sister stood beside him, wretched.

"I will lift up mine eyes unto the hills; from whence cometh my help?"

Beryl never was able to force herself to enter the door of that unhallowed, hastily constructed hut where the Seths died: not before they died and not after.

"He will not suffer thy foot to be moved; and he that keepeth thee will not sleep."

Guilt lay heavy in her chest. Some mornings she could hardly get up.

"Behold, he that keepeth Israel shall neither slumber nor sleep."

She grieved at the deaths of these children, at the fact that their bodies could not be washed and properly shrouded for fear of the disease that killed them. She grieved at the cheap boxes in which they were buried, coffins which could hardly be expected to protect the corpses for even a year. She grieved at the pathetic wooden crosses upon which Avery carved their names and date of death with so much care to so little effect.

"The Lord himself is thy keeper; the Lord is thy defense upon thy right hand . . . "

She could not sleep at night for thinking of the childish bodies lying in the darkness with the crickets calling and the coyotes howling.

"The Lord himself is thy keeper . . . the sun shall not burn thee by day, neither the moon by night. The Lord shall preserve thee from all evil." She wished she were dead, too.

"Oh merciful Father, whose face the angels of thy little ones do always behold in heaven; Grant us steadfastly to believe that this thy child hath been taken into the safe keeping of thine eternal love . . . "

So she listened to the reading of the burial service – decent, even reverent, but hurried, for no one knew if the contagion lingered in the air – and sought protection in its words from her imagined guilt and from the grief of the father and son who stood over the hole in the ground. They were only just recovered enough to come and see this last child buried next to four other crosses that signified funerals they had been unable to attend. She wondered where they found the strength to stand.

"Jesus saith to his disciples, Ye now therefore have sorrow: but I will see you again, and your heart shall rejoice, and your joy no man taketh from you."

Perhaps it was because they leaned on each other. They did not cry, but they clung together, arms linked, the tall child every now and again resting his head on his father's shoulder. It was unusual to see men hold together so, not least a father and an almost grown son. It did not seem quite British. But it was, Beryl thought, eminently right.

"In sure and certain hope of the Resurrection to eternal life through our Lord Jesus Christ, we commit the body of this child to the ground. The Lord bless her and keep her, the Lord make his face to shine upon her and be gracious unto her, the Lord lift up his countenance upon her and give her peace . . . "

One week later, Mr. Seth and his son left for Russell, where they determined to stay until they were well enough to return to Scotland. Neither could bear to stay in Victoria. Mr. Seth cursed the entire venture as "a folly and a lie," though he said he bore Mr. Grant no ill will, as "he couldna' ha' known the evil of the place beforehand." Grant did not reply to this indictment; he would not argue with a man who had paid for his dream at the cost of five children and a wife. The send-off was no less dismal than the welcome had been, though most of the colony was there as a tribute. Mr. Seth expressed quiet gratitude to Dr. Watson and those who had helped the family, but to Avery he gave a small package – a handsome hand mirror that had been his wife's. "Something to thank ye for your caring hand. It'll na show anything lovely back at us anymore – but here's hoping that someday it'll reflect some joy for ye. God bless ye, young man." The Seth boy wept.

"Almighty God, Father of mercies and giver of all comfort; Deal graciously, we pray thee, with all those who mourn that, casting every care on thee, they may know the consolation of thy love; through Jesus Christ our Lord. Amen."

None of the Victoria colonists ever fell ill from the contagion that wiped out the Seth family. After they were gone, Grant ordered the hut where they had suffered burned. He watched the smoke rise into the sky like a bitter Abraham upon whom no mercy had been shown, and from his mouth he spit the taste of ashes.

Two days later he left for New York City.

The banner that had spanned the veranda of Victoria Manor; the red, white, and blue ribbons that had festooned the windows, doors, and posts; and the Union Jack and American flags which had whipped companionably in the Kansas wind – all should have been stored in the back closet of the station. Too much conviviality had, however, resulted in champagne on the ribbons and even wine stains on the banner, so that after the eminent gentlemen and journalists from England, Scotland, and New York City (all of whom had toured the Victoria Colony, examined the land, the cattle, and the crops, interviewed the colonists, and arrived at a most flattering conclusion regarding Mr. Grant's endeavor – and, indeed, Mr. Grant himself), after they had departed in all the splendor of a special coach provided by the Kansas Pacific (never having heard of a family named Seth or having visited the row of graves that looked east to the Mississippi), Edwards arranged to have a laundress in Hays clean all the decorations. He put them, along with a crate of two-dozen cut-crystal wine glasses, graciously on loan from Tommy Drumm's saloon, in Jason Mayes' new buggy, ready for the trip to Hays the next day.

That buggy was parked beside the frame of Hunter's new store the night of the fire. This structure was a good ten yards or more from the ragged line of plowed ground that encircled the settlement like a moat, and it remained a mystery how a spark managed to fly so far and turn the shiny new vehicle into a torch. Nonetheless, at just past one-thirty, a.m., Mrs. MacDonough, her infant in her arms, let out a shrill cry and pointed to the flames which had broken rank and managed to find their way past the exhausted front line. Five or six men ran to the burning buggy; two grabbed it by the tongue and pulled it away from the store. The maneuver was dangerous: the very haste with which they dragged the vehicle fanned its flames higher. Inside, flags and ribbons disintegrated; Tommy Drumm's beautiful goblets exploded in violent shards of heat. One man struck at the buggy with a rug; in a moment the rug itself caught on fire and with horrific speed the flames ran up it and clutched at the man's arm. He screamed as his sleeve kindled; another man pushed him to the ground and threw himself on top of the burning clothes, smothering them. Meanwhile three women – Mrs. Baldwin, Mrs. Randall, and Meg Grant – came running from the manor house with buckets of water which, ignoring the men, they lunged at the fire. In a few minutes the buggy fire was contained. Hunter's half-constructed store and the other buildings were, for the moment, safe, but the buggy and all its contents were lost.

Will Newland's arm was blistering where his sleeve had kindled; he winced as Cabot supported him back to the manor.

"I'm grateful, Cabot," he croaked.

Cabot shook his head. "Had to do it. Need all the righteous friends I can get. And then there's your sister." His voice was a mere rasp.

"Where is she?" asked Will.

"I don't know."

Meg came gasping alongside them, clutching her empty buckets. Her braid swung over her shoulder. Cabot gave it a yank.

"Child, what business had you coming out with your hair hanging and your skirts flying? You could have gone up like a roman candle. Does your uncle know what you're about?"

Meg felt tired and sick, but she gave him a saucy grin. "'Twasn't me rolling around on the ground and smoking, now, was it?"

"Where's Beryl?" Will persisted.

Meg frowned. "I don't know – she was with us early, before the fire got close, and then she ran off."

Will stopped. "Ran off where?"

"Well – into the fire. I think she went to look for you."

Cabot burst into swearing. "Haven't any of you bloody women any sense?"

Will just looked at Meg. "When did she go?"

"I told you. A long time back."

"Damn. Damn." He cradled his injured arm with his good hand. "Someone has to find her." Then he looked into the blackness and the smoke and the flames which were at last beginning to move beyond Victoria. Except for a few lanterns that seemed to stagger about of their own accord, the fire provided the only light. There was no sign of dawn.

"Let's get you to safety first," said Cabot. "Then we'll send someone after her and all the other unruly wenches." He eyed Meg meaningly, but she was watching the lascivious flames and listening to the shouts of resistance that rose against the roar.

It was Douglas Keith who found Beryl. The morning light was just beginning to break in the east. Once it escaped the grim line of flame that was still visible on the horizon, the sun came up a frightening scarlet: the filtering effect of ash, smoke, and dust. She stood in a pool of this uncanny light, at a place where plowed ground ended and scorched prairie stretched away for miles. The earth still smoked beneath her feet; she held in her hands a damp sack that she had used to beat the flames. Her green dress hung limply from sagging shoulders: torn, singed, and stained with soil and ash. A scarf of uncertain color bound her brow and hid all her hair. Her face was grimy, her eyes shrunken inside puffy red lids. She looked as bad as any of them, Keith thought. She turned when she heard him approaching but then faced back again toward the wasted plain.

"Are you all right, Miss Newland?"

"Yes."

"Your brother is worrying about you; sent me out to find you. We heard from soldiers that a woman had been helping them on the north edge of the break. They said you wouldn't return with them."

"No." She was silent a moment. "The Americans weren't afraid to teach me how to help them with the fire. I was glad. I wanted to fight. When it was over, they told me I must come back with them. One of them tried to order me." She smiled to herself, slightly. "I told him that I was an English citizen, and he could not order me to do anything. He seemed to like that and did not force me."

Keith came to her and took the filthy sack from her hands. "Why didn't you come? You must be fair tired, lass."

"I was waiting for the dawn. To see if Johnnie Baldwin was right."

"Johnnie Baldwin?"

"He said they would all be burned. And he was right."

Keith grabbed her arm and looked into her face. "Who are you talking about? We're all safe."

Beryl turned her eyes to his face; they looked, he thought, as frigid as the North Sea. "The Seths, Mr. Keith. They died and were buried out there in that lonely place and then this fire came and burned away every trace that they ever were. We shall never be able to find where they are buried again."

Keith pressed his lips together and looked into the smoking distance. The devastation was bewildering. Vultures circled. After a moment he spoke. "We'll find the site again and put up a stone tablet to honor all of the bairns, one that cannot burn or blow away. Don't worry, Miss Newland. They'll not be forgotten."

"What do you mean? They've already been forgotten. Which of you men ever mentioned to the delegation from New York that we'd lost some of our own already, that the bodies of British children lie under this soil? Do you really think that would not have interested Mr. Ferguson of Aberdeenshire? Mr. Skirving of Edinburgh?" Her voice was full of contempt. "You – all of you – acted as though they never existed." She shifted her gaze to the miles of black land. "And now they don't. They are burned away to nothing."

She shook off his arm and turned back toward the town. Then she stopped and asked, "My brother – he's all right?"

"He injured his arm, but he's all right. Just wanting to see you. Everyone is all right."

But when they returned to the manor, they found the body of young Major Tilson laid out on a table in the station room. He'd been found dead against a far fence of the corral, pinned under his horse. Also against the fence was the corpse of a cow and a yearling calf. The calf had caught its leg in the hole of some animal; likely the accident had occurred while Tilson tried to save the creature and its mother. Tilson's face was black, but not burned beyond recognition. Vincent Spenser stood touching Tilson's charred remains like a sacred relic and wept. Captain Prescott sat next to the dead man, cradling his head in his hands.

Major Tilson was the first colonist buried in George Grant's cemetery, a sweeping stretch of meadow that lay along the southeast edge of the settlement near Victoria Creek. *"For a thousand years in thy sight are but as yesterday, when it is past, and as a watch in the night,"* read Neil Hunter. (William found he could no longer bear to act as chaplain. "It's too hard to believe" he said.) *"As soon as thou scatterest them they are even as a sleep; and fade away suddenly like the grass. In the morning it is green, and groweth up; but in the evening it is cut down, dried up, and withered. For we consume away in thy displeasure and are afraid at thy wrathful indignation. Thou hast set our misdeeds before thee; and our secret sins in the light of thy countenance. For when thou art angry all our days are gone: we bring our years to an end, as it were a tale that is told."*

Douglas Keith played Tilson's bagpipes. After the last moaning notes died away, a meadowlark trilled back from over the blackened earth. Then there was only a shuddering of wind, and silence.

Chapter VII

Throughout the summer the wind pushed hard over the land. Birds struggled in flight. Clouds folded over themselves in luxuriant masses or were carded into wisps that stretched the length of the sky. Moisture was sucked from the soil until it cracked; the swirling dirt ground itself to an eye-scratching fineness. At night, when women combed their hair, they combed out grit like splinters of glass. They listened to the wind push incessantly at shutters and doors, banging and breathing heavy. It did not cool the brow. It blew hot. It wearied them almost to death.

The initiated complained little, however, aware of the coming cold that would turn the heavy-breathing wind to a howl. Like muskrats, they gathered their food and thickened their walls and braced themselves for the storm. When at last it arrived, they burrowed deep, and they did not raise their heads to look for the sun.

Richard Cabot's land contained a large pond ringed with cattails. Many of the Britons boasted ownership of what Vincent Spenser christened "self-important puddles," but Cabot's body of water was respectably long and deep. It delighted him not only because it provided drink for his livestock (he had a herd of sixty English Cotswolds grazing the plains by September), but also because it attracted wildlife and enhanced the hunting. In late summer he fished its murky depths and pulled out catfish: big, brown, and grotesquely tentacled about the jowls. Fried up with eggs, they were a delicacy. In fall, migrating geese congregated on the pond's shores. Ian Duncan, adept at both the style and substance of Yankee storytelling, bragged that at Cabot's pond he shot a goose dinner for each and every colonist in only five minutes. Antelope came and sometimes stray buffalo. Garth Mason spent much of his free time there, field glasses and notebook in hand. He sketched and recorded observations for an article entitled "Beasts Big and Small of the Great Plains" while Cabot, who liked to join him, smoked and, from a distance, watched the progress on the stone house and barn he was having built.

"I say, Mason, seems to me one bird is much like another. You have sixteen sketches there, all labeled differently, and every damn one looks the same."

"If you knew what to look for, you'd know they're no more the same than sixteen different people would be. And it's not sixteen. It's only six."

"Those fowl are as alike as Chinamen."

"Which proves my point and not yours."

"Well," said Cabot, "no offense, old man, but it seems a dreadful bore."

Mason smiled benignly. "It's as much a pleasure to me as watching the ladies is to you."

Cabot took the cigarette from his mouth and brushed his thumb against his lips. "Couldn't be."

"I assure you it's true. And just now I have a better field for study than you do, so I am of course the happier man."

Cabot regarded his cigarette. "I'll concede that the quantity of my specimens is certainly limited. Not to mention the quality. So far, I must say that the English goods are superior to the American. And damnably rare."

"That will change," said Mason, studying the wing of a thrush against a checkering of cattail stems. "Mrs. Hunter is certainly a lovely lady."

"Well, yes, and rather inaccessible. I'm not so desperate as to hunt down married women. At least not yet. Hunter is too good a chap anyway."

"Yes," said Mason. "He's a good man."

They were silent for a few minutes. The autumn air was brisk. Mason looked supremely happy. From the summit of contentment, he looked down at Cabot's restlessness. After a moment he said, "There's Miss Newland."

"She's too good," said Cabot.

"You could reform."

"I'd rather not."

Cabot stood gazing to the west, watching the stone walls of his estate grow against the sky. His blond hair blew over his brow and into his eyes. They were a dreamy, speculative blue. Mason was struck by the splendid isolation of his beauty and youth.

"She's too good," Cabot said again. "Or maybe not good enough."

Mason frowned. "What do you mean?"

"She's not confident in her goodness, certainly not confident enough to save me along with herself. But a fascinating study, and not just because she's handsome. Which she is. Lovely limbs, though she covers herself like a sister of charity." He gave a sensual grunt. "But you know, that's just it. She's a woman intelligent enough to recognize her own inconsistencies, yet she refuses to acknowledge them."

"What inconsistencies?"

Cabot took a drag on his cigarette and shook his head. "Never mind, Garth. You just study your birds and fieldmice and leave the more complex organisms to me. But don't misunderstand me. I think very highly of Miss Newland. Someday she'll find someone deserving of her. It's already obvious I'm not the only one who finds her well worth watching."

Mason felt irritated, uncertain why Cabot was critical of Miss Newland. He did not know the Newlands well, but the sister seemed to him comely, gracious, and agreeably serious in a group where half the young people seemed disposed to nonsense. At last he said, "She's a brave woman. She fought that fire with the courage of a man."

Cabot took off his cap and let the wind push the hair out of his eyes. "Expiating her sins. I call it foolish."

Mason paused in his sketching and then closed his book and stood up. "I must get back to the stable." His voice was rather cold.

"As you wish," said Cabot and threw his cigarette gracefully into the pond. They began walking back toward the half-constructed house. "Do tell me about that new stallion of Grant's. I've heard it's a beauty."

Garth Mason was a gentle person, too gentle to rebuff Cabot's friendliness. He was also an enthusiastic equestrian – he managed the Victoria livery stable – and, after a moment, he rose to Cabot's bait like one of the pond's hideous catfish. "Oh, he's a beauty. Sixteen hands high, sleek chestnut coat, bright eyes. A real gentleman's horse. 'Lord Clyde' Mr. Grant calls him. Would you believe he's descended from 'Nugget of Gold'?"

"What, the one who won a prize at the Oxford show?"

"The same."

"Came from England then?"

"Along with that last dozen rams."

"How many sheep does he have now?"

"I couldn't tell you. Keith might know, or Duncan. Maybe a couple thousand?"

Cabot grinned. "Damn. And I've been so proud of my hundred head."

"Grant's ambitious, that's sure. Just purchased some Berkshire pigs and two more bulls. He talks about operating with fifty-thousand animals by next year at this time." Mason looked down at the buffalo grass with a doubtful expression. "How the land will support it, God knows. The fire is already forcing him to relocate for winter."

Cabot shrugged. "He's a gambler. You don't get rich by playing coppers. Where's he putting up the cattle?"

"Down in the Kaw Valley, near Junction City. Davis and Staples are leading the drive. Did you know Grant went with them?"

"Did he?" Cabot raised his eyebrows.

"Never underestimate him," said Mason. "You missed a grand sendoff: Grant mounted on Lord Clyde, looking as though he were leading them all on a western crusade. A fine-looking man. A real king."

Cabot smiled and strode over the ground silently for a few minutes. Then he said, "He's one of them, you know."

"One of what?" asked Mason.

"One of the ones watching her."

Mason stopped, puzzled for a moment. Then, in spite of himself, his eyes lit up behind his spectacles. "You don't say?"

"I do," said Cabot, and then he laughed at Mason's shamefacedness.

There was no minister to marry Neil Hunter and Julia Murray when she arrived from Scotland in late September, so they were married by Judge McGaffigan in Hays City. Daniel and Jane MacDonough stood as witnesses, and then they all walked down the dusty street to the New York House for a wedding party. The burned and barren prairie provided no flowers, but the British women raided their trunks to dress the long wooden hotel tables with linen, silver, and crystal. Buffalo steaks and gold-roasted geese sat on the board. The bread, which had refused to rise, was disappointingly flat, black, and gritty, but canned peaches nestled in china bowls, and at the end of the table a great bucket of lemonade glistened, compliments of Tommy Drumm's saloon. By late evening, when Neil and Julia escaped from an impending chivaree by slipping out the back door, mounting a pair of horses, and racing them far into the darkness, the hilarity of the guests was clearly being nurtured by something more pungent than lemon water and nuptial joy. If Mr. Drumm had a hand in that, he never took the credit.

Tommy Drumm was by this time a great friend to the Victoria colonists, the accidental destruction of his goblets in the fire notwithstanding. Unlike Dalton's, which catered to sullen soldiers and hard-hewn teamsters, or Mose's, which entertained Blacks and Mexicans, or Hound Kelly's, which served Irish railroad workers – and only served them whiskey straight-up – Drumm's attracted the brand of western immigrant that liked to consider himself a cut above. The appointments of the saloon were elegant – cut red crystal, sterling silver glass holders, and a polished bar above which stretched a shining mirror – and the clientele was, or had been, illustrious: in earlier days Tommy's mirror had reflected the faces of Wild Bill Hickock, Calamity Jane, and General George Custer. The English were pleased to see their own reflections in that same mirror, to be reassured of their role in the history of that frontier, and to conclude how eminently civilized and superior that role was. Between St. Louis and Denver there was said to be no finer drinking establishment. Drumm made special trips to the former city to pick up fine liquors and to study the art of alcoholic concoction; to please the English he made an impeccable "Shoo-fly" for which he bought a special cow so that the milk he mixed in would be rich and sweet. Drumm never drank himself, and he quietly stopped pouring for any gentleman who had had a bit too much. His saloon breathed culti-vation, and if it was not quite on par with a London club, many of the English ranked it a close second.

It was characteristic that when Drumm heard a newly arrived homesteader named Leonard Bell was in fact a minister seeking a place to conduct services, Drumm offered his saloon. The Reverend Bell, at first dubious, agreed after a meeting with Drumm where Tommy spoke of his mother, the homesteader spoke of salvation, and they both cried. Word quickly spread that on the third Sunday of October a service of Christian worship would be held in Drumm's at 10 o'clock in the morning. Despite long-standing antagonism to-ward anyone who poked their nose into the state of their souls, the inhabitants of Hays – who were becoming more respectable by the day – quickly became enthusiastic about the church service. Many who had been lounging at Tommy's on Saturday night, drink in hand, were present again on Sunday, hair slicked back and mouth dry. Many others who had never before set foot in a saloon crossed the threshold that morning with an avid, if somewhat guilty, curios-ity. Though the ornate bar had been covered with sun-bleached sheets and the polished tables had been pushed back to make way for rows of sedate benches, the great mirror remained uncovered. The citizens of Hays looked at themselves in some embarrassment, each gawking at the other, at the place, and not least at their own faces, which stared back at them like a relentless revelation.

Shortly before ten, a small contingent from the Victoria Colony arrived. People turned expectant eyes on them as they entered the saloon-turned-church. They were already noted in town for their money, their fashionable attire, and their aristocratic lineage. The latter, at least, accounted for their manners, which those who were more likely to patronize Hound Kelley's or Dalton's called "damned snobby" and those who enjoyed (or at least aspired to) inclusion in the Tommy Drumm crowd called "cultured." A half dozen young men and three women were part of the group. A dark-haired, sturdy-looking man with a pretty, plump, blond girl on his arm led the party. Her cheeks were pink from the gusty October wind, and her brown eyes were frank and friendly as they looked over the seated congre-gation.

"Just wed, them two," said a grizzled old man, nudging his partner. "Ain't she a rose blossom?" The partner grunted agreement. Behind the couple came a young girl in a blue dress and a coat the color of wine. Long red braids hung over her shoulders and down her back. "The Baron's heiress," went on the grizzled informant. "And that's his overseer – Duncan." He pointed to a husky, bright-eyed fellow with a cap set jauntily on his brown curls.

He was silent as the other six people entered. His partner did not like to seem too interested in something he knew little about, but after a moment he licked his cracked lips and growled, "And them folks?"

"Don't know fur sure," admitted the old man reluctantly. He pulled at the collar scratching his neck. "But fine to look at, ain't they? 'Course, they ain't been here long," he said. He looked speculatively at the broad-shouldered, round-faced man with a benevolent expression, and at the handsome gentleman with an ironic cast to his lips who followed. "Plenty 'o money there," he muttered studying the tweed jacket and noting the sensation the gentleman caused among the young females seated on the benches in front of him. "Them curls'll quiver the rest of the service, I'm bettin.'"

The curls seemed no less excited by the next gentleman who entered, blinking hazel eyes as he tried to adjust to the room's relative darkness after the sunlight outdoors. His hair was golden brown under his bowler, his cheek bones high, his jaw wide and well-shaped. He laughed as he introduced the woman with him to Drumm. She was slender and wore a green mantle and hat. Over the hat she wore a white veil. She lifted it from her face and let it fall around her shoulders before she shook hands with the saloon keeper, revealing coils of black braids and grey eyes. "Lovely orbs," observed the informant, "but ain't real chipper, eh?" The next moment she smiled, and the resemblance between her and the laughing young man became more apparent – much to the relief of the quivering curls. "Gotta be her brother," said the old philosopher. "He don't look at her the way I reckon most young fellows would. That last gent, for instance. God, what a doll." He gestured in some amazement toward a pale young man with wispy side whiskers who stood behind the woman. He wore a silk top hat and a handsome dress coat accented with a pair of gold buttons and a narrow collar of deep purple velvet.

Between the lapels of the collar, a small red tie was visible resting on a ruffled shirt front. He wore kids gloves and white spats.

"They do grow 'em with fancy feathers," observed his partner dryly.

"Must be a lord or a duke," said the old fellow doubtfully.

The other grunted over his folded arms. "Glad we don't grow 'em over here, that's all I gotta say."

The group from Victoria found room to sit near the back, next to a family with three small children. The father was a farmer, with a long, long beard. The mother, who sat closest to the open space on the bench, had a painfully thin face; she looked hungry. But her dress was a neatly starched calico, and, after a moment's diffidence, she beckoned to Julia Hunter, who smiled and sat next to her with a ready interest in her jolly baby. Neil sat next to his wife, then Meg and Beryl. The ladies' skirts took considerable space on the bench, leading to some debate over who should sit next to Beryl and who should stand behind the others for the duration of the service. Mason and Duncan willingly enough went behind the Hunters and leaned against the wall, the latter cheerfully observing that "they've blanketed Miss Fillmore," referring to the painting of a rose-lipped, bare-bosomed lass who usually looked out at Drumm's patrons with coy embarrassment. Today she was draped, frame to frame and up to her indignant eyebrows, in a decorous tablecloth. Cabot, putting on a sanctimonious face, went and stood by Duncan. He took great satisfaction in the number of young women who gazed his way, and even more satisfaction in returning the gaze of one or two of them. Avery and Will were left to decide who would sit, who would stand. Avery wanted to sit next to Beryl. He approached her and crunched the brim of his silk hat between well clad fingers. He wished she would smile at him. She seemed oblivious. He hesitated. Will watched for a minute, then grinned, shook his head, and deliberately sat down on the edge of Beryl's skirt. She turned a withering glance on him and moved over, pulling her dress from beneath his pant leg.

"Oh, do forgive me, my lady," he said in a low voice, laughing. Then he looked up at Avery, who wore a chagrined expression along with his ruffled shirt and red tie. "I say, sorry old man. Did you want to sit here?"

"No, that's all right, Newland." He sounded so sincerely disappointed that Will was both surprised and a little remorseful. After all, it didn't matter to him whether he sat next to his sister or not. But Avery went on, "I'll stand back here and keep Cabot in order. He's clearly contemplating breaking at least two of the commandments already."

Neil Hunter listened to the banter of the young men and watched his wife dandle the hands of the baby (the plump little hands made him think of her breasts, soft and full and sweet; he caught his breath for a moment at the still-new wonder of her), but mostly he scanned the crowd of men with narrowed eyes, imagining beards, noses, sunburnt cheeks and truculent chins covered with scarves and masks, trying thereby to recognize in this gathering of the godly those dim faces that had come upon him one evening and stolen Michael Fletcher's horse out from under him.

Horse thieves were a perpetual threat on the plains, more aggressive than the Indians and without the Indians' righteous cause. Mostly these thieves were cowards, sneaking off with tethered animals in the night. That was how six ponies were stolen out of the Victoria corral. Justice was a dubious venture in Ellis County, but Sheriff Ramsay, at least, had a reputation for being young, fearless, and of unflinching integrity. Hunter, who along with Keith was in charge of the colony during Grant's cattle drive to Junction City, called him in when the ponies disappeared, and he and Ramsay swore they'd find the criminals before the sun set. Michael Fletcher loaned Hunter his other horse – a good-looking mare named Sweet May –for the ride, and she proved a game companion. They spent a hot day trying to pursue the thieves across the prairie by following tracks that had been blown to dust. By the time the shadows grew long, they conceded defeat. They separated about a mile from Victoria.

Dejected and a little distracted – he was anticipating night and the chance to lie in the arms of his Julia – Hunter rode along the creek bed, which was heavy with brush that had escaped the rampaging fire. The wind never stopped; it just grew chillier as dusk fell. The branches shivered and cracked. Sweet May, sensing home, began to pick up the pace a bit.

At first, he thought it was his eyes playing tricks in the dusk, those dark shapes that rose out of the creek. But it was three men on horseback – one riding the little black pony which had so offended Beryl Newland months before. Their hats were pulled low, their faces were covered, and their guns were cocked. Hunter's rifle, the one he'd been given to kill savages and which he had held at the ready all through the long day, was tucked helplessly behind him in the saddle. He stopped. Then he spoke.

"Looks like you lads have found some of our property."

"Don't it now," said one – a tall one – pleasantly. "Well, you know: finders, keepers."

"That's hardly sporting."

"Ain't in it for sport, Johnny. Now that's a fine-looking animal you're on right now. We could use that animal. Ponies are tough, but ain't nothing like a fine thoroughbred." Neil sat still in the saddle.

"Why don't you get down, young fella, and let us have a look," said another of the men – shorter, older, with a portentous belly filling out his flannel shirt. He raised his gun as he spoke.

Neil had no choice. Sweet May meant nothing compared to sweet Julia. He silently swung off of the nervous animal, keeping his hands well clear of his rifle. He stepped away from her. She turned to look at him. The brown eyes seemed baleful.

The tall man got off his horse and went up to her. He spoke to her kindly and gently, all the while keeping his gun on Hunter. She was placated and knickered a little. Crickets started to chirp in the creek bottom; the sound made an eerie duet with the wind in the branches. Neil wanted to feel angry, but all he felt was philosophic. He had no choice. There were three of them and one of him. He only wondered whether they would shoot him. His hands went clammy at the thought, but outwardly he stayed calm. He watched the tall man take the rifle from the back of the saddle, admire it a moment, and then open it and deliberately dump all the bullets onto the ground. Picking them up and pocketing them, he tossed the gun to Hunter.

"Saddle we need," he said, "but a man without a gun out here is a dead man. We ain't murderers." Then, as an afterthought, he added, "Unless we got to be." He led Sweet May over to the other animals – she felt comfortable in the familiar presence of the ponies – and tied her behind his horse.

"I appreciate you sparing me the rifle."

"Yup," said the tall man. "I'm gonna have to ask for your boots, though. Can't have you gettin' home too quick. If you look another mile or so down the draw tomorrow, you'll find 'em waiting."

Hunter felt a sinking, but he quietly removed them, handing them to the man closest to him, the third man, the man who had never spoken. This man was slight; his hat was too big and covered part of his ears. Hunter wondered if he was a boy. He noted the long languid fingers as he handed the boots over.

"Be sure to check 'em before you put 'em on," went on the tall man. "Gotta watch for snakes around here."

"You're most considerate," said Hunter. He couldn't quite keep the sarcasm out of his voice.

"Aim to please, don't we boys? And now we'll say good night, mister." The tall man touched his hat. The other two just looked at him, but then the silent, slight one whispered to the older one, "Got guts, don't he?" His voice was high behind the dusty scarf. George started. Surely, he thought, it's a girl.

Before he could look again at the speaker, the three took off across the prairie with the horses running behind them. They moved fast and left him choking. He watched the thieves race into the horizon, and then he looked up at the evening star, just visible in the sky above them. He wondered where they'd drop his boots. He had a hole in one of his stockings. It would be a humbling walk to Victoria. And how to explain to Fletcher.

Fletcher was peeved, but not inconsolable. He was abandoning the Victoria project, going back to England. He hated the heat, he hated the flatness, he hated the work, and, not least of all, he hated having been bashed in the head. Sweet May was a fine horse, but he had to leave her behind anyway and Neil Hunter promised to make good on his loss. Indeed, Neil laid out considerable money after his adventure. He not only recompensed Fletcher for the loss of his horse; he also paid him a considerable amount to keep quiet about how he'd been ambushed. Being robbed was no shame, but riding for miles and miles over burned and barren prairie when the desperados were camped within a couple miles of Victoria – that he was ashamed of. He could not bear to have Julia know. He wanted to bribe Keith to keep quiet too, but Keith got angry and asked him why he would be such a fool as to think of paying a friend to keep confidence. Did he think so little of his friend then? Neil felt doubly shamed and took much less comfort in his wife's loving arms that night than he had anticipated – not least because she railed him soundly for forgetting his boots after "cooling his feet in that poor excuse for a creek." The heat must have affected his head as well as his toes to have done such a thing.

He got a little angry. "I spent my day searching for horse thieves. It's a wearying job, and no great pleasure."

She was quiet a minute, carefully folding under and stitching the hem of a linen shirt. "Well, you didn't find them now, did you? Seems you lost them and the boots as well."

But of course he had lost and found them both.

So he sat in the saloon that October morning, trying to recognize a potbelly, a courteous voice, and a hand with long, languid fingers. He found dozens of each. Frustrated, he looked at Sheriff Ramsay, sitting near the bar next to his wife – an attractive woman with reddish hair – and wondered if he, too, spent his time watching faces, listening, trying to reconstruct the elusive features of someone who stole, or raped, or killed. No, he thought, watching the Sheriff rise for the opening hymn. He lives in the present moment, and at present he's taken up with worship of his God. But Mrs. Ramsay? She was a tall woman who somehow seemed small. Her eyes constantly wandered the room, emerald, shifting, anxious. She's looking, Hunter thought. Looking for the face, the hand, that will take him from her. Julia pulled on his sleeve. Hunter stood up, watched the lean and lank preacher go behind the bar. "O God our help in ages past," he sang along with the others. The singing was tentative – people struggled to remember the words, to find the tune – and then grew stronger. "Our shelter from the stormy blast, And our eternal home." He felt heartened by the singing; after all, the loss of the horses was not so much, and he had found his boots. But when the song ended and he saw again the troubled wandering of Mrs. Ramsay's eyes, he felt what he had felt that night by the creek: that nothing is sure and nowhere is safe in this world.

The words of the letter came accompanied by a weird whistling of wind that haunted the manor house sitting room like the voice of a child. Beryl felt its pestering and tried to curl away from the sound beneath her shawl.

. . . . Robert has become truly grumpy with worry. He asked me to send you a copy of this Mr. Kerr's letter. I told him I do not think that it can be true, or Mr. Grant would hardly be coming back to take more colonists to the settlement. How do you find it? You haven't written for so long. Are you well? William seems quite taken with the life, doesn't he? We were glad to hear that his arm healed quickly after the fire, and that your cottage was spared. Dreadful, that Major Tilson was killed. I've heard that his family is devastated. Won't you write and tell us what you think of Kansas now? I look at the piano in the drawing room and miss you; I don't know how miserable I'll be when we go to the house in London. I'm trying to persuade Robert to find a new place. I've heard that Mr. and Mrs. Sedley's will soon be available. Very elegant — and the nursery is large and bright. The old place seems so dark. But Robert seems set on keeping it since your father died there. A stupid sentimentality (I think). What happy memories did your father ever have of that house? But it's no use telling him that. Won't you write? We do need to know how <u>you</u> find Victoria. We will be sending a holiday box soon. I shall not forget the tea, and also some patterns for the fashions just coming from Paris. (Skirts are getting tighter — they say the bustle will soon be passé. Can you imagine?) Is there a decent dress maker in that Hays City, or must you wear flour sacks? Hideous — I cannot remember who told me they dress like that in America. Perhaps Mrs. Warton. Did you know Amy is engaged? To a Mr. Lamont. The wedding will be quite the affair, I'm sure, though Mr. Lamont hasn't half the money of Mr. Cabot. Amy's mother is still angry that Mr. Cabot left with his £70,000. William mentioned a wedding at Victoria. What did you wear? I am comforted that your clothes cannot have worn out <u>yet</u>. He of course gave no details. Just said the bride and groom ran away after the dance. Well, I cannot blame them, though I did wonder where they ran to. <u>Don't</u> forget to

*write us. Please tell us Victoria is not what the enclosed letter suggests,
or we will have to come and fetch you in person. I mean it.
All my love, and that of the children too,
Marian
P.S. I am glad that you have learned to shoot.*

Beryl's fingers were cold. She carefully unfolded the newspaper clipping that accompanied Marian's letter. The print was small. She squinted to see it and bent her head and hand close to the lamp.

After a few minutes she folded it back up, put it in the envelope with Marian's letter, and went to her room. The small chamber was chilly despite the heavy stone walls. A slender skin of ice floated on the water in the pitcher. She folded her shawl on the bed and then took a heavy red coat and woolen scarf from the clothes cupboard and put them on. The letter she slipped into a deep pocket of the coat.

Outside, wind ran like a razor over the ground. There was no snow; everything except the overcast sky seemed sheared to the bone. The dull earth stretched for miles. Mr. Grant's long corral was empty of the famous sheep and coal-black cattle. Beryl walked on frozen mud and dung. The ground beyond the wide firebreak the men had plowed was still ashen; there was no vegetation to graze on. Wild animals were scarce. Antelope were rarely seen now that winter had come, and even the jack rabbits seemed to have migrated. Lean coyotes howled for hours at night, miserably hungry. The young Britons swore, for the days were long and the hunting damnably poor. Other people, who had come to Kansas not to hunt but to make a living, swore as well, possibly for more compelling reasons.

Beryl walked to the edge of the settlement and stood facing into the wind. It was so strong that she had to struggle to keep her balance. Still, she took pleasure in contending with it. Her cheeks became mottled under the whipping veil, her lips stinging and then numb. A kind of sleet began to fall. And still she stood there, facing the wind.

"It's a lie," she said at last, clenching her teeth. "Whatever has happened, it's a lie."

Michael Fletcher's defection was in no way related to the newspaper article that called Kansas "The Plain of Death," though he left at a time when there was considerable uneasiness among the colonists. Grant had been gone for a month already, and his absence was keenly felt. He had of course been away from Victoria before – to travel to St. Louis, New York, or Kansas City. But his return to England and Scotland seemed to take him to another world than their own, a world they had given up, relinquished – at least for a time – in favor of this flat playing board where they were exposed like chessmen, where every move had to be calculated and where any small mistake might sweep them off the table. It grew terribly cold. Snow came, and drifts formed high enough to keep them locked in with each other, with their thoughts, and with their doubts.

For those who had already moved out onto their land – and at least half of the colonists had done so – the isolation was difficult during these storms. Getting to the privy could be the major drama of the day, and the primary conversation could be with a horse or a hunting dog. Vincent Spenser stayed in the drawing room of his half-constructed mansion, talked philosophy with his cook and his manservant, and found it one of the most pleasant winters of his adult life. Few were so fortunate. The Baldwins struggled on their homestead, caring for the few livestock, trying to entertain the children when they were well and keep them alive when they were sick, and writing letters home to Scotland about all the promise of the new world with numb fingers and weary faces. The Wyatt brothers played cards and quarreled and calculated over and over again the money they had lost when their crops burned to the ground. For those in town, the majority of whom were housed in Victoria Manor, loneliness was less a problem than the continual boardinghouse atmosphere, which some adjusted to better than others. There was little privacy; there were small annoyances and petty intrigues and insufferably thin walls. Most of the colonists hid themselves in books and magazines, in amateur theatricals and sing-alongs, in tall tales about the buffalo they had bagged and in dreams of the empire they would build. Some of them hid in drink. A far greater number than Grant would have wished.

But Grant was not there – and the letter was. Beryl Newland was not the only one who received a copy of the offensive document, and it was quietly passed from hand to hand, inspiring indignation, protestation, and a measure of fear. After all, some things in this letter that had been sent to and published in the *Courant* were true: the land was desolate, the settlement lonely and isolated, and if Grant did not call himself "Sir George," there were those among the locals who did. On the other hand, argued Neil Hunter, the soil was rich and had proven it could grow crops, the cattle and sheep had fattened on the "stunted" grass, and the settlement was near a fort and a major railroad which connected it by only half a day to the cities of Kansas City, St. Louis, and Denver.

"How long was this Mr. Kerr here? As long as it takes to travel through by train. There's no evidence he ever stopped to really examine our situation, to talk to any of us. Why, Mr. Scot-Skirving and the others from the delegation spent time with us, studied our plans and the land itself. They were glowing in their report – and it's not to be forgotten that the delegation saw the place before the fire, and not after, as this presumptuous Yankee did. The letter is dated the seventh of October."

"The presumptuous Yankee seems to have an equally presumptuous British cousin interested in discrediting the project. I wonder about the motive," said Garth Mason.

Keith shook his head. "That's a hard one to figure. Only there's no denying that our friend Mr. Curror seems to have lost his enthusiasm." Curror was one of Grant's representatives in Scotland; in the preliminary planning stages, he had been the liaison between Mr. Grant, the Baldwins, and the MacDonoughs. And later, the Seths. "Skirving writes that there's been words at the Haddington Farmers Club. They're calling Kansas a 'damned unhealthy hole,' or some such, and Curror's letting 'em do it. Something to do with a family from Fife being wiped out by the climate on the plains."

Ben Davis looked disgusted. "The Seths got the fever on the Mississippi. Kansas had nothing to do with it, other than being the place where they died."

"In some ways I think this is worse," said Hunter, raising the letter to read a portion. "'. . . *the only opinion I heard expressed about Grant's settlement was that it was <u>a sell of his and the railway</u>, and pity for the poor* *people who bought land from them. People going from green, wooded, and watered hills and vales of England and Scotland will be sold surely.*' It's a direct attack on Grant's character."

"Not to mention a rather ironic statement coming out of Pittsburgh," said Oscar Jones. He had relatives in New York and had traveled extensively in the eastern states. Captain Prescott nodded in wry agreement.

Daniel MacDonough stood by the window of the station, looking out at the blowing snow. "Why these slanders? What has Curror got against Mr. Grant? Publishing these attacks – why it's poisoning the plant before it's even had a chance to grow."

Randall, who had been warming cracked hands at the stove, looked up. "Well, you've got to admit, gentleman, this is not exactly the paradise Grant promised. I'm not saying these attacks are warranted, but they're also not entirely off base. What's important is to set the record straight."

Keith nodded. "Somebody with a connection to the *Scotsman* – that's where the battle's being fought now. And Curror is leading the charge. If we can get a letter off soon – why they might publish it before Grant leaves again. The important thing is to encourage good folks to come – and the best way to do that is to show that good folks are here and doing well."

MacDonough was prompt. "Let me do it, Keith. Folks know me at the Farmer's Club, and they know I've taken my wife here."

"Are you a good literary hand?" asked Will. He'd been hoping to do it himself; he took pride in his writing and was eager to wield his pen against the Scottish naysayers. But Keith shook his head.

"What's needed is not literary skill, but good honest forthrightness. I say Danny's the man for the job."

"Grant should confront them directly at Haddington. Let them impugn his motives to his face and see what happens," said Randall.

"Aye," said Keith, "but it's the word of one who bought, not one who sold, that they'll be wanting. Mr. Grant can talk himself blue, but they'll have none of it if they're set against him. The letter's what's needed. And for all I ken, Mr. Grant may be planning to appear with Mr. Scot-Skirving as well." Which was possible, but Keith doubted it.

"I'll write a draft: you examine it before I send it," said Daniel. The assent of the men crowded the room, almost pushing out the cold and uncertainty that lurked in the corners, just a wall's width away from wailing wind.

Jane sat nursing the baby while Daniel worked at the table under the glow of the lamp. She listened to the scritch-scratching of the pen, the suckling at her breast, and the low moan under the eaves. The hour was late. She wondered if Daniel would be writing all night. He was not a fast writer; the words did not come easily, for all their earnest honesty. The ghosts of his despair, in the days of his wife's depression before Victoria was born, were not completely exorcized. They rose at his elbow and taunted him so that every now and then he glanced up anxiously at Jane, who sat nursing and looking out on the moonlit plain.

Her face was pale in the glow of the moon. Her hair hung in long black waves over her gown; the mad-medusa locks of her lying in were tamed. She hummed while she nursed, so softly that at first her singing might have been mistaken for the sighing wind. Her hands were large for a woman; capable; not at all delicate. They wrapped themselves under the baby's back and bottom like a sturdy nest. The child was sleepy; the first pangs of hunger were gone. She dozed in her mother's arms, sucked a little. Jane felt the nibbling lips with tender satisfaction. She grew dozy too and leaned her head against the back of the chair. Daniel wrote. Then, in the excitement of some dream, the baby suddenly bit down on her nipple. Jane started and gave a small scream. Daniel jumped in alarm; Victoria began to cry. Daniel half-rose; the ink of his pen pooled onto a small portion of the paper. He hastily blotted it.

"What is it, Jane?"

She looked at him with a perplexed half-smile; she could never understand the vague dread that seemed to hang behind his queries after her comfort, her health, her happiness. She had little recollection of last spring, only the sense that something heavy, some incubus, had crouched over her heart for long, homesick months. She did not remember the childbirth at all. When she met Elizabeth

Cavendar at the store in Hays some months later, she had been delighted, had felt like she was meeting again some genie of good from her childhood, though she could not understand the connection. She remembered the deep-blue eyes, the magical voice, but could not explain why they should seem so familiar and dear. Mrs. Cavendar asked how she was feeling, studied the baby a good long time, and then observed, as if it should have some significance, that Victoria was quite a queen.

Jane nodded but looked at her a little blankly. She wasn't quite sure how to receive the odd, unsmiling expression that suddenly came over the woman's face. There was something of Daniel's dread in it. It had made her uneasy. She felt that her husband and the midwife knew more of her than she knew of herself, or at least thought they did. They had no right to presume, she thought. It was not fair of these people to question her happiness, just as it had not been fair of them to question her sadness. She would have nothing to do with Daniel's ghosts. "Why 'tis only that she's bitten me with those wee teeth. They're sharp, they are, just like a kitten's."

Daniel sat back down. He laughed a little, as Jane calmed the baby, and rubbed his eyes. "I'm tired of this job, that I am. I start to question myself when I get to thinking over things too long."

"What worries you? You're not doubting Mr. Grant, are you?"

"No," said Daniel. "Though at times it comes back to me how he promised to pay passage and then didn't." He took Victoria from Jane's arms and she snuffled against his shirt.

"Why didn't he, I wonder," said Jane, gently drying her nipple and then laying the bodice of her nightgown back over her breast. "He's purchased so many, many animals. He seems to have no lack of money. And his promise to Vicky – why it's more than handsome."

"Well, the animals he certainly has. Whether the little one ever grows to see any profit from his investment, we shall see." The skepticism in Daniel's voice struck Jane. He was ever the optimist, always believing the best of people. What had happened that he should be doubting now, just when he was commissioned to defend the colony? It occurred to her that she had, perhaps, been rather too caught up in herself.

"I think you can have faith in him, Daniel. Think of his concern for everyone who invests with him. Think of how he rode in that dust storm to bid each one of us a personal farewell before he left for home. After all, he has our money – or the promise of it. He has no more need to be wrapped up in our lives.

"Yes, though our success is his success. And he's laird of the manor, after all. Perhaps it's all just pride."

Jane's dark brows drew together. "Where has this come from, the demon making you talk this way? You've always told me that the ground here is good for growing, that the air is healthy, and that in a few years we'll have a town here to be proud of, with a school and a church. You've always had faith in Mr. Grant's vision. Always. What has happened to make you say these things?"

"Janey, I cannot defend the man unless I look the opposing arguments square in the face." He wanted desperately to confide his fears to her. It was late, he was tired, and he was bothered by ghosts. He needed a friend. But he was afraid of the ghost that was hiding in her.

He sat for a minute, listening to that low moan by the window, and then got up and laid the sleeping baby carefully in the crib. She was well wrapped in blankets already, but he took another and tucked it around her. The night was so very bitter. Then he turned toward Jane. She stood up and came toward him; the motion was like an embrace. But he put his hands against her shoulders and held her away.

"Janie." He hesitated, quite afraid. Then he blurted, "The fire, Janie. The deaths of the mother – and the children – and the young major. What of that?"

There was no unholy resurrection. Jane simply looked exasperated. She was cold. "Those are terrible, terrible things. Of course they are. But what have they to do with Mr. Grant? We knew there were risks in coming here – just as those people knew. He didn't need to write them down for us to know. We came because of the hope for better, Daniel, not because of the promise. So he broke his promise about paying our way on the ship. Well, that was poorly done. He showed perhaps that being a laird must be in the blood after all. But Mr. Grant has not taken our hope away. Why, I believe there's no man with more hope in the entire colony."

Daniel felt buoyed a little, by her spirit even more than by her words. He persisted, however. "We cannot eat hope. We have funds enough for now, but if these men are right, and this is a bad place, why we might lose everything."

"So, then we will go home and eat humble pie. Very well then, Daniel MacDonough. We must eat what the good Lord sends us. I'm going to bed." She pulled away and began turning down the coverlet.

"Janie."

She stopped.

"Mr. Seth ate something more poisonous than humble pie. It did not kill him, but I'm sure it would kill me."

"My darling," she said. Then, after a moment, "But you must not let your personal fears influence how you speak on behalf of the entire group."

He stood looking at her. "No."

He went back to the table, turned out the lamp, and came back through the moonlit darkness to her.

"It's time to rest," he said.

"Yes," she said. "Long past."

They lay down. He wrapped his arms around her. She cradled his head in her hands as she had cradled the baby a little time before.

"He will come back," she whispered, "and you'll feel better again."

"Yes," said Daniel.

They were silent a few minutes, and then she said, "The wind never stops, does it?"

"No," said Daniel.

She shivered a little and then rested her soft, dark head against his shoulder. "Maybe in the spring. Maybe in the spring."

Chapter VIII

Beryl met the Witleys through Elizabeth Walker, wife of one of the officers at Fort Hays. Her husband, Gerald, was a good-humored, heavy-set man who led a calvary of Black soldiers – buffalo soldiers, they were called – stationed there. He spent much of his time out with the men and was considered a good leader by those under his command. "Capt. Walker ain't no Simon Legree," observed one of his soldiers. "Treats us like human beings. Name oughta be Lincoln. Don't care whether our skin is black or white. Just cares that we're men." In fact, Capt. Walker was completely cognizant of the color of his soldiers' skin, and he made his calculations based on the belief that these Black men would work harder, go further, and be more loyal than "any damn Whitey" in the regiment if they were treated decently. He had publicly sympathized with their anger over the lynching of three Negroes from the 38th back in '69, and he remained a staunch defender of their "inestimable service" when whites from Hays rumbled about a shooting in a bordello or an altercation on the street. "Most of these men are good people," he told his wife. "I won't allow them to be scapegoats for the trouble of folks prospering off of their money and their protection."

Betsy did not share her husband's enthusiasm for his soldiers, but she held it up to others as an example of her husband's "incredible devotion to his calling." She was a dark-eyed, dark-haired woman with pert, quick movements that caused her earrings to dance when she made an assertion or offered an opinion. She was intent on making her home in the officers' quarters a model of refined living and spent considerable time pouring over *Godey's* and *Peterson's*. She had lace curtains at her parlor windows and an elaborately embroidered lambrequin on the mantel, where a small display of fine Delft china was carefully arranged. A pair of matching chairs – an armless low one for her and a tall-backed throne for him – were situated on either side of the fireplace, and under the south window stood a small, marble-topped table. A ruby-globed parlor lamp sat on it, and displayed next to it was a large, open Bible. Every day, Mrs. Walker carefully turned the page. Presumably she read from the book every night, so Beryl found her distress curious when a warm gust of wind whipped the pages out of place one afternoon. "I shall never be able to find where it should be," she lamented. Certainly she seemed unlikely to consult her husband in the matter; she never allowed him to touch the book to make room for his papers or pipe. "You have a desk for that, Captain Walker. The Word of God is sacred." A stitched sampler in a gold frame near the door to the apartment seconded the sentiment. "Order my steps in Thy word," it said in a bright cacophony of yarns, "And let not any iniquity have dominion over me."

"Our Melinda made that," said Betsy Walker. "She was only five then. Children should be taught to remember that God is with them always." Beryl nodded.

"Of course, it is difficult, being so far from them," she went on.

"Why don't you bring them to the Fort?" asked Lydia. "It must be lonely for you to be without them."

"Oh, I wouldn't think of endangering them by bringing them out here," she said. She snatched Christopher Randall up from the floor where he'd been toddling and smothered him with kisses. "But you're a scrumptious little boy! Just like my Timmy." Mrs. Walker reveled in the child's delighted laughter. She did not notice the expression on Lydia's face.

Beryl did. "I cannot imagine a much safer place than a fort. And the air is so healthy here."

"Hmmmm. But so far from the benefits of civilization. I would never deprive my children of that."

"But to be deprived of their mother?" asked Lydia. Her gentle voice had just the tiniest edge of steel.

"I must sacrifice," said Betsy. Her big brown eyes welled with tears. "I must be with my husband."

"Of course," said Lydia, softened. "But couldn't you live apart from him for just half the year? Winter here seems terribly brutal to me. I'd think you'd welcome a chance to go back east and be by your darlings."

The tears were quickly blinked away; Betsy Walker's eyebrows rose into a cynical arch. "Do you think it's a good idea for a husband to be without his wife for so long? I don't."

Beryl looked down into her cup of tea. She gives Captain Walker little credit, she thought. Beryl had met Captain Walker the night of the fire. She understood why his soldiers respected his leadership. He treated them all as his equals – herself included. He had not questioned her ability to battle the blaze any more than he had that of his men; he had simply accepted her as a partner in the fight and turned his focus on the enemy. Beryl liked him and had gladly accepted the invitation to meet his wife. She enjoyed visiting the fort and rode out as often as she could. She especially loved sitting on Mrs. Walker's porch which, like all of the others fronting the long, disciplined line of officers' quarters, was draped in the summer by a canopy of morning glories. The quarters flanked the parade ground. Beryl found herself starved for music, and she could stand on the porch for hours watching the soldiers march and listening to the band play. "You're so funny," Mrs. Walker would say. Beryl would simply shrug and smile. Mrs. Walker was generous and effusive in her offering of friendship, but she did not seem to fully appreciate her husband or the advantages that life at the fort offered.

Mrs. Walker was clearly as starved for culture as Beryl was for music, and she clutched at it with both hands in the form of the English immigrants. Beryl suspected that was how she came to know the Witleys. The Witley brothers were not part of the Victoria colony – a fact that played against them when they first came to Hays. Anybody so evidently rich (they brought along a French manservant, his fashionably dressed wife, a cook, and an overseer – and that before they had purchased a penny's worth of land or had a kitchen to call their own) and so evidently English (Henry bowed when he paid Mrs. Chambers the rent, causing her to blush and bluster for half the morning) surely belonged at Victoria, and if they weren't there, then they must be charlatans.

But money spilling in the land office and a round of drinks at Tommy Drumm's soon set them up as "all right sort of chaps," and when they began building their three-story white house on 3,200 acres a few miles south of Hays City, it became the destination of an afternoon's diversion for the better part of the spring of 1874. Mrs.

Walker easily persuaded her husband it was worth a buggy ride to see how these rich Englishmen intended to improve the country. She was not a shy woman. After sitting beneath her parasol and calculating the eventual size of the house as well as the extent of the gardens being laid out on the rattlesnake-ridden prairie, she boldly approached the two distinguished men directing construction (after all, they were neighbors), introduced herself, welcomed them on behalf of all of Fort Hays, and collected a cornucopia of information out of which she fed her husband and the other wives at the fort for a month.

"They did not think much of the country at first. Too bland. But the younger one – that's Mr. Henry Witley – said the greening of the grass just changed his mind, and he knew it was right to stay when he found wild roses growing near the creek. 'An omen of the beauty that can flourish here,' he said. He tipped his hat very prettily as he said it, which I thought was overdoing it a bit." The earrings tossed beneath Mrs. Walker's ears. "But you know, he's completely in love with the daughter of an English actor of some sort, and his brother – that's Mr. Arthur Witley – said he's going to bring her back as soon as the house is finished. I suppose that marrying an actor's daughter might be a step down for the son of a wine merchant" – she looked at Beryl and Lydia, uncertain how these things played in England – "but the father is dead after all, and Mr. Arthur said the girl's father writes plays as well as acts in them. Perhaps you all have heard of him? Buckstone? Anyway, Mr. Henry's even putting a white picket fence around the house, and great red, white, and blue stakes, as tall as you are, Captain, to mark the property. I thought that was very decent of him, to use our national colors. Of course, he said that red, white, and blue are also the colors of the Union Jack, and I said it was another good omen, that it should fit both his old country and his new. His brother offered us each a drink of water with sliced lemon in it and asked a lot of questions about Indians, and then Captain Walker told him buffalo soldier stories till I was afraid they would become quite bored."

"I've yet to find a Brit or an American bored by Indian massacres," replied the captain.

"Well," said Mrs. Walker, "if we must have savagery, let it be Caliban instead of the Cheyenne. Mr. Henry said that perhaps his wife would perform some cuttings from Shakespeare for us. She's quite an actress herself, you know."

"We'll see," said her husband.

Alec Hunter was twenty years old when he came to Victoria with his brothers Jim and David in the spring of 1874. Far gone with consumption, he was not expected to live until his next birthday. His cheeks were a hollow, hectic red; his eyes glassy; his cough harsh. His brown hair seemed to be thinning, and his shoulders, hunched from clerking at a Manchester bank, sagged over his chest. He weighed less than his new sister-in-law. She, in fact, was somewhat dismayed when she saw him emerge from the train. He was so weak he could not stand alone; he walked supported between his brothers.

"Whyever have they sent the boy?" murmured Julia to Neil. "He's no more than a skeleton."

"Perhaps his lungs will wear better here, where the air is dryer. 'Tis what Mother and Father are hoping."

"Perhaps," she said, trying to pattern her expression into something more welcoming. "Champagne air."

Alec was self-conscious about his condition and seemed as often flushed from embarrassment or humiliation as from the harassing cough. He said little about his illness, however, only remarking that it was easier to breathe in this open place. He was not loquacious or demonstrative, but he was clearly moved by the country where he found himself. He sat in a chair on the stoop of his brother's store, a blanket across his knees, and watched the town grow around him. He often remarked on the sky. "Looks like you could step right up to heaven," he observed. "There's nothing to hold you back but gravity."

"Aye, and the pull of those of us who'd just as soon keep you here," said Julia gruffly. It was a potentially sentimental statement; she was sorry as soon as she uttered it. She was fond of her youngest brother-in-law, not least for the sake of a sister back in Scotland whom she knew had a particular affection for this frail specimen of the Hunter clan. But she didn't want to encourage morbid thinking.

She gave him a great basket of nuts and bolts to sort, pushing it into his lap with asperity to make up for her show of softness.

He groaned. "My lungs are sick, not my mind. You treat me like a blooming cretin."

Julia misunderstood Alec in thinking that when he spoke of heaven, he was looking towards death. Quite the contrary: the heaven-reaching sky increased his devotion to life. He was no less ambitious than his brothers, only more aware of his limitations. When he spoke of the sky, he spoke of what he thought he might achieve, given the chance – and his desire to achieve it in this place.

Mr. Grant understood this. He listened to the boy cough and thought with aversion of the home-country he had experienced over the winter. The frost-misted glens of Scotland were undoubtedly beautiful, the grey cities undeniably brilliant with their myriad lamps, carriages, and people. But the old world had seemed to him clammy and close, like a musty cellar where one stumbled in the dark against dank walls. He found it as hard to breathe there spiritually as the boy did physically. In Edinburgh, in the office of Donald Curror, he had thought he'd choke. The disordered files, the grey hairs falling loosely over the secretary's haggard brow, the purse-lipped distrust and closed-mindedness of Curror himself, conspired against him like the frustrating fogs that obscured the streets. Grant could not, for a while, see the way clear, no matter how much Scot-Skirving called Victoria an Eden in the rough (a possibly pardonable mixing of metaphors) and Mr. Curror a stinking Brutus.

The fog was always there, sometimes shaping itself into the limp body of one of the Seth children, sometimes shifting like smoke waiting to reveal the charred face of Major Tilson. Evil things were written in the papers, and Grant read them at night beneath candles that could barely break the heavy air. He closed his eyes and tried to see again the station house, the people that had huzzahed and shot their guns merrily into the cold from the depot as the train pulled to the east. There had been sun on that day. He sometimes believed he had not seen the sun since. He was unable to conjure the faces he sought or hear their voices. All was muffled, all obscured. There was only the fog, wrapping about him like an evil shroud until he felt he could neither move nor breathe ever again. He met friends and pursued business with his accustomed vigor, but only when he returned to the United States, and more truly to Kansas, did he realize that for four and a half months he had not been breathing. When he at last gulped in the clean wind that was running warm over the greening earth, the pain in his chest was like that of a swimmer who had been holding his breath for too long. The relief and the shock came together with a potency that he thought might kill him. But the bliss of breathing again was unmistakable.

"When you are better, my boy," Grant said to Alec Hunter, "come to see me. I will have work for you. Real work," he added, curling his lip in sympathetic contempt at the basket of nuts and bolts.

"I'll do that, sir," said Alec.

Whether she was an actress or not Beryl could not discern at that first meeting, but that Cynthia Buckstone Witley was beautiful and charming was immediately evident. She was tiny and blonde, like a Dresden doll, with great blue-violet eyes and lips like a ribbon of pink Christmas candy. She upstaged Lydia Randall's pale elegance, fading it the way the dawn does the moon. Her high cheekbones, delicate wrists, and lithe figure made Betsy Walker's pretty brown curves seem coarse. Mrs. Witley's voice was surprisingly low for such a small woman, but it poured out like a mellow wine. When she extended her hand, Beryl found it soft and perfectly manicured. Each finger was enhanced by a jewel, testimony, Beryl thought, to Henry Witley's besottedness.

Nor did he seem to be the only one besotted. Will Newland tried not to stare at Mrs. Witley as though he'd never seen a female before, but he succeeded miserably. The open Bible and the bright sampler both failed him as objects of undivided attention, as did his sister's shoes. He at last surrendered and spent the rest of the afternoon gazing at the small, perfect specimen of womanhood and wondering where she had been when they were both in England. Probably London. He had been at Oxford, groaning under his theology studies and flirting with Liberalism. For the first time he regretted that he had not visited London more, that he had rather neglected his sister.

Beryl would have enjoyed going to the theater, and he himself might have met Mrs. Witley while she was still Miss Buckstone.

Jack Randall was also very attentive to the young bride and offered to refill her coffee three times while his wife's cup sat empty for over an hour. He never noticed Mrs. Walker's irritation at his cavalier handling of her Spode coffeepot; he never looked at his hostess at all. Even Mr. Grant seemed to find new fonts of enthusiasm when Mrs. Witley sat near him. He waxed eloquent on the superior quality of Aberdeen sheep while she nodded, smoothed her soft muslin gown over her knee, and made prescient assents.

Henry Witley watched, pleased that his wife should be adored, possibly more than pleased that she inspired lust. She was, after all, quite completely his. He played with the Randall baby and every now and then exchanged a desultory remark with the other ladies on the cost of mahogany or the difficulty in finding a respectable pattern of china, but he made no move to engage his wife. Let these men chatter with her; she came to his bed.

The only males unaffected by Cynthia Witley seemed to be Captain Walker and Arthur Witley, who were arguing about some battle in the American civil war; James Avery, who actually did find Beryl's shoes an acceptable object of attention (but who marked Randall's neglect of his wife with vicious satisfaction); and Richard Cabot, who later told Garth Mason, "There are certain kinds of women I do not get involved with. That is one of them."

As the afternoon wore on, Beryl grew weary of the talk in Mrs. Walker's parlor. She noticed that Will seemed to be exerting a herculean effort to please Mrs. Witley and decided he was ridiculous. The topic was steam plowing; Will carried on a passionate monologue. Mrs. Witley listened and nodded her head, causing a stray yellow curl to rub itself against her bare neck with the insinuating grace of a cat. A purring cat. Will grew distracted. His argument faltered. Randall saw his chance and broke in with a romantic plea for walking behind the plough the old-fashioned way, which seemed to Beryl more absurd yet. Mr. Randall had yet to do anything more significant in his fields than listen to the men he hired to do the work offer their opinion and shrug his shoulders. But leaning against Mrs. Walker's carefully coiffed mantle, he held forth with the poetic authority of a man who had broken sod in the noble tradition of Abel.

Will scoffed. Mrs. Witley nodded, absorbed and absorbing. Beryl sighed and listened to Mrs. Walker discuss silver with Henry Witley. Deadly, decided Beryl. It might be a good thing for a woman to care about plowing and a man to care about the pattern of fork he eats with – but these people seemed utterly witless.

Avery had fallen asleep in Captain Walker's chair. His mouth hung slightly ajar. He actually did much of the work on his embryo ranch – or tried to. He'd been thrown from a horse only the week before. He was dead tired, and an ugly bruise under his left eye made him look like a forlorn schoolboy. Cabot had long since disappeared with Captain Walker, Mr. Grant, and Arthur Witley for a tour of the guardhouse. Beryl wished she had gone along. She glanced at Mrs. Randall, who was studying her fingers through the lace edging on her blue cuffs. Her eyes were blank. Christopher had been put to sleep upstairs and would not be likely to wake again for some time. Beryl set down her coffee cup.

"Lydia, shall we go for a walk? It's so lovely outside."

Mrs. Randall started and looked a little uncertainly toward Mrs. Walker. "If no one minds, I'd like that very much."

Beryl stood up. "Mrs. Randall and I think of going for a stroll. Would anyone else like to come?"

Mrs. Walker's earrings bobbed emphatically. "Oh no, but you girls go ahead. I'll stay and take care of the little one."

Mr. Witley shook his head. William glanced at Mrs. Witley. She laughed – a sound that seemed to drip over her lips like warm honey – and said that she was tired just now; she should have lain down with the child. Which one asked her husband, grinning askance at Avery. Beryl turned. She was decidedly tired of these people. Will settled back in his chair. "I'll wait for sleeping beauty," he said.

Mr. Randall at least had the sense to get up. "I'm ready for a stretch," he said, running his hands through his black hair so that it stood on end. "I'll take a quick turn-round with you, Lyddie, and then come back and fetch the boy. Or I might go after Grant and Walker while you take your turn."

Outside, the fort was alive with horses and soldiers, white and black. As Beryl walked with the Randalls down the wooden sidewalk in front of Officer's Row – a long line of ten houses - the men working or lounging in front of the enlisted men's barracks, the young ones in particular, noted the English women. Many were hungry for the company of a woman, though not entirely in the carnal sense. Those inclined that way could satisfy their appetites in the brothels of Hays City easily enough and did so on a regular basis. It was the company of a "respectable" woman they craved, a woman they could talk to about their ideas, their worries, and their homesickness without paying for the privilege. They missed their sisters and their mothers, their aunts and their cousins, their old sweethearts, even their schoolteachers. Many loved life in the west and, despite the low pay, the marginal food, and the possibility of dying with a tomahawk through their skull, would not readily go home, even for a woman. But they nonetheless gazed at Beryl Newland and Lydia Randall the way a thirsty man gazes at a glistening dipper of water.

Nor did their love of the west mean that desertions were rare. On the contrary, officers were constantly complaining about the loss of men and upping the punishment for those who tried to end their term of service prematurely. It was, after all, so easy to find employment at a ranch or on a farm. There was always more work than the boss could handle, always a need for more hands, and never any need to offer more than a name and a readiness to go at any job. Many soldiers kept this option in the back of their mind while they drilled, dug ditches, fought fires, and hunted Indians. They found it easier to do their duty knowing that, if they dared, it was possible to abandon it. In the meantime, they understood that a uniform lent more glamour to a sweating, tired body than a worn-out shirt and a pair of Levis. How else to explain the pretty gals that set up housekeeping with those bastards in Officers Row? There was more than just the hope of promotion in a well-polished button.

Beryl looked at the soldiers speculatively as she walked beside Lydia. Her interest was more historical than they might have liked: the older, weather-worn soldiers caught her attention more than the young handsome ones. They were the ones who had almost certainly witnessed the war between the states and who had likely participated in the battles with the Sioux and the Cheyenne that she had read about while nursing her father. Will twitted her about getting a twisted history back in England from sensationalist newspaper accounts that were little better than penny dreadfuls. He contended that the Indians were primitive peoples who had to move before civilization, but that they shouldn't be faulted for fighting. Beryl believed that. But the soldiers at the fort, the old ones who had lived to dig arrows from their hides and bury not just comrades, but women and children, would have none of it. Most of them did not like to talk of what they'd seen, but they were stubborn in their opinion that the only safe Indian was a dead Indian.

Mrs. Walker, not surprisingly, knew many stories. One morning she had told Beryl, in an eager, hushed voice, the tale of a couple who lived at Parks Fort, only forty miles west of Hays City. The young woman, named Mary, went on a long buffalo-hunting trip with her husband. Her mother, who Mrs. Walker thought lived in Hays City, had tried to convince her not to go. "The girl had lost a baby," said the captain's wife, "and was trying to forget. Well, the dog came back alone. Then two months later somebody found the corpses of her husband and brother-in-law, all shot up with Indian arrows. She must have been carried off and is presumed killed – or worse." Betsy's Walker's whisper was portentous. "Her brother wanted to go after her, but the army wouldn't let whites go into Indian Territory, not with guns. Captain Walker says we must follow the law, even if the savages don't. Anyway, her brother went mad and had to be imprisoned at Fort Dodge. Then somebody else wanted to ransom her, but General Sheridan said that doing that would just reward the Indians for stealing women and, after all, if she wasn't dead, all her friends were, and she was probably – well, she probably wouldn't want to come back after they'd – used her."

Beryl was horrified.

"This must have happened a long time ago?" The stories she had read dated to the time of her father's death; Mrs. Walker's narrative seemed very much like those stories.

"Only the summer before last – before you came."

Beryl felt something inside her shrink, shiver down to a hard core of cold darkness. After a moment she said, "I don't see why they didn't go get her." She sat on the porch in the purple and green shadows of morning glories and stared out at the blank hills beyond the busy space where men marched. That woman could still be alive, wandering out there, waiting for deliverance, waiting for God to answer her. Waiting for something that would never come.

"She's probably dead, or as good as. She may have borne an Indian brat." Mrs. Walker shuddered.

"But wouldn't you want them to rescue you?"

"I'd kill myself if the savages didn't do it. And wouldn't count it a sin, I assure you."

"I don't understand."

Mrs. Walker grew exasperated. "You poor child, the people she loved are all DEAD."

"Not her mother."

Mrs. Walker was silent.

"I don't suppose," ventured Beryl after a moment, "that white soldiers ever – I mean, they don't 'use' the Indian women – "

"I have no idea what you mean, and I am certain you have no idea what you are saying." Mrs. Walker's eyes spit sparks. "What would our brave soldiers want with *dogs*, Miss Newland?"

Beryl, walking beside Mr. and Mrs. Randall on that June afternoon, remembered Betsy Walker's words and suddenly heard the whisper of Shakespeare's Shylock: *Thou call'dst me dog before thou hadst a cause, But since I am a dog, beware my fangs.*

She did not, she decided, like Mrs. Walker.

Mr. Randall left Beryl and his wife near the guardhouse, a long, low building made of yellow blocks of limestone from which issued the sounds of men complaining, laughing, and hollering at each other. Beryl wondered how many prisoners were inside and what could interest a gentleman in such a place. She and Lydia stood, uncertain of their course for a few minutes, and then Lydia suggested they get a drink of water at the well house before going any further. There they met Cassandra Tyler who, after a tiring morning of baking, was glad to accept Lydia's invitation to walk in the open air.

Cassandra Tyler was the wife of Sergeant John Tyler: a wiry, energetic man with bright eyes, long curls, and a mustache modeled after General Custer's – though he would never admit it. They were older than the Walkers and had no children. Mrs. Tyler had followed her spouse from one fort to another across the great plains since the end of the war. Born in Virginia, she was a tall, graceful, calm-eyed woman with greying hair who still bore the soft twang of a Blue Ridge fiddle in her speech. She was good friends with Elizabeth Cavendar, whom she had met shortly after arriving at Fort Hays. When they got together, their conversation was a song.

She spoke in an easy, quiet way to the two English women. She was not dazzled by their nationality the way Mrs. Walker was. She took them like she took everything that crossed her path, whether exceptional or dull: with quiet, matter-of-fact acceptance. All ties with her birth family had been broken when her husband joined the Union Army, and she bore that pain without complaining and without losing her faith in the goodness of people. Yet that hardship might have explained her unusual inability to exclude others. She did not gossip and rarely criticized. It was said that she not only liked the buffalo soldiers who put in their time at Fort Hays, but that she had also defended a Chinaman and once even spoken on behalf of native children being held in the "Indian pen" at the guardhouse. She might have been dismissed as a saint except that she would not attend services, not even after the chapel building was hauled in from Fort Harker. "They just wanted it for dances anyway," she said. "I couldn't make an honest prayer there, not unless I was doing a waltz."

She proposed to Beryl and Lydia a walk that led away from the fort and up a wide bluff called "Lonely Grave Hill." The wind was blowing, as usual, but it was gentle and cool. The sun was warm, the sky blue. Birds sang. Big grasshoppers jumped against the women's dresses, and flying bugs whirred across the partially overgrown path. Beryl saw some butterflies, but not many. There were no clouds. There had not been clouds for weeks. The buffalo grass was starting to parch. By late summer, Beryl remembered, it would be completely brown. But it was drying out sooner this year.

"Will is worried about our crops," she said. "He's beginning to think up schemes for irrigating."

"What's he doing now?"

"Sometimes he gets rather desperate and crazy and hauls great buckets of water from the creek in the wagon. Red Thompson helps us."

Thompson was a middle-aged Yankee who had had to retire from his life as a cowboy after being lamed by an angry steer. He had little use for cattle after that and, as Will seemed disinclined to work with animals (watching one branding session at Grant's ranch had cured him of any romantic notions about ranching: "It's all blood and offal and cruelty," he told Beryl. "And that's before they butcher the beasts."), he was happy enough to act as Will's primary field hand and advisor. Will paid well and gave him a handsome horse to ride, and though Thompson called him "a durn pig-headed red coat," the two got on well together. He knew a lot about Kansas. He'd grown up in a town called Atchison where the hills and fields were "as rolling and green as England."

Beryl wondered how he could know what England was like. But he seemed wise in so many areas where she and her brother were ignorant that she was willing to accept his assertion on this point as well. "Thompson humors Will," she went on. "Even I know that you can't water one hundred acres of corn by hand. We just have to wait for rain."

"It's a dry year," said Cassandra. "Worst I've seen for a while."

They walked on. The path turned, and they came upon a prairie dog town. On seeing them, the little animals set up a warning chatter. Their chirping spread back into the grass, where small mounds of dirt marked the entrance to their burrows and tunnels. Most of them dived into the holes, peeking out at the women with shining black eyes.

"Well, Lisbeth is not lonely then," remarked Cassandra.

"Who is Lisbeth'?" asked Lydia.

"Elizabeth Polly," said Cassandra. "Though who knows if that's her real name. She lies here towards the foot of the hill. They say she wanted to be buried at the top, so she could look over the fort, but the ground was too shallow. They hit rock and had to move her further down."

"What did she die of?"

"Cholera. She and her baby." Cassandra walked a little way off the path, her eyes sweeping the ground. "Watch for snakes," she warned. Then she continued, "The boys say she was married to Ephraim. He was steward in the hospital until last year – got himself accused of stealing money and some medical instruments, although Sheriff Ramsay didn't find anything when they searched his home. He and his wife took off for Texas after that."

"I thought you said she was dead."

"The one before is dead – if she was his wife at all. I think the boys just say that, to protect her. I can't say for sure since she was already dead three years when I came. But she was good to those boys. They say she died nursing them when the cholera struck. A lot of them died along with her. Them, and I guess her baby."

They came upon a narrow, sunken spot in the ground, over which a warped and weathered board was laid. A wooden marker stood at one end, but nothing was written on it, at least nothing that the women could read. A cricket chirped from somewhere under that board. Lydia knelt beside the grave.

"They say she walks," said Cassandra. "The army moved the graves of most of the soldiers that died in the epidemic to a military cemetery back east. They say she's looking for her friends and weeps every dusk because she cannot find them."

"Why didn't they move her, and the child as well?"

"She's not military personnel. Though they might have done it if Eph had pushed for it. But he didn't care. He'd married Kate Hannon by then and had other things to think about."

"Women get forgotten out here, don't they?"

Cassandra looked at Beryl, surprised. She pushed a strand of hair back beneath her bonnet. "She's not forgotten, Miss Newland. The boys at the fort have never forgotten her. How would I know of her if they didn't tell me her story? We can't be certain of her name, and who knows what her relation to Mr. Polly was. But we know someone good passed this way. Folks don't forget out here. They sometimes have to leave people behind, but they don't forget. And especially not women and children. Not ever, that I've seen. And I've been all over these plains."

Beryl shook her head.

"I've heard she used to walk to the top of the hill every morning, always wearing a blue cloak," continued Cassandra. "That's why she wanted to be buried there. It's a pretty view. Come look."

The women turned and climbed to the bluff's crown. From that height they realized that the surrounding country was really not flat at all. There were swells and valleys; the land was a pallet of color where green shadowed yellow, and where white and purple flowers created patches of brightness against the blowing grass. Beryl took off her hat and veil, and then, on a whim, pulled the pins from her hair and let it stream out in the wind. She lifted her arms to the sky in a delicious liberation.

"Oh, this feels so much better! I was so cramped in that awful little parlor I thought I would scream!"

Cassandra laughed. "You look like the Wild Huntress."

"Who is that?" asked Lydia, who had also removed her hat but kept her pale hair tucked into its net.

"Perhaps you'll meet her someday. Tyler claims he did, though I'm not sure I believe him. She lost her husband to an Indian – or maybe a rival lover – and lost her mind as well. She rides all over the prairie wearing black, her hair flying, seeking to avenge her husband's death. Though those who've talked to her say sometimes she doesn't seem to realize he's dead. She runs with the buffalo and shoots in the air to make them go faster. The men are half afraid of her. Rather like poor Lisbeth." She smiled and shook her head, half pitying, half skeptical. "Both harmless, but they make for pretty tales around a campfire."

"Everything seems to be a story out here," mused Lydia, sitting down and dreamily pulling the petals off a blossom of wild rose.

"That's what happens when you go off on an adventure," said Beryl. "And sometimes you get to be the heroine. Isn't that why you came, Lydia?"

"I came because Jack wanted to come," said Lydia. "Papa begged me to stay behind in England, but I said I couldn't do that. And I'm sure he'd disapprove if I died out here so that I could become a heroine in some western romance."

"The stories here are brutal," said Beryl.

Cassandra Tyler listened to them and then laughed. "Y'all are so young. Life here is the same as anywhere else."

"Women get left to the wolves here," said Beryl.

"There are no wolves in England?"

Beryl shrugged and began collecting the white chalky stones that lay on the ground. When she found a sharp, particularly pointed one, she let the others drop and stood up. "It's time to head back. The sun's getting low."

"Yes," said Cassandra. "Supper."

The three wended their way back down the hill. Beryl ran ahead and, at the foot of the hill, she looked again for the grave. She was unable to find it until the others had caught up with her. She stepped on the board that stretched over the dead woman's resting place, and then knelt upon it. It creaked and shifted ominously.

"Beryl, for heaven's sake, you'll fall on her," said Lydia.

"I'm being careful," she said. Then she took the sharp rock she had gathered at the summit and began scratching with it on the weathered headboard. It wrote like chalk; she retraced all her letters, so they stood out brightly on the dead wood.

ELIZABETH POLLY
WIFE OF EPHRAIM
DIED

She stopped and looked at Cassandra. "When do they say she died?

"Well, the cholera came in '67, so it must've been then."

She wrote 1867.

"You've forgotten the baby," said Lydia.

Beryl frowned; there was little space left on the board, she had written so big. At last she squeezed under "Died 1867":

with child.

She stood up and stepped off the board. It creaked hideously. Then she examined her handiwork.

"It will wash off," she observed.

"There won't be rain any time soon," predicted Cassandra. "Another month like this and even the blue will be baked from the sky. Y'all watch."

They waited a while longer at the lonely grave, keeping Elizabeth company. The cricket still sang beneath the board. Down by the dead, Beryl thought. The shadows lengthened further, and at last the women turned away.

They walked back to the path. At the prairie dog town, the creatures chattered as before. Beryl stopped, tied her hair away from her face, and put her hat and veil back on. When she was done, she looked back toward the grave and then toward the summit of the hill. She looked for a long time.

Cassandra watched the two English women, the pale aristocrat who stood with such grace in the blowing grass and the dark-haired girl who arrested them all with her waiting eyes. At last Cassandra said, "You're not going to see her. She's not walking there anymore. She can rest. She's not forgotten."

"I guess not," said Beryl. After a moment she linked arms with the others. Together, they returned to the fort.

At Vincent Spenser's gala celebrating the completion of his house – a great three-story mansion looking over Victoria Creek – the topic of Indians came up again. The result was a skirmish that left no one dead, but plenty wounded.

Most of the evening was spent admiring Spenser's home. A wide porch ran along the outside perimeter, looking onto a tennis court and a broad lawn of carefully trimmed buffalo grass. Wooden deck chairs were set up along its length so that a large party could relax there in the cool of the evening. Many of the men settled themselves with their cigars and threatened never to go any further. The children ran back and forth along the veranda and pretended they were on the ship again. The women, curious to see how the bachelor had designed his house, were more eager to get inside.

The high, long hall they entered ran the length of the building like an indoor porch. Stuffed buffalo, antelope, and coyote heads stared down with shining glass eyes at a massive gun rack wherein all manner of pistols, revolvers, and rifles were cradled. Meg Grant was taken aback by the number of guns. She counted one hundred and two, and politely asked why so many were necessary. Couldn't one hunt just as well with three – or maybe five?

"One can *kill* effectively with a single rifle," said Spenser, stroking his mustache with thumb and forefinger. "But the art is in *how* one kills, and art always depends on the right tool. A rifle, for example, is a brutal instrument for killing a man with. It blows his head apart. A pistol can do the job much more cleanly and is therefore much to be preferred."

"But surely you're not meaning to go out hunting men?" protested Meg. Even Beryl's eyes widened at his example.

"Not ever, Miss Grant," said Spenser. "But I've found that no illustration ever serves as well as that which uses a human."

Beryl thought another illustration might serve perfectly well, but she merely shook her head and turned her attention to the drawing room.

It was a splendid room, large and airy with white draperies around the windows and volumes of books bricking the walls. Beryl could hardly take them all in, but she saw a complete set of Shakespeare and of Tennyson, Newman's *Apologia* and *The Idea of a University*, and Gibbon's *Fall of the Roman Empire*. Many books bore Latin titles on their spines that she could not translate. None looked new; they seemed to have been in Vincent Spenser's possession a long time. It must have cost a great deal to ship them from England, she thought. But then everything must have cost a great deal. A massive leather sofa and several high-backed chairs were grouped at one end of the room; at the other end, in front of the broad stone fireplace, sat a long mahogany table with a chair positioned behind it. Clearly it was here that the master of the house spent most of his time. Even with guests expected, the table remained strewn with books and disordered piles of papers that were held down by quaint paper weights (the jawbone of a bear, for instance). The blotting paper was well-used; the pen holder, once an elegant gold, had been blackened by splashing ink. Beryl toured the room in a slow circle, her green gown trailing over the exquisite tracings of an Egyptian carpet. There was no piano, and she felt some disappointment. She found the room otherwise satisfying. It felt like England again.

The dining room was handsome as well; a heavy walnut sideboard with angels and animals carved into it set against one wall. On it, an array of meats, cheeses, breads, puddings, and fruits all waited in dishes of polished silver. A great mirror hung above them, reflecting huge, crimson-draped windows that looked out onto Mr. Spenser's walking court and a chandelier whose pendants shattered the candlelight into a dazzling brightness. The table was laid with gold-leafed china. The room shimmered. Set there in the middle of a vast, desert-like plain, it seemed a mirage. Avery was tantalized beyond all self-control. He smuggled a plate from the table and covered it with a delectable shaving of ham and a spoonful of pudding. He stood in a corner of the ammunition room (it came next after the dining room, rather than the kitchen – a deplorable accident of architecture, the women agreed, and one to be expected of a man) and put a forkful into his mouth. Then another. Only after five mouthfuls was he able to convince himself that it was real. He went to find Spenser.

"Your chef is a prince," he said, wringing Spenser's hand. "He cooks with real butter. I don't know how, but he does it. God bless him, and God bless you!"

Upstairs was a tile-lined bathroom containing a great porcelain tub and four large bedrooms. All the bedrooms had fireplaces in them, but only two were furnished. After the opulent rooms downstairs, the furnishings and bedclothes in both seemed simple, even ascetic. The beds were of iron, the washstands of a design common to a decent hotel. The bureau was tall and somber, the oak closet large and plain. The wallpaper was a subdued blue and white stripe in one room, rose and white in the other. There were no mirrors, but all four rooms had crucifixes hanging on the wall, and in the room Vincent Spenser evidently used, a string of rosary beads was coiled up next to the bed. Cabot, who had followed the group of explorers up the stairs, nudged Beryl and pointed toward a what-not hanging on the wall in Vincent's room. On it stood a small statue of the Blessed Virgin.

"He wants to rile me," thought Beryl. She studied the blue robed image quietly for a moment and then said in a cool voice, "Very pretty. I wish I had one." She took a blossom out of the wildflower corsage she had made to decorate her gown, laid it before the statue, and brushed past Cabot into the hall.

Cabot's eyes lit up. He turned and followed her, catching her elbow as she climbed the stairs to the next floor. "He'll think you meant it for him," he whispered, laughing.

She stopped, and a blush spread down her neck and over her shoulders; she could feel it. But she teased herself into a smile. Her color, after all, could be blamed on mounting the steps in such heat. She turned on the stair, facing Cabot's laughing blue eyes – they seemed very close – and said sweetly, "Maybe I did." Then she kept climbing.

"My god," said Cabot to himself, catching his breath. "What an adorable liar!"

They climbed yet more steps after passing through servants' quarters on the third floor. At the top was a trap door. The group went through it onto a small porch, railed on all four sides and graced with a low bench for sitting. In a flat land, the perspective from such a height was exhilarating, even dizzying. Meg Grant, her hair up and her skirts reaching to her ankle, jumped up and down with delight, waving to the envious Baldwin children who ran through the yard, across the tennis court (upsetting Will Newland's game with Ben Davis), and into the house, wanting to find their own way to the top. Vincent Spenser reached under the bench and pulled out a pair of field glasses, offering them to his guests so that they could see the layout of his flocks and look for their estates through the magnifying lens. Daniel and Jane MacDonough eagerly took him up on his offer and laughed delightedly at the Manor House looking like a toy in the distance. Mr. Grant sat on the bench, wiped his brow, and glowed with pride, telling Spenser he was a credit to the colony, a king of the plains.

Beryl raised her eyebrows in some amusement at this hyperbole, but she was also impressed. A year ago, such a mansion in such a place would have seemed impossible to her. She went and stood by Mr. Keith and Mrs. Hunter, who were studying the layout of Spenser's buildings in relation to the river. She looked to the east, to the place where she and Will and Mr. Keith had spotted the antelope during their first days in Victoria. She remembered her fear at being alone when they left her, and her even greater fear that she was not alone after they were gone. She thought of the woman named Mary and found herself straining to see something on that endless reach of grass that was probably lost forever.

"Why are you shivering?" asked Keith. "It's a warm evening to be feeling chill."

"Oh – Mrs. Walker told me about a woman who was carried away by the Indians, her husband killed. They never got her back again."

Mr. Grant was watching her as she spoke. He paused a moment, and then reached out his hand to clasp her glove. The blood-red ring was brilliant against its whiteness. "'Tis all history, my lass," he said. "Nothing to be worrying over anymore."

"It was only two years ago," she said, pulling her hand back, "and less than fifty miles from here. At this very season. I don't believe, Mr. Grant, that the calendar is any longer here than it is in Europe."

The conversation on the porch died. The silence left them all exposed, like chicks clinging to the edge of an eagle's nest. It seemed, as Alec Hunter had said, that they could step right up to heaven. But they had no wings, and the fall was very, very long.

Captain Prescott spoke.

"Renegades you'll always have. White or Indian. The law-abiding natives are down in Indian Territory, causing no harm. We can never account for people who choose to go outside the law, nor expect to be totally safe from them. Horse thieves, gamblers, murderers, savages — they'll always be with us. Just like the poor, you know." He looked self-consciously at the sprawling ranch beneath him.

Keith frowned. "I don't think it's fair to rank Indians with horse thieves."

"Why ever not?" asked Julia Hunter. "They all steal from innocent people and kill and make life miserable. They all stand in the way of Christian progress."

Keith tread carefully. "I'm not sure it's Christian progress to take a people's livelihood away. To take a people's land. There's many a wicked Indian, just like there's many a wicked Scot. But there's many a good man driven to extremities by a starving family. The Highlanders were called outlaws and bandits for generations."

"But they didn't rape women," cried Julia, outraged, "and then smash their skulls."

"Who's to say what they did," said Keith quietly.

Meg's face was pale; all the child-joy had bled from it. Beryl saw and wanted to comfort her, but she was trapped again in that cold core of darkness and could not move. She realized for the first time that she was not the only one who sat on this exposed plain and wondered. And that made her more frightened than before.

Avery did what Beryl could not and put his hand on the girl's shoulder.

Mr. Grant spoke at last. He spoke as if through a fog, his voice distant, sad, almost old. "You must forgive me, Beryl. I did not mean to make light of your fears. They're true enough. I know the story of the Jordon woman."

She looked at him, at the MacDonoughs who held close to each other, at Julia Hunter's angry face and Richard Cabot's grave one. She sensed Mr. Keith beside her and heard the laughter from the veranda beneath them. She looked at Vincent Spenser, dark and quiet, who watched her with that searching gaze she always seemed unable to escape.

"There's no justice in this world, Miss Newland," he said at last. "But God is just."

"Yes," she said. "But God did not listen to the prayers of that woman, or her husband. Is that justice? Perhaps it is. Perhaps it's what we all deserve."

She was trembling. Jane MacDonough came and sat down beside her. Julia Hunter's eyes, however, widened in disbelief, and Captain Prescott shook his head.

Spenser was not daunted. "Who can say what we deserve? But as for these people who have died – you must know that He has wiped every tear from their eyes."

"You believe that do you?" said Cabot, derisive.

"I do," said Spenser.

Beryl wanted to say "Amen" with him but could not. The cold, hard darkness gripped her too well. And who knew if the lost woman had even died? She might be suffering yet, praying to a God who was biding His time – a God who, like the U.S. Army, would not barter for damaged goods.

The children could be heard racing up the stairs, screaming glee-fully. Below, a shining black carriage pulled by white horses made a commotion in the yard: the Witleys had arrived. The adults on the high porch shifted and composed their faces; they began to descend. Beryl would not look at anybody. She stayed behind, sitting alone at the top of the house until the little Baldwin boys arrived and begged her to point out where on the plain the Manor house stood, and the fort, and their farm. Thomas almost dropped the field glasses onto Mr. Spenser's roof and was chastised by his brothers "for not look-ing at things proper."

"Let him look as he likes," said Beryl.

That night Beryl dreamed of a woman in a blue robe who ran alongside a herd of white buffalo. They were stampeding across Vin-cent Spenser's tennis courts, tearing up the ground. Beryl called to the woman to come to her: it was all right; she needn't be afraid anymore.

As if by magic the buffalo disappeared. The woman stood on the high porch with her, the robe framing her face, her hair streaming, while Beryl tried to write her name in the Bible with a piece of rock. At last she got it down and looked up triumphantly. "Mary," she said.

The woman smiled. And kept smiling. Her smile grew larger and wider. Beryl watched, first pleased and then uneasy. There was no warmth in the smile; there was no light. She tried to back away from the woman, but she was on the edge of the porch with only the sky beyond the railing. She dropped the book. She dropped the rock.

The smile stretched into a leer. The lips pulled further away from the teeth. Then the flesh itself pulled away from the jaw – from the cheekbones – from the eye sockets. At last, it peeled back from the scalp, taking with it the long, thick hair, until there was nothing left but an empty skull. "Mary," it whispered to Beryl and reached for her from beneath the blue robe. In its fingers it clutched a wildflower.

Beryl screamed for so long, Will told Avery, that he had thought he would have to go for help. Thompson came running from the barn, certain they were being attacked. The men shook her and rubbed her face with a damp cloth, but without effect. She seemed to be awake and asleep at the same time. She looked at something in the mirror so steadily that even Will got spooked. At last Thompson took whiskey and poured it into her mouth. Beryl choked and spit like a consumptive, spattering her nightgown with dark stains. But she stopped screaming. She came to herself. When she realized what had happened, she was embarrassed.

"I think it was a nightmare," she told Will. "I must have eaten something at Mr. Spenser's that was – too much." She kept apologizing to Thompson. He just patted her shoulder.

"Helluva nightmare, miss," was all he said.

Avery later asked, "Did she tell you what she dreamed?"

"No," said Will.

"It must have been terrible."

"Terrible?" Will replied. "I thought she had lost her mind."

Chapter IX

By late July of 1874, the land running along Victoria Creek and rolling on into the Smoky Hills was baked parched and pale, like clay in a kiln. Roots reaching for water sucked the color from leaves and stems. Blossoms withered. The whole world was faded – the trees, the grass, even the sky. Grant's colonists wandered their estates looking at the shriveled beans and dying corn. They rode in circles, meandering like ants in an empty bowl, stirring up the dust and listening to the bleating of thirsty livestock. They pulled at their mustaches and spit, partly in disgust, partly for the relief of seeing something wet on the cracked ground. Young men whose idea of chance had been based on the roll of a die or the speed of a horse suddenly found themselves pinning their hopes on something so much bigger than themselves – the infinite horizon and the relentless sun – that their very prayers seemed a kind of presumption. When the effort to hope, to pray, or simply to wait became too much, many of them – far more than George Grant cared to acknowledge – took solace in alcohol, sex, and general devilment. Their anger glowed under the stone foundations of Victoria, heating from beneath what the sun baked from above. There were days, Grant felt, when the whole enterprise threatened to crack into pieces like so much cheap pottery.

Even Will Newland's golden-brown brow seemed to tarnish under the punishing sun. Beryl sat with him at breakfast, watching the morning light tread over his face and into the shadows under his eyes. He sipped coffee and stared into the dawn that rose over a stifling earth. The birds still sang – one of Beryl's chief consolations – but Will did not seem to hear them. He hardly heard her when she spoke. She had spent much time alone and was not overly bothered by his distance; she brushed it away like crumbs of toast from the table. Obviously, the drought was worrying him. Both she and Will felt the imperative to prove to their elder brother that emigration to the States had not been a mistake.

But although Beryl was haunted by the cruelty of these plains, and particularly by the savage frequency and injustice of death, she nonetheless took pleasure in the wind and sky. Some mornings she woke up and the bursting feeling in her breast – she wasn't sure whether it was joy or love – almost shocked her. Perhaps, she acknowledged, it was merely relief. Whatever it was, it opened her to the small graces of this life – the song of the lark or the smell of dew on grass – and it made her more patient than her brother with the hardships. She accepted the drought as a grim but not unforeseen likelihood. She wanted to remind Will that it was not for nothing that people called this place the Great American Desert. Next year might be better. But watching his pale, brooding eyes and the nervous twitching of his boot, she remained silent. She wrapped her fingers around her cup, looked toward the portrait of their dead parents on the wall, and then, with her brother, turned her gaze to the dawn.

Will drank. Not always, not even frequently, but since late spring he had been drawn to liquor in a way he never had before. Beryl would have liked to blame it on his bad company, but Avery had given up alcohol since the long nights he'd spent with the Seth family, and Cabot seemed determined not to involve Will in his own pleasure expeditions. Indeed, it was Cabot, sober and unhappy looking, who brought Will home from Hays City late one night a few weeks after the party at Spenser's. Will was drunk, sick, and bloody from a tumble against a horse trough. Beryl could not handle him by herself; she had to have Cabot and Red Thompson help her. When they at last got him cleaned up, undressed, and settled (though moaning and muttering) into his bed, Beryl led Cabot and Thompson into the parlor where she stood, silent. The two men watched her, uncertain whether to speak or wait. At last she said:

"Thank you for taking care of him. He – " She broke off.

Red rubbed his whiskers with a calloused hand. "He'll be mighty low in the morning, Miss Newland. You let me see to things, hear? 'Taint no trouble."

"If you'll pardon me, Mr. Thompson, it is trouble and of Will's making. But I appreciate your offer. We'll wait and see how he's doing tomorrow. Now go back and get some rest. I need to talk to Mr. Cabot."

"Well, if you're sure you won't be needin' anything, miss." He eyed Cabot narrowly.

"No, thank you, Mr. Thompson. Good night."

When he was gone, Beryl was again silent. Cabot began to speak, but she interrupted him.

"Where was he, Mr. Cabot? How could you let him get into this condition?"

"I did not get him into any condition, Miss Newland. I found him this way, blubbering into a glass of whiskey out by the tracks in Hays. I am surprised someone threw him out without getting back the glass."

"Damn the glass." Beryl hissed, her tone snaking between tears and contempt. "Whiskey. I thought he at least had better taste." She wanted to stamp her feet, to throw something. Instead, she paced back and forth, walking a nervous circle. The night was hot, but she trembled and pulled her robe close with clenched fingers. "Why is he acting this way?"

Cabot, his hat in his hand, said quietly, "I don't know. He's always been rather the Galahad among us. But I suppose the weather – the lack of rain, the disappointment – must be hard for him."

"Is it any harder for him than it is for the rest of you?"

"Plenty of others are drinking. I can't claim to be a better man than he is."

"No."

Cabot flinched in spite of himself.

Beryl sat down in the rocker and bent her head over clasped hands. After a moment she said, "But you're not drunk. And Mr. Avery has not been wasting himself in those dirty saloons. Why should Will? What has happened to him?"

Cabot sat down, tired, and uncertain how to handle this woman's distress. "I can't take credit for not being in the same condition as your brother tonight," he said. "I suspect it's just luck. And as for Avery – well, he has a motivation that keeps him working like a devil and living like an angel, you know."

"I do not know," said Beryl. "What can he have that Will doesn't?"

Cabot looked at her, disbelieving and slightly ironical. He finally said, "Well, I think he has great hopes for the future. Will is feeling thwarted in many things."

"Oh come," said Beryl, "nothing has happened to him that hasn't happened to Mr. Avery. Why should his hopes be any dimmer than Mr. Avery's? He has twice Avery's brains and four times the energy."

Cabot raised his eyebrows. "You're very hard on James Avery."

Beryl flushed. "I don't mean to be. He's a good man. And –," she hesitated, " – I admit I've been surprised by how hard he works. Back home he seemed only to care about dressing and dining and – drinking. But he's proven himself much more than that. Truly, if Will acted with half his integrity – "

"You mustn't think that Will has lost any of his old integrity," interrupted Cabot. "Or self-righteousness. But, you know, being a sort of Galahad, well, Will needs his Holy Grail. I think he thinks he's found it. And it's out of reach."

"What Holy Grail?"

Damn, thought Cabot, I'm digging myself into a bloody ditch with this woman. It made him angry, her stubborn innocence. He was only a few years her senior, yet centuries seemed to separate them. The gulf irritated him, not least because he recognized that his interest in bridging the gap was growing. He did not consider this interest healthy. Certainly it was not comfortable.

He studied her, the fingers of his right hand resting lightly against his lips. The second and third fingers seemed to seal them and, at the same time, to suggest their parting. When he opened his mouth to speak, they rested there a moment longer, as if they would hold back the warm breath. Then his hand fell to his lap.

"You must forgive me for saying so, but I believe, Miss Newland, that Will – " He paused, his brow furrowing. "That Will has become smitten with Mrs. Witley."

Beryl had been leaning toward him, resting her clasped hands on her knees. Slowly she drew herself back, her hands parting from each other, seeking the arms of the chair. She said nothing, but her chin tilted up in a way that Cabot recognized. He braced himself.

"Smitten? Smitten? You think him such a fool, then, as to get drunk over a woman he scarcely knows? And a married one?"

Cabot remained silent.

"He has confided in you?"

Cabot shook his head. She watched him, her eyes narrowing.

"I have seen no sign of this infatuation."

"I think you have."

She rocked. "It's impossible."

"Why?"

She stilled the chair, tense before his parries, grappling with possibility. Then she thrust it off. "How foolish of me to appeal to you," she whispered. "You, who can only see lechery as the motivation for anything in this life."

"That's unfair," interjected Cabot.

"It is not," she said, her voice rising. "You carouse with loose women. And you brag of it – incredible! You care nothing for yourself, nothing for your duty, nothing for the reputation of your family or your friends. When a good man like Mr. Spenser arrives, the first thing you do is besmirch his honor, spreading rumors that he's here because of a – a – tryst with a barmaid. How could I expect you to see anything in my brother's weakness but more of your own?"

Cabot stood up. He moved and spoke with his customary grace, but his face was flinty. "Mr. Spenser is a good man. Mr. Spenser is also a drunkard and the father of a bastard child. Your assumption that if a person is one thing he cannot also be another is infantile and unworthy of a woman with your intelligence. I do not perhaps conduct myself in ways that you find creditable, Miss Newland, but I am a true friend and an honest one. Your brother is a fine boy who finds himself infatuated – possibly in love – with a woman he can never have. It's because he's a fine boy that he feels he can never have her; a less honorable man would easily find a way around the small detail of marriage. Have some pity on him. And for God's sake, learn to be more honest yourself."

Beryl stood, but without her antagonist's grace; the rocking chair kicked away from her hand. "Thank you for bringing home my brother, Mr. Cabot. That will be all." She flung the words at him.

He put on his hat. He went to the door and, without turning to look at her, said, "Good night, Miss Newland." Then he passed into the darkness, leaving her to the company of her retching and miserable brother.

Up until that night, Beryl had determined to have little to do with the Witleys. Perhaps she had no truly good reason for this. The elder brother, Arthur, was always courtly in his manner. He followed every correct form. Yet when he spoke to people, particularly women, Beryl thought that his eyes often seemed blank, as if he did not really see them. The words were right, the posture was right, but the eyes were dead. He seemed an automaton. She was surprised, therefore, when she once saw him out in the great, red-roofed barn at Mount Halcyon, a man in shirt sleeves with mussed hair, surrounded by dogs, horses, and stable boys. He spoke excitedly; his eyes glowed. She could not believe it was the same person. She said so to Will. He shrugged. "He likes men and animals," he said.

Everyone at Mount Halcyon, the Witley ranch, liked animals. It was said they owned the finest horses west of Topeka, Mr. Grant's thoroughbreds notwithstanding. Maggie and Lou, their matched team, ran with the grace of ice dancers. Paris, the Lexington Stallion whom Henry Witley presented to his wife, was stunningly handsome. Cynthia remarked that her brother-in-law was only mildly interested in her existence, but that he was entranced by her horse. She laughed that Arthur accompanied her on her long rides over the prairie for the pleasure of spending time with the stallion. Her own passion was for dogs – not just the Pekingese and poodles that lounged in the two drawing rooms of the Witley mansion, but also for the pointers and spaniels that roamed the ranch. Henry complained that he could not enjoy a tête-à-tête with his wife because of the constant and jealous presence of four-legged chaperones. He solaced himself by holding the Persian cat – a great blond mop of fur – up to the canary cage and watching it fix its golden eyes on the tiny bird inside. When Cynthia protested that she would set the dogs on him and the cat both if they couldn't behave, he threw the cat down and said, "Do let 'em sic the cat, darling; then perhaps I can find my way to you."

The cat led a precarious existence.

Will liked the cat; it stretched itself out over his lap on the hot summer afternoons and purred. The draperies at the bay windows were invariably closed to keep the room cool, so that the mahogany and chintz, the blond man, the blond woman, and the blond cat were all bathed in a shadowy haze of gold and green. Will did not find it hard to find a pretext for visiting Mount Halcyon; as the crops withered, he spent less and less time on his own farm, leaving the chores to Thompson. He did not, however, like to visit alone. Though he asked repeatedly, Avery and Cabot rarely accompanied him. Avery professed to be too busy, and Cabot was unenthusiastic. So, Will came to depend upon Jack Randall, Jason Mayes, or Oscar Jones. The latter two usually spent their time smoking outside with Arthur or Henry, while Jack Randall frequently chose to join Will and Mrs. Witley in the drawing room. Will was not eager to share his audience with Mrs. Witley, but he tolerated Randall because he sometimes brought Lydia along, which was somehow comforting, and because he did not come often.

Of course, the logical choice to accompany Will out to Mount Halcyon was his sister. Early in the summer, she expressed little interest in such expeditions. Her mornings were spent working in the house, gardening a small patch of thirsty land near the creek, or driving into Fort Hays, where a laundress washed their clothes and linens for what Beryl felt was a reasonable price. The summer afternoons left her listless and prone to headaches; she preferred to rest in her room during the hottest part of the day. Riding in the scorching wind did not appeal to her even if it meant going to Victoria to visit Lydia and Meg, by now her two closest friends. The drive to Mount Halcyon was even less appealing. Never comfortable around wealth, the ostentation of the Witleys both intimidated and repelled her. She was impressed by the winding walnut staircase that climbed away from their front hall and stunned by the copious cupboards and culinary accouterments at the service of their French chef. She was appalled to see that the chef, his wife, and all the other house servants (and there were at least a dozen) lived in a bright white house set away from the mansion, a house much bigger and more opulent than the cottage she shared with her brother. Beryl was English enough (and hence class-conscious enough) to find this disturbing. She felt guilty when she compared her own snug cottage with the dirty sod houses most American homesteaders had to settle for out here; the idea that servants might be living in greater comfort than respectable landowners and hard-working homesteaders struck her as a sign of some grave disorder. That the Witley servants might be working just as hard as the homesteaders and with only half the respect was something she came to realize only gradually. In the meantime, she was certain that many a homesteader's wife would welcome spending her days polishing silver in a place like Mount Halcyon, and her nights sleeping beneath a ceiling out of which no rattlesnake was likely to fall. To be sure, Vincent Spenser's handsome home and Mr. Grant's new villa rose like lovely mirages on the hot, barren hills, but Mount Halcyon seemed to Beryl more fantastic yet: a bizarre pleasure dome, mis-placed and mis-dreamed out on these prairies. The land, she thought, will not respond kindly to such presumption. It will eat these foolish people alive.

So, partly because she did not understand them and partly because she found their conversation tedious, Beryl always chose to stay home and rest when her brother felt inclined to wander over to the Witleys for an afternoon. She changed her mind, however, after the night Will was brought home dead drunk. Cabot's revelation had, in truth, not been much of a revelation. He was right: Beryl was not quite honest; she had sensed Will's growing fascination with Mrs. Witley. She had seen him appeal for her attention at the Walkers. She had marked how he trailed her at Mr. Spenser's party, a tall shadow tied to a blue and white skirt. She had noticed that he could never find anything good to say about Henry Witley, whom he called vain and selfish, and that he could never stand to hear Cynthia Witley criticized. Beryl ventured, once, to suggest that though Mrs. Witley was beautiful, she didn't seem to think much on her own; she merely parroted back others' ideas. "Of course, that makes her immensely agreeable," she added.

"I can't think what you mean. She's a brilliant woman. You needn't dismiss her just because she's not always pushing her thoughts into other people's faces."

Beryl and Will were down by the creek. She'd been studying some strange worms – possibly caterpillars (she was not sure) – that were creeping around on the underside of the cottonwood leaves, chewing away the shade little by little. She turned to look at him, though, when she heard the defensiveness in his voice. "Oh," she said. "Well, she's good at looking like she's listening anyway. But perhaps you're right."

"Of course I'm right," said Will testily. He stripped a branch from a nearby tree and whipped the air with it. The worms which had been clinging to the leaves flew off into the grass where they coiled themselves up like the fossilized larvae preserved in his father's study. "By God, if a woman is beautiful, another woman will never give her credit for anything else."

"That's not true. I credit Lydia Randall and Jane MacDonough with many things – and I think them both quite beautiful."

"Jane MacDonough you feel sorry for, and Lydia Randall is not beautiful, she's aristocratic. That's not the same thing."

Beryl's mouth hung open; she could hardly understand this strange discussion. "I certainly do not feel sorry for Mrs. Mac-Donough – she has a lovely baby and a devoted husband. What should I pity? The birth of Victoria was terrible," (here Beryl could not quite suppress a shudder), "but birth is always hard. I pity any woman in childbirth. Why, I shall probably pity Cynthia Witley in childbirth."

Will became still. "She's expecting a baby?"

Beryl pushed away the black hair that kept blowing across her face and put her hands on her hips. "Why, Will, however should I know? We're not on intimate terms. But I suppose she and Mr. Witley will have a child sometime soon. Why wouldn't they?"

Will did not answer. He knelt by the trickling creek – he could hardly believe it was the same place where water had been rushing last spring – and splashed the sweat and grime from his face. He dried it with a handkerchief. "You really don't know her," he said.

"No," replied Beryl, "I don't." But, she concluded, it was time to do so. The next time Will asked her to visit Mount Halcyon, she would go.

The red roofs of the Witley ranch were visible for some miles. As the Newlands approached on their horses, Beryl observed an infant windbreak of elms and pines around the houses, the barn, and the stone corral. The deciduous trees drooped. Their leaves fell off and flew like torn paper in the hot wind. The evergreens, far from their native mountains, were browning from the bottom up. "They look homesick," she said to Will.

"Just damned dry," he said.

In England, Will would never have sworn in his sister's presence, much less when speaking to her. Now when he did it, she scarcely noticed. She marked it today, though, and remembered Rev. Seeley's confidence that she and Will would help bring "Christian civilization" to Kansas. "Good and faithful servants, heh?" She sighed.

An elaborate, wrought-iron sign stood over the gate to the ranch. "Mount Halcyon Stock Farm" it read. Beryl appended, "Abandon all hope ye who enter here." She was richly irritable. Her head ached. Hordes of canines raced at her as she cantered up the carefully paved drive. "They must raise nothing but dogs," she thought. But out in the corral she saw several head of russet-colored cattle, and past the spindly trees, in the distant meadows toward the creek, she could see many more. The heavy smell of manure spread itself on the hot wind. "Halcyon indeed!"

Will was not cross: His face was bright with expectation. He was dressed handsomely; only his sunburn marked him as a farmer rather than a gentleman of leisure. He dismounted gracefully and helped Beryl from her horse with chivalrous attention. The great house was barricaded against the sun, every shade pulled, but their knocking brought a quick response. The butler, a tall Dover transplant named Hared, was pleased to tell the Newlands that both Mr. and Mrs. Witley were at home.

Beryl entered the elaborate hall, which still smelled of new wood and carpets, convinced that nothing could unite her to Mrs. Witley. But the key to their relationship became apparent as she and her brother passed into the golden green drawing room. She saw it shining in the shadowy half-light.

"A piano!"

Mrs. Witley, who had risen to greet her guests, extended a small hand. "How nice to see you, Miss Newland. Yes, the piano just came a few days ago. Isn't it lovely? Do you play?"

Beryl touched Mrs. Witley's hand and did not quite let it go as she moved across the room. She stood before the square ebony instrument hardly breathing. She could not keep from reaching for it, first for one key, then for another. She caressed each gently, tentatively, like a holy thing. Her eyes glistened. "Not for so long. Not for so long." She was whispering.

Cynthia Witley put her arm around Beryl's waist. Her soft blond hair came only to Beryl's shoulder. Will watched, pleased but also envious. It crossed his mind that he should have stuck with his music lessons. But then what use was a violin to a fellow?

"Will you play?" asked Cynthia.

Beryl blinked quickly and looked down into Mrs. Witley's face: pretty, perfect, a flower opening to the morning. The exquisite cheeks blushed like the petals of a tea rose. Beryl, distracted by the piano, was nonetheless struck by its beauty. Then, after a moment, she realized the art in it: the delicate painting of lid and lip, the dusting of powder, fine as gold pollen. Yet she could not arm herself against it. This small, glowing person had a piano and was asking her to play it.

Cynthia Witley pulled out the stool for Beryl and then stepped away from the instrument. Will sat down on a leather chair and leaned forward expectantly.

Beryl paused for a moment, and then removed her hat and gloves. She pushed the seat back a bit further from the piano and sat down, sweeping her skirts across the floor and away from her feet. She lowered her dusty right boot to a pedal, feeling for the response; she slid her fingers over the line of black and white keys lightly, like a blind man poring over a page of Braille: recognizing, reading, drawing sustenance. Then she leaned in; her hands found their place; she played.

Her fingers, remarkably, did not stumble. They ran over the keys like children across the fields of home: sure-footed, joyous, intensely alive. Yet the music was dark. Fire, death, loneliness, and fear broke out of Beryl's body as from Pandora's box. Cynthia Witley stood transfixed. Will forgot himself, moved first by the music and then by something familiar that sang behind the tempest of notes: the trees sighing around Lindenhurst and the hushing of his mother in the night. For so long it had been night. He missed his mother. How strange that this music should bring her back again.

In the hall, a group of servants gathered. They said nothing, they only listened. One woman sobbed quietly.

Beryl finished. Her hands moved from the keys and came to rest in her lap. She sat still for a moment. Her shoulders shuddered, once. Behind her, a curtain billowed ahead of a hot, gusty breath of wind and then was inhaled back against the window frame, all the life sucked from it. A dog barked in the yard.

"Bravo! Bravo, Miss Newland! I say, Cynthia, you'll never get lonely for England with a musician like that in the neighborhood."

Beryl looked up to see Henry Witley leaning against the doorway. "I think that something in me needed to get out." She paused. "And I think it's gone now. I'm not sure I can do that again. Ever." She closed the lid to the piano.

"Oh, don't!" cried Cynthia, rushing forward and pulling back on the lid with small fingers. "I've been so wanting someone to play while I sing – and Henry fumbles ridiculously – there, you know you do, darling, so don't grimace like that – Do you think you could, Miss Newland?"

Beryl's body was limp and spent. She wanted to rest still and silent, watching the serene reach of the sky. But here she was, in a drawing room, in society, just as surely as if she were in London. She wrenched herself back from the distance. The sky contracted into a cloud-reflecting mirror.

She nodded yes. Cynthia glowed. She opened a small cabinet and pulled out some sheet music. Beryl studied it and then smiled at her hostess, fitting once again within the boundaries of mahogany and chintz and teacups. "I'm not much of a sight reader, but I'll try," she said. After a moment they began.

Beryl fumbled more than her previous execution might have led Mrs. Witley to expect, but the latter was delighted nonetheless. Mrs. Witley's performance was brilliant and bright; lyrics trilled from her lips like spun sugar; her eyes flashed, and her curls tossed. It was a saucy little number. She alternately sang to her husband, to Will, and even to Beryl, who found herself laughing. Her husband chuckled and warbled right back at her, but Will could only watch with helpless, adoring eyes. When Beryl caught sight of his face after the song was complete, the amusement fled from her own. She looked in alarm at Cynthia. Mrs. Witley seemed largely oblivious – or at least unaffected. She was an actress used to a worshiping audience; she smiled charmingly at Mr. Newland. She smiled just as charmingly at Beryl; she smiled no more charmingly at her husband, who seemed quite aware of Will's condition and was clearly amused by it. Beryl's reservations returned. She abandoned the piano to sit next to her brother. How to pull him from the nakedness of his idiocy perplexed her. At the very least he ought not stare.

To do William credit, if his face could not hide his infatuation, his words could and did. Everyone chatted while Hared served refreshments. Will spoke well and sensibly. He said nothing untoward, kept to strictly impersonal topics, and engaged Mr. Witley as much as Mrs. Witley. The tendency to show off, to assert his ideas and prove his initiative that Beryl had observed in Mrs. Walker's sitting room was not evident. Perhaps he now felt more assured of Mrs. Witley's esteem. Then too, perhaps Mr. Witley's presence acted as a tonic. Beryl could not be sure.

"By god, the heat's oppressive and hard on the cattle. Grass around here's tough, but I'm not convinced it'll keep the creatures fat and happy once it starts to die. What's the situation at your place, Newland?"

"Bad," admitted Will. A shadow fell over his brow. "Not much livestock to get thirsty, but the crops are blowing away. Thompson and I are working on a plan to divert water from the creek. I'm afraid it'll only be a crude kind of irrigation. We don't want to drain the creek; too many people depend on it. Some of us have talked with Grant about a cooperative effort to get the crops watered. He's sympathetic but keeps telling us to wait it out. Weather like this can't last. I don't know." He shook his head.

"Ah well," said Witley languidly, "Grant's a rancher; he can move his livelihood to water. Doesn't need the water to come to him."

"No," agreed Will. "He keeps telling me to invest in sheep. But agriculture appeals to me more than ranching."

Mrs. Witley spoke. "If you want to farm, of course that's what you should do."

"He told us we could grow grapes and peaches here," mused Beryl. "We never believed that, but we had hopes for wheat. And the plants looked quite handsome even a month ago. But they're so thirsty now, I've begun to feel sorry for each of them individually."

"That's a lot of sympathy, Miss Newland," said Mr. Witley. "How many acres do you have planted?"

"A hundred," said Will.

Witley shook his head. "Well, it's a hard year to get started. But we won't starve, will we, my Cindy? Plenty of wine in the cellar and bread on the board. Next year will be better."

Beryl looked toward the windows where the curtains blew. "Too many people out here have nothing to depend on. They have no one helping them from home."

Witley shrugged and reached for one of the sugary confections concocted by his cook. "These Yanks camping in holes in the ground must be wishing they could shed their skin like snakes. The trains heading east will be full of 'em if the sun doesn't stop its blistering. Don't know how they hold up, living the way they do." He chewed on his cake, and then stopped. "I say, you people are well set, aren't you?"

Will replied with some irritation, "We're fine, we're fine." Which was true – the support from England was certain, if not overly generous, as long as Robert's patience held out. But the gap between the Newlands' situation and that of their hosts galled Will; it in some way emphasized the gap between him and Cynthia. Will Newland was an Oxford man, every bit a gentleman, and that ought to have been enough. But sitting in that green and gold drawing room, he wished he were a titled millionaire.

"Ah, well, good then," said Witley, settling back into complacence. "Grant must have a tidy sum set aside. His villa's going to be a handsome place. Not too far from you, is it?"

"No," said Beryl. "Only a short ride. Our land borders his south of the creek. The house should be finished in a couple of weeks. He plans a soiree in honor of Meg when it is done. She will be coming out."

Mrs. Witley, who seemed to be wilting under the grim talk and the heavy heat, perked up. "Ah, is she? How exciting! Of course, all the lads will be after her! She must be quite an heiress."

Beryl stiffened. "Meg will be invaluable to whomever she marries, regardless of her dowry."

Mrs. Witley immediately realized her mistake but did not retract her point. "Oh, of course. She's a sweet girl. Her excellent prospects will only give her a better chance to find a young man worthy of her. She'll not have to settle for anybody. She can marry for love."

"I hope she would be sensible enough not to marry for mere money even if she were poor."

"It can be quite sensible to marry for money," said Mrs. Witley. She looked at the treasure of rings glittering on her fingers. "Romance is the luxury of those who are well cared for. Love might grow in poverty, but it has a hard time blooming."

"Now what would you know about marrying for filthy lucre, my dear?" said Mr. Witley, lifting his brandy and closing one eye to look at her through the distorting glass of the goblet.

She raised her eyebrows and cocked her head. "I know only about marrying for love, but not everyone has had my luck: to find love and luxury together. I've known girls who've married for love and had to live in near squalor, and I've known girls who've forsaken love and married for money. The latter seem to me luckier."

"How can you say that?" protested Beryl.

"Because the ones who marry for money may be lonely, but they don't go hungry, and they don't have to see their children grow hungry. That's why."

Beryl frowned. "Yes, but . . . " She looked to Will for help. She realized she would have to take back her assertion that Mrs. Witley had no ideas of her own. She certainly was not afraid of disagreeing with another woman. Would Will be disillusioned with this pragmatism? He did not meet Beryl's eye. He was gazing at Mrs. Witley.

"It's too bad that anyone should have to forego the one or the other," he said.

"Yes, rather." Mrs. Witley's face became momentarily tragic. "But Miss Grant will be spared that lot in life. She can choose and, with the help of her friends, choose well. I should think, Mr. Newland, that you might want to court Miss Meg. I'm sure neither Miss Newland nor Mr. Grant would be adverse. What say you?" She leaned toward him playfully.

Will flushed. "I assure you I would never think of it, Mrs. Witley." He looked angry. Mrs. Witley studied him for a moment and then laughed, a sound as sweet and light as petals tossing in a breeze. William did not explain why he would never think of Meg Grant and Mrs. Witley did not ask him. Beryl wondered if it was because she already knew the answer. She watched the Persian lace itself in and out of Will's ankles. A smudge of fur clung to his cuff. The creature purred and looked at Beryl with gold, knowing eyes. Beryl looked back and then lowered her head in shame.

The morning of Meg Grant's coming out was hot; the sky was brassy and cloudless. She sat on the floor by her bedroom window in a fawn-colored chemise, her red hair streaming to her waist, looking westward at the grass stretching away from the villa and northward toward the bluffs that lined the creek. Her expression was thoughtful, but not pensive. She was neither sentimental nor melancholy. She was looking forward to the evening but was too practical to take a romantic view of it. She could not really imagine marrying any of the men she had met at Victoria, and she was even less able to imagine any of them wanting to marry her. She was not a pretty girl: her face was freckled in a charmless way, and the lashes on her brown eyes were pale. She was an heiress, but she didn't see why that should lure anyone when every man expected to make his own fortune in Kansas anyway. She liked Mr. Cabot, but he was too handsome (and, Lydia kept telling her, too dissipated – though his behavior didn't strike Meg, at least, as much worse than anyone else's); Mr. Avery was sweet, but he was too skinny, and besides he was in love with Beryl; and Beryl's brother seemed to hold himself altogether too high for any woman, as far as she could see. Her cousin Clay was too harum-scarum; Mr. Keith was too old; and Ian Duncan, well, any man who took you out to collect buffalo chips was problematic as a lover. She was not disappointed at what she considered rather uninteresting prospects and gave it little thought. As she looked out at the hot morning, she only wondered whether Mrs. Walker was really handy enough with a needle to make the elaborate gown her uncle had ordered from Paris fit her lean and boyish body. She did not want to feel a fool.

The gown was a filmy white thing, with swaths of tulle and gauze draped elegantly to one side and fastened there by a spray of beaded silk flowers that cascaded over the hip. Tinsel was braided into an ermine cuff that ran along the edge of bare shoulders and nestled over the breasts. It was, Meg thought, an amazing concoction. She had never owned such a dress. Her uncle's generosity touched her;

she felt behind it some pride in her, possibly more in himself. After all, it was a gown fit for court presentation. At the same time, to appear in such a dress in the wilderness of western Kansas seemed to her silly, even bizarre. The temperature would probably be near 100 this evening. The fur collar – if that was what one called a trimming that ran so low as to make one feel utterly naked – could only seem ridiculous, no matter how pretty in itself. She wondered what the big game hunters would think of her, sporting such a hide on such a night. Well, it gave her small bosom shape, anyway. She sighed.

Her hair was sticking to her neck. She drew it away with her hands, lifting its great weight high and balling it on top of her head, twisting the long locks around and around each other until the entire crown of hair could be held in place by a single pin. The style was not becoming; it revealed too much of her broad, freckled brow, shiny in the warm air. But it was cool, and she did not care how she looked. She was her mother's child, a girl of frank and candid countenance, cheerful and sensible and rather plain. The more dashing features of her father and her uncle could not be traced in her face; their strong and romantic ambitions seemed also to have passed her by. Like any child, she gloried in the freedom and adventure that life on the frontier promised, but as a woman she had no illusions about the land, the storms that beat it, and the dead that it swallowed. She had seen and heard enough in the last year and a half to convince her that Kansas was no arcadia, that its beauty and bounty were matched by its brutality, and that the people here were like people everywhere: suspicious and self-interested, generous and cruel in equal measure. Her father had died singing a love song to the grey-green Scottish hills where his bones were buried; her uncle gazed upon these scorching American hills with a similar ardor. Neither, she thought, really saw where they were. She looked at the dry ground that split and cracked beneath the tough grass and smiled to herself. Here was a good place to walk, she thought. But this was no celestial city; the roads were paved with dung, not gold. And that suited her. That suited her just fine.

She rested her chin in her hand. It was so terribly hot; the air shimmered above what her uncle optimistically called the lawn. Ian

Duncan passed through the yard carrying a large tin bucket of water. One of the dogs followed at his side, trying to shove its snout into the silver wetness and yipping discontentedly. "Get on, ye mongrel," laughed Duncan. "Go wet your dry nose elsewhere; we'll be wantin' none of that scum in our drink." He pushed away at the dog, who yipped again and then sat down and grumbled to itself, scratching its ear and shaking its head, puzzled to be foiled. Duncan went on, whistling. For a while the dog watched the man, and the girl, from her window, watched the dog. The animal yawned, bored, and then suddenly came to attention, raising its nose to the wind. It stared to the northwest, and, after a moment, began to whine, low and uneasy. Duncan turned. "Now what'll be your problem, my lad?" he asked. He followed the dog's gaze. Meg too raised her eyes to the sky.

She exclaimed in spite of herself, thrusting her head and shoulders out the window for a better look. "Rain, Ian, rain!" she called down delightedly, taking her arm from the sill to point at a glittering cloud in the metal sky. It sparkled and moved like nothing Meg had ever seen before. It was beautiful, a shimmering spray beneath a waterfall. She clapped her hands for joy; she imagined the cool drops streaming down her face, over her body, dripping from her garments onto the dusty, discontented earth like a baptism, settling its uneasy soul. "Rain!"

He turned to her, and yelled up, "Only you'd be glad for a storm to come a-ruining your party, miss. Clay, Keith, come look! Where's Grant?" He turned back to face the welcome vision, his posture smiling. Then suddenly his back stiffened. He put his hand over his brow, straining to see better. Then he hollered, "Keith!" The name broke from him like a scream.

Meg stared at him, uncomprehending. She lifted her gaze to the darkening heavens. She heard, she did not see, the men come running. Then a voice.

"Shut the window, Meg. Shut the windows. For God's sake, cover the well, Duncan! Move! Now!"

The girl struggled with the sash; when she at last got the window to close, it came down hard, cracking one of the new panes of glass. Through the brokenness she saw her uncle standing bare headed beside the dog, staring at the sky, his breakfast napkin still in his left hand. His right hand covered his mouth. The ring on the first finger shone like a bright spot of blood in the sun. Then the light grew dim, and the cloud fell to the earth.

Mrs. Walker stumbled from the wagon and into the villa, sobbing, screaming, tearing garments from her body before the servants could calm her. For almost half an hour the object of her visit was forgotten. By the time Meg found the package which had been carefully constructed to protect its contents from the dust and wind, part of the wrapping had already been eaten away. She pulled the paper off frantically, stamping furiously, only half aware of the crunching under her boots, of the slime that was staining the floor.

The white dress was still a vision, but it crawled. The insects were already at work in the delicate folds. They clawed at the gauze as they ate; the silk flowers might have been real given the relish with which they were devoured. The lovely ermine edging on the bodice moved; red legs, yellow antennae, tiny blue heads with busy jaws decorated the collar, a bizarre accent to the silver threads that braided their way through the fur. Dull, yellow-brown stains marred the fabric of the gown.

For a moment Meg tried to shake the dress, to brush away the small creatures which clung to it as if to a blooming shrub. Then she gave up, her young face pinched, her brown eyes full of tears. In a fury she punched the expensive dress into a bundle and ran through the front hall, out of the French doors, and onto the veranda where she stood for a moment and then threw the gown out onto the creeping ground. Mrs. Tyler followed, tried to stop her, but Meg pushed her away and ran back into the hall sobbing, "Folly! Folly! Folly!"

Grant, who was trying to comfort the distraught Mrs. Walker with some tea, watched her run up the stairs. Mrs. Walker watched too, and then, for a moment forgetting her own terror, murmured, "Well, I never. I thought she didn't much like the dress. Such a waste, beautiful thing."

A few miles away, Beryl stood in her parlor, clutching her arms to her breast like a person who is cold though the room was sweltering. She stared in horror, not at the hordes of insects that crawled over the cottage, stripping the foliage from the morning glory vines, creeping in the cracks in the walls and the windows in search of fodder, but at her brother, dirty, red-eyed, smeared with black, reeking of smoke and liquor. He drained glass after glass with something like vicious satisfaction and glared at her.

"Can't burn-em away, though Thompson and I burned plenty of the bastards. Burn the whole damn farm down to kill them if I could. Burn the whole damn state. But they're here. There are too many of them. Bloody legions from hell. A plague, sister, a plague like the scourge of Egypt." He filled the glass again, slowly, for a moment pensive and mournful. His hazel eyes welled. Beryl was moving to put her hand on his shoulder when he burst out, "But what the hell did I do wrong? What the hell did I do?"

She quailed before the anger and anguish and self-pity that spilled like venom over his blackened lips, stunned to hear again the voice she thought she had laid to rest. Not all the thousands of locusts, their thousands of jaws chewing away the last parched remnants of the Newlands' dreams, could cause the girl this despair: to see her brother degenerating into a drunkard who swore and sobbed with the voice of his father.

Will alternately snarled and sniffled. Beryl shrank against the wall, stunned at the way the wide, heaven-reaching sky had so suddenly and completely collapsed into a small space where frightened men and starving insects competed to see which could eat away the greater part of her soul first.

PART II

"Why do I love" You, Sir?
Because –
The Wind does not require the Grass
To answer – Wherefore when He pass
She cannot keep Her pace.

Because He knows – and
Do not You –
And We know not –
Enough for Us
The Wisdom it be so –

Emily Dickinson

Chapter X

The Kansas spring of 1876 bloomed richly. The scars of fire, insect, drought, and blizzard were obliterated by spreading waves of grass and white, yellow, and purple flowers. Over the lost graves, larks soared and sang, jubilant. The turquoise sky made death and sorrow seem like lies – though a skeptic, standing in the sun with a warm and gentle wind caressing him, might have said it was a country given to lies.

They looked all the more absurd, then, these people disembarking from the train wearing fur coats, caps pulled over their ears, and shawls tied tightly under their chins. They looked ready for a Siberian winter, a trip to the Arctic, a sledge ride into woods populated by wolves and other creatures of ice and snow. They huddled together. They looked at the British idlers on the platform, elegant in light jackets, fashionable bowlers, even one tennis outfit, and then turned quickly away. They were ants. They would not be distracted by grasshoppers, triflers unacquainted with the want and care of living. They were ants. They could not be fooled by the sun.

Grant's report to the Kansas State Board of Agriculture in December of 1875 was enthusiastic and charged with optimism. The locust invasion – which had accompanied the drought of '74 like a hideous consort on the arm of an already unwelcome guest – had been unable to do its worst: a late frost the following spring killed millions of larvae while they were still buried in the ground. Grant defied the horrors of the previous year. He bought 5,000 sheep in Colorado and by the end of July had 8,000 head, including 195 English rams and their offspring. Vincent Spenser, joined by his brother Bernard, also invested in a large flock, and Lord Petrie, new to the colony from Argentina, made massive livestock investments. Grant bragged of $1,600 in personal profit despite the drought and the hard winter that followed (when snow so encrusted the ground that he was required to ship in corn to feed his animals). He intended to add 1,500 breeding ewes to his flock in the spring. He maintained that he would soon own the largest stock farm in America. His experiment on the Kansas prairies, he assured the Board, could only be counted a success.

Ben Davis said little in public, but in private he questioned Grant's sanguine assertions. "He's not giving his numbers strictly right," he told Keith. "He didn't factor in the 2000 animals we lost. We can't control 'em all out here. Not enough fences, not enough shelters; too many wolves, too many coyotes. Factoring the losses in – it changes the profit numbers altogether." Davis sighed and rubbed his eyes. "I don't see how Grant can be callin' it a success."

Keith took a drink and licked his lips. "He's a businessman, Davis. Any venture that isn't a bust is a boom. It's early on yet; he sees no reason to call it a failure. It takes a while to make a fortune."

"Aye," said Davis, "but wool ain't silk, and Kansas ain't London."

"Are you thinking of bailing out, lad?" asked Duncan.

"Not a bit of it," replied Davis. "But I'm wishing he'd be more of a realist. It's hard to argue practical realities to a man who always insists we're winning the race."

Duncan grunted. "He's not always so confident. Has a deal more faith in sheep than he does in men." He nodded sagely into Drumm's mirror.

It was a new mirror. It was not the mirror that had reflected the legendary faces of Buffalo Bill, Calamity Jane, and General Custer — or even, two years earlier, the humble visages of Ellis County gathered for the novelty of a church service in Hays City. The original had been shattered by an iron tea kettle, Nigel Wyatt's missile of choice one evening when, after several whiskeys, he saw his ghostly face sneering back at him from its depths and lost patience with its lack of flattery. The crash was tremendous. Tommy was beside himself, running in circles, pulling at his mustache, and wailing, "By the boot! By the boot!" Slivers of glass crunched under his feet, causing spirited debate among the drinkers as to whether he was screaming about the condition of his footwear or simply cursing.

After cuffing the offender and offering philosophic platitudes on the transience of all things – a form of consolation utterly lost on Tommy – Cabot, Spenser, and a few of the other Brits passed the cap and gathered enough to replace the mirror and then some. To his credit, Drumm replaced the glass only for what it cost and sent the balance to alleviate the poverty of a farm family that, in the grasshopper debacle, was not lucky enough to be comprised of remittance men from London. It was, Avery remarked, probably one of the few times good came out of anything that the youngest Wyatt brother did.

"It's true Grant wouldn't be thankin' us for spending our afternoon here when there's work to be done," said Keith.

Davis shook his head. "Aye, but we're not the ones spending our night's sleepin' on Tommy's tables. A man can't even go for a drink anymore and his reputation's ruined by those he's forced to associate with. If these fellows would work themselves instead of hiring others to do it, why they'd lose their desire to be catting about in Hays every night of the week."

Duncan was indulgent. "Lads will be lads."

Davis made a sound of disgust. "I'm younger than many of 'em, and I have better sense. Lot they learned at university. 'Gentlemen,' huh! Most of 'em have no more brains than billy goats in a barnyard."

Keith smiled. "No more manners anyway. But don't take it so to heart, Davy. Can't be responsible for everyone. Some must learn their lessons the hard way."

"Uhm. And drag the whole bloody colony down with 'em. Even the best acting like pigs at a trough."

"I say, Davis, you've the making of another Robert Burns. I've not heard so many homely similes for many a day. Makes me feel right at home, it does." Duncan's laughter rumbled. "But chirk up, lad. Many as seemed to be floundering are doing better. James Avery has proven more of a man than I'd have ever bet on. Damn his tailor though. Them waist coats just don't look right on a man milking a cow."

"He's a dandy, true enough," said Keith, "but a decent chap. Speaking of cows, you've heard about Randall and his bonny little jersey?"

"Would you be meaning Mrs. Witley by any chance?" asked Duncan raising dark eyebrows.

"Why never in the world, Dunc," replied Keith. "I'm no poetical sort like Davis here. I mean the jersey – that fine milker his father-in-law just sent him from England."

"Handsome thing – lovely eyes," nodded Davis.

"Like I said, Miz. Witley," said Duncan.

Keith ignored him. "Well, they say the night before last his man was out on the ranch past milking time, and Mr. Randall decided he'd try his hand at milking the beast."

"Randall? Go on!"

"It's true – and to his credit. Seems he sat down next to the jersey – wearing an apron they say, so his pants wouldn't get muckied – and set to it with great gusto. Got a fair bucket of milk too." Keith took another sip from his glass.

Duncan and Davis waited a minute, and then Davis shrugged his shoulders. "Well, what kind of tale is that, Keith? So Randall's becomin' a man. Bully for him."

"I'm not done talking, lad. Your problem is you have no patience, and it's telling, it's telling. But, as you seem to want a more exciting plot, I'll give it. Well, the cow gave him a good half-bucket of milk when she had the poor luck to be bothered by the flies. Seems she flicked her tail once or twice and got Randall in the eye."

"It's happened to many a better man," said Duncan putting his bearded chin into his hand.

"Your storytelling is vastly overrated," snorted Davis. "The bloke got some tail in his eye. Guess now he's ready to bust a bronco, 'sure 'nuf,' as the Yanks say."

"Randall didn't take to it kindly," continued Keith mildly. "When she did it a third time, seems he came charging into the house hollering 'No damned cow can get away with that,' got his wife's pearl-handled revolver and shot her."

"God, his wife?" said Davis.

"You're daft, Benny boy," said Duncan. "Though I will say your delivery is wanting, Keith. You can't mean he shot the poor jersey?"

Duncan's horror at the loss of the beast was hardly less than Davis's at the loss of the wife.

Keith nodded. "More than once. With his wife's gun. Through the heart. Or maybe it was the head – but it's a shame either way. That cow was worth several hundred."

"I'll be damned." Duncan frowned and then, thinking on it a bit more, began to chuckle. "By Jove, that's a rum tale. Truth to tell, I thought better of Randall than that."

"Like shootin' himself in the foot," said Keith. "A bad scene. His boy followed him to the barn and took on terrible at seeing the creature bleeding to death."

Davis shook his head. "Randall's a hard one to figure."

The three men sat silent for a few minutes, pondering. Then Duncan, who'd been eyeing the voluptuous Miss Fillmore with lazy interest at last said, "Well, Will Newland's got back on track anyway. Thompson said he's working hard as hell on the farm, and not mooning about where he oughtn't be."

Davis grunted. "I wouldn't stick to growing grain, but he's stubborn. You know, I heard Neil Hunter say them Russians are intending to farm. Using their wives to pull the plows, no doubt," he added contemptuously. "Or harnessing the bairns. Never saw so many children. They'll die by the dozens out here."

Keith's face grew thoughtful. He studied a patch of sunlight that fell against the counter of the bar. "I think not."

Duncan nodded agreement. "I tell you, Davis, I can tell a strong animal when I see one – and them Russians look sturdy. Comely, too, if you know what to look for."

Keith kept his brown eyes on the sunny counter. "Germans, actually."

"What?" asked Davis.

"Germans," said Keith. "Germans from Russia."

"Well, that explains it," said Davis pulling back his chair.

"What?"

"The smell. Kraut." And he laughed, running his hands through his dusty hair before putting on his hat.

Keith rose. "I wouldn't make too much fun, Davis. We'd be lucky if we had more like them in Victoria. They're not the sort to shoot their cows."

"Huh. Just sleep in the barn with them."

Duncan set his glass down. "Sometimes, lad, I think you're no better than the other billy goats in Grant's yard. 'Deed I don't."

"Oh, but I am," said Davis, his cheerfulness restored. "Kraut!" And the young Scotsman snickered to himself all the way out of the saloon.

"They walked out onto the prairie chanting their beads. No horse or cow, just trudging on their own feet, carrying their bags and trunks – even the tiny ones. It was incredibly picturesque. I'd paint a picture of it if I only had the talent."

"A little sad, I'd say. So superstitious, so poor. How will they survive?"

"You mean without cut crystal and fine china?" Cabot's tone was amused. "Jolly well, I'd guess. No distractions." And he popped a biscuit into his mouth.

The two women looked at him. "I'm hoping you'll be paying for that, Mr. Cabot," said Julia Hunter.

"Why, Mrs. Hunter, I intend to buy all of them. The whole bunch of 'em, for my parrot. And he'll not mind the bugs in them like some of your more fastidious customers."

Her hands whipped to her hips. "Mr. Cabot, there's no vermin in our crackers, and I'll thank you not to be making jokes in such poor taste. It's an insult, it is." Her blue eyes blazed over rosy cheeks.

Cabot laughed and then bowed. "Forgive me, madame. An unpardonable impertinence. Your goods are worthy to set on the table of the Queen herself. I'm never so happy as when I'm eating a biscuit from Hunter's." And he popped another in his mouth to prove the point.

"Better buy them while you can," she said crossly. "Those new people seem to live on nothing but hardtack. I shall need to order more soon."

"Hardtack, eh?" said Cabot. He whispered his fingers against each other to brush the crumbs away. "About what I'd expect, seeing the way they live. Perhaps that's the name of their village. Hardtack. Well, Polly will be sorry to have a rival for her biscuits."

Jane MacDonough shook her dark head. "They call it Herzog. And you oughtn't to speak light of their hardship, Mr. Cabot. They're just looking to find a living in the world, same as us."

"I'm not looking to find a living, dear lady, I'm looking to find an entertainment. And some of those pretty little Russians just might provide it." He examined his nails complacently.

Jane looked at him with shrewd eyes. "You play the roué, Mr. Cabot, but I know better. And so does our Vickie, don't we love?" she said to the tiny raven-haired child who was reaching for a stack of tobacco tins.

Julia snorted. "Handsome ain't wholesome, that's what I say. Shall I wrap these up for you?"

"I seem dreadfully unpopular today," sighed Cabot. "Yes, do. I shall go over to Hardtack and try to woo a peasant girl with an of-fering of cracker. My witticisms are utterly wasted here."

"They don't know English," said a voice from the back of the store. "So, they won't know how weak your wit is. Might just be the thing to change your luck, Cabot." Alec Hunter's dark head popped up behind some crates.

"Shouldn't you be out punching cows?"

Just then the door to the store opened, causing a sensation among the flies napping against the screen. They spun dizzily around Beryl Newland's head as she entered.

"Grant's given me the day off," answered Alec. "I thought I'd help Julie and Neil out. 'Morning, Miss Newland. How're the roads this morning?"

"Good morning! Passable, but there's a bad patch just past the old railroad cemetery. The mud there is like quicksand. Good morn-ing Mrs. Hunter, Mrs. MacDonough. Oh, and Mr. Cabot."

Beryl was glowing from her ride. Her face had filled out in the year and a half since the coming of the locusts. The shiny black coils which had once crowned her head were gone; a single long braid hung far down her back like a schoolgirl's. Her riding habit was a deep blue, unfettered by ribbons and trims; her hat was also simple, a cross between a fashionable cap and a homely sunbonnet. It shaded her eyes from the bright prairie light but avoided the look of a blindered horse. She had tied its rose-colored ribbon coquettishly under her left ear. She looked younger than she had when she left England, at least in the half-light of the store.

Cabot, seeing her, lost his comfortable urbanity. He avoided Beryl's face, though he nodded briefly. "Your brother is well?" he asked.

"Quite, thank you." She paused. "He'd be glad if you came out to see him sometime."

"I was thinking of doing some shooting Thursday next. If he'd like to join me, we could make a party of it."

"I'm sure he'd be glad to; I'll mention it."

The others in the store watched their exchange with interest. It was old news now that Beryl blamed her brother's difficulties on Richard Cabot, and while many sympathized with her position, few blamed him. Cabot's was a friendly, easy-going kind of personal debauchery. He enjoyed pursuing women and drinking himself into a state of sophisticated inebriation, but he was not much interested in corrupting others. His devilish reputation among the mothers of young innocents, male and female, was vastly overstated, and as secrets are not long kept in small communities, most of the colonists at Victoria recognized that he was a rather average English gentleman. He respected virtue when he saw it. He respected Will Newland, loved him like a brother, and, without contempt, called him a self-righteous prig.

Will was not particularly popular among the colonists. That he should fall in love with a married woman, and an actress at that, gave even people who bore him no active ill-will some satisfaction. Still, when he took to drink there was surprise and possibly a little disappointment. Not everyone knew he was heartsick over Mrs. Witley, but everyone knew about his drinking simply because it was so out of character for him, and so in character among the other young men. He might be irritating, but he was also among the most dedicated of the emigrants to Victoria. His fall suggested more serious faults in its crust than even skeptics had imagined.

And there was, as well, his sister. She seemed much alone. In the months after the grasshoppers ravaged the country, she was seen far from home, walking the barren hills or standing silent before the stripped trees and the half-frozen creek. Her black hair streamed in the wind. During the long, bitter winter of 1874-75, her eyes grew shadowed and anxious. Her cold hands, clasped together like death, hid themselves in her lap; her skirt rustled with the absentminded kicking of her boot against the floor. She was gracious and pleasant to speak to in company, but troubling to watch. It was said she confided in no one but Lydia Randall and Meg Grant. They told no tales, so she remained a mystery – a romantic mystery, because it became apparent that for her sake Mr. Grant, Mr. Avery, and (even though he would not acknowledge it) Mr. Cabot worked hard to encourage Will, to occupy his hands and his mind. They reasoned with him, argued with him, and appealed to his pride. Their efforts were aided by the gentle summer that followed the drought year. Crops prospered; rain fell. Gradually William took renewed interest in the estate; seemed bent on proving himself – or perhaps justifying himself. Life in the cottage must have improved. Beryl's nervousness waned; her limbs grew round, her eyes hopeful. Will once again became insufferable – and all seemed well.

But Beryl would not warm to Cabot – nor he to her. It was not active dislike; it seemed, rather, that each felt wounded by the other, somehow threatened. Perhaps they saw each other too clearly. Cabot knew that Beryl did not consider him a gentleman; Beryl knew that Cabot did not consider her honest. He felt attracted to her despite his own best judgement. He wanted to make her respond to him some way, any way. He fought the desire. It seemed unhealthy. He was not, he was sure, in Will's condition: he was not in love. Still, he was angry with her – the more so since she refused to recognize any merit in him and seemed eminently disposed to favor Vincent Spenser.

Cabot had nothing personal against Spenser. He was not likely to hold a bastard child against a man – or a woman, for that matter. If Spenser drank to solace his loneliness, and if it occasionally caused him to fly into a rage and beat his dog or his horse (something Beryl could not know, and Cabot would not reveal), that was something for Spenser to work out. Or for his older, milder brother Bernard to deal with: Bernard, who was said to have come from England to protect his sibling from his demon self. But the demon was the exception, not the rule. Spenser seemed a good sort – a bit too moody, a bit too intellectual, and more than a bit too superstitious (for how else could one characterize a Papist?), but also hospitable, generous, and given to impulsive acts of compassion. There was no reason not to like Spenser.

Except, of course, that Beryl obviously did. She would not, like an American girl, take unchaperoned buggy rides with him, but they walked together at picnics, conversed at parties, and danced together at balls. They actually looked like brother and sister — much more than she and Will did — with their dark hair, pale skin, and graceful way of moving. When they danced, which Cabot saw them do at the Witleys' and again at an officers' dance at Fort Hays, they synchronized easily, responding to the rhythm of the music and each other's bodies. Of course, as there were few women in these parts, Beryl danced with many men: with Avery, who took her in his thin arms with nervous vigor and commented every few seconds, "What a lark!" so that Beryl ended up laughing at him, at his exaggerated state of decoration (he'd taken to wearing lilies, having heard it was the vogue among the *avant garde* in London), at his inexplicable surges of euphoria and embarrassment, and at the uncertain expression in his eyes. Avery recognized the affection in her laugh; he knew it was not the affection he sought. His lily drooped. With Garth Mason, who talked to her shyly about birds and horses, his round eyes glowing through round spectacles; with Nigel Wyatt and his albino brothers, who glided like specters against the warmth of her body; with Douglas Keith who towered over her dark head and every now and then twitted her about his grandmother the witch; with Thomas Carrigan who bubbled, and Jason Mayes who boasted; with Ben Davis who bantered and Captain Prescott who spoke of home; with Mr. Witley who presumed, somehow, in the way he gripped her waist, leaving her confused and unhappy; with Mr. Grant who smiled at her in a fatherly way — or so she thought — and was courtly, like a prince or a king.

But she danced most often with Vincent Spenser, who drew and repelled her at once. She could rarely meet his eyes; they looked too hard into hers. Not the way Captain Denton's had — there was none of her former suitor's insistence, and certainly none of his well-deep sorrow — but in a searching way that made her feel as if Spenser would like to read the inside of her mind for the same reason he would like to read a knotty volume of Carlyle: for the challenge and interest of it. But he interested her, too — of that Cabot felt sure. She never danced with Richard Cabot, perhaps because he never asked. She seemed largely oblivious of him. And when he wasn't watching her, he thought little of her in return. The problem was, there were few other women on this frontier outpost to watch.

There was always, of course, Mrs. Witley. She was a bewitching object of contemplation – all blonde ringlets, shining and soft, that, despite being lifted off her neck, clung coyly to its nape, insinuating the pleasures of seduction. Her gowns were confections, mysteriously fashioned to suggest innocence while revealing the delicious lines of her hips, the bare loveliness of her shoulders, of her nestled breasts. Her laugh traveled low and sweet across the roomful of voices; she inclined her head deferentially to whatever man she talked to, and to not a few of the women; she knew the art of how to move, how to gesture, how to turn her eyes for maximum effect. Cabot admired her craft, even felt a physical rise when their bodies brushed in the turn of a waltz. But he preferred looking to having. He did not trust any woman so profoundly self-conscious, so determinedly in control of her effect on others.

She could hardly be unaware of her impact on young Newland. Will's face when he danced with her was noticeably contorted, as if he were straining against a heavy object, a gargantuan impulse. Cabot, seeing the longing in his eyes, put a cigarette to his lips and felt a stab of pity. Newland wanted the Witley woman, wanted to wrap himself around her and inside of her, and he neither could nor would do it. He would follow the way of honor, as he had been doing for over a year. And it was killing him. *La belle dame sans merci.* Better not to dance with her at all, thought Cabot. It's too hard on you, old boy. No other man seemed so helpless before her. The other bachelors vied good-naturedly for a chance to whirl her around the room, and the married men, though they preened their feathers and strutted like cocks when she was on their arm, seemed untouched beneath the surface. Captain Walker was merely courteous, Neil Hunter rather bored; Mr. Randall was somewhat ironic, and her own husband smugly proprietary. She allowed him to be; she submitted to his hand with provoking docility. It was part of the act: the tantalizing, untouchable mistress, the Helen of Troy. Play Paris at your peril, thought Cabot. At your peril. And he watched no more.

"I will call when the weather looks auspicious. Until then, good day, ladies, Mr. Hunter." And Cabot left the store, his package beneath his elbow.

"He needs a good woman, he does," said Julia Hunter firmly as she went behind the counter. "He's a fine man, but no direction."

Beryl's eyes clouded, but she laughed and took off her gloves. "He has a smart and pretty cousin back in England. I'd say she's the very thing, if ever he can be taught to look at her – and if ever she can be convinced to salvage such a wastrel."

"You're rather hard on him, you two," said Jane MacDonough dandling some bright yarn in front of Victoria. "I'd like canned peaches please, Julia, and a pint of molasses."

Julia went after the molasses while Alec came to the front of the store with a crate of canned fruit. This brown-skinned man was a different person from the sickly boy who sorted nuts and bolts in a blanketed chair two years earlier. The wide sky had done him good. He had put on bulk, and the glassy shine of his eyes had given way to a healthy brightness. He hardly ever coughed anymore and hadn't seen blood on his neckerchief for months. He put the heavy crate down lightly, with little effort. He spent most days working out on the Grant ranch, riding after sheep and tracking down lost cattle. The store work was a mere favor to Julia for having put up with him when he had been such a burden. She had thought to bury him; instead, she was to see him marry her sister next spring. His recovery sold them all on this country. No Hunter would ever go back to Scotland.

"I've heard Cabot plans to marry your little one there when she comes of age. Am I witnessin' a mother's approval?" asked Alec.

Jane gave him a wry glance. "I'm not one for losing my head, now. And Mr. MacDonough would likely be difficult about it. Let Mr. Cabot marry his English cousin or some other nice lass – little girls will keep for little boys. May-December marriages bring a flurry of trouble in the best of circumstances. There now, Vickie, you've made a mean knot. I shall have to buy it all, Mrs. Hunter. It will take some work to undo that tangle."

Beryl approached. "Some sugar please, Mr. Hunter, and some white flour. And a tin of kerosine, too."

She began counting out coins on the counter when the door to the store opened again. Everyone grew quiet. She looked up and, seeing the expression on Alec Hunter's face, turned.

The woman wore an old woolen shawl and a shapeless calico skirt. Her black hair was long, wind-whipped into tangles as mean as the snarls in Victoria's yarn. A pair of scuffed, high heeled lady's boots were tied together and hung from her left shoulder. Her feet were bare; mud stained her heels and toes. Her skin was bronze, almost black. Her eyes were completely black; the lids hung weary over the irides, and a worry-crease sliced the skin between her brows. Her lips were set in a strong line. They were fine lips, shapely and wine-colored. They made the beauty of the whole face. When Beryl gasped, it was not from fear.

Children clung about the woman's bare ankles; little boys, Beryl guessed. They were in rags but wore sturdy moccasins on their feet, brightly beaded and handsome. One child saw her looking at them and grinned. He stuck his foot out at Beryl and pointed proudly. She nodded and said, "Pretty."

"Pretty, yes," he repeated. He knew English, or else he had a good ear for imitation; there was little accent in his speech. Beryl wondered where he'd learned it.

Julia saw neither the woman nor the children; she saw only the man, his hair trailing over his shoulders, his mouth grim and toothless. She wondered where the gun was, where Neil was. She thanked God that Alec was at the store today. The butcher knife is just beyond the pickle barrel, she thought. I can get it if I need to. She tried to speak – she must ask what they wanted – but her voice came out in a croak. Beryl raised smiling eyes from the child and looked at her in alarm. Then she, too, saw the man. But no one came to kill with a woman and children. And they all looked so hungry.

Alec, wary, smiled with his mouth but not his eyes. "Can I help you?"

The man drew his hand out from his robe; it was gnarled, arthritic looking. Perhaps it had been twisted by a wound; a scar curled from the back around to the palm. He pointed at the tobacco, the box of biscuits, the sardines. As he moved, the smell of animal skins made the air of the store musky. Alec handed him tobacco and a couple tins of sardines, but the biscuit box was empty. He looked at Julia.

"Mr. Cabot took the last," she whispered. "We have no more."

Alec frowned and showed the man the inside of the empty box. The man made an exasperated sound and then looked at the woman. She said something in a low voice and the man turned back to Alec and pointed at the cornmeal.

"How much?" asked Alec.

"Eh," said the man and thought a minute. Then he held his hands apart to show how much. Alec measured it out for him.

"Anything else?"

The man shook his head. He reached into a leather pouch that hung from his belt. He pulled out coins and put them on the counter. Then he reached for the goods. Alec picked up the coins, puzzled, and said, "What the . . . "

The man, who had turned toward the door, looked back on hearing the tone of Alec's words. His eyes were wolfish. He's hungry, Beryl thought. He's so hungry.

Julia took the coins in her hand, studied them for a minute, and then lifted her chin. She forced a smile. It broke her face like the cracking of an egg. She nodded vigorously. "It is good. Good." She spoke loudly, as though to a deaf person. She nodded harder and raised her hand in farewell, willing them gone.

The man narrowed his eyes, looked at the woman. She shrugged and ushered the children toward the door. He paused, then followed her.

Suddenly, a bright flash of color flew through the air and hit the woman on the shoulder. She whirled. The tired eyes had opened wide – black disks of surprise and anger. She looked to the floor. It was the snarled ball of yarn.

Victoria clapped and crowed. "Toy," she cried. "Toy!"

The woman continued to look indignant, but the grim man with her seemed inclined to laugh and the boy – the one so proud of his moccasins – picked it up and said "Toy, toy," to the little girl. They seemed mutually pleased. He got ready to toss it back.

"No," said Jane, coming forward. "You take it. It's a toy for you."

The child studied her, now frowning. He was an open-faced, happy-looking child, but he had lived long enough to know that one did not get anything for nothing, especially from Whites. He considered the yarn, marveling at its brightness, and glanced at his mother.

Her face evened out. She nodded. He took off his moccasins. "Yours," he said and handed them to Victoria, who said "Toy!" and clapped them together.

"No," Jane said. "No! The child needs his shoes."

The mother looked at the yarn and then looked at the shoes.

"I can make him more; his feet grow fast, and he is ready for bigger ones. The string is a nice color. The trade is fair. Take it, little fox." She handed the mop of yarn to the boy, and they walked out the door, the other child enviously eying his brother and wondering what his own moccasins might have brought.

The Britons stared.

"She knew English," said Julia at last. "She could have saved us some trouble had she wanted. Do you think he did too?"

"What beautiful beadwork," said Beryl, taking one of the slippers from Victoria. The little girl slipped the other over her hand like a leather mitten.

"God knows what language they all talk. What about the coins, Julie? They're not American."

"They're worthless, but they're American. Confederate."

Alec took them up, examining them shortsightedly. "So they are. Must've gotten them from one of the soldiers at the fort. Not much good to us. No fair trade there."

"Whoever gave that man those coins wasn't trading fair either. But these moccasins, the handiwork on them – all for a bundle of crimson thread – You've a treasure there, Vickie." Beryl handed the slipper back to the child.

"Treasure, pah," said Julia. "Dirty beasts. Between the aborigines and the Russians this place won't be fit for a Christian." She looked ready to cry. "Alec will tally things for you. I'm going to go find Neil." And she slipped into the back room. Her brother-in-law watched her go.

"Well, it's too bad," he said at last, gathering money from the women. "She's no likin' for the neighbors, that's sure."

Beryl moved to the window and gazed out at the muddy street where a few horses were tied and a dog nosed around a puddle. The Indians were gone. Grant's settlement was as yet small; the natives had walked in and out again without anyone else seeing them. They left with one less pair of shoes and carrying a bright tangle of scarlet yarn. Their road ended somewhere other than Victoria.

The bell could be heard ringing for miles. The Spenser brothers heard its call to prayer reaching over the plain to the bluffs of the creek, where it echoed in competition with the gurgling water.

"Well now they've put us to shame. Tolling the Angelus after six weeks, and here we've been two years and not even a church."

Vincent turned his horse to the east. "*The angel of the Lord declared unto Mary. And she conceived of the Holy Spirit. . . . And the Word was made flesh. And dwelt among us. . . . Pray for us, O holy Mother of God, that we may be made worthy of the promises of Christ.*" He bowed his head.

Bernard crossed himself. Then he said, "Let's go see."

"Why not?"

It took little time to cover the few miles leading to the settlement north and west of Victoria. Where two months before there had only been winter-blighted prairie grass, there was now a clearing with seven long, low soddies and one partially constructed wood-frame building. Chickens scuttled and clucked in the dust; a cow tied to one of the soddies gave the visitors a baleful look. Gardens were already underway near several of the structures, where women and children dug onions and seed potatoes into the surprised dirt. At the sound of approaching horses, the women straightened their aching backs. Then there was a sudden rushing of skirts and wailing of barefoot children. Most of the women retreated into their sod houses and stood with their children at the windows and doorways, watching.

However one woman, in an elaborately embroidered shawl, shrieked at her boys, running and pushing them into a dugout with something bordering on hysteria. Then she ran to the cow and began pushing and shoving at her. The animal looked indignant, let out an unpleasant bawl, and firmly planted its legs in the grass. The woman pulled at the cow's horns; the shawl fell from her head revealing a tumbled gathering of gray-gold hair. When she realized the animal would not move, she knelt in the dirt and sobbed.

Men converged on the scene, seemingly from nowhere, though they must have come from the fields being plowed on the edge of the settlement. An old man with gaunt cheeks went to the weeping woman, spoke roughly, and pulled her to her feet. She ran to the door of the dugout, where she crouched against the thick, dirt walls like a cornered muskrat. A young girl came from the shadowed doorway and put her arms around the elder woman. The girl did not appear frightened. She scowled at the newcomers from beneath yellow bangs.

The old man went forward to meet the strangers bearing a sharply pointed shovel. Several other men, young and old, clean-shaven and bearded, joined him until the Spenser brothers found themselves facing a phalanx of about twelve Russian farmers, some of them looking affable, but most with truculent expressions.

"By Jove," said Vincent under his breath. "By Jove."

"Well, it won't do to lord it over them, Vince." Bernard dismounted and Vincent followed his lead. "You've been here longer," said Bernard. "You talk to them."

Vincent considered. On a square of land in the middle of the settlement, a huge wooden cross was erected. Next to it, from a crude A-frame of wood, a bell hung. Beneath it, a dog stood tense, ready to charge at a word.

Vincent took off his hat and walked to the men, extending his hand. "I am Vincent Spenser. This is my brother, Bernard. We heard your bell and came to welcome you to Kansas."

The men looked at him. A moment passed while the only sound was the scratching and clucking of the chickens. Finally, a well-built, broad-faced man came forward and shook hands with the Englishmen. He spoke.

Bernard looked at Vincent. "That isn't Russian. Sounds like Dutch."

"No," said Vincent. He spoke again, this time in German.

The men's closed faces opened a bit. One of them answered, then another. The Germans and the Briton had to listen to each other carefully; a difference in vocabulary and accent made for some confusion. Bernard, who had only seriously applied himself to the romance languages, found himself frustrated, confined to trying to interpret gestures and intonations and the expression on his brother's face.

"*Ich bin Franz Geist*; this my son Henry. This is Andreas Herman; Franz Krause and his sons; Peter Hoffmeister; Johannes Storm; Joseph Braun; and Nicholas Hammerschmidt. The others are in the fields." He gestured at the horizon. "You speak of our bell. You are Katholik?"

At Vincent's affirmative, his reception grew still warmer. "Well, willkommen in the name of the Blessed Virgin and the Christ Child. Himmel Gott, it's good to know we have Katholik neighbors. We thought to find only pagans here."

"Well," said Vincent, "There are plenty of that sort too. You have a priest?"

"Nah. We've written the bishop; he will send us a priest."

"I'm disappointed. It's been a long time since we've attended the mass."

"Sure. Come in then. Our homes are humble, but you're welcome to food and drink."

They entered one of the sod houses, a large but plain structure. The pride of the settlement was undoubtedly going to be the wood-frame house of Aloysius Dreiling, but it was far from finished. Nicholas Hammerschmidt was willing to boast of his wife's housekeeping for the guests, however. He was a slight, scholarly-faced man with the hands of a laborer. His wife – his second – seemed little more than a girl. She was round and pretty and looked harried. She was noticeably pregnant, and a toddler wound under her skirt. Several older children, from Hammerschmidt's first wife, stood behind her. The girl was in charge of them all, in charge of the house, and now in charge of serving unexpected company. Though her brown hair threatened to tumble over her ears, and her apron was well smudged with garden dirt and wipings from the toddler's nose, she moved efficiently among the men. She offered them beer in shiny cups and thick slices of bread, still warm, with a generous spread of grape preserves that had been carried from Russia.

The soddy, despite its construction, was clean and sweet smelling. And quite empty. A bedstead, a table, and a trunk covered with a quilt constituted the whole of the furnishings. A rag rug lay on the hard-swept dirt floor. A crucifix, draped with a well-worn rosary, and the portrait of a stern-visaged matriarch hung on the wall.

"My first wife," said Hammerschmidt proudly. "A tough and pious woman." Vincent nodded, wondering whether her features were preserved as a warning to her motherless children or to their stepmother. It was a face to run from at night.

"I say," he said after a pause, "you've made a tidy place here, Mr. Hammerschmidt, but you might spread a sheet against the ceiling if you have any to spare." He pointed to the low earthen roof. "It will protect against snakes, you know."

Hammerschmidt clapped his cup onto the table. "I never thought of it. The evil things are everywhere; they scare the children in the outhouse. We hardly dare put our shoes on in the morning for fear serpents have crawled into them." He shuddered. "You have snakes where you come from?"

"Nothing like here. I'm from England. It's a cool, damp place. Prairie rattlers wouldn't find it hospitable."

"We saw England from the ship," said Mr. Krause, "but only the coast. Germany we went through on the train, and saw many things – great forests, castles. Very different from the steppe, yah."

"Why did you come from Russia?" asked Spenser.

"Old Empress Catherine promised us, when we came from Germany, freedom from soldiering. Well, now that she is long dead the government begins calling up our boys to be soldiers.
So, some of us go to Brazil, some to Dakota. We come here."

"You miss Russia?"

"You miss England?" replied one man rather roughly. He evidently thought it a stupid question.

The broad-faced Geist said more cordially, "You ask us too soon. Of course we miss Russia. Our families, they weep for us like we are dead. The priests and altar boys, they led us from our town as they would lead a funeral, as though we were corpses in our coffins. Russia is gone from us. The Volga—you have seen the beautiful Volga River in your travels? – is like a dream of heaven lost." He was quiet for a moment, rather overcome.

Spenser was stunned to see that Geist and several other of the men were actually crying. He fidgeted uncomfortably, taken aback at the sight of another man's tears. "Keep a stiff upper lip, old man, a stiff upper lip," he wanted to say – but he somehow knew this would be the wrong thing. These men were not Saxons, nor even Teutons of Europe. They came from the East; their tears were no less exotic than their clothes. They mourned unashamedly. Vincent felt his throat grow tight watching them. He could not even look at his brother. And it was good he did not, for Bernard, who had little conception of what was being said, was appalled to find himself in a circle of weeping men. He looked at the girl-wife in desperation, but she was also crying, muttering and hugging the toddler to her swelling belly. After a moment, he gave up and glared fixedly at his beer and pumpernickel, taking surreptitious bites out of the bread and fighting the urge to belch. He was a big handsome Brit, and it was a rum situation for a man of his nature and nationality to find himself in. A rum situation indeed.

The tears did not last long, however. Theirs was an honest sorrow, not a sentimental indulgence, and the new country was the men's real preoccupation. They asked about the soil and the rain; they listened to the stories of the drought and shook their heads over the damage wrought by the locusts; they heard with interest the narrative of Mr. Grant's ranching venture and wondered aloud whether such rich a man might not be looking for laborers. The Germans were anxious to find ways to earn money for farm equipment and seed, for livestock, and for boots. Spenser told them that the British would welcome hard workers. Americans, he said, were a poor source of labor. When asked why, he replied that they were too independent; they would work under no one; they would serve only themselves. Which was, of course, a gross oversimplification growing out of the injured pride of the Britons, who found that no Yankee would stand for being treated with the condescension due an English manservant or an Irish maid-of-all-work. Americans were cursedly rebellious; it was in their blood. At the slightest provocation, they gave notice. The Germans did not question Spenser's explanation; it accorded with their experience.

"They like money too much; they serve themselves, not their people. They think they know best and will listen to no one else." Joseph Braun, a sunburnt young man who must have had his convictions branded into him at an absurdly early age (whereafter his brain, like that of many provincials, shut itself to other possibilities forever), summed up the indictments against his new compatriots very neatly. "*Protestantisch*," he said, and settled himself with his pipe. "Protestants."

Spenser thought there might be something to that.

The Volga-Germans' perception of their British neighbors might have remained positive had they not been doomed to experience the ritual hooliganism of the pagans. The Spenser brothers joined the Germans for worship at the wooden cross every Sunday, or almost every Sunday, and Mr. Grant came out with Neil Hunter and Douglas Keith to offer aid to the new colonists along with the promise of employment. But the attitude of most Britons in Victoria, and the majority of Americans in Hays City, was that the "Roossians," as they stubbornly insisted on designating them, were ignorant, dirty, and superstitious, hardly an asset to a rising Anglo-Saxon nation. They were good for a buck and a joke, and little else. In Hays City they were tolerated because they were steady and generally well-mannered patrons of its businesses and because they had settled far enough out on the prairie to be an occasional, not a chronic, annoyance. The inhabitants of Victoria, however, had less patience, if more reason, to be hospitable. Constitutionally bred to believe in their cultural superiority not only to other Anglo-Saxon nations, but also to any other race or people on the face of the earth, the Britons of Victoria resented the fact that the Kansas Pacific compelled them to share the same stretch of country – or almost the same, for the dry hills near the North Fork could never have the value of the estates facing onto Victoria Creek – with a group of poor, ill-educated immigrants from backward countries (the wonders of Goethe and Tolstoy not withstanding). These people made good servants, but one should not have to acknowledge one's servants as fellow landowners. The Germans were a small but significant blot staining the fantasy of a pure British empire on the virgin prairie. Granted, they were less of a blot than the Indians – but then they could not be kept on reservations.

Besides which, they worked so damned hard they made a fellow look bad.

Exactly who organized the drunken afternoon raids on "Hardtack" remained a mystery. The motivation was partly vengeful – the Russians had no right to make their superiors look like sluggards –

and partly, even mostly, lustful. The German women gathered their aprons and front skirts up before them like baskets when they worked in their gardens, providing incomparable views, it was rumored, of shapely calves and dainty ankles. If one drinks enough liquor early enough in the day, even the dirty feet of a milkmaid will seem alluring. So it was that, on more than one occasion, the noble sons of England (or at least three or four of them) mounted their steeds and raced to the Russian village where they spurred their horses in drunken circles, shouted lewd comments at the frightened women, and took potshots at the gardens' melons. Their need for sport, if not sex, surfeited (usually signaled by one of the gallant knights vomiting), they reeled off into the sunset to collapse against a tree, a barn, or (if they were really lucky) their own front door.

The Germans were terrified by these rampages. They were a scarred people from a brutal land. Within living memory, they retained tales of the Kyrgyz, nomads who rushed down from the hills to raid German villages on the Russian steppe: raping, stealing, dismembering, and dragging souls away into slavery. A watermelon exploded by the bullet of a fun-loving Briton was merely a sweet, sticky mess unless one had grown up listening to how the heads and bellies of babies were split apart by the spears of the Kyrgyz. Then the red pulp splattered against the ground took on a symbolic significance that no pampered son of Britain could appreciate.

When it became known that the Germans warned each other the young gentlemen were coming for yet another afternoon of sport by yelling in the streets of Herzog, "*Die Englische Kommen! Die Englische Kommen!*" the hilarity, especially among the Americans at Tommy Drumm's, broke all bounds.

"You Brits are a sorry lot. Couldn't keep a tinsmith from spoiling your attack in 1776, and now can't even sneak up on a bunch of women and children without giving yourselves away. Call yourselves empire builders. Ha! Have ya seen a bit of Roossian leg yet? Have ya? Here's twenty dollars saying ya haven't!"

What the British boys said to this taunt is not recorded. But they never did see any "leg" – or calf, or even ankle. After the first attack, the soddies were always shuttered, the doors always bolted, and the streets always deserted when Johnny Bull came roaring into Herzog. This disappointment could only be borne a few times before the joy bled out of the hunt. And even if the Germans had not proven so adept at hiding from marauders, the young men would have found little to titillate. A German girl might lift her apron, and even her skirt – but beneath that was a petticoat, and beneath that another, and under that a set of long drawers, and then, at bottom, a pair of droopy stockings. If they wanted flesh, the young men would do better to attend a ball at the Witleys'. Herzog was not on display. Not for her own, and certainly not for the pagan.

Chapter XI

Perhaps it was a penance. It might also have been an unlikely defiance, an aggressive one-upmanship. Grant sometimes saw it that way. He would sit out on the veranda after tea, breathing in the brisk air and watching the russet trees shed their color into the creek. He smoked his pipe. His dog – his favorite, a collie named Faith – sat with her head on his knee. His face was tired. Yes, it might be sheer bloody defiance: Don't judge me. And don't presume, you who call yourself a success, you who would build a city of God on the plains and instead lord it over a tiny town given to vice, pleasure, and drunkenness, a town unchurched and unholy; don't presume to judge me. See what I do while you buy cattle and sheep and watch the souls of men waste away. See me erect a house of God.

His niece inclined to the other view. Mr. Spenser was not so mean-spirited. He was merely generous, and he was also, no doubt, feeling some compunction for his behavior. He wanted to set things right with himself, with his brother, with his God. And probably also with Beryl Newland. Vincent Spenser was truly a gentleman: an impeccable dresser, an excellent sportsman, a well-read scholar. But since coming to Victoria he had proven his accomplishments extended equally to darker habits. He suffered from fits of melancholy when he refused to see anyone. He paced the lawn outside his house in the early morning, deaf to the birds, blind to the brightening sky. He brooded, a monk robed in a wine-colored dressing gown, reckoning with wrongs that no one could guess, his expression an unwholesome mixture of contempt, disgust, and sorrow. He found solace in drink. He was quiet when he drank, whether alone or in company, but it was a dangerous, sullen quiet that masked a temper made more combustible for being doused in brandy. He drove a man's head through a glass window once. After that incident Mr. Grant wrote to Lord Herries suggesting that the young man might benefit from the tempering presence of his brother.

And Bernard was a good influence: he made Vincent feel less lonely, he was an optimistic companion, and he was both psychologically astute and physically strong enough to curb Vincent's more violent tendencies. On the other hand, he too enjoyed his liquor, so that while he protected his younger brother from acting out his antisocial impulses, he perhaps encouraged his brother's drinking rather than braking it. They became jolly drinking partners of a Saturday night and were found together in the pig pen of a Swedish homesteader one Sunday morning, sleeping off the effects of an ambitious evening. They had their arms around each other like little boys in their nursery bed.

Vincent's melancholy drove him to drink; his shame at having been drunk drove him to deeper melancholy yet. He was, however, a Roman Catholic: he believed in the repeated forgiveness of an ongoing sin, if only the sinner was truly sorry. And if his church gave him reason to hope that he could always be better tomorrow, his regard for Beryl Newland also helped him. She had an uncompromising aversion to alcohol. She could scarcely speak to her own brother on the days following his debaucheries, much less to those who had less claim on her affection. Vincent Spenser felt it was worth fighting for her esteem. He knew that she liked him in spite of his Roman religious convictions – or perhaps, in a strange way, because of them. For although she had been reared on a rigorous English prejudice against Catholicism, she felt in his faith an answering echo of her own. If she did not understand the crossing of hands and the mumbling of beads, she sensed the thin but mighty cord that bound Spenser to his God, a cord that stretched agonizingly but nonetheless did not break when its owner grappled with a fallen world. She listened patiently to his discourse on Cardinal Newman, to his explanation of why that eminent man came to embrace Catholicism, not because she could ever imagine following in his steps (a point she made very clear) but because of her immense respect for Spenser himself, her sense that he was, somehow, a good man at bottom, a man who had something to teach her. His faith was greater than hers, and if her life was more correct, her spirit was less easy. He paced and drank and battled his demons; she tried to ignore hers and, by refusing to confront them, gave them the strength to gnaw more effectively at her soul. It was comforting, therefore, to be with him. She felt, somehow, that he battled for them both. She sat gratefully in his shadow, not always able to meet his searching eyes but always fortified by the conviction and kindness in his voice. Whatever he might be with others, with her he was unfailingly good.

So she, at least, seemed willing to accept that his motives in this last instance were pure, that in his gift to Herzog he had not meant to make a commentary on Mr. Grant's leadership at Victoria. If, as was said, Beryl would be attending the German chapel with them next Sunday, then Meg maintained to her uncle that it must be all right. If Beryl trusted Spenser, then he should.

Grant grunted. Perhaps. But still, he would contact the Episcopal Bishop, Vail. It was time to break ground, to build their own Anglican church. The right church. The church that would be a tribute to the Queen, that would give her subjects somewhere to congregate other than the establishments lining the tracks in Hays, something to do other than get drunk, and fight, and destroy property. The church that would acquit George Grant to himself.

Sheriff Ramsay and his wife lived in a small clapboard house with a white picket fence and pressed chintz curtains at the window. The tiny front yard was not, like most in Hays City, a dusty waste of grass. It contained two flourishing shade trees and was cultivated with flowers, including a cluster of hollyhocks that boldly opened their scarlet blooms to the sun. Bees whirred constantly around their heads. Standing at the gate, Beryl thought it an almost idyllic scene, one that would entice many women to believe life could be something better than just bearable on the frontier.

But the cries from behind the front door would have served as a caution.

Sheriff Ramsay was dead. He had been shot to death in Stockton while pursuing a horse thief. The men who brought the news — and the sheriff's body — did not know how to deal with Mrs. Ramsay's subsequent hysteria. After listening to them with a queer silence that made the bubbling stew on the stove and the wagon wheels in the street seem like a preternatural chorus, she commenced screaming: not a screech, but a high, toneless utterance that did not cease. Her jaw hung open like that of a dead woman, her expression blank except for the black hole at the bottom of her face. She began demolishing the room, calmly and methodically as if she were dusting and polishing furniture. The men were aghast. She did not weep; she did not struggle when they restrained her. She merely kept screaming and, whenever she was released, she began again to break and tear things: a pitcher, a hand mirror, a shirt she had been mending. She took the thin candles from the mantle and cracked them as though she were breaking a child's fingers. One of the men ran for a doctor, another for a preacher. Captain Walker rode to Fort Hays for his wife.

Mrs. Walker insisted that Beryl, who was visiting at the time, accompany her. When Beryl protested, saying that she did not know Mrs. Ramsay and did not want to intrude on her sorrow, Mrs. Walker said, "Well, you want to help don't you?"

Beryl felt she had no acceptable answer, yet her feeling was so often different from Mrs. Walker's. Mrs. Walker seemed so right, so generous, so eager in her impulses. Beryl could foresee it all: Mrs. Walker would comfort the widow; would provide food; would arrange for the funeral; would relay the sad news to the other women in Hays and at the Fort; and then, later, would describe the widow's condition with sympathetic relish. Everyone would talk about how kind Mrs. Walker was, how good, what a paragon of Christian womanhood, what a pillar of the community – and who could doubt it?

Beryl went to the Ramsay house. She stood quietly in its tiny parlor while Mrs. Walker spoke with Elizabeth Cavendar and her daughter, who had come to watch over the traumatized widow. The room had been tidied, but the shambles that preceded their coming was still evident. Broken crockery lay in the corner, and a half-torn curtain dangled at a window. The wallpaper of the room, a red pattern on gold ground, bled where water had been hurled against it. Beryl had seen human devastation before: her father's prolonged death; her brother's drunken humors; Jane MacDonald's agonizing childbirth. But Mrs. Ramsay's grief surpassed them all. The woman sat in a chair, her head hanging to one side. She no longer screamed

– the doctor had drugged her – but the anguished spirit that possessed her refused to give over and stared out of her dry eyes with undiminished intensity. Her mouth hung open; her breath came in labored gasps that might have been sobs in another. She did not move because she could not. She had been tied to the chair. Beryl was appalled. Through a door to the kitchen, she could see the sheriff's body laid out on the table. He lay under a quilt, a patchwork of birds and stars, green and yellow and pink. Beryl wondered if it came from the bed he and this woman had shared.

"Must she be restrained this way?" asked Beryl.

"They say so," said Mrs. Cavendar. There was displeasure in her voice. She held Mrs. Ramsay's hand in her own, stroking it gently as one might the cheek of a sick child.

"But why not let her lie in bed?"

"It's easier to control her on the chair. They'd have to tie her arms over her head in the bed. Here she can rest more – natural." The man spoke as though Mrs. Ramsay were not present.

"Why did they bring his body here?" whispered Mrs. Walker. "They could have taken him to the undertaker's. It would have been better for her."

Mrs. Cavendar shook her head. "He asked to be taken home before he died. They took him at his word. The undertaker's been here; chosen the clothes. He's gone for the coffin. I expect the body'll be moved soon."

Beryl removed her hat and gloves and sat in a rocker across from the other women. Mrs. Cavendar continued stroking the woman's hand; her daughter Rachel sat mending the sleeve on a man's white linen shirt. "For the burial," the girl explained.

Beryl watched her stitching, the way the frayed fabric was caught and tamed under the needle "Will family come for Mrs. Ramsay?"

"There's none to come," said Mrs. Cavendar. "Mr. Ramsay's from Pennsylvania – a far trek just to see a corpse put in the ground. His mother, she'll surely be heartbroken if she's still alive. He was the only son. Talk is she was not well; didn't want him coming west, but he had a good job with the Walnut and Big Timber. He was little more than a boy when he came."

"How could anyone so young get to be sheriff?"

Mrs. Cavendar shrugged. "Sheriffs didn't last long in the early days," she answered, as if speaking of a period decades before rather than five years previous. "Got killed almost as quick as they were starred. Some of 'em not quite so law abiding as might be wanted either. Wild Bill now: a picturesque fellow, but no saint. He abandoned his wife and baby son – turned feelings against him, it did. He was voted out, Lanahan voted in. Well, that one was shot in short order, ambushed by some as resented how he was trying to clean things up. Dirty business, dirty. Then came Mr. Ramsay, Lanahan's deputy. Young, sure, but a good, hard worker, and an upright sort. Had a pleasant way with 'im, too; always a friendly word for children and dogs. I think maybe those of us living here thought his youth would serve him well. Fate'd be cruel to cut down one so young and so good. And with a new wife, too." She inclined her head toward the haggard woman beside her. "It wasn't a pretty job when he started, either. Men shot each other for sport, they did, the way they'd shoot crows or rats. He knew what he was in for. And she did too. She didn't like it, but there – it was his duty. A woman has nothing to say in a man's duty. But he did a fine job, and raw as you may find it here, miss, I can tell you that life in Hays is a good bit more respectable since Mr. Ramsay served. It's a different world from what was."

Mrs. Walker shuddered. "When we first came. I hardly dared step foot in town; only a few dozen women in the entire place, and the respectable ones I could count on a single hand. Mary Ramsay worked at the hotel, cooking and waiting on guests. So pretty and happy. She never said much about where she came from, though. I asked, but she would never say. It made me wonder sometimes. She must have come from one of the cities; you know she's quite educated. There was talk of her teaching school, but by then she was courting Mr. Ramsay and was certain to be married."

"Sure, she was a pretty lass, but never happy after she married Sheriff Ramsay. It dimmed her light," said Mrs. Cavendar.

"Why?"

"Poor fool, she loved too much. When a man's job is to be ready to die on a moment's notice, it's only a fool as would give him all of her heart. And once your heart's gone, the only way you'll get it back is in little pieces." Mrs. Cavendar stroked the widow's hand more gently still. Then she looked at her daughter and added, "Take notice, lass."

"Seems to me there's no point in loving at all," muttered Rachel. "It's all loss. From Pa to this Mr. Ramsay. No good at all."

"Oh now, that's not true," protested Mrs. Walker. "Lord Tennyson says, *Better to have loved and lost, than not have loved at all.*"

Mrs. Cavendar's eyebrows climbed up her skull. "Pretty sentiment."

Beryl looked at the midwife's daughter, her thick brown curls pulled out of her blue eyes with a blue ribbon, her cheap calico made fresh and fair by her youth. "Oh, you'll fall in love too," she thought. "It happens to everyone." She turned from the girl to the widow – delicate cheeks, small chin, nicely-spaced eyes, a pleasing combination that agony had twisted into pieces which no violence could fit back together. To look too long at this deformity would be rude, unkind, like staring at a freak in a circus. Beryl turned her gaze to her lap, where her hands lay restless. "Everyone but me, thank God."

While the other women conversed in low tones about who could provide food for a wake, Beryl began to wander around the room. She picked the shards of crockery up from the corner where they lay. She went to the window and, taking some pins from her reticule, patched the torn curtain together. Then she pulled the curtains closed so no one could look in; she had noticed a steady procession of gawkers passing in the street. Since the curtain fabric was not heavy, the bright sunlight still passed through. Otherwise, the room was depressing. The air was fetid despite the open front door. A pail of lime sat in the kitchen, but it did not seem to be enough. The June day was warm; the body was deteriorating. Not wanting to go near it, Beryl went to a small room off the parlor. In it was an oak chest of drawers, a trunk, an iron bedstead, and a closet over which a curtain hung. A black gown lay on the bed, creased from being folded in the trunk; as yet no one had been able to calm the widow enough to dress her. Over the head of the bed hung a portrait, a painted tintype of Mrs. Ramsay and her husband on their wedding day. His long fair mustaches drooped almost to his chin; she wore a veil on her head and a dark dress which had been crayoned a rose color. Both wore serious expressions, but the bride's face glowed even in the artificial pose. Beryl could not look at it long. The dead man and the distracted woman in the adjoining rooms were a brutal answer to the hope trapped under that glass.

The pitcher on the chest was what Beryl wanted. She took it and went out of the house, walking around to the back where there was a pump. She filled the pitcher with water and then, with a knife, cut flowers from the garden, the most fragrant ones she could find. The blooms were varied and profuse; the plants were carefully arranged and tended, like in an English garden. She clipped some blossoms of wild rose, flicking insects from the leaves and petals. She found pungent marigolds with wide faces and put many of them in her pitcher. She added orange day lilies and daisies. Indomitable morning glories, so common here in Kansas, climbed along a trellis under an open kitchen window where a curtain blew. As she gathered blooms from beneath that window, she could see the body, an unwieldy, unnatural mass desecrating a table meant to hold cups and plates, coffee and bacon and bread. She could hear the kitchen flies buzzing in busy circles and shuddered.

Beryl moved from the shadow of the house to the far end of the yard where a high, unpainted fence ran along an alley. A trash pit was there, and a privy which had violets growing in the shade of its walls. She stooped to study their plush blooms, and then heard voices.

"Ya think it's true?"

"Blasted his whole face ta nuthin, that's what my Pa says."

"I dunno. That's not what my pap told my ma. Said it was through the guts. Spilled all over his saddle."

"Well, if we look, we'll know."

"Don't wanna see no dead body. 'Sides, Miz Ramsay's gone plumb crazy. She might catch us."

For a moment the young voices ceased, their owners evidently pondering. Then:

"Don't haveta' see no body, ya fool. See, they won't bury him in the clothes he was wearing. They'll have thrown them in the trash heap. So I'm bettin' a nickel if we can get in there, we can find them clothes. See if they're bloody and tore up and stuff."

"Say – betcha we could sell 'em for a pile of money."

"Who'd buy a pile of bloody rags?"

"Papers. My Uncle Tom says they'll buy any trash and publish it."

"Can't publish no shirt, dummy."

"Can draw a picture of it and tell a right hair-raisin' story. Would sell lots of papers."

"I think that's a dumb idea. Besides, the *Sentinel* is already writing a story. Lots of stories. What'd they want with a dirty old shirt?"

"Well, he's a hero. I think it'd be a great relict. Like – like the shirt Lincoln wore when he was shot."

"I bet we could sell it to Josh Merrit. He's got money. And he'll buy anything. Bought a frog offa Johnny Beckman, and it'd been dead for five days already. It was crawlin' something creepy."

"Why'd he buy a crawlin' frog?"

"Said he was gonna put it in his stepsister's bed."

"Ohh, that's a nasty thing to do."

"Did he do it?"

"Woulda got whipt if he did. I sure woulda got whipt."

"Thing is, would he buy a shirt from a murder?"

"Other thing is, how much'd he pay. It'd have to be a lot. We'd have to split it fair, three ways."

"We all going ta look in there?"

"Aw, I don't dare. These are new trousers. Ma'll hide me if I get 'em dirty or bloody."

"Silly, the blood will be dried. But you can't share if ya don't go in. Maybe yer yella."

"But it was my idea."

"Got a patent on it?"

"What's a patent?"

"Yer just plain ignorant. It's where you get a paper saying an idea is yers, and everyone has to pay ya ta use it."

"I can get a paper."

"From the guv'ment, Sam, from the guv'ment. Can't just be any old paper."

As the boys argued, they moved closer to the fence. Beryl could see one of them peeking between the slats of the enclosure. His blond bangs hung down into his eyes.

"Time's wastin'. Someone else'll be thinking of this, and our chance'll be lost. Let's go. If ya' don't wanna go in, Sam, ya can go to the window, and tell us what ya see."

"Is she really crazy?"

"I dunno. Just screamed a lot, that's what I heard."

"My Aunt Minnie screamed when my cousin died, but they didn't put her away nowhere. I heerd Dr. Hanson wants to put her away."

"Must be a lot worse than screaming."

"Come *on*."

There was a scrambling at the fence. After a moment, the first, a skinny, dusty-haired boy, pulled his way over and dropped deftly to the ground. The other, the blond-banged one, was straddling the fence when Beryl called out, "Is there something I can help you with?"

The retreat was disorderly and by no means a credit to their cause. The boy straddling the fence gave a wide-eyed look, pulled his leg back over and jumped onto the gravel and out of sight. The skinny boy gave a yelp, cried, "Don't hurt me, mum – was just trying to pay my respects, mum – don't hurt me," and backed up against the fence. His confederates were running away; their scrambling made stones fly. This boy, clearly not "Sam," for his trousers were worn and ripped, had been abandoned. He must have been nine or ten years old. Beryl thought of her nephew Charlie. He was now about as old as this scruffy child.

Beryl studied the boy. "Why would I hurt you? Now if you want to pay your respects to Sheriff Ramsay, the place to do it is at the funeral. You shouldn't go crawling behind people's houses. There's nothing respectful about that."

"No, ma'am," he snuffled. He looked at her anxiously, his eyes darting from her face to the corners of the yard, where he clearly sought escape. After a moment, he gathered courage and said in a frightened, formal voice, "I'm sorry, ma'am, for your loss."

The situation was rather pathetic, but Beryl found herself amused. "My loss is yours, I guess. He was a very good constable. But I'm not Mrs. Ramsay, you know. She's inside. And she'd be very sad if she knew you were climbing in her garden. Why don't you go quietly around the house and out the front gate. I shan't say you were here. And if anyone stops you and asks – why just say one of the ladies wanted your help getting flowers."

Relief spread over the boy's face. "You ain't her then? Oh, ma'am, I *am* glad." Then, realizing there probably wasn't something quite right about that comment, he added. "I'm sorry for thinking ta bother her, and I wouldn't want her to know."

"Nor your mother, I expect. You go along now, lad."

"Yes, ma'am," he said. He seemed rather awed by her; probably it was her English accent. He stood still for a moment and then took off his cap and bowed. After that he put his cap back on and walked very fast to the side of the house and on out to the front. He could not resist looking at the kitchen window as he passed. He must have seen the body, for his eyes widened and his pace quickened. Well, thought Beryl, he shall have his story for the papers after all.

For her part, she stood for a moment in the sunny yard with the heavy pitcher of flowers. Then she walked over to the trash bin and looked in. The flies were busy; the smell was noxious. No bloody shirts, only food scraps. She put down the flowers, took a shovel, and spread some loose dirt over the pit so the offal would not be exposed. Then she gathered the flowers up again and went into the house.

She had been busy perhaps a half an hour. The undertaker had come in the meantime; he and Mrs. Cavendar were in the kitchen now with the door closed. Beryl set the flowers on the table. Mrs. Walker looked approving; Mrs. Cavendar's daughter looked wistful. "Go on outside for a bit," said Beryl. "You've been sitting here a long time. I'll take a turn."

Rachel got up. "I'll take these rags out to dry," she said. She knew her mother would demand justification for the defection.

Mrs. Ramsay did not seem to see or smell the flowers that Beryl had brought. She remained immobile in the chair, her mouth open, her breathing coming in those strange gasps. Her pupils were still wide from the drug; she was far away.

Mrs. Walker had been making a list on a piece of paper. After Rachel went outside, she said to Beryl, "Perhaps we should pray over her. What do you think?"

Beryl could feel herself cringe. Mrs. Walker enjoyed a revivalist brand of American Protestantism that made Beryl, raised in the decorous distance of Anglicanism, uncomfortable. And while she knew how to pray for someone, she was not at all clear on how one prayed "over" someone. It was not something that she felt equipped for. "Oh – why not just read to her instead," said Beryl.

Mrs. Walker nodded agreeably. "There's a Bible over there," she said, pointing to a basket of yarns and papers next to the rocker Beryl had earlier been sitting on. Beryl got up and found a worn black volume with many strands of yarn bookmarking it like a rainbow. Written in the front cover she found the words *Mary Suzannah Wilson: her Bible. 1866. Columbia, Missouri, United States of America.* Beneath that, further down on the page was written: *"Married Alan Ramsay, Ellis County Sheriff, March 8, 1872, Hays City, Kansas. Until death do we part. First child born:"* There was nothing written after the last words. Either there had been a miscarriage or there had never been a pregnancy, and the inscription merely signified eagerness for an event that had not yet come to pass.

"She's from Missouri," said Beryl to Mrs. Walker, pointing to the inscription.

"Why so she is. I'll talk to Captain Walker; he may know how we can trace her family. Oh, read to the poor girl. I confess I can hardly bear to hear her shuddering another minute. It really is too dreadful."

Beryl sat down; she paged vaguely through the Bible until she came to Psalms. She frowned over the cramped lines of praise and woe until she thought she'd found something suitable. Quietly, she began to read:

Hear my prayer, O Lord, and let my cry come unto thee.

Hide not thy face from me in the day when I am in trouble; incline thine ear unto me; in the day when I call answer me speedily. For my days are consumed like smoke, and my bones are burned as an hearth. My heart is smitten and withered like grass; so that I forget to eat my bread. By reason of the voice of my groaning my bones cleave to my skin –

"Beryl," interrupted Mrs. Walker. "Can't you find something more uplifting?"

"Why, I don't know," said Beryl. "It's true to her state. And the psalmist does find comfort – as I hope she shall."

"Well, by all means skip to the comforting part. We have enough of the other."

Beryl sighed, squinted at the psalm, and then closed the book. "Perhaps none of them are right."

"Are you feeling well?" Mrs. Walker looked at her sharply. "Isn't the twenty-third psalm in that Bible?"

Beryl kept the book closed and refused to look at Mrs. Walker. She felt wretched for Mrs. Ramsay's sake. She didn't want to offer clichés. But a psalm is a psalm, she thought. So, she clasped her hands in prayer on her lap and, with a somewhat resigned voice, slowly recited the twenty-third psalm.

"That's better," said Mrs. Walker when she was finished. She stood up, looked over her list, and then set it on the parlor table and smoothed her gown. "I wonder if we can dress her," she said, walking to the bedroom where she stood looking speculatively at the gown on the bed. "It hardly seems decent."

"What, that she's not in mourning clothes? Does it matter? She can't go to the funeral, can she?"

"No." Mrs. Walker came back and sat down.

The women were silent. Except for the widow's strange breathing, the only sound was the ticking of a clock. It was a small noise that grew relentless as the minutes passed: time scraping at the surface of the room, at the skin of the people sitting there; a grating, maddening sensation. Beryl fidgeted. The sound reminded her of London, of ebony hands creeping across an empty face – no numbers, no hours, only blank days measuring themselves out tick by tick. Beryl gave up her earlier scruples and stared at the shattered widow. The widow stared back.

A tin fell to the floor in the kitchen. All three women started. The sound seemed to wake Mrs. Ramsay from her drugged state. Her eyes focused. She closed her mouth, then licked her dry lips. "Water," she said, her voice raspy.

Beryl got up to serve her, but Mrs. Walker was faster. She had the cup at the woman's lips before Beryl had even found the pitcher. Beryl sat back down. The widow watched her, a confused expression on her face.

"Who are you?"

"My name is Beryl Newland."

She looked at Mrs. Walker. "You I know. The busy one."

Mrs. Walker's earrings did a little dance. "It's Elizabeth Walker, Miz Ramsay, from the fort, here to take care of things. How do you feel?"

"Sick." She licked her lips again. "What happened?"

"You've been a little – beside yourself, dear. But you're better now."

"What do you mean?" The widow tried to raise her hands. Her face rearranged itself when she discovered that she was bound; not surprise, but a still, careful, vigilance came over it. "Alan?" she called.

Mrs. Walker put her arm around the woman's shoulder. "In the kitchen, my dear."

"Tell him to come here."

Mrs. Walker said, "He can't come, child."

"Why not?"

Mrs. Walker was, for once, at a loss for words. Mrs. Ramsay studied her. She then looked at Beryl, whose usually smooth face was crumpling.

"My dear," said Mrs. Walker at last, "he has died. He's gone to our Lord."

Mrs. Ramsay turned her eyes to the kitchen door. "He's gone where?"

"Why – " There was awkwardness in repeating the phrase; even Mrs. Walker felt it. "He's gone to our Lord."

Mrs. Ramsay may or may not have heard. She continued to focus on the kitchen door, watching. Waiting. Her head tipped a little to one side, slightly off center, but her eyes – they were green – remained clear and alert. Mrs. Walker exchanged a glance with Beryl and sat back down. No one said anything. Mrs. Ramsay watched the door for twenty minutes. The clock ticked. From the kitchen, the sound of movement, of low voices, came and went. Mrs. Ramsay gradually leaned forward; she seemed to be straining to hear. Her features twisted into discontent. But she did not fight her bonds and she made no noise. She just waited.

At last the door opened. The undertaker, a gray-haired gentleman named Jameson, came out first, followed by Mrs. Cavendar. She was wiping her hands on a towel. Her lips were pursed; they pulled into the toothless spaces of her mouth giving it a puckered look. Her shoulders stooped wearily, but her eyes were sharp as ever. She immediately saw that Mrs. Ramsay was awake and conscious. She put the towel on the parlor table and went and stood by her.

Mrs. Ramsay did not seem to see the people coming into the parlor; she gave all her attention to the kitchen. She still did not try to rise, just looked. Through the door, on the table, her husband lay. The quilt was beneath him now. He was dressed in a handsome black coat. Beryl recognized it from the wedding photograph. The collar of his shirt poked into the flesh under his chin. Had he been alive, he would have scratched at it, pulled it away in irritation. As it was, the only discomfort was the viewers'. He had not been shot in the face. His features were whole, though yellowy and waxen. His blonde mustache clung to his jowls, still wet from having been washed. Beryl found herself wanting to take Mrs. Cavendar's towel to dry it more thoroughly. A glistening drip trickled from the edge of the hairs and down into the constricting collar.

Mrs. Ramsay kept looking, leaning forward. Her fingers began working on the arms of the chair, curled under themselves, nails clawing. In only a few minutes the finish of the chair was scratched, the nails broken and threatening to bleed. But the widow seemed oblivious. She just kept looking and leaning. Mrs. Cavendar tried to still her clawing.

"Miz Ramsay," she said, "You stop that now. It's no good destroying your hands."

Something – perhaps it was the music of Mrs. Cavendar's voice – drew Mrs. Ramsay's attention. She pulled her gaze from the kitchen and looked at the midwife. "How?"

"He was shot, Mary."

Mrs. Ramsay stared back into the kitchen. Then, as if to herself, "They told me that. They told me that."

A long silence followed. Mr. Jameson, who had something to say, cleared his throat, uncertain whether to address the widow, Mrs. Cavendar, or Mrs. Walker. He at last settled on Mrs. Walker, who had risen expectantly.

"We can bring the coffin in, madame, and then, I think, the body will be transported to the courthouse so the town can pay its respects. Unless there's any other plan for the funeral . . . ."

"There is no other plan," said Mrs. Walker. "The minister is expected later. My husband and Deputy Enright have been spending the afternoon arranging things, I believe. I expect them soon now."

"Very well. It will take only a few minutes to remove the body; I will send to the sheriff's office for some extra hands with the work. Perhaps the deceased's wife would like to make her goodbye in that time?" He looked doubtfully at Mrs. Ramsay.

"He never listened to me," the widow whispered. "He never heard me. Always the others, never me. Why should I speak to him? He cannot hear me now. Never hear, never, ever hear. He will never hear me. He never did." She spoke to no one in particular. Maybe to herself. She was scarcely audible.

"I'll take care that she has her goodbye," said Mrs. Cavendar.

Mr. Jameson left. Mrs. Walker retreated to the bedroom, determined that now the widow should be made presentable. Mrs. Cavendar knelt next to Mrs. Ramsay and physically turned her face to her own.

"Are you feeling you'd like to go to him, lass? You needn't stay here and look from across a room. He's your own husband."

Mrs. Ramsay kept clawing the arms of the chair. The sound made Beryl's skin creep.

Mrs. Cavendar grew firmer. "Mary, if you're wishing to say goodbye, it's now you must be saying it. They'll come for him soon."

Mrs. Ramsay's green eyes remained dry and wide; she said nothing. Mrs. Cavendar's brow furrowed. She said to Beryl:

"Miss Newland, help me. I'm going to loosen the bonds; she needs to be saying her goodbyes."

Beryl obeyed Mrs. Cavendar. They undid the ropes around Mrs. Ramsay's wrists; the skin was red from being bound. They helped her stand; she leaned hard against Beryl. She was a tall woman — taller than Beryl, and much taller than Mrs. Cavendar. Her head remained tilted to one side; the strawberry-colored hair that escaped from her bun brushed into Beryl's face.

The midday sun had by now traveled to the back of the house and shone in those windows. It was around 2:00. The kitchen was small, and with the three women, the large stove, and the dead body on the table, it was crowded. A sickening sweetness hung in the air, a smell that did not come from flowers.

Mrs. Ramsay looked at the body – at the lips she had kissed and loved (that now were sunken and blue); at the hands that had traveled over her own body, cupped her breasts, and wrapped around her fingers in such glad fellowship (and that now lay cold and stiff, one on top of the other). She looked at the starched coat covering the chest where she had lain her head, the belly she had slid her hips against (the coat that hid two black holes in a lifeless hide); she stared at the long, stiff legs, trying to recognize the graceful limbs that had stretched alongside her own in bed. She studied the eyes, waiting for them to open because then perhaps she would understand the mystery of this thing; she might be able to accept that yes, this was her husband, the man who had laughed and teased and argued with her, the man who had, only the day before last, promised that once his term was up they would move from Hays to a farm and she wouldn't have to fear for him ever again. Yes, if he opened his eyes and looked at her, she would know it was him. But this dead body, that looked so familiar yet seemed so empty, that was not her husband. That could never be her husband. Her face hardened. After a few minutes she turned without speaking and, by herself and unsupported, returned to the chair in the parlor.

When Mrs. Walker approached her with the black gown, Mary Ramsay growled.

"Why, she ought not to be unloosed," said Mrs. Walker, putting down the gown. "She's not herself." Mrs. Walker bent and with great efficiency re-tied the woman's wrists to the arms of the chair. "It's for your own good, Mary," she said. Then she tucked the woman's red hair into a black cap.

The widow did not say or do anything. After a moment, her hands began their work on the unfortunate chair.

Mrs. Cavendar observed the proceedings with folded arms. "Tying a woman up like an animal. It's a mean thing to do, it is. Mother of God, forgive us."

When the men at last came – among them Captain Walker and the new sheriff – Mrs. Ramsay sat still and quiet. However, when the coffined body passed over the threshold and into the sunlight, she let out a cry. She tried to stand but was strapped down. She lifted herself by sheer force of will, bent like a hunchback under the load of the chair. Mrs. Cavendar watched her frantic straining for only an instant and then was beside her, ripping the knots from her wrists. Unbound, Mary Ramsay flew to the coffin, pushing between the startled pall bearers to reach the lid. It was not nailed down; it slid to one side, knocking and bruising the forearm of one of the men. Captain Walker tried, with his free hand, to push the widow away and almost lost hold of the coffin. The heavy body could be heard falling to one side of the box.

Mrs. Walker began to cry. Mrs. Cavendar said, "For pity's sake, put it down and let her look," but the men ignored her in their effort not to drop their load. Beryl and Rachel Cavendar coaxed and pled, trying to pull the widow from a scene that was rapidly changing from tragic to gruesome. She was stronger than they were. Mr. Jameson at last managed to pin her arms and pull her from the casket. She thrashed, her skirt tangling around her legs. The men, white faced, went on with their burden, moving fast.

As the coffin passed out under the shade trees and onto the waiting wagon, Mrs. Ramsay ceased fighting. For a moment she seemed as though she would fall to weeping, but then her face froze and her jaw dropped. The eerie scream began again, low at first and increasing in volume: unceasing, pushing against the walls and out the windows and doors of the little house. A sizable crowd was gathered in the street, some out of respect, many out of curiosity. The widow's traumatic struggle had caused great excitement, but the uncanny scream silenced them. The three children whom Beryl had seen earlier scuffled to the front of the crowd, gawking and gaping. The boy whom Beryl had spoken with, seeing her looking at him, grew shame-faced. He disappeared. The other two stayed, sucking in the scene.

In the meantime, the doctor came; he spoke to Jameson and then entered the house, angry. "Why did you women release her? She could hurt herself; she could hurt others. I have always been able to trust you, Elizabeth Cavendar. What were you thinking?" He flung his bag onto the table and opened it, rifling the contents in quest of a vial or a pill, some concoction that would silence the eerie cry.

"I tried to stop her, doctor," said Mrs. Walker.

Mrs. Cavendar gave the Captain's wife a death's-head look that chilled her speechless. Then the skull-faced midwife turned to the doctor and, her voice low under the widow's terrible descant, replied: "The woman has lost her husband, Silas Hanson. If you cannot understand that, I can. She's not an animal to be bound. He's hers, not yours. I say if she wants to burn down the house, let her. It's not for anybody else to tell her the proper way to grieve. And I'll not stay to guard your prisoner. Let that one do it. She's well suited." She gestured to Betsy Walker. "Come, Rachel."

Mrs. Cavendar took her lilac sunbonnet from the hook and tied it under her chin. She then went over and wrapped her arms lovingly around the rigid body of the widow. Mrs. Ramsay did not stop screaming. Mrs. Cavendar turned and left the house, her daughter following with a bowed head. After a moment Beryl took her jacket and quietly went after them.

The scream trailed the three women like the wail of a train whistle. Beryl heard it long after she had returned to Victoria. And that night she dreamed again of the wild huntress of the plains with her streaming hair and her cry that sang over the roar of a thousand racing buffalo. But the woman was no longer featureless. Beryl now knew that she had Mary Ramsay's face, and that under her blue cloak her gown was the color of a wild rose.

The church was not Grant's first idea for solving the problem of the young rowdies whose behavior had become the dominating spirit of the colony. Already in the summer he had begun casting about for means whereby to capture the attention of the prodigals, especially after the Fourth of July episode at Tommy Drumm's. Thirteen drunken Britons, including Will Newland, found themselves penned in the cellar after a table-splintering brawl, imprisoned by twenty equally drunken Americans who cheered that they had "whipped the English bastards again" and who insisted that they would never release them until they agreed to sing the "Star Spangled Banner" (an intolerable, impossible, term of release for any loyalist — and all the prisoners were, in their own words, "deshperately loyal," ready to die at a word on the glorious field of battle, even if the field was no better than "Tommy's shit-stinking wine shellar"). Judge Reeder, a local celebrity coming in for refreshment after some hot speechifying, found the saloon a shambles; agreed to intervene on behalf of peaceful Anglo-American relations; determined that all should sing the song of each nation in turn; and ended by seeing the Saxons and Yanks hugging each other, neither camp able to conjure a word or a tune (so fuzzy had their thinking become between booze and bruises) but all able to agree that they were "damn goo' fellas," that they "shoulden' never fight nowhere against sush goo' fellas."

The next day Drumm came to Grant with a damage bill of two hundred dollars. "These boys may be what you call gentlemen, sir," he said, "but they're bringing down the high tone of my place, and I won't have it."

Grant said little. There were limits on how much one could chastise grown men. He took one of his long rides, racing Lord Clyde over hills and across great stretches of grass, walking him through contented herds of sheep and standing with him in still creek bottoms. He at last convinced himself that the lads suffered from an excess of the sporting instinct and that the thing to do was to harness their energies by donating land on the east side of Victoria for the construction of a track for racing horses. Let them enjoy some of the pleasures they missed from home. "Ascot on the Plains," he said.

"Ascot, indeed," said Sarah Baldwin, punching her fist into the bread dough when she heard of the scheme. "Just see you keep your horses and your money at home on the ranch, Mr. Baldwin." She'd become rather dour during the three years in Kansas. The near drowning of her smallest son during a picnic at Mr. Cabot's had swept the smiling from her eyes forever. She believed in her husband, she even believed in the promise of this land, but she had no faith in the young men of Victoria and little more in Mr. Grant. "A more negligent, thoughtless lot I've never seen. How Mr. Grant can think that running horses around in a circle of dirt is going to promote better behavior I can't understand."

"I think he's just wantin' to keep them all under his eyes. The devil you can see is easier to fight than the devil you can't. If they're in Victoria, in his reach, I think he's hopin' to influence them. After all, horse racing is a gentleman's sport. If they're not drinkin', there should be no untowardness."

"It's teaching my sons to gamble, it is. What honor is there in that?" Mrs. Baldwin came from staunch Scotch-Calvinist stock. She could not see the sense of Grant's plan. "You just see that you stay at home, Mr. Baldwin."

He did, but few of the other colonists could resist attending so diverting an event. Everyone had their favorite horse, their darling pride, their worthy mount just waiting to prove its glory by winning the owner a hundred pounds or a prize hog. So, after a fashion, Mr. Grant's plan did lure the idle British boys home again where, in the sight of the ladies, they found they rather enjoyed behaving themselves. Grant's venture also lured many Americans to the site, some from as far away as Salina. The races, held every other Tuesday, earned a feature column in the *Hays City Sentinel*, where the doings were narrated with great drama and exaggeration. Beryl sent clippings of these articles back to England, inspiring Marian to write,

> *"Oh, Beryl, it all sounds quite dashing, but could Mr. Spenser's 'Nellie' really be the greatest steed in all Anglo-Saxondom? And if that wasn't rather overstated, I must say that we haven't seen in <u>The Times</u> that Victoria outdoes Denver, Kansas City, <u>and</u> St. Louis in refined entertainments. Robert says that if it is so, New York and Boston must be positively quaking at the prospect of such competition. He also says that he wishes Will would back the plough a little more and Mr. Avery's filly a little less. He refuses to send any more money to pay racing debts. You are not betting, are you? It's hardly respectable. They say that Lady Jennings lost £5,000 on a horse once; her husband wouldn't speak to her for a week. But that's possibly because he lost so much more. Her horse came in well ahead of his."*

Beryl did not bet on the horses. But she did attend the races. She sat on a white pony (now much more at home in the saddle than three years before, she straddled the creature like a man even in public) along with a line of other women – Mrs. Randall, Miss Grant, Mrs. Hunter, Mrs. Witley, and Lord Petrie's wife Angelina. Sometimes Mrs. Walker and Mrs. Tyler joined them from Fort Hays, and once the Irish midwife came, made jokes about the men preening themselves on their horses, and caused the ladies much merriment.

"Hie there, you're making the horses skittish," hollered Mr. Grant impatiently at them.

"Are we now?" said Mrs. Cavendar. She walked, businesslike, to the front of the box which had been constructed for him near the stands (or what passed for them, three rising levels of wooden benches on a crude platform) where he stood amid ribbons and pomp. Blair, her brown sheepdog, followed her, snapping at spectators' ankles as they went. "Well now, Mr. Grant," she said, "I must say you're a might skittish yourself, if you're gettin' your nose outta joint over the joy of a few women whose only entertainment is watching boys gad about atop poor tired beasts who'd just as soon be eating grass in the shade as hauling lunks about on their back in the heat o' the day. Are you afraid we'll see that you've nothing more important to do in a world of sorrow and starvation than to spur a gorgeous animal down a dirt road for the mere sake of makin' yourself feel big? Look at these young bloods out here riding in pink coats instead o' working with their sleeves rolled up like real men. Ah, they make a fine picture. But maybe it's them as is spooked by women's laughter, not the horses? Tsk. The poor dears."

"May I ask, madame, why you trouble yourself to attend a spectacle that so obviously offends you?" His tone was courtly, but irritation made his whiskers twitch.

"Why, for the pleasure of visiting with these fine ladies." She turned and bowed to them. Her dog gave a yap. "And I've got $20 on Mrs. Witley's 'Paris,' o' course. A woman has a right to win her living you know. Wouldn't bet on your animal," she said, gesturing toward Lord Clyde, whom Ben Davis was preparing to mount. "Too undisciplined. Like the whole crew: un-dis-ci-plined. If you don't break 'em right, you can't expect 'em to turn out winners after the fact. Mark my words." She looked up at him. The lines around his eyes were weary, and suddenly her shrewd, pert face became kind. "So I wouldn't waste my money and my life trying, Mr. Grant. I would not."

"I say, could we vacate the track for the race?" called Mr. Edwards.

Elizabeth Cavendar turned to Grant's secretary and gave an exaggerated curtsy. Then, lifting her cotton skirt like a fine lady keeping her silk out of the mud, she rejoined the crowd of women on their ponies. After a moment, the sheepdog reluctantly followed her. Mrs.

Walker, nursing an active hostility since the incident at Mrs. Ramsay's, shook her head in disdain at the midwife's behavior and made a point of cantering to the other side of Angelina Petrie (who was her current favorite because she alone of all the British women could boast an actual title). The others, though, seemed amused. Mr. Grant was much respected among them, however they might judge the other men, but the freedom of Mrs. Cavendar's speech was always intoxicating. She spurned convention; it seemed absurd to judge her by the usual standards. Her unwomanly words were like a cutting winter wind; crisp, direct, blowing the air clean and clear. The music in them was sometimes piercing, but the notes always rang true.

If Mrs. Walker glowered, Mrs. Witley sparkled. "She bets on my horse? I should bet on her any day!" she said to Beryl. "What a splendid woman."

Beryl wondered at Mrs. Witley's admiration, not so much surprised that Mrs. Cavendar's directness might earn the esteem of women who only dreamed of speaking as she spoke, but struck that it should be the exquisite Mrs. Witley, so much the master of her words and her body, who was captivated.

"She's very strong," said Beryl, somewhat equivocally.

"You don't like her?" asked Cynthia. "I should think you would."

"Why?"

"My dear, you speak the same language." Cynthia laughed and gazed pointedly at Beryl's gloved fingers, knotted in the reins of pony. "You talk with your hands, and she does with her tongue. But you say the same thing. I've never heard music speak the way it does when you play."

"I don't understand," said Beryl.

Mrs. Witley studied her and then said after a minute. "It's passion, my dear, and truth. But I suppose it is possible you don't realize what you say. That woman does." She nodded, facing her fine features back to the track. "I hope Paris wins. I shall get great satisfaction out of giving Mistress Cavendar her winnings."

"Passion!" thought Beryl. Aloud she said lightly, "Well I hope I have better manners."

"Not particularly," said Mrs. Witley, raising her eyebrows and glancing at Beryl's stockinged calves. "But that hardly matters to me. I think you and your brother both worry about your manners rather too much. If William would open his collar and unbutton his shirt, so to speak, he'd be quite delightful. He's such a charming boy. I do adore him. And he'd feel so much better."

Beryl stiffened, a hot flush rising along her neck. She couldn't think how to reply. She thought of her brother's miserable passion for this woman and felt something akin to hate. At last she said, "He does quite well to keep his shirt buttoned, Mrs. Witley. Especially in this place, where there are so few checks on a man's – or a woman's – decency."

"Decency!" exclaimed Mrs. Witley, her long-lashed eyes widening. "Was I speaking of decency? Heavens! You Newlands are so deadly earnest!" She laughed her low, trilling laugh. "It must be your belief in God. William told me you were trying to make him a preacher – poor boy! Well, I gave up God years ago and I've been much more cheerful since. You should read Swinburne; he understands. '*Thou hast conquered, pale Galilean, / The world has grown grey from thy breath.*' Ah, now you're shocked, I can see. But then this explains why you find Mr. Spenser so attractive: it's his faith, its wonderful smoke and incense and statues! All flame and shadow . . . . There now, don't protest, we can all see you're taken with him. I've even heard you are going to his church. He is of course very romantic, in a dark way. At least I've always thought so." She laughed again, then whistled to her horse. "Ah, there's Arthur. I must inspire him to win. Goodbye!"

She rode away before Beryl could answer. She was an accomplished horsewoman, moving gracefully across the field to where Arthur Witley sat upon Paris at the starting line. Will Newland was there with Mr. Avery and Mr. Randall. Once Beryl was able to see – her anger was blinding – she saw Mrs. Witley slide from her horse and tap Arthur on his boot. After giving her brother-in-law what seemed to be very particular advice, she turned to Will. She took his right arm into both her hands, looked teasingly up into his face, and laughed. Mrs. Witley was most inclined to speak her mind to women, that was clear. She had other ways of communicating with men. Will's expression was startled, elated; he was taken off guard. He started to speak but stopped and flushed. Randall, observing, did say something and it must have been unpleasant, for both Will and Mrs. Witley looked at him angrily. Mr. Avery touched Randall on the shoulder and spoke. Randall said something else – the harsh tenor of the words, if not their meaning, traveled as far as the stands – and shook off Avery's hand. Then Mr. Edwards was urging the spectators away from the track for the beginning of the race.

Lydia, who had heard some of the exchange between Beryl and Mrs. Witley, watched the scene between her husband and the others with evident anxiety. "There's trouble," she whispered to Mrs. Hunter.

Julia had not been paying attention. "What do you mean?"

Lydia shook her head and said no more. She put her arm around her tow-headed son, who looked at her curiously from his perch on the horn of her saddle.

Mrs. Tyler knew what Lydia meant. After a moment she quietly asked, "You and your husband know Mrs. Witley well?"

"Yes, I suppose."

"She's beautiful. Always creating a drama for herself and those around her, isn't she?" Cassandra Tyler's tone was not critical – she rarely criticized – but it was thoughtful. "She plays people like a fiddle."

Mrs. Cavendar, who had her arm through Mrs. Tyler's, said, "My mother used to tell o' fairies that made toys of people's souls. Their beauty gave them great power. That one is like that. But she's no fairy. Quite human. And running hard." The others looked at her. The midwife's dark eyes were wise in the sun bonnet.

"I don't know," said Lydia, barely able to speak. "But something is wrong. Something is always wrong." She looked at Beryl's angry face and the sober expressions of the women beside her. Then, in spite of her best efforts, the words spilled over her lips: "I hate it here. I do hate it."

A pistol shot tore the air. The handsome animals, released at last, streaked down the prairie as though the devil was at their heels.

On Sunday morning, Vincent Spenser and his brother Bernard came for Beryl at the Newland estate. She stood on the porch waiting for them, wearing a blue gown and a brown cloak. The fall air was crystalline. The grass was stiff with frost. Beryl's breath hung visible in the cold. Her hands were wrapped in a fur muff; the hidden fingers twisted nervously, but her grey eyes were calm.

When the carriage came and Vincent got out to help her in, the front door of the house opened, and William stood watching. His hair was uncombed and fell unkempt across his high brow; his shirt was open. Mrs. Witley would not have revised her wish for a less mannerly Will Newland had she seen him. He was strikingly hand-some, squinting out at the cold sun. His face was haggard, however, and unfriendly. He greeted the Spenser brothers shortly, then said to Beryl, "You're sure about this?"

Beryl was embarrassed and angry. They had quarreled over her decision to attend Catholic mass at the German community for over an hour the night before. But that was how it was with her brothers, she thought; she could argue herself blue and they never would ac-cept that she knew her own mind. She flushed as Vincent helped her onto the seat next to Bernard. When the lap robe was well tucked around her, she turned her face to Will and said, "I shall be back after dinner. There are fresh eggs on the table for your breakfast." That was all. Will scowled. The horses started and the carriage moved away on the slippery ground.

For a few minutes, Beryl said nothing. She felt shy alone with the Spenser brothers, chagrined at her brother's behavior and cold in the bright morning. Her feet were numb in her boots. Bernard, who was driving, chuckled cheerfully to the horses. Vincent was silent and watched the passing autumn landscape with a grave expression. The frost had dulled the harvest color of the foliage along the creek, but it made the leaves and branches sparkle. The sky was turquoise, clear in all directions. Crows cawed. Beryl felt the familiar swelling in her chest that morning in this place so often brought. She became absorbed by the distant sight of ducks – or perhaps geese, she wasn't sure which – soaring south in a great V. The group sometimes broke; occasionally some staggered; but the formation held. There was al-ways a coming back together, a dedication to purpose that allowed the flock to surge forward as one. She heard their calls far away. The sight and sounds of the dawning day allowed her to forget that she was participating in what she would have once considered an unthinkable, even despicable, act. Her personal prejudices and problems seemed very small in that landscape. She was not sorry to see them shrink.

The Spenser brothers chatted together quietly, leaving her to her thoughts. She did not really listen, caught up as she was in the morning, but then the drift of their conversation struck her, and she was brought down from the sky like a shot fowl.

"What did you say?"

Bernard looked at her, his placid English features startled awake by the urgency of her tone. "Only that they say she's died out there."

"I'm sorry – who has died out where?"

"Why the wife of the former sheriff. Ramsay. The law man murdered last June. Drumm says the woman lost her mind altogether when he was killed. The doctor sent her out east to Leavenworth, near Kansas City. Committed her to an asylum there. Thought it might do her some good. But she's died."

Beryl's face blanched. Her eyes grew brittle, the irises like smoky chipped glass. Vincent touched her arm in concern. "You didn't know the woman, did you?"

Beryl sat back and stared out at a sky suddenly gone gray. "I met her once," she said. "Just once." And she said no more.

Chapter XII

The child, an eight-year-old named Franz Braun, was killed by lightning as he sat on a horse that was being led home by his older brother. Because of the heat, the body needed to be buried quickly. The family had no money. Beryl heard from Julia Hunter that the German community was coming together as best it could to provide a decent burial, but that not a lot could be spared on the dead when the living needed so much. The lost graves of the Seth children had never ceased to haunt Beryl. Despite Keith's protestation, they had never been marked after the great fire, nor, she suspected, had anyone ever attempted to find the site. The thought of any child being buried among those barren hills, alone and forgotten, made her ache.

She went to Vincent Spenser. And, because there was little she asked for that he did not seek to give, the finest coffin in Pettimore's stock (Pettimore had taken to building them in his spare time from scraps of his best lumber) and a boy's suit from an establishment in Hays was quickly sent to Herzog, along with money for masses. The Germans did not take easily to anything that seemed like charity, but the boy's mother wept for joy and grief at the gifts. She wished to have the child photographed in his finery, but his face was blackened and in the heat the body swelled quickly. No memorial picture of that corpse, dear though it was to the parents, could offer solace. So, less than twenty-four hours after he'd been killed, the third-born son of the Brauns was buried next to the newly constructed church, one of the first Germans to lie in Kansas earth.

Beryl sat in a buggy, watching the spectacle with Vincent Spenser. She felt smothered by the presence of loss. The black scarves of the women formed triangles of sorrow over bent backs and hunched shoulders. Men stood hatless, their weary faces shiny from heat and grief. Children looked frightened. Their eyes were wide. That Franz's soul was in heaven with Mary and Joseph and even Jesus was no comfort. All they knew of their friend was his body, and that had become something terrifying, something to be thrust into the ground and out of sight as quickly as possible, like a mangled bird or a poisoned dog.

All the oppression of heat and fear and sorrow seemed to come together in a guttural hymn-singing that to Beryl, who could not understand the words, spoke less of hope than of resignation. She prayed that God might actually be more merciful than He had shown Himself to these parents, to this community; she prayed that He might give them His comfort; she prayed that she might not lose her ability to believe in His benevolence. The latter was becoming more difficult. As she grew older in this place, she seemed always to be seeing the skull beneath the face of joy. Something hissed to her that moments of beauty were accidents, that hours and days of pain were the norm. She prayed for mercy.

Then, above the doleful hymn, a descant rose, sweet and sudden. It startled Beryl from her reverie, and she turned.

A man stood at the edge of the assembled mourners. The man was not tall. He was compactly built, his features pleasing but unremarkable, his hair long and sandy. His eyes were strikingly pale, however, against the summer brown of his face. They reminded Beryl of the silver eyes of a husky she had once seen at Fort Hays. They were lowered much of the time, focusing on the strings of a violin that was tucked under his lightly bearded chin. He drew a bow over and across those strings. The grace of the movement made the wand seem part of his body, the action as simple as the raising of his arm or the lifting of his hand. His fingers, brown and calloused from work, played gently on the neck of the instrument. The hymn ended on a plaintive chord, but the violin seemed unable to stop singing. It seemed to go on even after the man lowered his bow. It contended against whirling dust for the last word.

When she turned to face forward again, the solemn procession of the pall bearers, the Latin incantations of the priest, the swaying of the censor, and the clicking of the mourners' beads no longer seemed strange under that scorching sky. They were the necessary accompaniment to revelation. The boy's father gave a cry of anguish as the dirt began to fall and Beryl felt her pity add poignance to something that she could not name but that she sensed had nothing to do with death and nothing to do with sorrow.

In a few minutes the subdued crowd began to move away from the grave. Spenser put on his hat and turned the buggy around.

"Who was that man?" she asked. Hot wind pushed the black veil against her lips.

Spenser did not need to ask whom she meant. "Anton Vonfeldt," he said. "The boy's cousin. He was in the band that played last October at the Gunther celebration."

"Oh," she said. "I hadn't remembered." But she knew she was not likely to forget again.

A young Volga-German musician, no matter how talented, would easily have been eclipsed at the party celebrating the coming of the Gunther brothers to Victoria. Neither the U.S. press nor the colony's founder could exaggerate enough the significance of these additions to Grant's community. The sons of the mayor of New York City seemed to command almost as much attention in America as Prince Edward did at home, or so it seemed to Beryl. Titles didn't impress her in England; status in the United States impressed her even less. She listened to Betsy Walker's excited speculations about where they would settle, and how soon they would visit the Fort, until she decided that she'd rather spend the chilly afternoons at home reading *Bleak House* for the seventh time. But Mrs. Walker merely reflected the enthusiasm of the Kansas newspapers which, dazzled that such celebrities should decide to take up raising cattle with the British aristocrats (who, one reporter insisted, would "soon learn the only real men are Yankees"), could not get over bragging about their coming.

Mr. Grant provided no relief from the euphoria. Somehow the coming of these Americans seemed to validate his project in a way that the emigration of all the younger sons of England could not. He talked incessantly about the recognition their coming would bring to Victoria in the eastern American cities, and how more wealthy young Americans might thereby be encouraged to join the enterprise. Money mattered. While many of the British emigrants were well off financially, an equally large number were younger sons in aristocratic families whose wealth had last been a reality (rather than just the illusion of a crumbling ancestral home) in the eighteenth century, or even earlier. Blood Victoria had in plenty. Money was not always so evident. And despite sanguine promises to the contrary, hard work was making very few of the emigrants wealthy – a reality possibly explained by the failure of many of the emigrants to put as much faith in hard work as they did in hard play.

In any case, the Gunther brothers, Michael and John, were fêted at a great gala at the Grant mansion. The good-looking red heads, aged 18 and 20, were treated to a night of dancing and drinking, eating and revelry, amidst the elite of Victoria and Hays society. The men were in full evening dress or military regalia. The women's gowns were exquisite. Only a few were out-of-date enough for the Gunther brothers to remark upon them before Cynthia Witley's entrance in a provocative décolleté ballgown. A seductive drapery of garnet shimmering with silk butterflies, the dress and its owner captivated the young heroes for the rest of the evening. The music, provided by local musicians, was surprisingly acceptable to New York ears, and waltzing couples spun for hours, turning the drawing rooms into a dizzying carousel. At one a.m., the dining room opened to reveal an overflow of exotic fare: French cuisine, compliments of Mount Halcyon; Indian dishes prepared by Spenser's cook Tabermann; and German-Russian food made by the women of Herzog. The roasts were succulent, the curries piquant, and the pastries laced in butter and cream and fruit. Champagne sparkled; the wine glowed ruby. The coming out for Meg which had been ruined by locusts two years earlier was in some measure atoned for here. The very air seemed intoxicating, sparkling with all the glory of the British empire and all the allure of the American West. The Gunther brothers breathed deep and with great satisfaction.

They received, of course, a very unreal impression of life in Victoria.

Drunk on attention and punch, the New Yorkers noted fashion faux pas and "western" slips in correct hospitality, but they were happily oblivious to the undercurrent of tension, of things gone and going wrong, that ran through the laughter and dancing and feasting like a subtle poison. Those who had lived in Victoria for any length of time were less lucky; they sensed the spreading toxin with uneasy dread. And George Grant, who played host with all the grace of a king, felt it slide into his pleasure like a paralysis.

Meg, now eighteen, wore her hair braided into a simple chignon that shone against the midnight blue of her gown. She wore a solitary strand of pearls. She laughed unaffectedly and enjoyed herself in a sensible fashion, neither eating nor drinking too much, and taking the flattery of men with a heavy dose of disbelief. There was still much of the child about her, however; she was not quite effective at putting off unwanted attentions. And that evening the attentions were coming from an unanticipated quarter. Nigel Wyatt haunted her like a ghost, clinging to her shadow, turning his pink rabbit eyes upon her earthy brown ones until she became flustered. He insisted on filling half of her dance card, leaving one of the Gunther brothers to ask Ian Duncan if it was true that the Grant heiress was as good as spoken for by the youngest Mr. Wyatt. Duncan's big shoulders and curly black head heaved indignantly at the suggestion, and the innocent Gunther for a moment thought the Scot would strike him. Duncan merely growled, however, that "Miss Grant would never look so low." But as the evening wore on Duncan noted that Meg good-naturedly bore Nigel's attentions and thought that she even seemed to be enjoying them. During one particularly melting waltz, Duncan felt sure that Nigel presumed. After they separated, he approached her.

"Miss Grant, you'll not be spending the entire evening with that lowbrow, will you?"

Meg, flushed with the warmth of dancing, turned stunned eyes on him. "Whatever do you mean, Ian Duncan?"

"I mean your uncle will be none too pleased if he hears what I'm hearing and sees what I'm seeing."

She felt that he had struck her. "But you've seen and heard nothing. I've done nothing but be polite. Which is more than you have done. At least Mr. Wyatt is not insulting." Her eyes filled and she hurried into the crowd, leaving Duncan certain that he did much better keeping company with the residents of the stable. He sought the sympathy of a laboring cow for the rest of the evening.

Meg sought out Beryl, who was resting on a bench in a small parlor where drinks and light sandwiches waited to refresh the guests. She was absently running her finger around the edge of a champagne glass. When Meg sat next to her, she smiled welcome. Meg smiled wanly in return and said, "My head hurts."

"Are you unwell?"

"Just tired from everything. I suppose I shall have to go find Uncle George in a few minutes. I'll be walking into dinner with him. Who will you be with?"

"I don't know. I haven't really thought about it." She glanced at her dance card. "Mr. Avery perhaps, or Mr. Spenser. Or maybe William. Have you seen him?"

"Not for a while. He was dancing with Mrs. Witley. They look very well together."

"I'm sure Mrs. Witley looks well with everyone."

"She's so beautiful," said Meg with a trace of wistfulness. "But that must be rather a bother. So many men wanting your attention, and not knowing how to get rid of them."

"Mrs. Witley seems quite able to control the gentlemen. And I suppose her husband can control them if she can't."

"Assuming he wants to," said Lydia Randall, who had joined them. The dislike was thick in her voice. Beryl reached her hand out to the woman in the soft yellow gown.

A crowd of men broke before the doorway as Mrs. Witley herself came in. On one arm was the younger Mr. Gunther, on the other Mr. Randall. Both of them were absorbed by her remarks; all three laughed heartily. Randall offered her a drink, which she took with an uncharacteristic giggle. She had had quite a bit to drink. Beryl did not like to think she was drunk, but a certain recklessness rouged her customary allure.

"Mr. Randall, you are so kind." Cynthia Witley took the glass, touching his fingers. Her words were commonplace; the invitation in them was not. Butterflies shimmered along her shoulder.

"I can never be kind enough, my lady."

Lydia stiffened and dropped Beryl's hand, but Beryl only noticed the expression on Will's face. He had followed the trio in and stood against the doorframe. He was a beefy red from too much wine; his hair was tousled from perpetually running his hands through it. He did not drink often now, but when he did it was terrible. "He will kill her," thought Beryl with sudden fear. "My God, he will kill her."

She rose swiftly and walked over to the table. "Mrs. Witley, how wonderful to see you! Do join me. It's been so long since we've had a chance to chat with each other. Let these men go off and amuse themselves by talking about horses. I'm sure Mr. Randall has all manner of advice for Mr. Gunther." Even to herself, Beryl's voice sounded tinny.

Cynthia Witley's eyes widened. She had no illusions about Beryl's feelings towards her. Something swept over that small, lovely face, an image slid too quickly in and out of a stereoscope to be clear. Perhaps it was contempt, perhaps relief; Beryl was not sure. But she did not care. She reached out and took Cynthia's arm, drawing the small woman from the half embrace of her companions. She did not look at either Mr. Randall or Mr. Gunther; she did not care what they thought of her intrusion. "Come and sit with me, Mrs. Witley. Now how is that charming Pekinese of yours?"

Cynthia settled herself on the bench, arranging her dress in becoming folds. When she looked up, she saw Will glaring at her. She smiled and said to his sister, "The poor thing died three weeks ago. Surely you heard."

"Oh no, did he? How very sad. But your husband will be sure to get you another."

"Hmmm," said Cynthia. Will walked, a little unsteadily, to the table and picked up a silver spoon. "And how is your pony doing?"

"Oh – they had to shoot him. The ankle was broken, you know."

"No, I didn't. How very sad." Will picked up a fork, and then stood motionless, watching the women. "But your brother will be sure to get you another."

"I have already found one on my own. Douglas Keith advised me."

"Did he? Such a fine man. You must be very glad to have him for a special friend."

"He's a special friend to all of us, Mrs. Witley."

Meg listened to their exchange, faintly sickened by the turbulence under seemingly still waters. "Isn't it a lovely evening?" she said struggling for balance. "Mrs. Witley, I do wish you and Beryl would sing and play for us. You make such lovely music together."

"Don't we though?" said Beryl. The raven braiding of her hair glistened as she inclined her head. She looked toward Will and her grey eyes glowed green in the gaslight. "But not tonight, Meg. Mr. Grant has other musicians here this evening. We will just enjoy them, and not draw attention to ourselves."

Cynthia Witley rose as her husband sauntered into the room smoking a cigar. "You'll excuse me, ladies, Mr. Witley has come to take me to dinner. So delightful to see you again, Miss Newland."

"The pleasure is always mine, Mrs. Witley. I only regret that our chat has been so short."

"I'm sure you do." Mrs. Witley's irony was delicately nuanced and not entirely unfriendly. She seemed more amused than anything as she took her husband's arm. "Good night, Miss Grant." She did not look toward Will as she glided away.

"We understand each other," Beryl thought. "And Meg understands neither of us." She glanced up at Lydia, wondering what she was thinking, only to discover she had gone. Mr. Randall and Mr. Gunther, too, were nowhere in sight. Will was glowering at the plate of sandwiches, leaning against the table and looking as though he might vomit or burst into tears at any moment. James Avery came into the room with Vincent Spenser.

"We've come to claim our dances, Miss Newland," said Avery preening the collar of his green evening jacket like a peacock. "And I think I have the pleasure first." He reached gallantly for her hand.

She took it, but clasped it very hard and looked meaningly at him. "Mr. Avery, I do think Will could use some – companionship. Would you be so good as to – ?" She wasn't quite able to finish the question.

If she had asked him to sleep in a bed of rattlesnakes, he'd have done it.

But he couldn't help thinking, as he took the silverware from Will's limp hand and Miss Newland walked into the ballroom with Vincent Spenser, that it would have been jolly nice if Spenser had been Will's best friend and if Avery had been the dark, handsome drunkard whom his sister seemed to prefer. He himself hadn't been drunk in three years. Much good had it done him. He sighed and bit off half a sandwich glumly before leading Will outside for some fresh air.

Meg watched them all leave and sat brooding for a while on the bench. Cabot saw her there, fetched her some lemonade, and joined her.

"Miss Grant? Do entertain me. Those barn boys, Davis and Mason, are debating whether importing sparrows will keep insects from eating an orchard. I am bored to tears and there's not a pretty lass in sight except you. But you look as though you've been spooked, child. What ghosts are you seeing?"

She shrugged her shoulders. "Oh, no ghosts. But everything seems so tangled sometimes." Nigel Wyatt entered as she spoke and walked expectantly toward her. "Well, maybe one ghost," she muttered.

Cabot glanced at Wyatt, raised his eyebrows, and then lifted her gloved fingers to his elbow in a proprietary way. His golden hair shone; he's such a lovely man, thought Meg, shivering a little as she stood. Nigel came to claim his dance, but Mr. Cabot shook his head.

"I regret, Mr. Wyatt, that Miss Grant is feeling a bit tired and has asked me to escort her to her uncle before we all go to dinner. She is obliged to sit out this dance. But I'm sure you can find another young lady eager to do a reel with you. One from Hays City perhaps. If you'll excuse us, sir?"

Nigel bowed with bland politeness as Meg left with Mr. Cabot. But a purple flush crawled from his collar all the way up into his thin, pale hair. He would not forgive Cabot's scarcely veiled reference to the redlight district in front of Miss Grant; he added it to the long list of affronts that he had suffered since coming to Victoria. He collected and preserved these wrongs, letting them simmer in the back of his mind over a white flame that occasionally flared. But when the blood drained from his face, he faded back again into the paneling of the room. And it would have taken a keen observer to spot the evil flicker of light that energized the man, that kept him from disappearing into the shadows completely and from being swallowed by them forever.

Peach juice ran over her hands until the knife was slippery and even the most timid flies could not resist trying to settle on her knuckles and wrist. The air smelled sweet, but the work was loathsome. The great sparrow experiment had saved the fruit trees at Spenser's farm, as Garth Mason had contended it would, but it had not kept insects from invading the fruit. Beryl was not sure how grateful she was for Mr. Spenser's generosity when she saw she must cut away three quarters of each peach in order to remove the bad spots and, worse, slice out the worms. At first she had resisted the job, but she discovered that if she embraced an inner ferocity and let her eyes lose focus so she couldn't really see the dark patches, she was almost able to ignore the way the sweetness crawled.

Meg absolutely refused to touch them and stuck close to the great kettle where the salvageable remnants stewed, bubbled, and spit sugar. Sweat poured down her freckled neck, but she preferred that to cleaning the fruit. "I'll never be able to eat the jam if I look at the bugs. You just let me stir."

So, Beryl let her stir and squinted at the directions Mrs. Baldwin had scrawled for her on a bit of paper. She glanced at the bucket and a half of peaches still waiting to be cleaned and sighed. It was all very well, running a home on the frontier, but she was beginning to think that preserves from the shelves of Hunter's store, no matter how expensive, were infinitely preferable to the work entailed in canning. Mr. Spenser had offered to have his cook prepare the fruit for her, but she insisted that she needed to know how to do such things. Well, now she knew, and she was not happy. Another bubble of peach lava exploded over the stove, and Meg jumped back. "I do think we'd do better if we put on the lid," she said.

"You can't stir with the lid on. Just keep at your business, lassie. And here's some more fruit for your pot." Beryl added a bowl of syrupy chunks to the rose-gold brew.

The job would have been easier if the day had not been so hot, but all the days of the summer had been hot and there was no counting on the next day of coolness. Thunderstorms roared over the land frequently, pouring sheets of rain onto the fields, so there was no fear of drought. But the storms never broke the heat, and humidity made the air thick to breathe. Cooking and washing became purgatorial. Only Meg's company reconciled Beryl to the task before her.

She let her knife tear open the fuzzy surface of another peach. "So they are really leaving?"

"That's what Ben and Ian say. Ben says they thought they could just come out and hunt buffalo and the wheat would take care of itself. Well, the buffalo are played out and wheat won't grow like magic. They are very nice lads, both of them, but I don't believe they ever really wanted to farm. 'Twas some notion of their father's."

"But what have they been doing all this time? And what about their land?"

"Mr. Edwards says they never even made the initial payment. Uncle George was so pleased to have them come, and their father is so respectable, that the entire transaction was carried forward on faith."

"Whatever have they been doing with their time?"

"Same as all the ones who don't want to farm or ranch do out here." She didn't need to elaborate: Beryl knew what that meant. "Oh, and did you know they were gone to Colorado for several weeks? Went hunting in the mountains. Actually, one of them – Michael, I think – is considering trying for banking work in Denver. Ian says it would be a good choice. Neither of them is much hand at hard toil, but he says they are smart, in a Yankee sort of way."

Beryl wiped her forehead with her sleeve and looked out at the shimmering bluffs where the figures of men working could just be made out. "And Mr. Grant?"

"He never says very much to me about business, but of course you can see he's not happy with them. I mean, they weren't here much longer than six months. 'Twasn't much of an effort."

"No," said Beryl. "They haven't even seen a harvest."

"On their land, there'd have been no harvest."

The women were silent for a few minutes. Meg settled her spoon and bent to the wood box to put more fuel on the fire. The inferno flamed her face; she shut the stove door with a slam. "Beastly day for such a chore."

"Is Mr. Wyatt still coming by?"

"Uhmm – sometimes."

"Do you like him, Meg?"

"What is there to like?"

"I don't know. I was hoping that you'd tell me."

Meg looked irritated. "The man comes and sits in my uncle's parlor, and I don't know what people expect me to do about it. His brothers are nice enough, and at least none of those Wyatt men are afraid of work. Their farm is looking better than most; Mr. Wyatt took me to see it after the picnic last week. But just because he wants to be my suitor doesn't mean that I'm ready for a shivaree. He passes the time. Not always agreeably. But there he is."

"Maggie," said Beryl setting her hands against the bowl, "your uncle surely can't approve your being courted by such a man."

"He trusts me not to be foolish. Which is more than some others." Beryl took it as a reproof to her, but actually Meg was glowering at the image of Ian Duncan, crossing his beefy arms at her from behind the horns of a great bull.

"Well, you've always been a sensible girl."

"And you and Mr. Spenser?"

"I like him. But I will never marry a man who drinks. Never ever."

"Oh." Meg watched Beryl's lips purse over her work. "Does he know that?" Beryl didn't answer. The flies circled her head, impatient but persistent. "Do you like being alone?"

"I'm not alone. I have Will."

"That's not what I meant."

"I'm not unhappy."

Meg didn't know how to proceed. Beryl could be stubborn.

A voice called from outside. "Beryl!"

Beryl put down her knife and covered the bowl of peaches with cheesecloth. She gathered the corners of a towel from underneath a pile of pits and rejected fruit, turning it into a great bag and carrying it to the door. "What, Will?"

"I say, do come and meet our new help. Spenser's recommendation."

"Just a minute." She went out into the glaring sun and crossed the yard to the chicken coop. There she tossed her sticky load over the ground to the initial dismay and ultimate delight of the hens. She washed her hands at the pump and rinsed the towel. After hanging it over a post, she walked to a small group of men gathered in the shade of the stable.

Will stood beside Vincent Spenser, Red Thompson, and a young man in a straw hat. Will was looking pleased, Vincent was looking pleased, and Thompson was chewing tobacco with patent satisfaction. The young man was drinking a dipper of water; his back was turned, and Beryl could not immediately see if he, too, looked pleased. But it was a relief to her to see Will smiling.

"Here she is," said Will.

The young man placed the dipper back in the barrel and turned. There were those strikingly pale eyes – blue as it turned out, even lighter than the sky. The man looked at her and smiled. He, too, seemed pleased.

Vincent took her by the elbow. "Miss Newland, this is Anton Vonfeldt, one of the Russians from Herzog. Your brother was saying he could use a good hand. Bernard and I have had none finer, and we thought we could spare him to you and Will for the rest of the season." Then Vincent spoke in German. The young man replied, nodded, and reached his hand out to her.

She took it briefly. "But this is the musician?"

Spenser spoke to the young man. Vonfeldt listened and then laughed out loud. Beryl had never seen anyone laugh the way he laughed. He tilted his head back so that the hat threatened to fall off and his pale eyes crinkled up at the heavens as though he were sharing a joke with birds or clouds. The sound that escaped from the lips of his wide mouth was amazing, unselfconscious in its jubilance. Beryl's reserve fell to pieces before it. She laughed too.

"He says he works for a living and plays for God," Spenser explained. "But he's glad you like his music."

She smiled at Mr. Vonfeldt – a smile that James Avery would have sold his soul for – and then became serious. "Tell him I am so sorry about the death of his cousin."

Spenser spoke and Vonfeldt glanced away briefly. He knew that this English woman was responsible, in part, for seeing that the child was buried well. The day of the funeral had been bleak for him. His sister's grief at the loss of her son, the knowledge of his parents' grief when they heard the news in Russia, tore his insides ragged. He had noticed very little that day; he had turned inward, letting his soul wail into the music. But he had noticed the slim young woman sitting in the buggy and had felt grateful to her and her companion. He had not anticipated then, however, that the grey eyes hidden behind her black veil were so sad or so beautiful. He looked back into them and nodded. The laughter was lost.

Beryl returned to the kitchen and did not speak. At last Meg asked, "Who was it?"

"A new man, from Herzog."

"Does he seem like a good person?"

Beryl picked up a peach and nuzzled it against her cheek. "Yes, very," she said. Then she turned it over and deftly cut out a bruised spot where larvae squirmed.

The Victoria Hunt Club had been founded in the March of that year, but although the members all ordered handsome red uniforms with blue derbies, and although their charter was regally done up with a gold seal by a Hays City printer, their excursions seemed doomed to disappointment. A snowstorm ruined their first hunt, and none of the British women, fearing to be stranded in a blizzard, would even agree to go to the ball that night in Hays. The dance went on with a bevy of American girls and the hunt was rescheduled, so all was not lost. But moods went sour when, on a brisk April day, the good-looking lads spent two hours scouring the prairie for antelope, bison, or even coyote, and found they could not even scrounge up a prairie dog. They mutinied, raced to Hays City, purchased a case of Prickly Ash Bitters from the drug store, doctored themselves until they hiccupped, and then paraded their ponies and greyhounds in the doors of one saloon and then out the doors of another singing "Mary Had a Little Lamb," leaving tidy piles of pony shit and not-so-tidy pools of dog piss behind them.

One of the members, Jason Mayes perhaps, counted it a "grand sucshessh." The *Hays Sentinel* published a vivid write-up for the edification of Hays City mothers and daughters. Tommy Drumm paid another visit to Mr. Grant. And Mr. Grant ground his teeth. Meg could not get him to unclench his jaw for a week.

But the venture continued and in early July, inspired by an unfortunate encounter that left a favorite spaniel dead and his chicken house several fowl the lighter, Mr. Witley, secretary general of the club, came up with the idea for a rattlesnake hunt. "It's just the season, don't you know. Dry and hot. Scare 'em out of their blasted holes by pouring kerosene down them – then shoot the bastards' heads off when they slither out. I haven't seen an antelope for months, but I've seen thirty or more snakes in the past two weeks. I say, I'll give £250 to the man who can collect the most rattles."

"I don't know, Witley," said Ben Davis. "Not very sporting, is it?"

"How many sheep has Grant lost to snake venom?" said Witley. "How many cattle?"

Davis was silent.

"You really loved that bloody dog, didn't you Witley?" drawled Randall.

"I did, sir. And I love my wife more. I'd like her to be able to walk in the garden of an evening without worrying that her sweet slipper will step on something unwholesome."

"Ah, Eve in Eden," whispered Avery to Cabot. "But he's too late. I'd bet my money the serpent's already gotten to her."

Mason looked uncomfortable; his naturalist instinct inclined him more to preservation than to extermination. "I don't care for the creatures, but I'm not keen on killing them where they are not a direct threat. And they clean out the vermin."

"I take exception. My dog was not vermin."

"They can be a threat anywhere, Garth," added Neil Hunter. "They can be on the prairie today and curled in a crate behind my store tomorrow. I say let's clear the country of 'em. The school mistress shouldn't have to worry about snakes in the rafters when she begins lessons in the morning."

"Now there's a stunner," murmured Cabot to Avery. "Have you seen her? I had no idea the lass was in danger. I must run over tomorrow and ask her if she has any dragons to slay. I think I'd rather enjoy playing St. George, you know."

"I'm ready to win that £250," said Randall, standing and cocking his pistol as if to prove his point. "And I shall make a necklace of the rattles as tribute to the fair lady inspiring this hunt."

"That'll not be his wife he's thinking of," snarled Avery under his breath.

"Lucky for her," replied Cabot. "If that's his taste in jewels, I can only wonder what hideous love tokens Lord Stannard's daughter has had to suffer."

"Did you gentlemen have anything useful to contribute to the debate," asked Mr. Witley. "The titter-tatter of little voices is rather deafening."

"I shall be only too glad to prove my prowess by earning a pair of snakeskin boots. I was merely expressing my enthusiasm, was I not, Mr. Avery?"

"Oh you were, Mr. Cabot. Without the least ambiguity. Your fervor is a model of British manhood."

"Indeed," said Witley. "What say you then, gentlemen?"

Though some declined to take part, the general consensus was in favor of the expedition. Snakes were too common a pest, and too gruesome at that, not to be popular quarry. And there was enough danger involved to make it exciting for impatient young men who found the everyday toil of colonial life a recipe for ennui. Many, like Cabot, enjoyed the idea of going out and hunting dragons. That Saint George could only have looked ridiculous in a red jacket and a blue derby hat did not concern them. They were, after all, British — and snakes were, after all, snakes.

Lord Petrie, early on a bright summer morning, blew his hunting horn with great fanfare, and the Victoria Hunt Club, some twenty strong, galloped out of town ready to do battle in ditches and culverts, under rocks and behind fence posts. If the ponies thought they were in for another lark with Prickly Ash Bitters, they must have been sorely disappointed.

It was a long day. Hunting snakes after all does not involve the same kind of racing and running that makes chasing wapiti exciting. One spends time beating the grass, pouring evil liquids down holes, and listening for the warning purr of angry beads. Nervous mounts rear in terror, and it is a hard test of one's marksmanship, shooting at a weaving skull not even as big as a beer bottle.

At a certain point, most of the Britons gave up trying to blow the heads cleanly away from the bodies. It was easier just to pump bullets into the nasty coil willy-nilly until the thing was dead. Of course, hides were somewhat marred in the process; Cabot's chance for snakeskin boots grew dim after the first hour. He was also unlikely to win the £250 so he could buy them from the bootmaker on Peachtree Street in Hays City, because he refused to dig in the shattered mess of meat and bone for the tail. He had only three rattles to show for his pains after a long day in the sun, but he seemed nonplused. "I killed at least eight," he said. "It would smack of mayhem to do more."

His fellows were less moderate. Witley brought back 12, Randall 26, and Lord Petrie 41. Jason Mayes had 9, Nigel Wyatt 17, and Neil and Alec Hunter together 20. Keith, Davis, and Duncan took part in the hunt as well. The latter steadfastly refused to wear club garb and showed up instead in kilt and stockings – a rather foolish nationalistic statement, as Keith saw it. "I'd not be baring my knees to their fangs," he said. Grant's foremen participated less for the sport of the escapade than because they felt it was their duty to lessen their employer's loss of livestock. Between the three of them, they produced 54 rattles.

The club's casualties were, all told, minimal considering the number of vipers that had been done away with: a dog with a swollen jaw, a broken stirrup, and a lost derby hat. Lord Petrie took home the £250 pounds and, to his credit, he spared Angelina the horror of donning a necklace of rattles at the next ball. All the rattles were collected in a huge box that Neil Hunter put on display in his store window. Children ran their fingers through the amazing collection when their mothers were not looking, and gradually a fair number of the rattles found their way into grubby overall pockets. Miss Maguire, the stunning schoolteacher whom Cabot was determined to impress, found herself trying to stem a flourishing recess trade in snake tail. She spoke to Mrs. Hunter about it, and the box mysteriously disappeared. The gentlemen at the Hunt Club expressed dismay when the storekeeper's wife refused to reveal where she had stowed the box; the rattles were, they insisted, Club property and "an impressive part of Club history." They belonged in an archive. Julia folded her arms and shook her blonde head in contempt.

"Some men," she said to Jane MacDonough, "will never grow up. Neil can be glad I put up with the nasty things for as long as I did."

Jane leaned across the counter. "Where did you put them, Julia?"

"Why, where do you think? I burned them." She became confidential. "I considered tossing them in the privy – but somehow I thought I might never be able to sit down again, if you know what I mean."

Mrs. Hunter and Mrs. MacDonough howled until they cried. Vicky watched her mother in amazement. The little girl missed the big box of rattles; when her papa took her to the store, he had always allowed her to gather some to play with on the floor. But then, small though she was, she was old enough to understand that the kind of merry abandon she was witnessing was rare and that it was perhaps worth the price that had been paid. So, without understanding the joke, she clapped her hands together, hooted, and felt glad.

The men pouted for a few days and then secretly rejoiced in the loss. Without any physical evidence to verify or refute, stories about the number of snakes killed became more and more exaggerated until the Victoria Hunt Club became a legend in its own time. Whether it was safer for child or woman to walk on the open prairie after the expedition was debatable; like the buffalo had once been, rattlesnakes were legion on the high plains. But the British boys felt ready to bust their buttons. Though the object of their next hunt was only jack rabbit, they proceeded without shame and without boredom. They had proven they could kill and conquer, and if they hadn't quite rid Victoria and her estates of the slithering monsters, well, they had shown they had pluck. They were, they assured each other at meetings, a credit to queen and country. They were the heirs of Saint George, the sons of Britannia, the very rock of Empire.

As the hot days continued, Beryl found herself listening. Birds calling, insects whirring, dogs barking, corn leaves rustling – she was present to the sounds of the farm in a way she had perhaps never been. Not for the sake of the sounds themselves, but because of what she hoped to hear accompanying them: the clank of a shovel, the blow of a hammer, the melodious whistling in the barn that assured her Vonfeldt was there.

She listened for him for perhaps two weeks before she realized that that was what she was doing.

He was a happy person. He came early in the morning, worked hard, and made a friend of Red Thompson by cracking jokes in German that somehow needed no translation. He knew even more about farming than the former ranch hand, and he seemed instinctively to understand how to respond to both the rancorous climate and the cantankerous cowboy. His hands had the same gift with green things and creatures that they did with the violin: he knew how to touch them so that they would grow. But where his hands were graceful, his feet were clumsy. They were big and seemed to have trouble finding a place to rest without getting bumped or knocking something over. He walked to the Newlands in boots but by midday was often working barefoot, something which bothered Will and made Red worry about snakes (one or two had been seen about the place even after the great purge). They didn't say anything, however, not sure how to communicate it without causing offense. He never came into the house and had his beer and bread by himself at a cool spot near the creek. By late afternoon he was heading back to Herzog; he had his own homestead there where he worked until dark.

Beryl didn't have much cause to deal with him directly. She offered him tea and a slice of rabbit pie once, which he refused, leaving her rather offended. Only later did she realize that it had been a Friday – and of course he would not eat meat on Friday. He brought her and Will a beautiful kuchen one Wednesday – a present from his sister – made with small, black berries which he called *schwartzbitten*. The berries grew wild by the creek; Beryl hadn't realized they were edible, though the birds kept busy at them. They were sour by themselves, but well sugared they were delectable. He gathered some of the bushes from the creek bottom and planted them near her porch. They could never really talk to each other. He showed her things and then went right back to his work, but she liked being with him. He laughed a lot, and that was welcome.

She took to working in the vegetable garden near the creek later in the morning than had been her habit, so that she could see him while he ate his lunch. He read a book sometimes; some days he fished, storing his catch in a pail that he took home with him. His dress was that of a peasant – a big blousy white shirt tied around the waist like a tunic or tucked into his pants under suspenders. She wondered why she hadn't seen him at the Catholic church the few times she had attended with the Spenser brothers. But then she was always stiff there, a little afraid to look around for fear of seeming curious or seeing something that would affront her Protestant sensibilities: a row of candles, a paganish side altar, a gory crucifix. Actually, the Herzog church was very plain; poverty kept everything bare. In fact, she hadn't seen him because she hadn't looked.

He had, of course, seen her.

Like Victoria Manor, the German church was constructed of limestone. The rough-hewn blocks glowed in the pale morning light. The bell, formerly confined to a crude frame in the middle of the village, now tolled from a high belfry crowned with an iron cross that stood silver against the sky. Several narrow windows ran the length of the building; they contained gold, imageless panes of stained glass. The wide double door was oak. It thudded behind the people as they entered, shutting out a chaos of horses and wagons and men. Flanking it, just inside the building, small gold dishes jutted from the wall, each containing a dipperful of water. Her first time at the church, the day she heard of Mrs. Ramsay's death, the liquid was icy and would have frozen except that worshipers kept dropping their hands into it – hands calloused, swollen, and cracked from work. The Spenser brothers removed their gloves and blessed themselves with elegant, tapering fingers. Beryl kept her hands in her muff.

Before her, in dark rows haloed by window light, knelt German families – old and young, restless and still. The women were hooded in long shawls. The men sat hatless, their caps and fur hats in their hands. Most wore long, heavy coats. Some of these garments were patched. No one spoke; the only sound was an occasional sniffle or cough, the whimper of a baby and the shuffling of heavily clad bodies. Children stood or sat, many barefoot, on the wooden floor next to their kneeling parents. There were no chairs or benches for the people to rest on, with the exception of a single polished pine pew that waited, empty, at the front of the church. Behind the altar table, a cushioned chair waited for the priest.

The Spenser brothers walked through the crowd of kneeling people to that highly polished pew. They, with the help of their father, had provided the funds to build this church. In gratitude the immigrants, who could afford no seating for themselves, built the handsome pew for the Spenser brothers. No one else ever sat there, not even when the Spensers were absent. It was reserved exclusively for

"*Die Englisches.*" For the children, its shining wood was of a piece with all the untouchables of sacred rite: the golden chalice, the finely embroidered altar cloth, the small, white, tasteless host that must never touch their hands or lips or teeth, but only their tongue, lest it be polluted. And when the English gentlemen entered in their handsome morning jackets, their knee pants and buckles, their white gloves with pearl buttons, they were no less spectacle than the priest in his stern surplice. The grey-eyed woman who walked before the men this Sunday in a blue gown and a brown cloak, who wore gold in her ears and flowers on her hat even after frost had blighted the grass and the trees, must, the littlest ones thought, certainly be the Virgin. They watched her with awed eyes. The older children, those approaching or well into their teens, were wide-eyed as well – not because they thought this woman was the Mother of God, but because she and her companions nonetheless hailed from another world: a world of fine clothes and jewels, of warmth and wealth and plenty. They might as well have come from heaven, these English. That they should have a special seat was as natural as that the Host should reside in the tabernacle and the Holy Water in the font. They must be treated with reverence. They had a high place in the order of things.

Beryl sat stiffly on that favored pew, while next to her Bernard and Vincent knelt. On the altar table, in the middle, stood a small gold crucifix. Two white candles, lit, glowed on either side. There were no other images, though Beryl had half expected a warehouse of statuary. Probably, she thought, these people were too poor to adorn their house in the grand Papist fashion. When at last the priest – a stern-lipped, brown-haired missionary named Valentin Sommersein – came in with two altar boys, one swaying a small censor on a chain, the people stood and sang. Incense rose thickly into the golden light. Its exotic scent overshadowed the odor of bodies and the smell of construction dust. The priest turned and blessed the people, then he faced back to the altar.

"*Kyrie eleison.*"

"Kyrie eleison."

"*Christe eleison.*"

"Christe eleison."

"*Kyrie eleison.*"

"Kyrie eleison."

The people, with bowed heads, mimicked or answered – Beryl was not sure which – the call for mercy. The sound filled the building, an ordinary, pitiful human cry raised to the level of high dignity by the imposition of Latin. Beryl admired the impact of the language. She also felt lost in its impersonality. The priest spoke and read in Latin – scriptures, supplications, all but the sermon, which he delivered in German. Beryl struggled not to yawn, regretted that she sat in front where she could see no one but the stern-eyed priest. Her mind wandered; every now and then Mrs. Ramsay strayed through her thoughts, lost; then the severe tones of the priest would exorcize the intruder, leaving Beryl bewildered. When he was done, he turned away from the congregation; he faced a bare wall and a small crucifix while he raised the Cup and the Host. Bells rang. Censors swung. People knelt, beat their breasts, muttered responses, and worked their beads.

Beryl wondered if they knew what they said, mouthing Latin in throaty tones behind her. She could only guess what was happening by following the order of the service and comparing it to the Anglican rite in her head. She might have been inclined to dismiss it all as so much mummery – a common enough indictment among her people – but she was perplexed and strangely drawn by the musical intoning of the priest (Rev. Sommersein was blessed with a lyrical tenor) and the absolute devotion of the men and women bent on the cold floor. They were not sheep at all – something she'd been led to expect – though the posture of each back and the tone of each voice bespoke a trust that would brook no questioning. This Catholic faith was the faith of their fathers (and their mothers, who submitted to the will of their men even as Mary had submitted to the will of the Almighty); they had carried it with them through hardship and famine, rampage and death; they had carried it from Bavaria to Russia to western Kansas. They found nothing to doubt, nothing even to ponder about their religion. Each Sign of the Cross, each *Ave*, was merely another stone cementing the mounting tower of their faith. Beryl sensed that Lyell, Darwin, and Huxley could not have touched them. Their faith was bedrock, uncompromising and unyielding. If Vincent Spenser's belief had seemed a thin but mighty cord spanning the breach between heaven and earth, here she found a great wall reaching to the clouds. She was not certain whether it was a wall for keeping out or for climbing; she could not assert that it was part of the celestial city. But, watching the immigrants come forward and kneel to receive the Eucharist, she stood in its shadow and wondered at its severe glory.

Vonfeldt watched the English woman at her first visit and wondered why she came. But she was outside his realm of reckoning, and the young man never thought of her again until he saw her at Franz's funeral. Then he once more wondered about her, but this time he did not forget her.

After he had been working at the farm for three weeks, Beryl heard from Bernard Spenser that Vonfeldt had begun playing at mass. She had felt little inclination to repeat her visit to the chapel after the first time, but she now felt her interest renew. She wanted to hear Vonfeldt's violin again. And, because he liked the new hand, William actually agreed to go along. Entering any church, much less a Catholic church, was a major step for him. The former candidate for the ministry had not prayed in two years.

Beryl was restless throughout the service. The four Britons were cramped on the small pew. It was hot. She could not follow what was happening, and she neither saw nor heard Mr. Vonfeldt. Will fell asleep twice. She felt angry disappointment sting her when the congregation rose for the final hymn. Bernard had been wrong. She bit her lip. The priest and the altar boys moved to face the altar and everyone's voices came awkwardly together.

Then, at last, it came from behind her, the instrument singing along with the people. The rendering was skillful, the voice singular. The violin wove in and out of the melody like a shuttle through the threads of a loom; it filled the building with a tapestry of sound more worthy of a European cathedral than a small stone chapel in the wilderness. Beryl yearned to turn and look, but she dared not do so as long as the priest and his acolytes remained before her. She listened and waited impatiently. When at last the procession from the altar had passed to the back of the church and the singing had ceased, she turned around.

There, at the back of the building on a small balcony intended to one day hold an organ, he stood, putting the violin into its battered case. He seemed absorbed in his activity and paid little heed to the congregation below. Beryl watched him unaware that she herself was being watched. The German women, all interested in the cut of her cloak, the fabric of her gown, and the shape of her hat, studied her intently. They noted her interest in the man on the balcony. Some smiled, pleased that one of *"unsere leute"* could earn the wonder of the English. The English acted too superior by far.

At last, he looked down and, seeing the Britons, he raised his hand in greeting. Will raised his in turn and then shook his head. "By Jove, Spenser, the boy is wasted tossing manure in our stable."

"He feels he's where he needs to be. His brother-in-law told me he studied for a few years with a teacher in Katherinastadt. Unusual for a peasant's son. But he's not ambitious. Would rather be with his family. And of course he can perform among his own people all he wants. These Volga-Deutsch are always dancing and singing."

Beryl still looked up, watching Vonfeldt. He seemed to feel her eyes and turned to glance one more time into the crowd. She was there, quietly gazing at him in her white dress, a black braid winding under her hat and veil, her gloved hands playing a silent arpeggio against her prayer book. He smiled at her, then suddenly felt like laughing. The pale eyes crinkled up, rising toward the rafters. He didn't see that she began to laugh with him, and he probably didn't need to.

He had been drinking in the vision of her for the entire morning.

Chapter XIII

"I tell you, Dick, it isn't Spenser." Avery was sitting against the edge of his porch, his soft brown hair, parted at the side, falling over into his eyes. He was notably devoid of finery. His shirt was cotton, his Levis faded, and his boots as patched and worn as the meanest homesteader's. The suspenders, a bright lemony yellow, would have been daring on another man, but on James Avery they bespoke a subdued mood, even depression. Yet his estate was prospering: his buildings were solid and handsome, his sheep were healthy, his corn thigh-high and shining in the fields, and his person much improved by work in the sun and open air. Not even his unpleasant turnip of a cousin would dare to call him pasty-faced now. But nonetheless his expression was like that of a crestfallen child.

Cabot rested on the railing, spreading his elegant legs along its length and letting his blond head bump against the post a few times while he considered his cigarette. "She's been letting Spenser trail her long enough. And if attending papist services with him and his brother isn't an encouragement, I can't imagine what is. But then, she never has come to the point with him. Or maybe he hasn't with her. Odd chap. If he wants her, he should say something. Of course, you want her, and you don't say anything. Positively mystifying. What are you waiting for?"

Avery shrugged. "It doesn't matter. It's not Spenser. I thought it was, but it's not. I had hope as long as it was Spenser. Because, as you say, he never did come to the point. But that was before I saw her yesterday. The way she looked. The way she looked at this man."

"Ye gads, Avery, the virginal Miss Newland looked at a man?"

"Don't be a bastard."

Cabot exhaled a blue fume of smoke. "Sorry, old man. Just a bit hard for me to believe any man can touch that woman. Never met such a self-contained bit of goods before. I've often thought she doesn't even see men. She clearly hasn't the least idea that you laid your heart and soul before her altar years ago. Any girl that blind–" He flicked ash at an ant pile. "I'd like to see the man that can get Newland's sister to look beyond her own nose."

Avery's chin fell glumly into his hand. He said nothing.

"I say, do chirk up. Have one of those cabbagy pies my little Russian cook sent."

Avery turned his head away. Cabot's eyebrows went up. "My gawd, Avery, you are in a funk. I've never known you to pass up a pastry." He slipped off the railing and stood looking down at his friend. "Surely you're wrong," he said kindly. "Tell me who this person is, and I'll give you fifty reasons why you may still win her." He gestured to the farm which Avery had built from his devotion. "What can he have that compares?"

"Nothing," said Avery. "Nothing but himself. But don't you see, Cabot, that's all she seems to want."

After the Sunday when Beryl again heard Anton Vonfeldt play, a new consciousness came to both of them. She still did not see Vonfeldt much; he was out on the land most of the time. He came early and went to the barn, where he and Thompson worked out their plan for the day. He rarely had any reason to come to the house to consult with Will. Will was erratic in his overseeing of the farm's affairs. He would throw himself into the work some weeks, and then for days at a time give himself over to hunting, fishing, or haunting the environs of the Witley estate. Thompson really ran the farm; he consulted with Beryl when Will was not around. Beryl learned a great deal this way. But she had no direct dealings with the new hand. She left the house to fetch and dump water, to feed the chickens and collect the eggs, to take her pony on a run. Vonfeldt generally labored in the fields. She saw him from a distance sometimes, toiling next to Thompson in the hot sunshine, but she did not ride out to watch them. She was only sure of seeing him at midday, when she worked in the garden and raised her eyes from the ferny carrot tops and the bug-worried potato leaves to watch him eating lunch, fishing, and spitting sunflower seeds by the creek.

She noticed that he did not read much anymore during his meal. She wondered at this, in part because she had been curious about what was in his book. But of course he read less, because he had grown aware of her presence across the meadow. He discovered that following the swing of her long braid from her shoulders and down the line of her back to her hips was more interesting than following the march of black words across a page. He realized that she looked his way frequently during her work. This often gave added grace to his manner of tossing a fishing line into the water; occasionally it caused him to trip over his feet. Once or twice, he was inspired to come to the garden and help her tote a basket of vegetables to the house. They could not have a real conversation on these occasions; they could only smile and gesture and sometimes exchange the words for beet or melon or sunflower. She always parted rather abruptly, which perplexed him a little. But he was happier for having been with her and went away whistling.

Even before he felt her admiration for his violin playing, he discerned that music spoke to her. He noticed how she stopped at her work and listened to birds, how she responded to the rhythm of the pump, how she cocked her head when he whistled or sang. Once he saw her dancing in the stable to some music in her head, and though he never heard her play a piano or organ, he guessed at it: he had seen her fingers running on the table in idle moments as if over keyboard of remembered music. He thought about that quite a bit. He wondered why the rich English girl didn't have an organ in her parlor. The English seemed to have so much. But perhaps she didn't have everything.

So, in part because he remained grateful for what she had done for his sister's boy, and in part for some reason he was not ready to articulate to himself, he made her a small halo of bells to hang outside near the kitchen window where she so often worked. With clever hands, he fashioned it from tin, molding the metal and making clappers from bits of glass. He polished each piece until it shone. When the instrument was done, he was perplexed for some days, wondering how to present it to her. At last, one morning when he was in the barn shoeing one of Will's horses, he saw her wander across the yard to get some water. He put down his tools and grabbed his bag. He met her at the well, smiled a good morning, and then took the gift from his bag and put it in her hand.

She stood puckering her brow at the shiny bits and pieces strung together in her palm. But then he lifted them, and the pile separated into tinkling parts that swung gently against each other. Beryl flushed, delighted. "Oh," she cried. "What a pretty thing!" He handed it back to her. She lifted her arm high so that the bells could dangle and sing. She could not think what to say; she didn't know the words in his language and wasn't even certain she could find them in hers. So she simply stood, looking a little awkward, with a dripping pail in one hand and the odd, musical toy in the other.

Vonfeldt laughed and took the pail from her, set it down on the step, and then, with a hammer and nail, attached a small bracket to the frame of the kitchen window. Beryl watched him. Shy about the intimacy of handing the chime back to him, she climbed up the short incline of the cellar door and hooked it onto the bracket herself. They both stood admiring it for a moment: the way the bright bells twisted and spun in the warm gusts of air, dancing each other into music. Beryl, who had once been made breathless by the pealing of Westminster and St. Paul's, found herself holding her breath.

"Thank you. You make magic with your hands," she said at last, holding her own small hands out before him to try and explain what she meant.

He wanted to reach for them and clasp them in his fingers. But instead, he looked at her and laughed. "Yes," he said in English. "Yes." And he went back to his work.

Beryl watched him, his white peasant blouse blowing from his wide shoulders, and then turned to look at the spinning bells. Excepting his violin music, she was sure she had never heard anything sweeter. Everything around this man seemed bright and beautiful, not least the dusty, sharp buffalo grass where he trod. She wanted to dance on it.

"What are you so happy about?" Will asked her at dinner, looking tired and feeling her joy irritate him like a probing finger on a sore spot.

"Nothing," she said, blushing. But she could hardly keep the singing from her voice.

Shortly before the defection of the Gunther brothers became common knowledge, a delegation of New York dignitaries – ministers, lawyers, professors, and journalists – came to Victoria to investigate and ultimately congratulate George Grant on the success of his experiment. The vision he had imagined five years before seemed within reach of realization. Victoria City was handsomely laid out; limestone houses, some big, some small, were arranged in neat lanes behind the main city street where, in addition to the Manor house and station, Pettimore's Lumber, and Hunter's store, there was a meat market, a drug store, a hotel, a blacksmith shop, a restaurant called the Alma House, and a half-completed church. An establishment known as "Tom Hill's Saloon" had managed to become a reality in Grant's town before the house of worship, representing a bitter concession by the founder. He comforted himself that the shanty-like structure was hidden behind the Alma House, whereas the solid foundation of St. George's was well in view. His guests remained ignorant that there was a house of liquor closer than the inimitable Tommy Drumm's in Hays.

Victoria seemed dusty but hopeful, the small trees in its front gardens emulating the high-growing cottonwoods along the creek in a way that promised great things. But the morning's ride in the country impressed the visitors most. They saw fifteen plows pushing up rich soil on Cabot's estate; wool twenty-one inches long sheered from the backs of Lincolnshire sheep at Captain Prescott's; cashmere goats roaming the meadows at Lord Petrie's; a hundred fruit trees blooming at Vincent Spenser's; and black cattle stretching to the edge of the sky at Grant's Stock Farm. The handsome mansions fronting the creek, surrounded by infant windbreaks of Russian Olive and elm, were a revelation. The yellow-gold stone framing elegant windows and reaching to quaint cupolas, the long esplanades draped in morning glories and climbing pink roses, the interiors rich in walnut and mahogany and crystal – all reinforced the idea that a gentleman could enjoy the freedom of frontier ranching and the cultured comforts of civilization simultaneously, that there was much for a young man to gain and little that need be sacrificed.

Which was, of course, just so much hooey.

To do him justice, Lord Grant (as one of the more fawning Anglophiles insisted on calling him in spite of constant correction) sought to be frank about the hardship that the colonists had faced. "It's a better place to ranch than to farm," he told the agriculture professors. "A few of our boys are giving it a go with maize and wheat, and the Russian immigrants to our north are intent on raising only grain, but the land supports livestock more reliably. The animals feed on natural grasses that are suited to the climate; when drought comes, those plants weather it, whereas imports must struggle. I'll not be fooling you, gentlemen. It's a dry land. We've been fortunate this year; rain has not been wanting. But in '74? That was a difficult season. If the good Lord chooses to send a plague of locusts – a rare enough thing, but we've seen it here – we can only sit back and watch them do their work. Kansas is a capricious mistress; a man needs sound financial backing and a constant devotion to win her. When she turns a cold shoulder, he cannot be fainthearted; he must woo with redoubled effort. And she comes around. As you can see, my friends."

A physician named Wismer, a long-faced, long-mustachioed fellow, looked appreciatively at his claret. "If I may say so, sir, you do seem to have the gal sitting in your lap. The young bucks seem game, and I defy the best families in Boston to entertain with your hospitality."

"A little debt goes a long way," muttered a skeptical banker.

"Aye, but the payback is great," said Grant, looking the banker straight in the eye. "I have no doubts about the success of this enterprise. I would not waste your time, gentlemen, if I did. Or mine." The garnet ring on his finger sparkled; his silver hair shone, and his voice was rich with all the intonations of British success and history and culture. The American, a small balding man with a nasal twang, understood his disadvantage and bowed his head to his host.

Jonathan Walton, president of one of the great eastern universities, adjusted his cravat in a shining gilt mirror and then smiled at Mr. Grant. "I cannot speak for these other gentlemen, Mr. Grant, but I must say I am favorably impressed. I'd not hesitate to send one of my sons to Victoria to begin his career. Indeed, if I consider a new start in life, I may come out myself. I assure you that when I return to New York, I shall personally undertake to see that all geographies calling Kansas the Great American Desert become kindling. If this is desert, then I'm a Chinaman." And, as the gold-bearded president clearly had nothing of the orient about either his face or his manner, the cruel slander that Grant's mistress had so long endured seemed measurably closer to being wiped away.

At luncheon the men enjoyed a feast of cold beef and pork, all Kansas raised, accompanied by a variety of exotic cheeses and fruits shipped in from the East. It was a party of men: Mr. Grant, the New York delegation, some dignitaries from Fort Hays, the commissioner of the Kansas Pacific, and a selection of the most successful colonists: the Spenser brothers, Captain Prescott, Lord Petrie, and (in a position unusual for him) James Avery. The mood was jovial. Scottish, English, and American flags hung from the high dining room windows, swelling now and then with the warm summer air that lazily passed over the open sashes. Mr. Grant proposed a toast to the Queen and to the glory of the Frontier; he was answered by an enthusiastic greeting of glass against glass. Dr. Wismer toasted Mr. Grant, wishing him blessings on his endeavor, years of long life, and "a fair lady as crown to his magnificent achievement."

A journalist at the end of the table, a bright-eyed fellow by the name of Jenson, called out, "Tell us, Mr. Grant, who the good lady might be. Surely there's a lovely muse inspiring you among the handsome women of Victoria?"

The British boys present noticeably came to attention. The Spenser brothers lowered their forks. Captain Prescott looked up from his bread. Avery felt a sudden clutch of jealousy that made him put down the delectable morsel he'd been enjoying for fear of choking; he had heard some of Cabot's theories on this point.

Mr. Grant seemed slightly taken aback by the question, but he responded smoothly. "All of my queen's daughters are an inspiration, Mr. Jenson. They bring the beauty and grace of home to these plains, and a bravery in the face of deprivation that makes what we men have to suffer seem little indeed."

The journalist was not to be put off. "Oh, but surely there's one who's extra special, Mr. Grant? Some dark-eyed beauty? An 'English Rose for the Scottish Lord Who Has Made Kansas a Garden'?" He

almost stood up at the excitement of possible bylines. He was digging in his pocket for a pencil.

The grizzled Reverend Armstrong of Brooklyn chimed in. "Tell
who the lady is, say 'Barkis is Willin'," and I'll unite you this afternoon, Mr. Grant. We leave at 4:15 for Denver; there's just time."

The men laughed. Mr. Grant merely smiled and shook his head.
If Beryl had been there, she would have said that the only woman
Mr. Grant cared for was this lovely, cruel land he had settled. It tantalized and enthralled him; like a clever mistress, it never gave herself
to him completely. She was certain that it left him no room for another love. And she might have been right.

But perhaps not. Avery narrowed his eyes at his plate and hooked
a worried finger in the pocket of his embroidered waistcoat. He, at
least, thought otherwise.

The wedding gave Beryl her first real insight into the community
from which Anton Vonfeldt came each morning. She had been to
services at the increasingly crowded chapel, and she had seen a funeral. But she had always felt outside those events. Because of the
formality of these occasions and because she did not know the language, she felt she had little sense for the people as people. Certainly,
many of the Russian immigrants were suspicious of the English and
avoided them. But Mr. Grant had hired several Volga Germans to
work in his house, and these workers respected and liked him for
both his generosity and his kindness. When the woman who cooked
for him and Meg invited him to her daughter's wedding, he understood the honor. The Spensers were also invited, and Vincent asked
Beryl to escort him. So, on a Saturday in late July, under a hot blue
sky, George and Meg Grant and Vincent Spenser and Beryl all drove
over to Herzog for the celebration.

The British were, as ever, handsomely fitted out. Meg wore a pale
green silk against which her red hair shone. Beryl wore a yellow
gown with white trim. The black braid that usually hung down her
back had been loosed into long waves and then lifted off her neck
and pinned high on her head. Spenser wore his invariable tweed
knickers, but Mr. Grant wore a handsome black suit that emphasized

his height and the silver curls that clustered at his collar. For that time and place, these people were exquisite specimens of fashion. Had the Germans been compelled to face them at Grant's Villa, they would have felt abashed. But this wedding was a day of the celebration for their own community. The Britons honored the Germans by their presence but in no way eclipsed them. They were footnotes to the festivities.

The crowd of guests gathered outside a large sod house on the east side of Herzog. A brass band of four men stood waiting in the sun, their instruments flashing at the sky. The British stood on the edge of the crowd across from the band. Inside the house, Vincent explained, the parents were blessing their children. After several minutes, a young man and a girl emerged from the house. The couple, a man named Peter Dreiling and a girl named Martina Brungardt, both looked very young. Beryl thought the bride must be only fifteen or sixteen; she looked small under the ribboned crown resting on her brow. She wore a soft blue dress which fit snugly around the bodice and arms, but flared at the waist into a rustling, full skirt over which a white apron was tied. The apron was embroidered with green and pink flowers and edged with lace. The girl's face flushed with excitement. The young man, who seemed only a few years older, was pale and serious looking. His dark eyes blinked at the bright outdoor light, but he smiled when the girl caught his hand. Everyone cheered and clapped, and then the band began a march. The attendants, two young girls bearing flowers tied with lace and two young men in dark, short-coated, tight-fitting suits, marched ahead. Behind them came the bride and groom, the couple's parents, and the rest of the town. Beryl and Vincent and the Grants walked near the back, weaving with the crowd to the church.

The marriage ceremony was a high mass with much singing and many prayers. One of the attendants, a yellow-haired girl who looked like she might be the sister of the groom, grew faint. She recovered herself after Spenser gave her his seat so she could rest on the favored pew for a few minutes. The bridal couple seemed dazed and awed at being the center of so much attention. The groom clutched his small wife's hand as though he would take her and run if he had the chance.

Beryl found the service long and hot. She spent most of it wondering what it must be like to stand before everyone and proclaim your love. During the hymns she let herself get lost on the sweet singing of the violin whose voice she now recognized so well.

She saw the violinist for the first time at the wedding dinner, which was held in what seemed to be a big meeting hall or storage barn. The bride and groom sat on opposite sides of a long table, not eating, and looking hungry and tired while the guests were served dishes that seemed exotic to Beryl: chicken stock with rice and buttery bread balls floating in it; vinegary head cheeses; rich brown roasts and cakes and kuchens, some of which she had tasted before at Mr. Grant's parties. The food was all very good, if richer than what she was used to. The succulent, buttery balls filled her mouth delectably and when she swallowed them, she felt as if her stomach must burst through her stays. Everyone consumed a lot of beer and wine, and she grew a little dizzy with the liquor and the heat. The raucous roar of laughing and joking was tremendous; she felt bewildered by it. Vincent Spenser was attentive and translated and explained for her when he could. She felt the relief of the couple when they at last left the table and went into a small side room to dine by themselves; she wished she could go with them.

As she watched them go, she spotted Vonfeldt, there by the door. Vonfeldt was dressed in the short-waisted, high-collared Russian suits common to the men. His sandy hair, which grew dull and tangled when he worked in the wind, was combed against his collar in shining waves. He stroked his closely trimmed beard as his gaze ran over the crowd. Then he saw Beryl. He smiled and nodded, that jubilant laugh glowing just behind his eyes. All her dizzy bewilderment seemed to go with a rush. She looked away and clasped a cool glass of water to her hot cheek. They must all see, she thought. They must all be able to see.

For certainly she saw what she had for many weeks blinded herself to. This young musician and laborer, with whom she could not even share an ordinary conversation, had become the center of her life. She waited for him in the morning; she waited for him at midday; and when she saw him leave in the afternoon, she waited for him to come at night in her dreams. All the years of meaningless waiting, all the years spent listening to ticking clocks and dripping rain, seemed to have at last merged into an urgent, breathless, pointed longing that tortured her most in the minutes before she knew she would see him again. Until his extraordinary blue eyes rested on her, she felt fractured and incomplete, as though part of her were cut off. When they did rest on her, she was afraid to look back into them because she sensed that if she did, she'd never be able to look away again.

It was all so inappropriate.

For the rest of the afternoon and on into the evening she was alternately seeking and avoiding those eyes. During the bridal march, she watched the men pinning money to the girl's gown and wondered if Vonfeldt would take a dollar earned at the Newlands' and pin it on the bride's body so that he could dance with her. She looked at the ruffled bodice of her own dress, imagined his hand there, and blushed.

Mr. Grant danced with the bride; he caused a sensation by pinning $100 to the girl's apron. Mr. Spenser danced with her as well, tucking some bills into the cuff of her long sleeve. The girl positively fluttered with green paper by the time all the men who wanted to dance with her had taken their turn. She and her mother and mother-in-law and sisters laughed as they unpinned the money, unwrapping her like a present. When her new husband had her in his arms again, he looked very proud. What other girl was pretty enough to earn so much, and who else could boast such generous friends and neighbors?

Anton Vonfeldt did not pin money on the girl. He played his violin, along with a fellow playing a hammered instrument called a zimlin and a heart-faced girl who strummed bright chords on a dulcimer. Beryl found the music disappointing. The idea of gliding to Mr. Vonfeldt's music was exciting to her, but the reality of the German "hochzeit" was less pleasurable. Her slippered feet were crunched several times before she felt able to do the hopsy steps of the dance with any confidence. But Mr. Grant was patient with her. Mr. Spenser, with whom she always danced so well, explained the moves. When she failed, Meg was there to share the confusion. And the music was, after all, Anton's. The violin, which she'd always heard singing before, now seemed to laugh, exhibiting much the same character that caused its owner to tip his head back at the sky, crinkle up his eyes, and let the joy roll out.

The eating and drinking and smoking went on and on. The very young danced, and then the older people. At the tables surrounding the dance floor, people gossiped and crunched sunflower seeds and played cards. Sometimes there was singing; the children ran about, laughing and screaming; young couples flirted. Many of the men grew drunk and maudlin – a state Beryl could recognize even without being able to understand what was said. Peter and Martina danced mostly together now, lost to the world in each other's arms. Other young couples were growing amorous. Occasionally one of the young men would speak to the band, lead a girl out to the center of the floor, and then leave her. As if by magic, the other dancers left the floor too and there she stood alone, serenaded by the instruments and applauded by the crowd. Spenser spoke to one of his neighbors, and then told Beryl and Meg that is was a sign of great favor for a man to do this for a girl.

"What if the girl doesn't like the man?" asked Meg. Uneasy visions of what Nigel Wyatt would do if such a tradition became common among the English rose before her.

Spenser laughed. "It doesn't bind her to him, and I suppose at the very least it makes the other lads realize that she's a lass worth pursuing."

"I suppose so," said Meg doubtfully.

As the evening wore on, Beryl grew tired, and her head ached. She sat languidly next to Mr. Grant, sipping a cup of coffee. Mr. Grant was enjoying the entertainment; he smoked his pipe, and his foot kept time to the music. It all made him feel young, he said to Beryl; it reminded him of weddings in Scotland. The weddings she had attended had always been fairly staid affairs; when Robert and Marian were wed, they simply had a quiet breakfast at Lindenhurst after a private ceremony at the church. This drunken hopping and whirling and feasting seemed far from anything in her world. She looked at Mr. Grant and wondered what he had been like when he was young. Like Meg, perhaps? Or his nephew Clay? Not that he seemed old; but she could not imagine him young, like herself. Or Will. Or Anton Vonfeldt.

As she studied him, she felt a hand on her sleeve. Startled, she turned and looked up into Mr. Vonfeldt's face. He was smiling at Mr. Grant, and then held out his hand to her. He said something in German and then, raising his eyebrows and puckering his face at his own pronunciation, he asked, in English, "You will dance with me, yes?"

The band was still playing, but the violin had been abandoned on a table. She looked at Mr. Grant a little absurdly, like a child asking for permission or guidance. He looked back at her, surprised and amused. "Well of course, lass. Enjoy yourself. Vincent is off with Meg, and my legs have done for the evening."

She stood up, a little unsteadily, nervous at feeling Mr. Vonfeldt's hand through her glove, his body near her side. They went to the floor. He stood before her. He was not tall; she could look straight into his eyes. When she did, she gasped a little and then bit her lip. But he seemed nonplused. His pale eyes crinkled, and he slid his hand around her waist. He lifted her other hand in his own and – at first tentatively, and then with confidence, and then with a kind of joy – they polkaed together.

That was of course the beginning. Once it became apparent that the English girl was willing to dance with the Germans, more than one young man asked for the honor. They were scrupulously polite and generally shy; the novelty of it seemed to attract them most, and few asked a second time. But enough young men remained around Miss Newland to frustrate Vonfeldt, especially as he was allowed little time away from the other musicians. They were already becoming impatient. The girl with the dulcimer was particularly vexed and motioned for his return. He came back briefly, but after seeing Beryl dance with five or six of his compatriots, he shook his head, resolutely laid down his bow and crossed to where Beryl stood on the arm of a young farmer. He spoke in German. The other man grinned at him, amiably nodded, and went to pursue another girl. Vonfeldt studied Beryl for a moment, then led her by both hands to the middle of the dance floor, bowed to her – and left her there.

A flame of color crept from the edge of her gown, along the curve of her shoulder, and up her neck. The crowd, after a broken moment of surprise, clapped. Or at least some of them did. Meg, next to her uncle, stood open-mouthed. Mr. Spenser turned to stare at the young German who had led Beryl to the floor. Then the music began, a gentle, lilting tune, and after a moment Beryl heard the violin singing above the dulcimer and the zimlin. She knew it was singing to her and she did not know what to do. She wanted to run to Vonfeldt and fling her arms around him; she wanted to run to him and slap him hard; and most of all she wanted to run away from him and from all these people, far away into the grass and sky and singing night where she would never be required to face anybody ever again. There was nowhere, nowhere, to hide.

But there was Mr. Grant's face: kind, encouraging, and, had she been able to recognize it, a little sad. She took courage. She was Victoria's daughter. She raised her chin and breathed in deep, trying to still the pounding in her breast. She kept her eyes on the hem of her gown and stood quietly until the end of the song. She looked graceful in her yellow dress, her black hair crowning her head, the music gaily circling round her. When it finished, she let herself look at the crowd; she smiled, a little tremulously, and seeing the bride and groom, curtsied. The girl smiled back at her, but Beryl thrashed inside like a bird trapped and clipped. Everyone seemed a blur. Then her eyes, wiser than her heart, found their focus. She saw Vonfeldt lower his violin from his chin and tuck it under his arm. He was gazing at her helplessly, his face anxious and questioning. She gazed back, her grey eyes wide. Then Mr. Spenser was at her elbow, Mr. Grant and Meg were before her, and she slipped away into a tumult of guests.

The music and laughter and drinking and card-playing continued. Vonfeldt jumped from the platform where he'd been playing, trying to see where the Britons had gone. He began to push through the people when he felt a heavy grip on his arm that forced him to turn. It was his brother-in-law.

"Hey! Little Anton! What the hell was that?"

Will suggested attending the play at the Krueger Opera House. This emporium of culture was neatly appended, in efficient frontier fashion, to the Krueger Brothers Dry Goods and Grocery in Hays. The idea to have an evening of theater had originated with the Witleys, of course. Cynthia, who as her father's child knew a good deal about such things, insisted that actress Louie Lord was a talent worth shedding tears for and that her touring dramatic company enjoyed renown in the United States. Mr. Avery, Mr. Cabot, and the Randalls would be members of the party, and they hoped the Newlands would join them too.

"What's the play?"

"Oh, I don't know," said Will carelessly. "Some melodramatic rubbish, I suspect. 'Lady Audley's Secret,' I think."

"No, really? How funny, to think it's come to the stage over here!"

"What do you mean?"

Beryl looked thoughtfully at her teacup, and then lifted it in her hands as though she were trying to see another room, another time, and an altogether different cup of tea. "Do you remember, Will, the first time you told me about Victoria? Do you remember the book I was reading?"

"Not really."

"Why, you accused me of reading nothing but sensation fiction. Well – that's what it was. The novel. *Lady Audley's Secret!* You know, I never finished it. Don't you remember – she'd thrown her husband into a well."

"Who had? The heroine? Good god – obviously highbrow material." He snorted. "But Mrs. Witley swears by the actress."

"I wonder if she knew her, when she was in London."

"Louie Lord? Not likely. She's an American."

"No, I mean the woman who wrote the novel. Mary Braddon. She's an actress too. She leads quite a scandalous life, actually."

"Well then I doubt that Mrs. Witley would know her."

Beryl was silent. Then she said, "Well, I think I'd enjoy going to an opera house, even if it is the second story of a dry goods store. And it will be fun to find out how the story ends. I have sometimes wondered."

Will, who was polishing his boots, looked amused. "Have you really? Making history in this great colony, and all the time pondering the fate of a husband killer?"

"Not all the time, Will. Very well, maybe not ever. But now that you have me thinking of it all again, I would like to go."

"Good," said Will. "Avery will be pleased. He says it'll be a great lark."

Beryl hoped it would be. She wanted diversion, something that would keep her from having to think or, worse yet, feel. She had evaded Mr. Spenser's questions about Mr. Vonfeldt's tribute to her by insisting – perhaps too strongly, she later thought – that Vonfeldt was a good worker who appreciated what she and Will had done for him and his family. Spenser listened, fixing her with that dark, searching gaze she'd learned to dread within the first hour of knowing him. But he said nothing except to observe that Vonfeldt was a talented young man. Mr. Grant was gallant about the entire episode; he said that he wished he had thought to honor Miss Newland so generously. Meg was quiet. Driving away from the sunset toward Victoria after the wedding at Herzog, she realized that never, ever, had she seen Beryl look at anyone, man or woman, the way she looked at Mr. Vonfeldt. But she recognized the expression: she had seen it on Daniel MacDonough's face when he looked at his Jane, on Julia Hunter's face when she was with her husband, and on Will Newland's face when he spoke to Cynthia Witley. The last comparison made her shudder. But she knew instinctively that to ask Beryl about what had happened would be the wrong thing to do. So she said nothing and felt miserable.

Beginning the morning after the wedding, Beryl threw herself into distractions. She refused to attend mass at Herzog again, riding into Victoria to participate in the Presbyterian service held at Julia and Neil Hunter's. The following Monday she spent a long, sticky day blacking the stove (and, inadvertently, much of her face), a chore which kept her indoors and away from her garden. On Tuesday she took down all the curtains in the house and scrubbed them, rubbing the fabric against the washboard so ferociously that her raw knuckles threatened to bleed and stain the very cloth she was trying to clean. On Wednesday she took her pony from the stables when she knew that Mr. Vonfeldt was busy and rode away to the Fort to visit Betsy Walker and Cassandra Tyler for the day; on Thursday she went to spend several hours with Lydia Randall and her son at their estate north of Victoria; and on Friday she roamed Victoria, consulting with Mr. Pettimore about the house she and Will were having built on their town lot and then shopping in the Hunters' store, where she chatted with Julia about furniture, the cost of fabric, and the baby that Julia and Neil expected the next winter. When she could find no more ways to fill her minutes, she rode back home and made herself tea and retired to her bedroom, where she lay on the white coverlet of the bed with the shutters closed. In the half-light of late afternoon, she tried to sleep, tried not to hear the tinkling bells outside the kitchen window, tried not to hear Thompson giving directions, and tried most of all not to hear Mr. Vonfeldt whistling as he headed back to Herzog.

She only succeeded at the latter, and that only because Vonfeldt found his heart for whistling had dried up. He trod away from the farm that day, as he had every day that week, in silence. But behind the shuttered windows she measured his footfalls. When he was gone, she knew she didn't have to hide any longer. Her misery was greater than her relief, however. She was not really hiding from him, after all. The problem was she could not escape herself.

She dressed for the play on Saturday night with an enthusiasm that was almost genuine. She seemed to be trying to prove something – perhaps that she felt it worth making herself look attractive even when there was no chance that she could meet Anton Vonfeldt. She piled her hair in a magnificent knot and studded it with bright rhinestone pins like those her sister-in-law liked to wear. She put garnet in her ears and spread a black lace mantilla over her head and shoulders. It made her look exotic, and not a little Spanish. She was pleased. She did not want to look English. She did not want to look like anything she had ever been.

The evening ride to Hays with her brother and Mr. Avery and Mr. Cabot was beautiful, the late-setting sun spreading gold and red against a purpling sky. They were all merry. They came along the road that led from Fort Hays; other wagons and carriages joined them on the way. When they got to town, they found the street outside of Krueger's grocery crowded with horses and vehicles and men and women in various degrees of evening dress. The building itself was big, three stories with an impressive molding that did not mask a false front. Cabot asked Avery to take Beryl inside while he and Will tethered the horses; the carelessness with which the suggestion was made did not fool Avery, but he was appropriately grateful. Will, who had already begun hunting for signs of the Witley carriage, said in a vague way, "Oh yes, would you, Avery? That would be a kindness to Beryl."

They entered the door of the grocery but then climbed some narrow stairs that took them to a long, foyer-like hall, handsomely papered and lit by a dozen gas lamps. Beryl lowered the mantilla to her shoulders while Avery rifled his pockets for the tickets. Beryl looked around curiously. She knew many people and didn't know even more. She still felt less acquainted with the Americans of Hays than with the denizens of the fort and her neighbors at Victoria. She waved to Captain and Mrs. Walker, who were standing with a group of soldiers near one of the entrances to the theater. Mrs. Walker had told her that there was some question as to how long they would be staying on here, since the government considered the Indian wars over and the work of the Fort essentially done. Betsy spoke of returning to her children in the east now that separation from her husband was more likely to be measured in months rather than years and half-years. Beryl felt a puzzled kind of regret.

Across from the doors to the theater, near a tall window through which the gold-red sky still shone, the Witleys stood chatting amiably with the Randalls. Mr. Witley was twirling his mustache and letting his monocled eye roam the crowd; Lydia, pale and thinner than ever, was intent on her program; the diamonds in her ears and on her wrist sparkled but seemed too heavy for her slender bones to bear. Randall, on the other hand, was stockier and more substantial than he had been when they first came to Kansas. He stood with his arms folded and made sardonic comments about the people entering the theater to Mrs. Witley. His hair still stood on end in the electric way which Beryl had noticed when she first met him back in Mr. Cabot's London drawing room. But he seemed to her less compelling than he had been then, more off-putting. Perhaps Lydia's tired expression influenced her. Certainly his energy flowed unabated, and Mrs. Witley seemed riveted. But then, Beryl reflected, Mrs. Witley could seem riveted by a tumbleweed.

She knew that Will would want to join the Witleys immediately, but she felt no inclination. "Could we go in and sit down, Mr. Avery? It would be nice to get away from all these people."

Avery took her gloved hand and wrapped it through his arm. Beryl's simple elegance stood out against the flamboyant cut of his velvet evening jacket and the elaborate pattern of his silk scarf. He'd never minded much what others thought of his apparel. He liked color and style and fashion, and he dressed in order to please himself and irritate his mother. But with Miss Newland on his arm, the black lace setting off the white of her shoulders and accenting her unadorned gown beneath, he suddenly wished he were wearing something less showy, less pretentious, less Parisian, perhaps. Something unassuming. Something not exactly like, but closer to, the kind of thing that a Russian peasant might wear. Though God knows he wasn't sure what that might be. He led Beryl into the theater and to their seats, considering and rejecting possibilities.

He had seen Beryl and Mr. Vonfeldt together only once, and not even on the Newland estate. He'd been in Victoria, waiting outside Hunter's store. The young Russian musician came down the street leading a horse and cart; in the cart were some children cradling baskets of eggs that they hoped to sell. The man made endless music, it seemed to Avery, with his chirruping to the horse, his laughing at the children, and his friendly greeting of those he knew. Avery's own good nature responded to the light-heartedness of the other man. "There is a fellow," thought Avery, "who would understand how to have a lark."

Beryl came out of the drug store just then, her long braid swinging below the waist of her skirt. She blinked at the brightness of the sun and, blinded for a moment, almost stepped in front of the man leading the horse. She caught herself at the last minute, and he pulled the animal to a halt. The abrupt movement jolted the cart, causing one of the children to lurch and let out a sharp angry cry that his eggs would be broken. Vonfeldt said something incomprehensible to the boy that made him pout. Then he touched his cap to Miss Newland, bowing slightly. She smiled at him (this was before the wedding dance), and there was something so open and so dazzling in the way she smiled that Avery found himself blinking in much the same way she had when she came into the sun. He could not believe this was the same girl he had known for four years and longer, the same woman who went about with such sad eyes and who seemed to take the general pain of life into her heart like a personal, soul-rending secret. The vision of her smile cut through him. That she could look so happy – and that this peasant with bare ugly feet and pale eyes seemed to inspire it! Avery would have sold every ruffle and button to earn an expression half as bright. He did not know who this person was, but he knew suddenly, and with the certainty of death, one fact: that the man who married Beryl Newland would not be Vincent Spenser.

Watching her face in the dim light of the opera house and re-calling that afternoon, he could find none of that bright joy. Beryl smiled. She was witty. But her eyes were cloudy and did not really seem interested in what they saw. She responded to Avery's every remark, but somehow, he felt, she did not really hear him. He sensed that she was listening for something else, something that no opera house, no matter how fine the performance, could satisfy. He ran through a catalog of ideas, trying to think of a comment or question or observation that might bring a truer smile to her face, something closer to the dazzling expression he had seen in Victoria. But the effort merely tangled his tongue. He ran his hand nervously over his combed back hair and blurted out, at last, the obvious, the only thing that he could have said and still been true to himself: "I say, but I'm hungry."

"Mr. Avery, we just ate before we left."

"I know, but those cabbagy things that Cabot's cook comes up with – they never agree and he's forever trying to foist them on me. I sneak them to the dog. I suppose they give the creature fearful gas – but then, it's either him or me, what? So, I go hungry, and the spaniel gets a belly ache, and Cabot goes trotting off for his after-dinner smoke feeling all is right with the world, never guessing the horror he's wrought. It's enough to drive a man into decline."

Beryl stared at him and then burst into laughter. It was not daz-zling, but her eyes brightened and at least she seemed to see and hear him. "Mr. Avery, you do suffer, don't you?" She settled into her seat, pulling a fan from her reticule.

He sat next to her, rather discontentedly. "Perhaps I do." He was quiet for a moment, frowning at his program. "If I did suffer, I don't expect you or anybody else would notice."

"Why Mr. Avery! You sound quite pitiful. I shall have to make you a pie or something to cheer you up."

"Would you do that for me?"

Something about the tone which he wrapped around the question gave Beryl pause; her own experience of the last several weeks attuned her to nuances she had missed before. The fan stopped fluttering. For a long minute she kept her eyes on the velvet curtain which was closed in front of them and then she said in a carefully cheery voice, "Of course I would. I hope you know you can count on such an old friend. What shall it be: peach or apple?"

Avery looked at her profile, which seemed to him so lovely and so cold, and then said, "Neither. I think – neither." He slumped in his seat, symbolically if not literally turning his back to her. He had never done such a thing before.

Beryl glanced at him and then wrapped her gloves tightly around the fan, realizing for the first time what half the inhabitants of Victoria had known for three years. Something heavy seemed to fall in her chest and stick there. She began to kick her boot slightly. Nothing made sense anymore; everything she'd been certain of had proven uncertain. This revelation about Avery seemed sure to set the whole house of cards tumbling. The play could not divert her now, knowing what she knew. After the curtain rose, she sat stiff and still between Avery and Will, hardly blinking as the house hooted and roared and wept at the villainy and heartbreak on stage; Cabot's sarcastic comments could not even resurrect her fondness for irony. She was only touched once, when the gorgeous Louie Lord, her red tresses trailing like blood over a satin gown, cried before a stricken house, "I am MAD!" It was no revelation to Beryl; she felt as if she had said it herself. The admission did not mitigate anything. It was just a sad, simple fact. She could not even be glad when the play revealed that Lady Audley had not actually killed her husband. That just made the heroine a more pathetic example of a too-common type: a poor, messed up, desperate woman.

"Bit of a dodgy story, that, wouldn't you say, my dear?" said Henry Witley to Cynthia after the play was over. He put a soft white wrap around her shoulders while Avery, Cabot, and the Newlands stood by the side of their carriage.

"I thought it divine fun," laughed Cynthia. "I should love to play the part."

"Ye gads, my dear, I hope not," said Henry. "And God defend us from the Lord Audleys who might tempt you to such extremes."

Cynthia allowed her eyes to slide to Will's face. He slipped into their violet depths, then pulled himself back like a dripping dog. He clenched his jaw firmly, but his soul seemed to shake and shiver. "As if you could ever bear to tear yourself from me and give me the chance to be tempted," she said.

"True," said Witley cheerfully. "Not likely. I say, won't you all join us at the house? I've arranged for Miss Lord and the other members of the cast to gather for a small party. The Randalls have promised to come. It's not so very late, and we'll have a jolly time."

Will's pale features were stern. "Beryl and I must get home. We have a long day tomorrow." Beryl nodded, hiding her face under the lace veil.

Witley shrugged. "How about you, Avery, Cabot? Take the Newlands back and then do come and help me and my lady entertain our guests."

Cabot glanced at his companions and sighed. "Better not. All these little children need to go home and tuck their downy heads into bed." He yawned. "I must say I do feel I missed something tonight. I mean, jolly good performance, quite tragic and all, but hardly as traumatizing as my friends seem to have found it. I've never seen a happy group so utterly shattered. If you sniffle one more time, Avery, I shall be forced to wring out your handkerchief."

"Cabot," muttered Avery, "shut up. Let's say good night to these people and be on our way."

Cynthia raised her eyebrows to her husband but said soothingly, "You darlings must all be terribly tired. Another time, perhaps. Good night, Miss Newland, William. Come see us sometime soon – tonight has given me the most marvelous idea for a theatrical club. I do think, Beryl, that you'd make a ravishing Desdemona."

Beryl was so tired and upset that she could hardly answer. "Of course," she murmured. "Of course. Good night." Her civility was a gift to her brother. She understood better now what Will had been struggling with for two years; she knew it down to the raw knuckles that snagged at her gloves. She put her arm through his and turned away.

"Well," said Cabot whistling. "And a merry time was had by all." They found his buggy and silently got in. He rode quickly through the calm night, eager to leave his dreary company behind. When

Avery was gone and he had crossed out from the gates of the New-land farm, he let out a long breath. "Praise be," he hollered to his horse. "I say, praise be that I am NOT in love. Give us lust every time, eh, old stud?" He whipped the animal into a run. They ran a perilous race along the creek bank. The buggy crossed the water with a great deal of splashing and cursing, and then the horse galloped for the high road. There, on the open plain, the winded animal slowed to a canter and then to a lazy walk.

Cabot reached under the seat and found a flask. He was not in love, and that was good. But his interest in Miss Newland had not abated. He found her distracting and desirable – he could admit that in the middle of the night with brandy in his hand – and, meandering slowly over the dark prairie to his estate, he spent more time than he would ever care to admit pondering who the man might be that Avery insisted had captured her affections. The stars wheeled to different corners of the sky while he rode and drank. And when dawn began to creep against the eastern rim of the earth and his flask was empty, he admitted defeat. He crawled down from the buggy and, resting his aching gold brow against his horse's white mane, he acknowledged that, however pleasant it might have been, the man who had won Beryl Newland was not him.

Chapter XIV

The Reverend Epis Emerson sat quietly in the leather chair across from Mr. Grant. His caramel hair curled in worried clusters against a high temple. But the expression under his fine, narrow brows was placid. Almost vacant, thought Grant. He shifted uncomfortably in his own chair and then said to the minister:

"You understand, Rev. Emerson, that what I'm hoping to avoid is a schism of any sort. I want to end the division between Presbyterian and Anglican in this town. Such a small community cannot, I believe, afford to be divided in its worship. So while I want a man who will be in full communion with the Church of England, I'm also seeking someone who can be doctrinally – open. To Scotch Calvinism and such."

"Are you a Calvinist, sir?"

"I understand it. I grew up among those people. I'm living with many of them now."

"But you don't consider yourself a Calvinist?"

Grant impatiently pushed away the dog which had been resting its head on his knee. "I'm hoping to bring believers together in this church. What I consider myself is of little purpose."

"Not to Jesus Christ."

"Oh my God," Grant groaned. Why the Bishop had recommended this man he could not fathom. Emerson was British, and perhaps the American prelate had thought that would be a plus with this congregation. But he struck Grant as painfully thick-headed.

Rev. Emerson smiled, a little sympathetically. "Mr. Grant, I'm trying to see where you situate yourself. Understanding you, I can better understand this congregation. But forgive me if I say you seem to want me to unite people whose beliefs are a bit of a hodge-podge. You have Church of England, you have Scottish Presbyterian, you have Roman Catholic, and, from what I've observed, you have a majority of agnostics and atheists. You wish me to draw them all together? We can put them physically under one roof. But I doubt that

I am up to the task of either uniting them spiritually or keeping them from warring with each other."

"Then why the hell did Bishop Vail send you?" exploded Grant.

Reverend Emerson licked his lips. "Mr. Grant, perhaps he sent me because he knows that I understand what it means to fail and be forgiven. Is that a trait that might be useful to this community?" The eyes, which had seemed rather blank, suddenly looked full and hard at Mr. Grant.

Grant started to stand up, felt a strange twinge, and fell back into his chair. He exhaled heavily. "Well," he said, frowning. "The Catholics are not an issue." He did not answer Emerson's question. The answer seemed too obvious to waste his breath.

Emerson let his eyes slide out of focus again. "I will do my best, Mr. Grant, with what I have to work with." He reached down and petted the dog.

"I ask no more, Mr. Emerson." But both of them knew he did.

Ye Merry Cricketeers met every other Thursday for a series of matches and a dinner at the Manor house. Grant usually presided over the matches; like the racetrack, the games embodied his efforts to direct and satisfy the less healthy appetites of his "lads," as he called them. The day when he interviewed with Reverend Emerson, however, he was not present. The games were played with no less ardor in his absence, but the tenor of discussion at the midday dinner shifted noticeably.

"Fine game, Fred, but if Mayes had been here, you'd never have conquered."

The eldest Wyatt brother laughed. He put some more bread and beef on his plate. "And where was he? He's never missed yet."

Alec Hunter shook his head. "He told me his father's getting a bit tight with the allowance. He had to let his foreman go. So he's having to do the work himself."

Ben Davis hooted. "What work? They've never broken ground, and he calls keeping a dog and two old cows raising stock. There's nothing to do on that place. Might as well let the Injuns camp there. At least the land would be put to use."

"Well, it will be rough on the old boy," said Cabot. "He'll have to drink alone now – and the other fellow was such a good sort. Probably why he missed the match. No one to wake him in time this morning."

Gerard Staples nodded his head. "Aye, and he owes me money. I'm afraid I'll ne'er see it now. The help from home has been getting scant for me too. Damn frustrating."

Nigel Wyatt gave Staples a rabbity look. "Doing badly with those sheep, are you?"

Gerard scowled. "Oh, they drank some scummy stuff from a pond and by Jove I go out and find half a dozen dead. God awful country, I say. Can't even trust the water." He threw his napkin down and put his cap on his head backwards. "Some days I really do think I'd have done better in Australia. The Bush could hardly be worse. And just when I need it, England says they can't send as much money. Damn."

Randall kicked a bowl of salt down the table with his palm. "What I say is, they don't understand at home what it takes to keep a farm going out here. Seems support for everyone is being cut off when it's most wanted."

"Ah," said Avery. "Mrs. Randall's papa not putting forth so much anymore?"

"He's a bastard," said Randall. "Thinks a man can grow an estate on air. But if Lyddie'd put in more of an effort . . . "

"Ah," said Avery again. "I somehow knew that any problems must be Mrs. Randall's fault."

Randall turned toward Avery. "And I suppose nobody sends you money from home? You earn your frilly blouses by yourself?"

Avery raised cool eyes to Randall. "As it happens, the remittances from home ended six months ago. I'm sending money back to Lancashire now."

"I am impressed," Randall said contemptuously. "Don't get me wrong, I'm not afraid of a hard day's work, but I do have other things to do than push dirt around in a circle."

"I've noticed," said Avery. "Most of them involve going in a circle around Mrs. Witley."

Will's hands stilled. Henry Witley, who had been pouring himself a glass of wine, stopped. Cabot pushed his chair back from the table.

"Don't want to get my face ruined when things start flying, don't you know," he murmured to Garth Mason.

"Mrs. Witley is a lovely lady," said Captain Prescott. "I'm sure we all orbit around your wife, Mr. Witley. We drink to your luck on winning her." He raised his glass and looked hard at Avery. After a moment, Avery raised his glass, and the others followed suit.

Witley put the bottle on the table. "Indeed," he said. "I'm not sure whether Mr. Avery compliments my wife or slanders her. But I shall choose to interpret it as the former. Cheers, gentlemen." He said nothing to Mr. Randall at all, merely narrowed his eyes.

Arthur Witley shook his head. "Cynthia rides a lovely horse. She's a fine mount, she is."

"That," whispered Cabot to Mason, "is what I believe Avery was saying."

Mason lined his fork carefully next to his plate, his round face troubled. "Bloody nasty thing to say, Cabot. You think she and Arthur . . . ?"

"Oh, good heavens no," said Cabot, almost laughing. "She's quite safe from Arthur. No, that's not what I meant at all."

Mason shook his head, and said in a low voice, "Sometimes, Cabot, you strike me as an unsavory character."

"Certainly not, Mason." Cabot brushed his gold hair back. "I merely make observations."

Vincent Spenser broke in. "A dangerous business, sir. For you and your friend."

"Avery," said Cabot getting out a cigarette case and offering it to Spenser, "is untouchable. Beyond a deplorable taste in dress, he's quite an angel."

"He should guard what he says, " said Vincent quietly. "Not all these boys are gentlemen. I wouldn't trust them all to play fair. In fact, I know from experience that they don't all play fair." He took the cigarette in his right hand and looked at a scarcely healed wound that ran from the thumb down toward the wrist.

Cabot's blue eyes widened. "I say, that's a wicked cut. How did you come by that?"

Spenser raised the cigarette to his lips and put his glove over the injured hand. "A rather interesting game of cards, shall we say." He shrugged and elbowed Bernard, who sat next to him. "My brother saved me from worse. Always a good chap for stepping in when things get ugly." He looked down the table at Nigel Wyatt for a minute, and then back at Cabot. "I wouldn't trust too many of them."

"It's gotten a bit testy around here. Perhaps American manners are rubbing off. Well, I suppose Avery's become a bit careless."

"Why?"

"Disappointed in love," said Cabot turning pointedly to Spenser. "You know how that feels."

Spenser sat back in his chair and gave a crooked smile. "Not really, no. Perhaps you could tell me."

Cabot measured him. "I've never been disappointed in my life." He stood up. "Shall we? I'm getting cramped in here. And my animal has a loose shoe. I'd be glad if you'd take a look at it, Mason, before we begin again."

Mason wiped his spectacles on his napkin, and then replaced them. "It's going to be a rough game this afternoon."

"I think so too," said Cabot languidly. "We shall all have to watch our skulls."

Bernard watched them leave and then said to Vincent, "Ever feel like you're among the Zouaves again?"

Vincent ground out his cigarette on the flowered china in front of him. "More and more all the time. But damn if I can figure what all the warring's about."

"And who is this woman Avery is losing his better judgment over?"

Vincent stood up. "Beryl Newland."

"Beryl Newland?"

Vincent nodded.

"You've known this?"

"Not much of a secret, Bern."

"Huh." said Bernard. "I seem to be a bit out of things."

Vincent shrugged. "You haven't been here as long."

Bernard studied his brother. "And now he thinks he's lost her. To whom?"

Vincent put on his cap. He gazed for a moment out the window, toward the railroad tracks that stretched away to the west. Bernard thought his eyes softened a little – but then perhaps not. They may have just been adjusting to the change in light. "I couldn't say. But I do know who it isn't." And he looked at Bernard.

They'd never spoken of it before. "I say, I'm sorry, old man," said Bernard.

Vincent shook his head. "There's nothing to be sorry about," he said.

The brothers went outside. They headed toward Mason's livery, where the ponies had been resting. The sun was painfully bright.

"Vince?"

"What?"

"You don't think it's Vonfeldt, do you?"

Vincent stopped. He squinted, frowning.

"I mean, think of the wedding dance, you know."

Vincent didn't look at his brother. "What do you think?" He walked on.

Bernard let out a low whistle. Then he stopped. He saw Will Newland strolling with head down toward the stables. There was a model of English manhood, he thought. Tall, handsome. Moody looking, perhaps, but nonetheless . . . . Bernard shook his head. Impossible that the sister of such a man could prefer a short, ignorant Russian. And then there was his own brother, such a good-looking, intelligent specimen, and the son of Lord Herries. He gave Vonfeldt credit – he was an extraordinary musician, a solid worker, and a good man. But hardly the type that would appeal to a cultured Englishwoman. Which left the mystery of who was breaking Avery's heart unsolved. Prescott? Keith? Some American?

Then he saw Witley and remembered a more pressing problem. He ran to catch up with Vincent. "You know, Vince, we're running low. Were you able to collect on that debt?"

"Not yet."

Bernard bit his lip. "Witley is going to sell that horse to someone else, unless we can pay for it soon."

Vincent went into the barn and examined his pony. He rubbed its handsome nose. "Go to Father."

"Can't do that. He says he's given as much as he's willing for animals."

Vincent checked his saddle, and then cinched it a bit more snugly. "The Germans need an addition."

"So what? You do get off the point."

"Tell him the Germans need an addition. To the church, you know." Vincent stood up. "Don't you think they need an addition?"

Bernard, ever fleet of mind, stared at his brother. Then he said, "Aunt Clara was right. You did inherit all the brains."

Vincent shrugged.

"Of course, it might be a sin."

"It might," said Vincent. In the half-light of the barn his expression was slightly sartorial. "But not if it's a very good horse."

"By god, it is," said Bernard delightedly clapping his brother on the back. "It sure as hell is."

Beryl could not stay out of her garden forever. Her own cowardice made her ashamed after a while. She was not even sure what she feared. Perhaps it was simply facing Vonfeldt again. But it was ridiculous to hide in the house when there was a farm to run. And she had to run it. Will was lapsing into apathy about the estate again. He was away more and more. Beryl was not sure what caused Will's defection; he did not come home drunk. But he was absent for long periods during the day, and sometimes overnight. Occasionally he came back with a deer or a handful of rabbits, so she guessed he might be hunting. She was afraid to ask him, however, in part because he was so touchy, and in part because they had developed a kind of working relationship that would have seemed impossible to her four years before: they asked each other little about their lives, and they intruded even less. Their experience in Kansas had taught them the many things that could not safely be said between them, and they had learned that the way to avert confrontation was to avoid discussion. So, they talked little, especially about personal subjects. This made life peaceful. It also fostered worry and a terrific loneliness.

When William came home with a rattlesnake bite one afternoon, Beryl could not avoid Vonfeldt any longer. Will came galloping in on his horse, leaning awkwardly over to one side. She came out onto the porch. At first, she thought he was drunk. She could feel the anger rushing up inside her, but then she saw the pallor of his face and the way he was clutching his forearm to his breast. He had managed to tie a handkerchief in a tight knot above the bite, but his limb was swelling like the belly of a dead cow. He could not talk clearly; he seemed as affected by the heat and the horror of his hard ride as from the snake bite. He fell against her. She cried out in fear and pulled him into the house. She could not get him as far as his bedroom; he collapsed on the floor, the dogs nuzzling and whining in his face. Frantic, she fetched some water, wiped his sweating brow, and coaxed him to drink. Beyond that, she had no idea what to do. She ran from the house.

At her request, Red Thompson had gone to Wichita to explore the possibility of buying sheep. This was against Will's wishes; he maintained that he was a farmer, not a rancher. She countered that since he wasn't home to farm, and since farming was so hard and the land so difficult, it made better sense to go into raising wool. When Will yet again disappeared for half a week, she sent Thompson on his errand. Now the hired hand would not be back for another day and a half.

The only help was Vonfeldt, who continued his dogged work in the fields when Thompson was gone. That afternoon she did not know where exactly he was on the farm. She screamed his name. She ran past the stable, the dogs running with her, barking in excitement. In the fields, the maize was now quite high. It was taller than she was; she could not see above it. She dashed into it, following the rows and calling. No one answered. She began tearing through the stalks, the leaves whipping against her face. Her braid tore and tangled over her shoulders, sending loose strands into her eyes. She realized too late she should have taken a horse; she could see nothing except the evil green leaves, the tassels that brushed her face like cobwebs, and the mocking sky. She screamed and screamed for help and began to cry. She could scarcely breathe in her panic. Will would die. Will would die because she did not know what to do, and she hadn't thought clearly. She ran and ran.

Somewhere in the fields, Vonfeldt heard her screams and the dogs' barking. It was the dogs who helped him find her. He called and they rushed to him, jumping and running. He dropped his hoe and ran through the field after them, his bare feet following the furrows and the sound of Beryl's cries. It took him only a few minutes to find her. She clutched him, weeping and screaming and crying "Will! Will!" She could not be more coherent. She pointed back to the house.

They were not far from the main buildings; in her panic Beryl had become disoriented, but Vonfeldt knew the fields well and holding her hand he ran through the corn, following the dogs out of the maze. Once they escaped from the field, he dropped her hand and raced ahead. Inside the house he discovered Will crumpled on the floor. At first Vonfeldt thought he had been shot, then he saw the swollen arm. He bent down and lifted the limp man over his shoulder. He found a room with a bed in it and took William in, letting his body fall onto the mattress. Beryl found them, Will lying grey on her bed, Vonfeldt frantically pulling at the handkerchief tied around his arm. At last he took out a knife and cut off the makeshift tourniquet.

He turned the arm gently and looked at the fang marks. They made large twin gashes; this seemed to please him. She did not understand why, but he was glad to see it had been an adult snake. An infant's bite was almost certain to be fatal. He looked around quickly and saw water in a washstand. He looked at Beryl and rubbed his hands together in a furious pantomime. She hurried to get him soap and a rag. Quickly, he washed the wound. Though it was too late to do much good, because most of the venom had surely circulated into the system already, he took his knife and sliced between the fang marks, lowered his lips to the wound, and sucked the blood out. After a moment, he spat it into the basin. Drops of blood clung to his beard. His eyes above his bloody mouth were pale as a wolf's.

Making an impatient, angry sound, he said something to her in German. She could not understand. He held up the rag, shaking it at her. She went and came back with a pile of fresh towels and linens. He washed the wound again, and then ran outside. After a few minutes he came back carrying a small bowl filled with mud from the creek. Adding fresh water from the pitcher, he made a kind of paste. This he smeared on the bite, and then wrapped it in the linen. The arm was swelling horrifically; an angry red line was mapping its way along the underside. He bisected it with the clean cloth pulled quite tight, though not so tight as to cut off the circulation.

Will moaned. Vonfeldt looked at Beryl, again said something to her in German, and gestured with his hands. "I don't know what you mean," she cried.

He looked angry at her frustration and pushed past her. She followed him into the kitchen, where he tore open cupboards and pulled out drawers. Beryl thought he would tear the house apart, but at last he exclaimed triumphantly. A bottle of whiskey; it had been tucked behind the coal scuttle. Beryl looked at it stupidly; she'd had no idea it was there.

Grabbing several glasses, some sugar, and a spoon, Vonfeldt ran back into the bedroom. He stirred together spoonfuls of sugar and a fair amount of whiskey in one of the glasses. Then he lifted Will onto his arm and raised the drink to his lips.

Will sputtered and spit but managed to swallow most of it; he was more than conditioned to alcohol. When the glass was empty, Vonfeldt turned Will on his good arm and rested his head sideways on Beryl's white coverlet. He feared Will would vomit, and he did not want him to choke. Then he stood still, breathing hard. He knew no more to do. They could only let the poison run its course and hope that Will survived.

Beryl looked at Vonfeldt, wide-eyed and trembling. Then she turned her eyes on her brother and began sobbing, falling to her knees beside the bed. "Oh, Jesus, help him. Dear Jesus, save him."

Vonfeldt knelt beside her, putting his arm around her and holding her to him. She cried for several minutes, praying and leaning against him. As she calmed down, he took his handkerchief from his pocket – a dirty blue bandana which she accepted gratefully – and then helped her sit in a chair. She wiped her tears, and shook her head a few times, as if to clear it. She pulled her hair away from her face. Her chest continued to heave convulsively, but she felt better. She looked at her brother's pale, sweating brow and wiped it with a clean cloth dipped in water. Then she looked at Vonfeldt "Doctor?" she asked.

He frowned. He wanted to tell her that all they could do now was tend him and wait; he doubted that a doctor could do more. He paused a moment, thinking, and then, putting her hands in his, he looked into her grey eyes and spoke to her in German. He knew she did not understand the words, but he hoped that she understood the meaning.

"He will not die?" she asked.

He is strong and young, he told her.

She seemed satisfied. She knew that Douglas Keith would be coming by later in the afternoon. For the moment, though, she trusted Vonfeldt. She had seen him nurse animals through sickness. She was confident he would see Will through, if he could be seen through at all.

Vonfeldt did not stay beside her. He went to the other side of the bed and sat quietly against the wall. Every now and again, he got up to feel Will's forehead. He loosened the tourniquet a bit. When Will began to gag, he lifted him so that he could throw up into a bowl that Beryl held. They cleaned him together and waited while the afternoon clouds sent shadows across the window light. At last Beryl closed the shutters, as she had every afternoon, to make the room more restful. This time, however, instead of closing Vonfeldt out, she closed him in with her. Neither of them noticed. Their entire attention was on the sick man.

Douglas Keith arrived shortly after 4 p.m. The dogs barked as he rode into the yard. Hearing them, Beryl ran out.

"Will's hurt – he's been bitten," she cried.

Keith dropped from his horse and rushed into the house. In the darkened bedroom, he saw Will lying, curled and groaning, on Beryl's bed. Behind him stood the Russian musician who had been working at the Newlands. Keith looked at Will's swollen arm and the wrapping, checked his pulse, and lifted his eyelids to study his pupils. He gently pushed Will's hair back from his face.

"Where did it happen?"

"I don't know – he came riding in, slumped on his horse. Mr. Vonfeldt helped me take him in and take care of him. Will he be all right?"

Keith looked at Vonfeldt, trying to gauge his opinion. Vonfeldt shrugged a little but nodded. "You've sent for a doctor?"

"Not yet; we didn't know what more he could do."

"Not much, I don't think. Stop the pain maybe. Though that concoction should relieve some of the agony." He sniffed at the glass Vonfeldt had given Will.

Vonfeldt watched the Britons uneasily for a few minutes. Since Keith had come, he felt out of place. His focus had entirely been on the sick man, but now he felt the awkwardness of being in this darkened room with its soft, feminine coverlet on the bed, the dress draped over a chair, the books in a language he could not read on a small table. He no longer belonged here now that someone equally capable could watch Mr. Newland. While Beryl and Mr. Keith talked, he quietly turned and left.

Beryl noticed. She asked Mr. Keith to stay with Will and then ran to the porch. "You're not going?" she asked, forgetting for the moment that his English was poor.

He turned and looked at her. "Chores," he said haltingly. Then he thought for a minute and said, "I go for more help."

"Oh. Yes." She struggled, about to cry. Then the tears spilled. "I want you to stay."

He stood in the yard, his feet bare and dirty, his hair blowing against his beard and over strained lips. "No," he said. "But tomorrow, yes."

She looked at him, shaking like a lost child. Her fingers clutched at her apron and twisted it; there was no music in them, only agony. He, too, struggled and then spoke to her, low and sweet, in German: "I will not fail to come. Do not be afraid. God will be with you, and I will pray for you every minute of every hour. In that way I will be with you too."

Then he turned and ran for Victoria.

The news that Will Newland was down from snake bite spread quickly once Vonfeldt reached Victoria. George Grant and Meg rode out to the farm with the doctor who, as Vonfeldt and Keith had predicted, could do relatively little, but who did know the signs to watch for. Keith stayed when they arrived, doing the chores that ordinarily Thompson or Vonfeldt would have done. Grant sat with Will and the doctor. He listened to the labored breathing and to semi-coherent ramblings about snakes and rocks and Cynthia Witley, stroking his head as a father would a son. "Be brave, Will," he said. "Fight the good fight for your sister and for yourself."

Will cried at one point, sobbing as though his heart would break: "I am a bad man. I am a bad man. Oh, forgive me, forgive me."

Grant's face contorted; he knew what this guilt was about, and it angered him. Gently, he held the boy. "It's not true, lad. Not a bit of it. You are a good man, Will Newland. One of the best." He clenched his teeth and writhed at something that ate him from the inside, not so unlike the poison that contended in Will Newland's system.

Meg stood by Beryl in the parlor, combing out the tangled hair and rebraiding it. Beryl said little. She gave many shuddering breaths; she jumped whenever Will called out; she would not eat. Occasionally a far-away look came into her eyes. Then she would come back to herself and begin to weep. Meg made her tea and cut her some bread and butter.

"Please eat, Beryl. You can't take care of Will unless you take food."

Beryl at last nodded and put the bread to her lips.

"What happened to the kitchen?" asked Meg.

"He was trying to find whiskey to give him."

"Who was?"

"Mr. Vonfeldt."

"He was here, then?"

"He helped me."

Meg sat quietly, listening to a cricket call at the coming of dusk. "They said a German came into Hunter's store and could hardly speak for running. It was good Mr. Spenser was there. He understood what the man was saying."

"Oh," said Beryl. She started to cry again and could hardly swallow the bread. She forced herself to stop. "I'm so glad you and Mr. Grant came. It was very kind of you."

"It must have been hard for you before Mr. Keith came," said Meg. "You couldn't talk with that German. You must have been frantic."

Beryl's eyes suddenly flashed. "He's not 'that German.' There's no one I can depend on as I can Mr. Vonfeldt. I didn't need to talk. I knew I could trust him."

Her tone was sharp; Meg stumbled at the sting. "I only meant -"

"You mean you don't know him. Not at all."

Meg raised a flushed face. "And what makes you think you do? Because he plays a fine fiddle and makes you queen of the dance?"

Beryl stood up. She turned and went silently into the bedroom.

Meg stayed in the parlor. She sat in the rocker, staring at the lamp. For the first time in four years, she wished that she had never left Scotland and never seen this flat, dark land. She wished she had never met Nigel Wyatt, the pale shadow who haunted her days like an inexorable fate. She wished even more that she had never lived to see Beryl in love, never lived to taunt her about it. Even after Will was well – and that took several weeks – the breach between the women was not healed. It was a wound, in fact, which cut deeper and bled more deadly than any that a rattlesnake could give.

The idea for a pleasure barge was conceived on an August afternoon in the Witleys' drawing room. The Newlands were not there. Will was still recovering from his injury and Beryl now had neither time for socializing nor reason for wanting to escape from the farm. But Mr. Grant was visiting with Meg and Ian Duncan and the new minister, Rev. Emerson. Jack Randall was there as well. And, after a short time, they were joined by Nigel Wyatt, who had heard that Meg was at the Witleys and took the chance to make a call and enjoy an "accidental" meeting.

It was an awkward conglomeration of people, but Cynthia Witley was never one to be daunted by such a challenge. She and the Persian both sat on the sofa looking delectably soft and leaving the impression that they could be counted on to curl up ever-so sweetly in one's lap. Her husband sat on the floor next to her, looking lazy and eating cherries from a bowl. Occasionally he spit a pit at the cat, causing his wife to protest. At one point he hit the Persian square on the nose. The creature crossed her gold eyes in a fury, jumped to the floor, and curled up under a table where she eyed him coldly for a full two hours. Reverend Emerson watched from under his worried curls and delicate, narrow eyebrows. The expression on his face as he sipped his tea suggested that he found the Witleys rather freakish.

Mr. Randall and Mr. Wyatt sat next to each other on a spindly settee with puffy cushions, looking like negatives of each other. Wyatt was clearly out of his element in that room of gold and emerald opulence; his white hair and pink eyes took on a greenish hue from the draperies, and when the wind blew them open the sunlight spilled over him like bleach. Next to him, Randall seemed an inkblot: black hair, black eyes, black suit, and black mood. Wyatt was making an effort to behave well. He was not quite oily in his politeness, but Meg, who felt sick at everything, kept muttering "Uriah Heep" over and over in her head. On the other hand, Randall seemed out to pick a fight. He was rude to everyone: sardonic to Mr. Grant, sneering to Mr. Wyatt, truculent to Mr. Witley, and brusque with Mr. Duncan. Meg and the Reverend Emerson he ignored altogether; Mrs. Witley he stared at until even her exquisitely chiseled manners seemed to chip. But she was, after all, a good actress and she carried the conversation like the accomplished hostess she was.

"So, Mr. Newland will fully recover? I'm so glad. Where could the boy have been, Henry? I thought you had led a rampage guaranteed to rid the country of serpents."

"He must have found the one that escaped our avenging hands. I say, perhaps we should have another hunt. We don't seem to have wiped them out yet."

Mr. Grant shook his head. "Better not go looking for trouble. It's bad enough when it meets you head on."

"The truth is it's a god-forsaken land. Nothing but trouble." Randall snorted above folded arms.

"It's a fine land, but it's no playground. To make it pay, we have to be ready to work and suffer. It's like any business: it demands constant tending."

"I agree" said Witley. "But if I can hire someone to tend shop for me – why so much the better, eh Randall?" He laughed. It was not exactly a pleasant sound.

"Leave your cherries untended and some else will come pick 'em," said Randall. "Assuming you can get them to grow in such barren soil."

"I find that my cherries are growing quite well, thank you." Witley popped another in his mouth.

"Your metaphors are getting tangled, gentlemen, and frankly I find none of them illuminating. Do let's change the subject. Mr. Wyatt, how are things on your farm?"

"We're doing well, Mrs. Witley. Expect a fine crop of wheat this year, and a good yield next too. I owe it all to Mr. Grant giving me the chance to turn my life around. I was headed wrong, but now I see my way clear. Hard work, manly pursuits, give a fellow everything he needs in life." He turned his pink eyes on Meg and blinked. "Almost."

Meg thought she would gag. Duncan, who had been wondering how a man could be expected to fill up on sandwiches the size of his thumb and who had been plotting ways to escape to the barn, decided he was better stationed where he was. He gave the dainty chair next to Meg a dubious glance, and then situated himself gingerly upon it. He leaned his head in a confidential manner toward her but said loudly enough for everyone to hear, "I may need to go hunting rabbit this afternoon, Miss Grant. What do you think?"

Meg's freckles were flooded in a blush. Duncan had called Mr. Wyatt a rabid rabbit more than once. She found herself torn between irritation at Duncan's continued assumption that she was unable to fend for herself and gratitude that someone seemed interested in getting the man off of her hands. Gratitude won out. "Some of them do seem to be nibbling at the gardens too much this summer, Mr. Duncan."

Wyatt (who might be pale but was by no means stupid) sensed an insult and ugly, hot anger rushed up his throat. But outwardly he remained calm and unconcerned, giving his full attention to his cucumber sandwich. Randall, on the other hand, looked at Duncan and Meg as though they were idiots. One, he was sure, shouldn't be allowed anywhere outside of a barnyard, and the other was so pulingly insignificant he couldn't imagine why his wife tolerated her. Perhaps because she was Grant's niece. But that hardly seemed a reason to respect her the more; it was, in his opinion, possibly reason to tolerate her the less. He snorted again and turned his stare back to Mrs. Witley.

Mr. Grant felt the poison rummaging in his chest and took up a cudgel against it. "You've made a place of beauty here on the plains, Mrs. Witley. I told Reverend Emerson that if he visited your home, he'd see what commitment and culture and taste can create even on the frontier. I trust he's not been disappointed."

"You have a lovely home, and I'm grateful to Mr. Grant for bringing me to meet you. I hope you'll come some Sunday and join the service at the Chapel in Victoria. The building is not finished yet, but the spirit is growing stone by stone."

Mrs. Witley looked at Reverend Emerson and began a pretty little speech, and then stopped, startled. She began again and finished her lines to perfection, uttering how delighted she would be to attend Sunday service and hear him speak. But as she spoke, she turned sharp eyes on his face, noting the large vacant pupils and measuring the tiny tremor in his lips and hands. Then she leaned back against the pillows piled behind her like a butterfly sinking into the petals of a great flower. "My land," she said aloud and began laughing. "I never fail to find something diverting out here. Just when I think I've seen it all and ennui must set in – I discover something new that I never suspected, and there the wonder is again."

Everyone looked at her blankly.

She laughed and said to Henry, "What shall we do for amusement now, love? These everlasting cricket matches and beastly hunts are getting boring. Have you any ideas? I mean, aren't there any lakes where we could go yachting?" In reply, Henry spit a pit at her.

"My dress! You incorrigible boy!" she exclaimed and slapped at him.

Mr. Grant sighed and wished he were home. Mr. Wyatt sipped his tea and decided that Mrs. Witley was like a useless dog: she needed a good beating to knock some sense into her. Her husband, he concluded, should just be shot. Randall continued to stare at her – though perhaps now with more reason – and Reverend Emerson began counting the crumpet crumbs on his plate. Only Duncan and Meg looked interested, Meg because she thought there might actually be a lake within a reasonable distance (such was her knowledge of Kansas geography) and Duncan because he actually had an idea.

"The nearest lake is a fair trek from here, ma'am, but I think you might be able to make a loch that would be ship worthy."

"Really?" She dropped the offending pit into an ash tray. "How?"

"Dam the Victoria."

"That's what I say," growled Randall.

"No, man, dam the creek. You could easily do it from where your land is situated – be able to make a deep enough flow that you might be able to boat all the way to the fort and back."

Grant looked at his foreman and frowned. "Damming for pleasure seems a foolish way to handle a creek in country pining for water."

Duncan nodded. "You're right, sir. It'd be a poor way to handle the creek in dry years – but in a wet year like this one? Still be plenty of water for cattle and homesteaders downstream."

Henry Witley was sitting up now. "I say, what a jolly scheme."

"Oh, Henry, we could get a steamboat, just like on the Mississippi!"

"That would be something to see," laughed Meg. "What an absurd notion!"

"Absurd," echoed Wyatt, glad to think that he and Meg agreed.

"What's absurd about it? Takes a bit of engineering know how is all." Duncan pulled a pencil from his pocket and, turning a magazine upside down on a low table, began drawing a plan. Witley put down his bowl of cherries and leaned over to see. "Get a good quarry to give you the stones, and you'll have no trouble at all, see?" said Duncan.

"Norton's," said Witley, speculatively. "We've gotten quality rock from there."

"So, you do think it's possible?" said Cynthia, almost squeezing her husband in her excitement. Randall glared at her. "Don't know why not, my dear," said Witley. "Draw me up a formal plan, Duncan, and we'll talk some more. That is, if Mr. Grant doesn't mind loaning you to me for a bit."

Grant smiled genially with his mouth, but his eyes were fatigued and displeased. Always play, never serious endeavor to build up the country. In the back of his mind was the village of Herzog as he had seen it on the day of the wedding: solid buildings, carefully tended gardens, wheat reaching in disciplined lines to the horizon. And all of it built from nothing except strong muscles and determination. He understood that way of achieving; it was how he had become a master merchant and then one of the most renowned purveyors of silk in London. These children – for they did all seem to be children

– had money handed to them like so much candy and they squandered it on toys. A pleasure boat, he thought. One more diversion from work. He was tired of trying to concoct wholesome entertainment to protect these young people from more dangerous pursuits. They found their way into trouble anyway. He gazed at Mrs. Witley, poised like a bright bubble on the edge of her couch, and thought of Will Newland. He could taste the sourness in his mouth. She noticed his eyes and, unable to read his thoughts, smiled at him. But another pair of eyes she divined better, and they pleased her less.

"Mr. Randall, if you cannot stop looking at me in that disagreeable way, I shall have to ask you to go out to the barn with Arthur and spend your time among the bulls."

Witley gave Randall a narrow look and then said, "Where is Mrs. Randall today? We miss her company. She's able to keep you much more cheerful, old man."

Mr. Grant felt the sour taste grow stronger. "Let's walk in the garden, Meg," he said heavily. "I'm feeling the need for some fresh air, and the afternoon seems to be cooling now."

Meg rose. "Of course, uncle. I'll get my parasol. Won't you join us, Rev. Emerson?" She felt sorry for the minister, who clearly had no desire to see any more culture or taste at the Witleys. And she could tell he hadn't discovered an ounce of commitment.

Nigel Wyatt quickly stood. "May I join your party?" he asked.

Meg hesitated, not wanting to be impolite but bursting with the desire to be untroubled by him. Duncan looked at her face and then said, "Wyatt, let's take a turn in the barn. Arthur has a handsome new horse that I know you'll be interested in. And I'd be glad to consult with you about a few things. How to handle pesky rabbits, for instance."

Ian Duncan was twice as big as Nigel Wyatt; the latter followed his husky animal bulk to the barn like a sulky wraith. The interesting thing was, Cynthia noted to her husband a few days later, that Arthur claimed he had never seen them in the barn – and certainly they never returned to the house.

"Must've gone off hunting together," said Witley, uninterested.

"I think," she said, "that only one of them was hunting."

"Ah, really?" he yawned. "Catch anything?"

"I don't know," she said. "But Meg Grant has the most beautiful white fur cap. She showed it to me today."

"Well, jolly good. Wonder how he found a white pelt in summer. Ah, well, she'll be warm this winter."

"Hmmmm," said Cynthia. "And Mr. Wyatt will, I suspect, will be rather colder."

"Hmmph. Got rid of him at last, eh?"

"Perhaps. He certainly wasn't skulking around the Villa when I was there. But if I were Ian Duncan, I'd watch my back."

"I say," said Witley, at last showing some real interest, "you don't think there'll be trouble before we've got the dam finished do you? I'm depending on Duncan."

"Your self-interest is positively inspiring."

"All for you, darling. All for you."

The cicadas' cyclic whir churned through August and into September. Will convalesced slowly, reading and occasionally taking a ride along the creek while Beryl harvested with Thompson and Vonfeldt. The work was hard; she was not used to it. Will had always done much of it before, and never before had they had such a good yield. Beryl's arms ached at night and her skin burned and then grew brown where she rolled up the sleeves of her dress. She cursed her corsets; the sweat and dirt slid down between the stinking whale-bone and her skin; she felt she could neither work during the day nor become clean at night. At last, frustrated, she kicked them under the bed and dressed without them one morning. She felt naked un-der her chemise and feared she might look naked to others, but she could breathe, and she could work, and she felt infinitely cooler. None of the men said anything (not that they would even if they noticed), and as she was always properly laced up when she went into town on Sunday, there were no women to be any the wiser. Meg did not visit, and Lydia was recovering from a miscarriage. Beryl of-ten felt alone in a man's world.

Yet she also felt happier than she had ever been in her life. She toiled with Thompson and Vonfeldt, ate with them, and joked with them. Neither seemed quite comfortable with her presence at first;

Thompson thought he would choke having to say "Miss" every five seconds, and Vonfeldt wondered how he could get any work done knowing she was so close to him. But they got over their inhibitions and her help was welcome. When the hired teams with harvesting machines came to the farm, she stayed indoors and cooked as best as she could for them. She was not a great success, but then the men were hungry and not particular. After the machines were gone, she joined Thompson and Vonfeldt out in the barn and the field. They relaxed enough to begin teaching each other their languages: Beryl taught Thompson and Vonfeldt English, Vonfeldt taught Thompson and Beryl German, and Thompson taught the other two American — "which is real, true, English and don't be fooled by that missy here," he insisted. They laughed quite a bit during their breaks and even while they worked. Will listened from the house where he was reading and writing letters and felt a little more at peace with things.

Thompson was a good fellow, hardworking, friendly, and frank. He was an old cowboy, however, and while somewhere back in his past he'd had a romance and (though he'd never admit it even to his horse) a wife, he was well beyond the time when he could recognize the signs of a man and a woman coming together. And as Beryl and Vonfeldt were fighting the tendency quite a bit themselves, he could hardly be faulted for not realizing what was happening.

Perhaps Vonfeldt began his active wooing, without even allowing himself to acknowledge what he was doing, when he began to bring his violin to work with him. It was of course a ridiculous thing to bring to work, but he rationalized that he could practice while he walked to and from the Newland farm. Beryl had once listened for his whistling; now she listened for his violin. And that violin, with or without its owner's conscious consent, was making love to her. The music occasionally touched her with its laughing, but more often with its longing. She and Vonfeldt could speak to each other only awkwardly even as they learned more of each other's language; she learned a little about his sister, his parents, his life in Russia in the city and in the country. But listening to him play, she learned worlds about what felt like his soul; and she knew, instinctively, that his soul was almost always singing about her.

This was no parlor courtship, no man coming to sit for an hour and watch while a woman played the piano and poured tea and talked about the weather. They dug in the ground for potatoes until their fingernails were black and husked corn in the barn while the sheaves cut at their dry hands. Their bodies were sweaty, and the flies bothered them so that they could not rest for long. The dogs and the horses kept them company. And they worked side by side, more conscious each day not only of a growing fondness for each other, a genuine liking and joy in the other's company, but also an almost painful awareness of each other's bodies. Their arms brushed in the garden; their legs bumped as they passed down the narrow rows; their hips rested together as they sorted turnips. Beryl found this distracting and disquieting. She had lived and seen enough on the frontier to understand things that she would not have understood had she stayed in London. She was not happy understanding all these things, especially when she saw them within herself. She knew that she had despised Cabot for his behavior with women without fully comprehending what passion was. And although she retained no illusions about the unholy evil of lust without love, she also realized that desire bites hard.

She worked with Vonfeldt and felt an incredible tenderness for him, an incredible gratitude for his laughter and gentleness. But she also grew aware of another feeling, a strange, frightening feeling of power, strange because it was new and frightening because she enjoyed it so much. When her back ached from work and she stood and arched it back over her hip, she knew that Vonfeldt's eyes watched her, hungry. She felt her breasts fall against her shirtwaist as she bent and realized that she loved the feeling of them hanging sweet and loose, that she wanted him to see how she loved it, that she wanted him to touch them, that she wanted to press them against his chest and feel his breath on her neck and his hands on her hips. And when she raised her grey eyes to his pale ones, she could see that he wanted all those things too.

She worked in a kind of stuporous dream as the Indian Summer came, only half aware of anything that did not concern Vonfeldt. Will seemed much better; the harvest was going well; the sky was blue and wide. The larks that caroled over the turning grasses were almost as charming as the strings which sang for her each morning and each afternoon. She prayed sometimes, thanking God for this amazing, beautiful thing that had taken all the heaviness from her heart. She wondered if Vonfeldt prayed the same way.

Which showed how far apart, really, the worlds were that these two people inhabited. When he went back to Herzog in the evening to work on his own farm, to laugh and live with his own people, he was stricken by a dark sense of sin. After the wedding where his brother-in-law had warned him not to get involved with the English woman and had reminded him, harshly, that he was betrothed to a girl in Russia, Vonfeldt fought his desire and growing affection. But he found himself surprised and unhappy and then, oddly, lonely when Miss Newland herself seemed to avoid him, when she no longer talked to him or watched him work. That she seemed to be spurning him turned his resolve into something like anger and his desire into something more nearly resembling love. Then when she came to him for help the day her brother was poisoned, when she turned to him with those anguished grey eyes, the trick that his heart had played on him was complete. He was not just running for Will Newland's life the day he raced to Victoria. He was running for his own, trying to out-distance a love that he knew was going to catch him and for which he was likely to pay the rest of his life.

So he went home every night to the dark of sin and shame. He was betraying the girl in Russia. He was betraying *unsere leute* by coveting something beyond their faith and beyond their ken. His sister complained that *die Englisches* were conceited and looked down on the Germans, "as though bare feet and hardworking hands were anything to be ashamed of!" He knew this was true. He knew, too, that Beryl Newland was not Catholic and did not, at bottom, understand his faith. He wept some nights, praying to the Virgin to take his part in this fight. The priest told him in Confession that the Protestant girl was a snare, a trap of the devil to take him from the true faith and to separate him from his people. Vonfeldt tried to believe this, and when Beryl's shape came to him in his dreams and he imagined holding and touching her body until he became hard and inflamed, he could almost accept it. But when he saw her in the mornings, the way her face lit up when he came into sight and the trusting way she looked at him, he said to hell with the priest. There were many good reasons for not getting involved with this English girl. But sin was not one of them.

So they worked together, contenting themselves finally with thinking about the current moment and not about what would follow. She was less certain than he that their love must end in unhappiness, so she enjoyed the days more fully. She had come to the frontier to escape the confines of her world; if she wished to go away with a German, then she would do so. She had left England behind. She did not reckon that Russia had come with him to this place.

On a brisk, blue-skied day near the end of that September, they worked together among the crabapple trees at the edge of the Newland land, along a bank of Victoria Creek. Thompson was elsewhere, busy with the sheep he'd purchased for Beryl, so they were alone. They climbed the stunted trees and filled their pails with the fruit. It was a light job after the hard work of the days before. The breeze blew cool and clean and made Beryl feel as if she could fly. She sat among the branches of the trees and picked crabapples, watching them stain her fingers red and swatting at jealous bees and flies. She wore a straw hat of Will's around which she had wrapped a white veil. Her sleeves were rolled up to the elbow, and her skirt, an old brown one that was stained with berry juice and barn work, hung soft between her legs, cradling the pail. Vonfeldt worked in the next tree. He was much faster than she was, although he spent more of his time eating the fruit than Beryl did. They sang together a little – he was teaching her a German folksong, and, in their halting way, they spoke of the coming winter. She felt perfectly, joyously happy. When he threw his head back and laughed, she laughed with him, full-throated and unself-conscious as a child.

He poured his pails of fruit into bushel baskets on the back of the wagon. The wagon was heavy; it held several barrels of stones which they would be carting back to the main house to build up a stable wall that was breaking near the foundation. The horses were tired from hauling and cropped grass gratefully. One of them raised his head and knickered a little as Vonfeldt poured in the load. Vonfeldt turned and looked at Beryl, laughing down at him from the tree, the bright sky behind her, and he suddenly knew that now was the time. Tomorrow, it would be worse.

"Come down now."

"Why? We can get so much more." She gestured to the tangled branches of the tree.

He stood quietly for a minute and then said. "The stone must go back. I will not be here tomorrow to help unload."

The breeze blew the branch where she sat, and the veil swept softly against her cheek. "Why not? Do you help your sister and brother?"

"Yah." He hesitated. "My time here is done. I must work on our place now."

Beryl's face stilled, as though she'd been slapped. "You won't come back?"

"No. We have our own work."

She took a breath, her eyes fleeing to the horizon above his head, away toward the Smoky Hills. For a moment, she remembered the young woman named Mary, carried away by the Indians, never rescued, never heard from again. She had not thought of her for a long time. "You will come again next summer."

He unconsciously stepped back from the tree where she sat. "No. Next summer I will be married."

Beryl's pail fell. Crabapples scattered like marbles. They got lost in the grass and rolled under rocks. He looked up at her.

Her face was frozen and hard. She felt cold and dizzy. Humiliation had slapped her numb, but she could still see. She saw that she was ridiculous, perched in a tree in front of this man. She saw that she was ridiculous, working side by side with him like a common laborer. She was ridiculous and disgusting, thinking what she had thought and dreaming what she had dreamed. An involuntary cry escaped her, the cry of an injured animal.

Vonfeldt's pale eyes grew wide with her pain and with his. "Come down."

She looked at him, shaking her head, scarcely aware that her body had begun to shake too. A cloud seemed to pass before the sun. Everything was grey. "For God's sake, Beryl, come down." She shivered in the branches.

He went up to the tree and began to climb towards her. She kicked at him, but only for a moment. Her sense of dignity was coming back through the numbness. She need not be any more ridiculous than she already had been. As he reached for her, she wrenched away and jumped to the ground.

He came down after her and grabbed her arm. She turned her face from him.

"I had to tell you."

"Why?" she burst out angrily, whipping back to face him. "Why? I was so happy. I was so happy." She broke down, sobbing.

He pulled her to him, now crying himself. "My heart. I had to tell you. I had to tell you." He kept saying it over and over, all the time straining her to him, until she looked at him with shattered eyes. He kissed her through the veil and then tore it from her head and kissed her on the lips, the eyes, the neck, the hands. He felt her body, her lips parted and open beneath his, and all those hours of yearning should have been realized. But what he felt most of all in this moment was her terrible sorrow and his terrible loss. The desire to love her body seemed to be carried away in something bigger: the desire to love and comfort her soul, the thing inside this woman that he would have given his life to protect long after her beauty was gone and she was old and ugly and her mind was lost.

"Beryl!" The steps were running, fast. "Beryl!"

The rage in the voice tore them apart. Beryl jumped, the shock jolting her from Vonfeldt as if she'd been struck. She knocked hard against the wagon. The horses, startled by the yell and the movement behind them, backed up. It was a slight motion, but the wagon had not been braked. It began to roll, the heavy load urging it down the incline. Beryl could not move quickly enough. Her skirt caught in the rear wheel. She fell beneath it. Vonfeldt screamed and lunged at the wagon. It pushed over her with a sickening lurch. He managed to grasp the side of it and tried to brace, then stumbled and dropped against the turning wheel. The horses staggered. The load dragged them toward the creek. The vehicle crashed against the fruit trees, sending a shower of crabapples like red hail onto the ground and onto the man and the woman who lay there. One of the barrels toppled from the back of the wagon, breaking through branches and smashing apart in the water below. The horses grunted and stamped to regain their footing. Then everything was quiet. The wind hushed through the leaves and a blackbird called.

Will Newland stood with his right hand over his mouth. The letter which he had been clutching in his left hand dropped to the grass and blew away.

Chapter XV

Night closed in. No twilight, no stars. Just blackness. People stumbled and fell. But though it blinded, the dark did not obliterate other senses. Blood still felt wet and warm on the hands; it still tasted sharp on the tongue. Insects, shrinking from frost, still fought against silence. Crickets still called from under rocks and rotting trees. Wind still hissed over the grass. And, out on the emptiness, trains still wailed. That was the sound that tore the dark apart, separating those who could hear, those who were still warm, who still breathed and moved and reached for light, from those who could not be touched, those who were stiff and cold and grasped at nothing. The wail came and then trailed away, getting lost in that blackness until those who were alive could hear it no better than those who were dead. The living grew still in their beds and by their fires, straining to catch what was gone. Their limbs grew stiff and cold with fear. Light and life pass and do not come again. Only night comes and remains.

James Avery burst in the door, pale and winded from his ride. The lamp dazzled his eyes so that, for a moment, he could not see. Cabot rose from the chair near the table, the chair from which Beryl Newland had chided him about her brother's drunkenness. Avery's cry broke from him like a sob.

"She's gone?"

Cabot's voice was hoarse. "Not yet."

"My God, my God, my God." Avery clung to Cabot, biting his hand to control the trembling of his mouth. "And Will?"

Cabot could not speak. The elegance, the satire, the pretense had been ripped from him. His shoulders began to heave. Avery put his brown head against the golden one.

After a moment, he spoke again, hardly a whisper. "It is sure she will die?"

Cabot swallowed. "No. But she's very bad."

"Then she may live?"

"She's very bad."

"Would Will – " Avery stopped and swallowed. "Can I see her?"

"I think so. Come."

They went to the bedroom. The door was open slightly; candle-light flickered inside. Cabot gently pushed the door, and it swung wide. Dr. Watson was bent over a basin in the corner, washing his hands in the shadows. Seeing Cabot and Avery, he nodded. Lydia Randall stood beside him, holding a towel.

Will did not raise his head. He sat on the other side of the bed, holding the injured woman's right hand in his. He seemed to be looking nowhere, though his eyes were glued to her face. The shadows pressed upon him unkindly. His hair was receding at twenty-four; he looked older than Cabot by ten years. On his arm the fang marks showed like a brand.

In the bed, the woman's face was ashen, the lips pallid and a little bluish. They were parted, as if she would like to say something, but the breath came through them in shallow, meaningless gasps. Her grey eyes were halfway open but unseeing. She looked like a boy: her long hair had been cut off, leaving her with short, unruly tufts that clung close to her skull. There was a bruise on her right temple, but it did not look serious, Avery thought – no more than a bump from a cupboard door. But her left arm lay across the bedding, thick with bandages. Blood seeped through them, leaving scarlet spots on the white coverlet. He could only guess what injuries the coverlet hid. Her gown was open at the neck; her throat fluttered with each gasping breath.

Avery looked piteously at her broken body, but what made him want to rage was the expression of sorrow that gashed her face. It was a wound that could not be closed. No doctor could sew it shut; no cotton could staunch the life that bled from it. Lydia gave the towel to Dr. Watson and came to Cabot and Avery. Together, they went back into the parlor. Avery struggled to control himself. Lydia sat silent, the waves of her pale hair drawing down all the lines of her face. Cabot touched her on her arm.

"Are you all right, Mrs. Randall?" Cabot noticed the way her thin hand rested on her belly; it was the way he had seen women who were pregnant holding themselves, instinctively protecting the child within. But that child, he knew, was dead.

She nodded. "Just tired."

Avery turned. "What are – how is she hurt?"

"Dr. Watson thinks two of her ribs are broken. He fears that one punctured her lung, collapsing it. She has a concussion and her hand – her left hand – the bones seem to be utterly crushed, though we cannot be sure because of the swelling. And Dr. Watson suspects bleeding on the brain."

"How did it happen?"

"She was with the German. The horses spooked; the wagon rolled out of control. She fell underneath."

Nobody spoke for a moment. Lydia went on. "Will went for Thompson on one of the horses; they brought her here."

Avery did not want to ask the next question, but he did, his brown eyes pained and dogged beneath the hair that fell into them. "And the Russian?"

Lydia folded her hands. "He tried to stop the wagon. But it was too heavy. He was unconscious when Thompson got there. But he could speak by the time they got back to the house."

"Did he say what happened?"

"He could not be understood. Or that's what Will and Mr. Thompson say." She sounded as though she thought otherwise. She picked at the lap of her dress. "Mr. Spenser came by earlier this evening. He told us that the man has a broken shoulder. Or perhaps it is his collarbone, I don't remember. He's not doing well, but he's expected to mend."

"The damn fool."

"It was an accident. Mr. Spenser said the boy is wild with concern for her. Quite beside himself." She lowered her eyes.

Avery felt jealousy tear at him; he turned his back on Lydia and walked to the mantel where he fiddled with some curios, trying to master himself. Cabot watched them both, his face jagged with unhappiness. He took his watch from his pocket. Two hours until dawn. One hundred and twenty minutes. Seven thousand, two hundred revolutions of that thin gold line which ticked, silent, under the glass. And then what? What good would the coming of the sun do? "I don't know why we are here," he said. "I really don't know."

Lydia stood up to go back to the bedroom. "Will is comforted by our presence. And Beryl must feel it too. It can only do good, Mr. Cabot."

Cabot shook his head and put a hand over his face. That was not what he meant. Not what he meant at all.

By St. Crispin's Day that October, Indian Summer passed from the land. Frost glistened in the early morning sunlight. The wind was cold; the leaves along the creek shivered, life draining from them in golds and reds. Douglas Keith and Red Thompson hauled corn into the Newlands' barn and stacked hay tight against the wind and rain for the coming winter. The broken wall of the barn stayed broken. Thompson piled dirt against the cracking foundation and hid it from sight. The stones that had been gathered for the purpose, those that hadn't fallen into the creek, had been brought back to the farm but rested unused. For a while, it was thought they might be used to mark a grave like the one behind the house, the one that Beryl New-land had unwittingly sat upon the day she first visited this site.

But there was no grave. Beryl opened her eyes to the cold sky through her window and heard the tin bells tinkling, lonely, outside the quiet house. For a moment she wondered, and then the oblivion which had wrapped and shielded her was stripped away, leaving her naked and defenseless before the pain of each breath, the sear and throb of her arm, the assault of memory.

She made an effort to move her head. Her eyes searched the corners of the room. She could not gauge the time. At first she thought she was alone, and then she saw Will slumped asleep in the chair. His face was peaceful, but, looking at it she seemed to hear again his raging voice coming at her, tearing from her something that mattered more than life. She cried out. The sound was bruised and scabbed and broken; it frightened her. She understood in that instant that she had been unlucky not to die.

Will started and Lydia Randall rushed into the room. "Beryl!" Lydia cried. "Sweet Beryl!" She bent over the girl. "Oh hush. Hush. Try not to move, dear."

The doctor came in and sat beside Beryl, feeling for her pulse and touching her forehead. For the first time in days, his eyes lit up. "Are you in pain, Miss Newland? Can I get you something?"

Beryl looked at him. "Anton?"

The doctor looked at Will and Lydia. Will's jaw tightened. Lydia spoke without hesitation. "She means the young German man who was with her."

Dr. Watson took Beryl's right hand. "I haven't seen him, but I've heard that he is doing fine. He broke his shoulder in the accident, that is all."

Slow, weak tears clung to Beryl's lashes. Her breast shuddered; the physical pain was clearly great. Then she croaked out, "Me?"

"You've broken a couple ribs and . . . " He hesitated.

"My arm," she whispered. "Is it broken?" She looked down at the bandages. They were clean, but she saw bloodstains on the coverlet. She tried to lift her hand, but the doctor stopped her.

"No, leave it," he said. "It's badly injured. You must try to keep it still. But we will see to it; you needn't worry. Let me give you some laudanum."

She looked at her hand. "I don't want to sleep."

"For the pain, Miss Newland."

"No," she said, lifting her eyes to the ceiling. "Thank you. Please go."

Lydia and the doctor looked at each other. Lydia stooped, kissed Beryl gently, and then went to the door. Dr. Watson stood up to follow. "I'm just in the parlor. I will check in on you."

"Go," she said. But she was not looking at him. She was looking at Will.

Will looked back at her. His relief was eclipsed. The rage at what he had seen by the creek, under the crabapple trees, rekindled at the defiance in her eyes. She was without shame; she did not regret having let that German make love to her. When he had seen her crushed beneath the wagon, when she had almost died, Will thought he could never recover from the loss. But now he listened to that weak voice telling him to go and he felt his hand quiver. He had wanted to kill Vonfeldt. If Thompson had not been there, he would have done it, would have smashed that man's skull while he lay unconscious in the grass. Because it was Vonfeldt's fault that his sister lay maimed. It was Vonfeldt's fault that she, who had always seemed to Will so brilliantly, untouchably pure (and therefore not worth worrying about), was now sullied, besmirched by associations with things in himself that he had spent years trying gouge out or drink away. And she felt no shame.

"Go," she whispered. "Go."

He went.

Cynthia Witley and Elizabeth Walker strolled with Mr. Grant through the shriveled vines and dead green leaves of his garden. The sun was gentle. Though their cheeks grew pink, under their cloaks the women scarcely felt the brisk breeze that tossed the Russian Olives around the villa. The cold was new enough that leaves had not yet fallen from the trees, but they were growing dry on the branches and made a constant, anxious rustle against each other. All the soft whispers of summer were gone.

"Their misfortune has been appalling, incredible," said Betsy Walker, shaking her brown head so hard that the earrings under her hood jingled. "How can they manage?"

Grant watched the tide of black cattle that moved on the hills far beyond the windbreak. He smelled winter in the air, though it was only autumn. "Douglas Keith is working with their man; he will see them through with the new livestock. And Mr. Newland is doing much better." Physically, he added to himself. Emotionally, he had his doubts.

Cynthia took her small, gloved hands out from under her cloak and held them before Mr. Grant. The violet in her eyes was intense. "But she will never play again, Mr. Grant. It's a tragedy! What will she do? What will she do?" Her sorrow and wonder touched him. He had not known that this charming little actress had any genuine feelings.

"Dr. Watson thinks they may have to take the hand."

"No, surely not that!" Mrs. Walker's voice rose half an octave. Her steps quickened in agitation. "I must bring them food. And medicine. And the boys at the fort – well surely they can come up with a subscription or something."

"Your neighborliness would be welcome, I'm sure, Mrs. Walker, though it can't necessarily save the lass's hand."

Mrs. Walker shook her head. "I'm sure that your Mr. Keith is a good man about the farm, but there are altogether too many men out there. Talking of cutting off hands! Appalling! I shall go with chicken soup and see about things."

Mrs. Walker always had something of the cyclone about her once she got an idea. Mr. Grant and Mrs. Witley exchanged glances. "Now, my good woman, Mrs. Randall is tending to Miss Newland like a mother."

"Ah, Lydia's an angel. But a high-born woman like that – how can she know how to nurse and cook? Why, can the lady even coddle an egg?"

"I believe, Mrs. Walker, that she can coddle an egg," said Mrs. Witley, amusement making her melancholy face winsome. "She certainly coddles her husband. I think it would be ever so kind for you to put together a basket for the Newlands – and I shall add some delicacies from our kitchen. But perhaps it would be better if we just send it along with Mr. Grant for now. It's so soon after the accident, excitement would probably not be good for her. And you know, Mrs. Walker, you are rather exciting."

Betsy Walker turned and looked at Mrs. Witley, skeptical and confused and vaguely flattered. "Well," she said after a minute. "We Americans are more exciting than you English, I suppose. Very well, I will send some goodies over with Captain Walker, Mr. Grant, and you see that Miss Newland gets them. Let me know when she seems better. I would like to say goodbye before we leave."

"You are going?" asked Mrs. Witley.

Mrs. Walker nodded. "We're returning to our children and folks in Indiana before the captain is reassigned to another post. This fort won't be operating much longer. The country has gotten too safe, I guess. Though after Custer – well, I'm surprised the government assumes anything."

"Oh," pouted Cynthia. "With the fort closed half of the fun of Kansas will be gone."

Mr. Grant laughed. A ruddy, robust color washed the grey care from his face. "Why Mrs. Witley, we shall still be here. May I assume that we in Victoria constitute the other half of Kansas fun?"

"You know," said Cynthia, giving him a coquettish smile, "that you have certainly provided a great deal of entertainment."

"Oh, don't be sad, Mrs. Witley," said Mrs. Walker. "The fort will not be closing immediately. The boys will be around for parties and dancing a while yet. And of course Mr. Grant's people will be here forever."

Mr. Grant bowed and smiled, but the grey settled back into the lines of his face. Several dozen colonists were returning to England for a visit this winter. He was a realist; he predicted that half or more of them would not be coming back. And of those, many had not paid up on the land as agreed to in the initial charter. All financial defaults fell on him. He looked again at the cattle beyond the villa, grazing on land that stretched unfettered in all directions. He turned his eyes to the sky where clouds moved and geese winged south. "I cannot fathom what it is they want," he thought to himself, "if it is not this."

Mrs. Walker returned to the house to bid Meg goodbye. Mrs. Witley remained in the garden with Mr. Grant for a few more minutes. She seemed to want to say something to him. He waited patiently, taking out a cigar and gaining her permission to smoke.

At last, she said, "Mrs. Randall nurses Miss Newland? Who takes care of the little boy?"

"Why, the lad's father of course. Why do you ask?"

She bit her lip. "I think it cannot be him, Mr. Grant."

Grant stopped and a crease centered itself between his brows. "What do you mean?"

"I've been rather – bothered, Mr. Grant."

"In what way?"

"Mr. Randall – well. Mr. Randall cannot be watching his son be-cause – because he is always watching me!"

The wind whisked a dry leaf across the path; it got tangled against a trellis where blood red berries hung.

"You must forgive me, but I don't think I quite understand."

"I mean that – that when I get up in the morning and go to the breakfast room he is lurking in the trees beyond the window, and that when I take the dogs out he is waiting to accost me, and that when I ride, or go to town, he follows me and – and that when I try to sleep at night I cannot because I know that he waits in the darkness! Mr. Grant! Make him stop!"

The silver-haired man bent down to look into her face. "Can you know what you're saying, Mrs. Witley? Mr. Randall is respected in this community, and his wife – why, he is devoted to her."

Cynthia's soft, pouting lips – the lips that men wanted to kiss – suddenly stretched back from her teeth in a hard line. "I do know what I am saying, Mr. Grant. I'm telling you that I own a pistol and I know how to use it. And I will use it on the respectable Mr. Randall if he does not leave me alone."

The wind gusted and skipped around them while they stood facing each other. The purple fringes of Mrs. Witley's shawl fluttered against the curves of her cheek and chin. Her eyes had become like ice. Mr. Grant had the impression that if the purple fringes brushed those violet eyes, they would freeze there.

"Surely this a matter for your husband, Mrs. Witley?"

"If I could speak to my husband about this, I would not be here with you. Please. I appeal to you as a gentleman, as the leader of Victoria. Mr. Randall must listen to you. Stop him from harassing me."

She conveyed little of the distressed heroine in her voice. She made her request quietly. If there was any desperation in her plea, it was well masked, perhaps only revealing itself in the nervous playing of her gloved fingers. Mr. Grant looked at her for a long time, the tired lines in his face growing deeper.

Then he took those fingers in his hand and bowed. She put her arm under his sleeve and slowly, very slowly, walked with him up the steps of the villa.

Lewis Watson shook his head in frustration and stared grimly out at the dying earth. Better to nurse plants and trees in this place; he was certain they grew less twisted than the humans out here, and certainly they were easier to deal with. "The safest thing is to take it off. The bones are shattered and the chance of infection, deadly infection, is too high to take a chance."

"But there is no gangrene now," said Vincent Spenser.

"Not today. But tomorrow? I'm telling you I can't set those bones and make it right; the only thing I can recommend is cut off the hand clean, and let the arm heal."

"She can get infection from an amputation as well," Spenser countered.

"So, you'd take that risk on the off chance that she can preserve the mangled thing and have it hanging from the end of her arm the rest of her life?"

"Are you Americans always so delicate?"

"I speak plain blunt truth. Sorry if it don't suit. But I watched that woman almost die once. I'm not interested in repeating the experience."

"Cut if off," said Will, grimly. "The doctor is right."

"You haven't even allowed the woman a chance to look at it." Spenser's face was pale from the effort to contain his anger. "At least let her see it."

"I'll be damned before I'll let one of those people in to see her."

"You have to stop blaming Vonfeldt for an accident he did not cause."

"The hell you know about it."

"I know plenty about it. More than you think, Newland. I'd be careful about casting blame."

"Then you know she showed no respect for herself, her family name, or her place as an Englishwoman."

Watson, irritated enough at the battle over treatment, raised his eyebrows another two notches at this thickening of the plot. "Hey here, fellas, we have enough problems without arguing about the lady's good name. Which seems to me unimpeachable. Could we get back to the point?"

Spenser ignored him. "She fell in love with him, and he with her. It is unfortunate for both of them, but neither has done anything dishonorable. If you persist in impugning your sister's character, I assure you I shall call you out as I would any other bounder."

"Aw, shit. Ain't you Brits just something." Watson rubbed his nose in exasperation, but he also backed away a step or two. He knew Spenser's reputation. Spenser had been involved in a duel before; his brother had extricated him from that imbroglio. But the dark, quiet-eyed intellectual had as strong a taste for violence as he did for drink, and Lewis knew that he'd indulge it given the justification.

Will trembled with anger. "He's a peasant with dirty feet."

"He graduated from university in Saratov. You, I believe, have not graduated from university at all. His outward appearance may be coarse, but he has talent and decency equal to any gentleman."

"If he'd been a gentleman, he'd have stayed away from her. He would have understood his place and hers."

"As you have with Mrs. Witley?"

The question was asked in a low voice; Watson may or may not have heard it. But Will heard. The knives were clearly on the table.

"You overstep, sir. I have never, never conducted myself dishonorably toward Mrs. Witley. If your right arm causes you to sin, then cut it off!"

"As you would cut off your sister's? For God's sake, man."

"She's my sister. She's nothing to you. I thought you meant to be her husband one day. Now I find that all you've been is her pander."

Spenser hit Will so swiftly that even Watson, who was watching, couldn't tell how exactly the blow was delivered. Will slammed against the parlor mantel and would have fallen but that Spenser caught him by the collar and held him in the air, one hand crushed over his mouth. "By God, Newland, you take your own filthy mind and smear its excrement over everyone else. If she weren't in the next room, I would beat the crap out of you right here. But I will tell you this: I honor and reverence your sister. If I had thought myself worthy of her, I'd have asked for her long ago. As it is, I devote myself to her as a friend. And I will not, I will not, allow you to assume the worst of her." He lowered Will, letting him fall in a chair.

Spencer went and stared out the window, his breast rising and falling with the force of his passion. When he turned back to Will, his tone was almost pleading. "I understand what you've been going through, but don't you see that the fine thing in you that has kept you from doing wrong is also in her? She and the boy fell in love. It's doomed to nothing. His people will never allow it. Given the loss she must endure, at least give her a chance to come through it whole in body. Let the woman look at her. It can't hurt. Watson can be present."

Will could scarcely hear, Spenser's blow had been so violent, but finally he answered. "Just make it when I'm gone. I can't bear the sound of their talk."

"Thank you," said Spenser and left.

Watson came over to Will. "You okay?"

Will nodded. Watson looked after Spenser. Then he said, "A witch doctor? You've agreed to let a Russian witch doctor look at her?"

Will rubbed his shoulder. "Humor him," he said. "And then be ready to do your work. I – I don't want her to die."

Beryl was staring listlessly out the window when the woman came. Lydia led her in.

"Beryl, someone to see you."

The woman was tall and stout and wore a black scarf. Her silver-brown hair was parted in the middle over a smooth, serene brow. Her eyes were large, the color of a warm sea. She did not smile; she held her folded hands before her as if in prayer. They were worn hands, with dimples at the knuckles. They stood out, brown and freckled, against her white apron.

Beryl recognized immediately that the woman was from Herzog. She made an effort to sit up that almost split her side open. Her right hand flew to the cropped hair on her head.

"*Ich bin die Riedel's Göte*, Anna Maria," the woman said. She approached the bed. Her eyes were quiet; they neither judged nor dismissed. They simply took in.

Beryl looked at Spenser who, along with Dr. Watson, had followed the women into the small room. Spenser went to the head of the bed and knelt next to Beryl.

"Mrs. Riedel comes from Herzog. She is a bone setter. She will examine your hand and see what we can do for it." Beryl's expression remained blank. "My dear," he whispered, "please let her look at you. Anton Vonfeldt sent her."

Something like a shock went through Beryl. Her eyes flew to the woman's face as though she expected to find Anton somewhere in those features. But all she saw was the serene brow, the quiet eyes.

Those eyes had seen Anton Vonfeldt, however, and had seen him recently. She gazed into them, trying to find the remnants of his reflection.

Mrs. Riedel unfolded her hands and gently bent and touched the bandage on Beryl's left arm. "Yah?" she said, looking for Beryl's permission.

Beryl, after a brief hesitation, nodded. The woman removed her scarf and sat quietly on the edge of the bed. Then she took Beryl's left arm in her hands and raised it gently. Beryl cried out. She bit her lip while Mrs. Riedel began to unwind the bandage. Beryl could smell the odor of sweat and vinegar and earth. She watched, with dread fascination, as the bindings around her wrist came undone. She had never allowed herself to look at the wound before.

There was still swelling; the forearm was thick and purplish yellow. Beryl's wrist seemed altogether gone, swallowed in swollen flesh. The hand was small, frightful, twisted; the fingers, puffy, curled like claws, some turned at impossible angles. Dried blood and puss caked parts of the back of the hand. The blackened nails seemed ready to fall from the ends of the fingers.

All the pain suddenly made sense. Beryl thought she screamed, but actually she made no sound at all. *Die Riedel's Göte* shook her head. "*Himmel Gott,*" she muttered. She got off of the bed and knelt on the floor. She held the wounded limb in her large right palm, close to her face. She studied it. Then, with the fingers of her left hand, she began to probe the wounded flesh with a soft, firm touch.

Beryl cried out and instinctively tried to jerk her hand away. Mrs. Riedel turned serene eyes to Mr. Spenser and spoke quickly in German. He listened, and then said to Dr. Watson and Lydia, "We need to hold her."

"But the pain," protested Lydia.

Spenser spoke to Mrs. Riedel again. She talked to him quickly, shaking her head. Then she looked at Beryl and softly stroked her healthy hand. "She says she needs to know what Beryl feels; she needs to hear her. But she won't do it if Beryl doesn't want her to."

Beryl was panting; not only was her limb screeching at her, but her cries had wrenched the broken ribs and injured lung, making them quiver with a pain that made her entire body vibrate. She looked, dazed, at Vincent, and then at the woman, who looked back at her with those eyes the color of a warm sea. The woman whispered to her in German, as Anton once had. Beryl did not know what she said, but the music of the words she understood. She whispered, "Yes," to Spenser and reached for Lydia.

Spenser put his arms around her shoulders while Lydia held her right arm and clutched her hand, kissing it. Lewis Watson, looking wary, stood at the end of the bed, holding her by the ankles. Carefully, as though she were lifting a small, precious baby, the woman took Beryl's injured arm back into her hands. Then, gently and firmly, her fingers once again searched in the flesh, looking for the shattered bones, feeling them in the torn muscle, pushing and playing them. Now and again the fingers paused for a moment, resting. Their owner quietly studied the hand again, her head to one side as though she were listening, and then she let the fingers go back to work: feeling, turning, adjusting, testing, as though she were tuning a stringed instrument.

Beryl's eyes grew enormous with the effort not to scream. At last, she let out a long, shrill moan. "Jesus, help me!" she cried, bracing herself so hard that Watson could feel the terrible tension in her legs.

Mrs. Riedel did not look at her; she was intent upon her work. After a moment she said, "Beryl!"

The girl looked at her. Mrs. Riedel said nothing more, but she stopped her hand for a moment; her face was fierce and determined. She reached to Beryl's chin, caressed it a bit, and then looked hard into her eyes. The demand that the girl be strong was written on the air. Beryl shrank away but could not escape her gaze. "Yah?" the woman said at last.

"Yes," whispered Beryl.

Mrs. Riedel turned to Spenser, said something in an abrupt, stern voice, and then turned that fierce look on the people around the bed. "Hold her," said Spenser, clutching Beryl more tightly. Watson clamped his hands around Beryl's ankles, his frowning eyes glued to the crushed hand. Quickly, Mrs. Riedel turned back to it; she was praying aloud in German. She looked at no one and nothing but the injured hand; her fingers, which before had been probing and massaging, now moved sternly against the flesh, reaching for the bones beneath, sliding and shifting them. Beryl screamed and arched her back in agony despite the broken ribs – and then she was silent. She had lost consciousness. *Die Riedel's Göte* kept working, moving as quickly as she could, feeling through the tender bruised skin, lining the fingers back up, pushing them, willing them, praying them home. She breathed quickly and deeply, as though she were running, but her brow remained serene. After a few moments, she stopped. She turned to Dr. Watson. "Eh?" she said, giving him leave to look.

He left the foot of the bed. He took a lamp from the side table to get more light. He bent low, moving the lamp over and around the hands of the two women. Tenderly, he felt Beryl's hand, felt through to the bones. Then he stood up.

"We shall see," he said. "I could not have done it."

The woman looked at Spenser, questioning. He translated. She laughed a little and shook her head. She asked for bandages. Together she and the doctor cleaned the wounds; she tied slender wands to two of the fingers like a splint. Lydia realized they were broken knitting needles. Then Mrs. Riedel stepped back and let Watson wrap the hand and arm once again.

"How long until we know?" asked Lydia.

Spenser translated. Mrs. Riedel stood up, looking thoughtful. She deferred to Dr. Watson, who said, "Maybe a week." He felt foolish. The way the woman had manipulated the jagged bone back into something resembling a healthy hand was close to miraculous. His feeling was emphasized when she stood next to him, towering over him by several inches. She had such calm green eyes. He thought of the tumult of the past two weeks, the arguments and accusations that had poisoned the grief and hindered the healing of this family, and he wished she had been present sooner.

She nodded and reached over, stroking Beryl's pale face and fingering her shorn hair. Then she bowed and left. Out on the porch, she turned to Mr. Spenser. Together they spoke German, their voices low.

"She is a nice girl, a strong girl," she said to Mr. Spenser. "But I have only made the hand look right, you understand. She will not, I think, be able to use it again."

Mr. Spenser looked down. "You know, she is a pianist."

"No. That is sure too bad."

Mr. Spenser spoke again. "Mr. Vonfeldt – how does he do?"

"He mends, he mends. But his heart is broken." She shook her head and clucked a little. "The young people, they are not careful with their hearts, and they do not understand."

"Will he come to her?"

"It will not be permitted." She looked at the shivering bluffs and pulled her shawl more tightly over her head. Then she looked into Spenser's face. "Next week, if she is better, I will speak to her. You will be here?"

Spenser sighed and looked to the east. "I return to England soon. But not before you come again. I will be here, to tell her what you say."

"Yah." She went down the steps to a poor-looking pony and cart. Then she turned around. "Be careful of your own heart, young man."

Spenser smiled a little and shrugged. "Too late," he said and went back into the house.

If Beryl expected Anton Vonfeldt to come to her, she showed no sign. She listened quietly while Lydia read to her and, when she could sit up, she watched the clouds pass over the land, pushing the south-flying birds ahead of them. Will came in occasionally, talked to her about the farm and asked her, in the most general way, how she felt. Then he left again. As she got better, he began to disappear from the farm again, as he had in the summer. Sometimes for several nights. She did not worry. She did not really care.

Lydia Randall slept in his room along with her little boy, who had come to join her when it became apparent that Lydia's help would be required for some time. Mr. Randall came once, when he dropped off the boy. He spoke with his wife briefly on the porch, came in and looked with compassion at the very ill Beryl, and then left again. Lydia spoke of him little. She seemed happier now that the boy was with her. Christopher was a bright, funny little thing who practiced his alphabet on a slate in the parlor and followed Red Thompson around as much as the gruff American would let him. When Red got fed up and told the youngster to go and find his mother, then he went to go find Mr. Keith, who never seemed to be exasperated by him and who taught him things about plants and animals and, occasionally, told him stories about Indians, or fairies in Scotland. Mr. Keith was more quiet and less colorful than Mr. Thompson, but the boy grew fond of him as the weeks passed.

The day that Mrs. Riedel was due, Lydia was helping Beryl dress when suddenly the child began shouting excitedly from outside.

"Mother, come see! Mr. Keith! We have company – oh and look what they've brought!"

Keith came out of the barn and squinted, perplexed, at the wagon rumbling toward the house. A man and a woman were in it. He did not recognize them. When he saw what was in the wagon, he felt his breath stop. Then he looked toward the house.

Lydia was helping Beryl out onto the porch; Beryl leaned heavily on her. Both of them blinked at the eastern sky, trying to make out who it was in the wagon. Lydia felt Beryl, who'd been leaning on her heavily, suddenly lift away, as if she would run down the road to the approaching vehicle. But of course she couldn't, and she collapsed back against Lydia and began sobbing. She reached her right hand out toward the vision.

"But who is it?" asked Lydia anxiously. She watched as her son ran up to the wagon, which stopped. The woman stood and bent over the side to talk to him, her green and blue skirt whipping in the wind. Then she faced the house and called out in a merry voice,

"Beryl, I've come traveling and I intend to write it all up for the magazines! How are you, my darling?!"

"Marian," whispered Beryl. "Marian."

Marian wept over many things before her husband that night at the Manor House in Victoria, but the gift they had brought had her crying the hardest.

"You couldn't know, Marian. Though why that fool boy couldn't have informed us – it's been six weeks since we wrote. Outrageous! And here she is, half dead and crippled, and he's nowhere to be found. Infamous! He conducts himself like an imbecile pup!" Robert's indignation was boundless, and his frustration nearly so. He itched to write a letter to the *Times* to express his outrage – but then that eminent periodical was not an organ for venting family spleen. Perhaps, he thought, an epistle attacking the practice of sending younger sons off to America would be suitable. Certainly he intended to bring the matter up in Parliament when he returned home. Meanwhile, he patted his wife on the shoulder and looked out at the dead grass stretching away from the town. "It was a fine gift. We could not have known."

"But, Robert – a piano! And she will never play again! All she can do is look at it and be reminded of what she's lost – oh, it's unspeakable."

"Marian, she still has one good hand. I suppose that there is music for people to play with one hand. It's tragic, but buck up, my dear. We can thank God she is not dead."

Marian wiped her nose on her handkerchief. "Yes, I suppose you're right. But she cried so."

"She's had a rough time. Why the hell she had to come out here in the first place – my God, what is there? Absolute desolation for miles and miles."

"Well, now, Robert, you're revising a bit. On the way to the farm, you spoke of how handsome the country was, and you admired the houses."

"I lied. I think the place abominable. And I intend to speak to Grant about it. And who was that peasant tending to Beryl? Don't they have surgeons in this country? They have to drag in midwives to offer physic to the injured?"

Marian bristled. "She is a doctor. At least I think so. Mr. Spenser told me that she healed Beryl's hand well enough that they were able to avoid amputating it. We owe the woman a great deal."

"Well, Spenser certainly gave her a great deal. He poured the gold coins in her hand as if he were stocking a mint."

Marian said nothing. Mr. Spenser had explained to her about the young German man and Will's fury and the accident. She wondered if Beryl would ever speak to her of it. And she wondered where Will was.

By the time Mrs. Riedel had arrived that afternoon, the excitement of Marian and Robert's arrival had been somewhat digested. Marian noted Beryl's agitation when the tall German woman arrived. Beryl, the German, and Spenser went into the bedroom and were in there for more than an hour. Beryl did not come out again.

The afternoon had become overcast. When Mrs. Riedel at last finished examining Beryl, the day was dark with an impending storm. The wind blew hard, and rain began to pelt the window. Beryl looked sadly at the newly bandaged hand. She knew now what others had known already: that her hand was saved but that it would never serve her again. It must always hang limp beneath her cuff, useless, as good as lost. As it had healed, the feeling in it had grown less; the nerves were damaged. The last thing she remembered touching – before she fell and the wagon pressed over it, leaving her only the sensation of pain – was Anton's rough beard, and his lips as they kissed her palm. What use could there be for her hand now, she thought bitterly. It would never touch him again.

Die Riedel's Göte was kind to her and brought her beautifully embroidered doilies as a gift. She spent some time examining Beryl's wounded limb. When the examination was over, she and Vincent sat down next to Beryl. The three of them were still in the small dark room, listening to the wind and rain whip against the shutter for a moment, and then Vincent spoke.

"You trust me, Beryl? Mrs. Riedel needs to talk to you about Anton Vonfeldt."

Beryl looked at her good hand, watched it clutch the blanket as if it were a thing separate from her. Her chin trembled. "I have always trusted you, Mr. Spenser." She did not raise her head.

Spenser took a deep breath and exchanged a glance with Mrs. Riedel. She took both of Beryl's hands, the good one and the bad, into her own large ones and began speaking.

She said that Anton Vonfeldt, when he was taken back to his home, raved and cried for a day and a half as if he had lost his mind. He wept for the English girl, swore that he loved her, that if she died, he would die too. His brother-in-law was patient at first and then hit him, to try and knock sense into him. This did little good and, in fact, much harm, so Vonfeldt's sister sent for the priest, who was with Vonfeldt for a long, long time. When the priest was done, Vonfeldt was reconciled to the fact that he must give up the English woman. He begged, however, that *die Riedel's Göte* would go to her, for he heard that she was terribly hurt.

Anton Vonfeldt was returning to Russia as soon as his shoulder was well enough, which would not be long. He would go to his parents' house, be reunited with his fiancée, and in the spring return to the United States with his parents and the girl's family. They would not be coming to Herzog, however; they would be settling in Arkansas.

Beryl refused to look at Vincent or Mrs. Riedel while she was told these things. She kept looking at her small hands resting in the big ones. She listened to the wind and rain, and thought she heard a struggle of bells through it, the bells he had given her. When Mrs. Riedel raised her chin to force her to look at her, her grey eyes were as wet and cold as the sky.

Mrs. Riedel spoke again, and, reaching to the floor, she lifted onto Beryl's lap a rectangular luggage case. She rested Beryl's good hand on it and spoke softly. Spenser's voice was almost inaudible as he translated.

"She says that he said to tell you he loves you, and that since he cannot give you his heart and his life, he gives you this."

Beryl remained motionless after he was done speaking. She knew what the box contained. For a moment she could not speak. Then she said, "Tell her to tell him that I love him." She struggled to finish what she had to say. "I will not forget him and pray that God will bless him. And I will not forget you. Thank you." She raised her eyes to Mrs. Riedel and to Vincent Spenser. Mrs. Riedel listened to Vincent, and then bent over and kissed Beryl. They rose and left her.

Alone, Beryl wept.

So it was that Beryl Newland gained in a single day what, in frontier Kansas, constituted a veritable symphony of instruments. And on that same day she faced the hard fact that none of them would ever make music for her, at least not in the way she desired, ever again.

It was perhaps unfortunate that Vincent and Bernard Spenser, and several other young Britons, left for their return visit to England while Robert and Marian Newland were still in Victoria. Spenser had become enough a friend of the family that Robert was necessarily invited to the going-away party in Hays City, a grand and very wet affair held in the rooms of Patrick O'Brien, apothecary, above the Mammoth Drug Store, home of the Famous Prickly Ash Bitters. The rooms were impressive – marble-topped tables, flowered carpets, and richly upholstered chairs. The billiard game below was amusing and reminded Robert of some of the best evenings he'd spent at his London club. O'Brien had hired a brass band and drinks flowed freely, from champagne to iced sherbet. The ladies were ravishing and got more so as the evening went on and the glasses were refilled. There was dancing and laughter, and there were multitudes of toasts to Merry Old England. At midnight the ladies retired, and O'Brien led a brigade of revelers to Tommy Drumm's for further refreshment.

But by the time the train had come at eight the next morning, hotel and tavern furniture littered the street and broken glass threatened to pierce the boots of Hays' more law-abiding citizens. Robert's head throbbed. He was indignant at what he considered lawless, ungentlemanly vandalism. The shooting of guns as Vincent, Bernard, and the others boarded the train and disappeared into the rising sun did nothing to improve his mood. He would not speak to Will – who showed up at last in the midst of the party – for the entire ride back to Victoria, and when he was ushered into Mr. Grant's office (he was not the first; Tommy Drumm had been there with a bill at the crack of dawn), he was in a terrific passion for so phlegmatic a personality. He had little sympathy for the founder, who looked tired and ill.

"So, sir," burst out Robert. "This is the conduct of our boys after four years of manhood training in the wilderness? Drunken, disrespectful, hooliganism? What I saw last night shakes my faith in the entire enterprise. My brother, an earnest lad, out wandering God knows where when his family is expected and worse yet while his sister lies ill?! A farm that is losing money, not making profits of any sort? My sister, a beautiful girl, maimed and sick? Where is this civilization you were boasting of? What in God's name have you been doing here all this time? I come to find my brother and sister a wreck!"

Mr. Grant sat back in his chair. Behind him, a window looked out on a wide line of prairie. The trees along the creek bluffs, gold and brown, shuddered in the wind; beyond them, the stone gables of a large house rose. In the distance, against grey sky, cattle grazed. Mr. Grant turned his chair to face that view and said nothing. When he turned back around, his blue eyes blazed, and he ground his forefinger into the desk as if he were shaking it in Robert's face. The garnet shone.

"Lads will be lads, Mr. Newland, a sad truth that sometimes muddies my plans. But nothing accomplished? Why, this may look like a wilderness to a man come from London, but if you'd seen what was here when we came? Nothing but bare ground and sky! No town, no farms, no ranches! We've made a miracle of the place; women waltz where wolves howled, and bairns learn to read and write where prairie dogs burrowed. Young men are raising cattle that are the boast of the country – the entire United States, I'm meanin' – and the Queen herself has helped to stock my farm. You're for calling me a failure, Mr. Newland? I defy any man in Britain to show me what he's accomplished in twice the time."

Robert stood, his stolid frame unmoved. "Eight years at home could not do to my brother and sister what this place has managed to do to them in half that time. Your success or failure is a matter of no concern to me. My family is my concern. And I want you to know that I intend to take them home with me when I return to England in two weeks."

"You've asked them?"

"No, but I shall. And I shall be surprised if they don't listen to reason."

A slight smile tickled Mr. Grant's lips. "Aye, but this is a land for surprises."

"A damned benighted place."

"I'm sorry you feel that way, Mr. Newland," said Mr. Grant. Then, as an afterthought, he added, "If you're seeking to talk to Miss Newland, you'll want to go to the Villa. She's come there, to spend time with my niece Meg until she fully recovers. Of course, I would be honored to have you and Mrs. Newland stay with us until you leave. The Victoria Manor is a fine place, but its accommodations are not spacious."

Robert half-turned. "Thank you, Mr. Grant. I will consult with my wife. But I hardly think that staying with you would be appropriate under the circumstances. And I believe that Beryl should be with her family."

Mr. Grant leaned over the desk. "What you fail to understand, sir," he said to Robert, "is that after four years together in this place, *we* are her family." His eyes snapped.

"We shall see. Good day, Mr. Grant."

On the way out he passed a small woman who pressed by him to get to Mr. Grant's office. Her light hair was lifted softly off her neck and tucked under a handsome lavender hat with a white veil that made her violet eyes more vivid. Her coat clung close to the curves of her body. Her gown was of an expensive fabric and surprisingly up to date in its styling. Robert could not help himself; he turned to look at her as she disappeared into Grant's office.

"A figure worth following, isn't it?" said a man near the door. His dark hair stood up on his head, thick and black. His brown eyes shone under scowling brows. He lounged against the wall, smoking a cigarette which, after a moment, he threw down and crushed under his boot. "Robert Newland, isn't it?"

Robert studied him for a minute, puzzled; then suddenly he remembered. "Jack Randall, I think. Good to see you." He reached out his hand.

Randall took it and held it for a minute. "I say, I am sorry about your sister's accident."

"I am too. Thank you for sparing your wife to her. Mrs. Randall has been wonderful. Beryl couldn't have done without her."

"Yes, Mrs. Randall is wonderful," said Randall. "The woman you just passed – she went into Mr. Grant's office?" Robert nodded.

"Hmmm." Randall dug in his pocket and got out another cigarette.

"Things going well on your estate?"

"Couldn't really say," said Randall. "My foreman takes care of that. Well enough, I s'pose. Long as Liddy's daddy keeps the guineas coming." He nodded to Robert and walked on into the building.

Marian received word that they would under no circumstance be accepting hospitality at Mr. Grant's house. The man was a charlatan or a fool, but in either case, lodging with him would be a mistake.

Marian wailed at the news. "But, Robert, there are bedbugs here! I cannot stay another night."

"Then we'll stay on the farm with Will. Now that he's back, it's better we stay with him, and with Beryl gone to Grant's there's a spare bed available. I'll have a chance to look over this 'investment' Will and Beryl have made. We'll see what we might be able to sell it for."

"What if they don't want to sell?"

He pulled a watch from his waistcoat pocket and checked the time. A train was passing outside the station; its roar made the glass in the windows tremble. He sat on the bed waiting for its noise to fade. Then he said, "They've lost a lot out here. But I don't think they have lost their minds. Yet." He thought grimly of Beryl's wasted eyes, his brother's angry face. "Oh, Mother," he muttered. "I'm so sorry."

Marian watched him and then began quietly removing the pins from her hair. They lay in a shining pile, like all the hopes she'd had for this trip: undone and useless.

Chapter XVI

Cynthia Witley's complaint against Jack Randall worried George Grant. He personally found Randall unpleasant. The charm of his outspokenness and the asset of his vitality had quickly worn away to reveal little more than poor judgment and an inability to follow through on bursts of initiative. And the skepticism with which Randall spoke of Grant and the Victoria project not long after their arrival in Kansas had evolved into an antagonism which could hardly endear him to its founder. Yet Mr. Grant had considered him a good member of the community: he knew how to delegate work even if he himself quickly tired of it, he took an active interest in the progress of his fellow colonists, he could be compassionate in spite of a pugnacious self-interest, and his wife, a superior woman in every way, believed in him. In fact, it was her faith that Grant depended on. To question or worse yet destroy that faith would be, he felt, the job of a blackguard, especially if Mrs. Witley's accusations were baseless.

But he did not like to believe that either. He embraced a chivalric view of women that would have done him proud had he lived three or four hundred years before, and if he had a hard time conceiving of himself as a knight in shining armor rescuing damsels in distress, he did feel he owed Mrs. Witley the assurance of his protection. That she had not turned to her husband troubled him; but then if the wife was ready to shoot Mr. Randall with a pistol, he could only imagine what the husband might do. And it would be best for all involved to avoid a messy, and probably unnecessary, confrontation of that sort. He had little sense for exactly how the Witleys ordered their domestic relations (the fact that Mr. Witley had spit cherry pits at his wife's cat, and even his wife, left him wondering), but obviously the attentions of another man could only upset the ship. If Mrs. Witley wished to avoid rocking the boat by keeping her spouse in blissful ignorance, Mr. Grant felt he must respect that wish.

He waited before speaking to Mr. Randall, however, wanting to see for himself some evidence that she was in fact, as she put it, being "bothered" by Lydia Randall's husband. He did not doubt the lady's word, but he thought perhaps she exaggerated the nature of Mr. Randall's attentions. The wedding of Alec Hunter and Barbara Murray would, he thought, offer an opportunity to study the situation. Such a public occasion might not provide proof that Mr. Randall was hiding in the bushes at Mount Halcyon – but then Mr. Grant had no stomach for lurking in shrubbery himself to test that part of the woman's story. It would be enough to see how Mr. Randall acted toward her at the wedding party. Mrs. Witley was an actress, but Mr. Randall was no actor. Grant felt certain that if there was something wrong about Randall's behavior toward Mrs. Witley, he would not be able to conceal it.

The need to watch Mr. Randall mitigated the pleasure with which Mr. Grant had anticipated this wedding celebration. He was fond of Alec Hunter, who seemed to have outgrown his consumption and the last remnants of his boyhood working at the Victoria Stock Farm. He was a natural rancher, as far as Grant could discern: he loved the land, he loved the animals, and he was not afraid to labor and toil in spite of tremendous odds. This unlikely candidate, who had come to Victoria with less life in him than Mr. Randall possessed in his thumb, was emerging as the most promising of all the young colonists. Grant wondered if it was because the boy had to work for everything – his health, his earnings, his success. He had not come to this place handsome, healthy, and rich. He only promised to leave it as such. If he ever left at all – which, Grant believed, was unlikely. If Grant could boast of a spiritual son among the colonists, he considered it Alec Hunter.

So he had looked forward to this wedding of his favorite with Julia Hunter's sister. And he was pleased that Neil, who had been hosting Presbyterian services in his home, agreed to have Rev. Emerson marry the couple. It boded well for the spiritual coming together of the community. He regretted that they could not marry in the chapel, but that structure was still growing, the walls climbing slowly against the dreary November sky. As yet it could not shelter the colonists in their time of joy.

Neil and Julia Hunter had a relatively large drawing room where they hosted services on Sunday mornings, but the number of colonists who attended those services was quite small compared to the number of people coming to witness the nuptials. The space proved cramped the morning of the wedding. Guests came early and crowded eagerly into the Hunter house. The gentlemen stood around the edges of the room; the ladies sat, their gowns filling the chairs, benches, and floor with yards of shimmering blues, burgundies, and greens. Children stumbled over the sea of fabric. Julia, nursing her three-week old infant in the back kitchen, murmured prayers of thanksgiving that the great hoop skirts of her mother's day were no more; only half as many women could have fit in the drawing room had that fashion continued. The windows were draped with white and yellow ribbons; roses stood in vases around the room, compliments of Mr. Grant, who had them shipped from a hot house in Topeka. When the Rev. Epis Emerson entered the room, he seemed rather stunned by the light and the spectacle. His worried curls seemed more worried than ever by the handsome crowd of people gathered before him.

Beryl Newland sat with Meg Grant near the front, a place of honor she shared because of her status as a guest of Mr. Grant. She was thin and pale. She wore a dark blue dress that was largely hidden under a rose-colored shawl. She could not wear stays; her body had not healed enough to allow for the crushing and strapping of a corset. She had taken to wearing loose, flowing gowns that Marian told her were "Aesthetic" and quite the rage among the more artistic women of London. Beryl was grateful for their comfort, but she felt certain that only Avery would appreciate their fashion properties and did not flaunt her avant-garde dress. She wore white gloves on both hands; her left hand rested motionless in her lap. Her short hair, which made her eyes look unnaturally large, was combed neatly around her face. She only showed emotion when Annie Carrigan, Thomas Carrigan's new wife, fresh from finishing school in Scotland, sat at an organ in the corner of the room and began to play a spirited and brilliantly executed tune (directly contradicting the couple's request for a staid Calvinist march). Something in Beryl's posture and the set of her face shifted, became hard. Pain might have caused it, but if pressed to explain, Beryl would have said it felt more like hate.

The bride was a pretty girl: blond, round, and rosy like her sister. She stood next to Alec, trembling and excited. Before them, Rev. Emerson began to read the service. He seemed to have trouble focusing on the page; his words slurred a bit. Neil Hunter looked at him sharply. But he read on without stumbling, warning the listeners that matrimony is "*an honourable estate . . . a holy estate . . . and therefore not to be entered into unadvisedly or lightly*" (Mrs. Witley smoothed her gown over her knee) "*but reverently, discreetly, advisedly, soberly, and in the fear of God*" (Neville Baldwin pinched his little brother on the sleeve, causing a small yip toward the back of the room). He continued. No one suggested that there were any impediments to the marriage (Will Newland stood stone-faced next to James Avery); the couple promised to love and cherish, in sickness and health, for richer and for poorer (Alec thought of the small wood shanty waiting for them among the brown grass) until they died. Reverend Emerson raised his hand above the couple in blessing (it shook slightly, as if with a spasm) and intoned: "*Send thy blessing upon these thy servants, this man and this woman, whom we bless in thy Name; that they, living faithfully together*" (Jane MacDonough watched Vicki pull the hair out of her doll's head and frowned), "*may surely perform and keep the vow and covenant betwixt them made, whereof this Ring given and received is a token and pledge*" (Lydia Randall turned the sapphire on her left hand so that it caught the morning light) "*and may ever remain in perfect love and peace together*" (Beryl gazed blankly at her broken hand) "*and live according to thy laws; through Jesus Christ our Lord*" (Cabot yawned in spite of his best efforts). "*Those whom God hath joined together let no man put asunder*" (Cynthia Witley raised a lace handkerchief to her eyes). "*I pronounce that they are Man and Wife, in the Name of the Father, and of the Son, and of the Holy Ghost, Amen.*"

Douglas Keith smiled and then noticed that Mr. Grant had gone grey and clutched at the windowsill; he put his arm around the man's back to support him. The couple received their blessing and the organ burst into joyous chords. Keith hustled Grant into the hall with Duncan, who sat him on a chair and loosened his collar.

"Are you all right, sir?" asked Keith, the cheering in the room behind him almost burying his question.

"I'm fine, I'm fine." His protestations were angry.

"If you'll forgive me," said Keith, "You look like you've seen a ghost."

"I've seen worse than that," muttered Grant.

"Can we help you, Mr. Grant?" Duncan bent his great, curly head to study his employer.

"No," said Grant rising. "Just a drink of wine, to settle me."

After a minute or two, he went back into the drawing room, where the newlyweds were receiving congratulations. Alec shook Mr. Grant's hand, and then threw his arms around him like a child. "I owe you so much, Mr. Grant. We can't thank you enough."

It ought to have been a sweet moment, but Grant saw only Mr. Randall's sullen stare fixed on Mrs. Witley and, when Mrs. Witley saw that he saw it, her strange, inexplicable look of triumph.

As winter crept closer, Beryl took to wandering Grant's estate. She could not ride; the movement hurt her ribs. But she walked for hours, bent under her brown cloak. She liked the loneliness of the barren November landscape. It gave her a chance to work out her grief without the distressing solicitude of people's pity. She knew that Vonfeldt was gone back to Russia. She sensed it in the dreary sky and the stripped trees. There was no music in the world but the eerily unhappy wind and the mournful bawling of cattle. Her loss was immense. She did not know how to grapple with it, so she walked. To those around her, these hours alone in the cold seemed morbid. Meg was uneasy, reminded of her friend's deep depression the winter after the locusts came.

But Beryl was not indulging her pain. Only once did she go to the place by the creek where she could see across to her own land, across to the crabapple trees where she had sat on an Indian Summer's day, thinking she could fly. She looked across the water at the twisted, skeletal branches – she could see where some were broken from the accident – and, removing her glove, she lifted her left hand up against the silhouette of that tree. She compared its crooked branches to the dead fingers of her hand. But *die Riedel's Göte* had done her work too well; the hand was limp and could not move, but after two months it was otherwise restored. The bones had healed in their right place, and Marian had insisted on exercises that kept the muscles from atrophying. To look at, it was still beautiful. Beryl let it fall and slid it back into her glove. "God is merciful," Marian said, but Beryl did not believe it. She turned away from the scene. Her eyes were dry, but they burned.

She thought about how she had once believed in God, had so devotedly and fervently accepted the idea that He loved his creatures, that not a sparrow fell without his knowledge. She remembered the soaring voices at the Abbey and the arrows of light that had burned through the darkness like prayers answered. She walked for miles and then sat on the hard, brown earth, remembering the German women going to the altar rail for their bread and how the triangles of color down their back had seemed to her holy, the obedience and reverence they betokened a sign of some great nameless good that suggested, in spite of evil, all would be well, and all manner of things would be well. She climbed the highest bluff she could find and looked toward the Spenser mansion, missing its owner and the thin but indestructible thread of belief that moored him to heaven in spite of the demons that she knew pulled him down. And she felt, when her traumatized spirit allowed her to feel anything at all, that she stared into a vast blank of nothing when she looked for God. Humans, tortured by fire and disease and death and love, meant nothing, were mere accidents of unhappiness that every now and then allowed themselves to be fooled into believing in joy. Life inevitably undeceived them. Deep down she had understood this before, perhaps. But then, as Cabot said, she was fundamentally dishonest.

She tried to explain what she felt, what she had come to understand, to Douglas Keith once, when she found him nursing a sick yearling in a bitter wind. The weary animal bawled in misery, its eyes rolling. Keith listened to her, gently rubbing the soft neck of the beast and watching the sleeting sky in the distance. Then he stood up and looked at her. His eyes were sober brown – she had forgotten, it had been so long since they had spoken together – and they studied her in that way she remembered, as if she were an interesting plant, or an intriguing animal. Or, perhaps, as if she were a person who mattered. "I think," he said at last, very slowly, "that you are not being brave."

And he walked away, leaving her there with the wind, and the sick animal, and the cold.

"So that's what she's saying, is it?" Randall laughed. The sound was mean and bitter. It crashed up against Grant's anger and broke into ugly pieces.

"Do you deny it, sir?"

"I deny giving her what she doesn't want."

Grant's fist smashed onto the top of the desk. His face was almost purple. "And what woman could want you hounding her in such an ungentlemanly fashion?"

Randall shook his head. "I deny hounding her. We need to talk. She knows that."

Grant folded his hands together on his desk, struggling for calm. "Explain to me, Mr. Randall. I will try to be fair and understand your position."

Randall grew less truculent as Mr. Grant grew quieter. He walked to the window and looked out at the town. Wagons passed below. The Baldwins' eldest son, now a big boy of twelve, ran across the street, his cap pulled low over his ears. A dog followed him, scampering gleefully. "She treats me unfairly and she knows it. She was glad enough for my attention, very glad, for quite some time."

"Meaning what?" said Grant, after a long pause.

"Meaning her husband is a cad. She wanted someone who appreciated her, treated her like a lady instead of like a trophy."

Grant waited.

Mr. Randall turned around and shrugged. "I gave her what she wanted. For almost two years. And then, suddenly" – he took his hand and flashed it through the air, as though he were knocking over a house of cards – "she didn't want it anymore. Just expected me to go away. She was done using me." His voice began to rise. "Played the pussy cat for two years, and then let out her claws. Understand me, Grant, she didn't even give me an explanation."

"She was your mistress?" Grant's voice was deadly.

Randall came up to the desk, spreading both arms wide and resting them on it so that his face came within inches of Mr. Grant's. He whispered viciously, "I'm telling you we were lovers. She wanted me. She took me wherever she could get me – seductive little puss – in the fields, in upstairs rooms, at parties and during dances. She wanted me. And she made me want her." Randall's face began to crumple, an awful, angry anguish making his voice hollow. "And then she suddenly said no more. No more. But it was too late. Too late to be left with nothing. And she gave me no explanation. Just – nothing." He sat back down in his chair, pushing his hands through his hair until it stood on end, and then said, in an almost conversational tone, "She's a god-damned vixen."

Grant unfolded his hands slowly, as if they ached. He did not take his eyes from Randall's face. "And Lydia?"

Randall said nothing. The clock on the wall struck three.

Grant stood up. "I can't believe it of Mrs. Witley. And I can't believe you would do it to Mrs. Randall."

Randall made an angry sound. "Believe it. She and I were going to go away together. Denver, Cheyenne. Make a new life. Liddy – Liddy doesn't need me. Lord Stannard's daughter. Fine and high. I was never good enough for her. Never. And he made sure I knew it." Randall's face flushed. "Cynthia Witley, though. She I'm good enough for. We understand each other. Or we did."

"You must stop following her," said Grant. "For her sake and for your wife's sake. Lydia is devoted to you. She's just lost a child. You have a son together. She needs you."

"I'll follow her until she gives me some satisfaction." Randall seemed not to hear anything about his wife. He had no room for her in his mind.

"I will talk to Mrs. Witley. But in the meantime, you stay away from her."

"Why should I?"

"Because if you don't, I believe she will kill you." Grant's voice was matter of fact. "I care little for your sake. But I should deeply regret it for your wife's sake. Now – I am tired, Mr. Randall. Good day. We will speak again."

Jack Randall sat motionless for a moment. "Like hell," he muttered. And then he was gone.

"You've spoken with him, then?" Cynthia Witley's face was bright and expectant, as though she anticipated news of a party or a present. She pulled off her red gloves and laid them on the table as familiarly as if she were at home. They were the only spot of color in the grim afternoon dark of the villa's drawing room. Even the fire in the grate did not share their warmth.

Grant rose but did not come to shake her hand. In the shadowy room, with his silver hair curling along his collar, he seemed both handsome and spectral. The ghost of Hamlet's father, perhaps.

"I have seen him," he said quietly. He put down his tea slowly. "I do not justify how he has persecuted you. But he says that you owe him an explanation."

"What? For what?" Her violet eyes flared like a gas light, then left her face duller and more wary.

"Mrs. Witley," said Mr. Grant. "Why could you not tell your husband about this trouble?"

"Because he is an extremely jealous man. It would worry him excessively – beyond its importance."

"You carry a pistol to defend yourself against Mr. Randall. That suggests a problem of more than minor importance. Would your husband have reason to be jealous of him?"

Cynthia looked at Mr. Grant for a moment, her small hand moving back and forth over the fur edge of her collar. "Mr. Randall has been telling lies," she said at last.

Mr. Grant shook his head. "I do not think so."

She sat down. "What has he said?"

"That you have been his mistress. That you wished to end the relationship when he did not, and that you gave him no explanation."

Her blond head twitched just slightly.

"If you tell me it isn't true, lass, I shall try to believe you."

She said nothing.

"I take it unkindly that you came to me to extricate yourself from a mangle that you put yourself in."

"And to whom could I turn?" she asked. "I was lonely and bored, and I didn't think when it started – and then – there was only you who could help when it was done. And you judge me," she burst out, angry all at once. "They all have lovers! Hypocrites! Half of these boys here are the products of liaisons in old country houses! The fine blood of England indeed! A jolly basket of bastards! And they come out here and whore and you act surprised when a woman comes to you in trouble? You're no better than the rest of them. Playing the lord over a bunch of filthy boys."

Grant folded his arms. "You are unhappy with your husband?"

Her distress intensified with exasperation. "Oh, no! It was just a diversion, to add some excitement to this beastly place. It could not hurt Henry as long as he didn't know, and it made me more content. He was happier because I seemed happy. No one was meant to get hurt. But Randall became wild, frightening in his demands. It had to end – it had meant nothing!"

Grant's gorge rose along with his ire. "I do not know what your upbringing was, Mrs. Witley, or in what circles you moved in England. But what you did meant a great deal to that man you ensnared. And it would mean a great deal to your husband. And it will mean a great deal to Mrs. Randall when she hears of it."

"Surely you will not tell them?"

"I will not tell your husband. That is your affair. But I fear I must tell Mrs. Randall, because I think she is the only one who might be able to control her husband. I can neither control nor be responsible for him. And I prefer not to see you driven to murder."

"I did not ensnare that man," said Cynthia. "He made love to me long before I ever paid attention. If I had wanted to seduce an innocent, I could have trapped Will Newland as quickly as a spider traps a fly. But he's a decent person and I wouldn't do that. At least believe that of me. Mr. Randall was no innocent victim, and if he represents himself as such, then he lies. It is not fair that you should blame me, as though I were some kind of – kind of seductress. I made a mistake, which I am sorry for and for which I have paid and will continue to pay."

Some shred of compassion stirred in Grant. "Perhaps you would like to talk to Reverend Emerson."

"What?" Cynthia laughed, in spite of herself. "The dope fiend?"

"Madame! You go too far. He is nothing of the sort!"

"He most certainly is," she said. "Oh, Mr. Grant, it's you who's the real innocent. It's evident in his very face, in his every action. I've worked with men and women addicted to opium. You think he came natural by those spooky eyes and that trembling hand? Why, I pity the poor man, but I'd as soon seek spiritual council from a – from a – well, I don't know what. But I hardly think the sick can heal the sick." She stood and looked at him. "You're a very King Arthur, aren't you, my lord? All Camelot crumbling around you, and you cannot see it." She stopped, not quite able to trust her voice. When he said nothing, she went on, "I am sorry for my part in it. Because I see that you have really believed in all this. Forgive me. And thank you for speaking to Mr. Randall. But please do not speak to his wife. Please." She picked up her gloves and left.

Mr. Grant listened to her go, and for some minutes stood alone and silent in the dusky room. Then suddenly his features contorted. He picked up a bottle of claret and threw it. It slammed against the fireplace, shattering and spilling its content across the white marble like blood. The fire hissed and sputtered. And in the doorway, Beryl Newland stood, her eyes wide.

When Mr. Grant looked up, he saw them and knew the comedy was complete.

"Why won't you believe me?" Beryl's voice was low, full of wonder.

"You've never liked her."

"That's not true. She's sometimes been very good to me. Only Mr. Grant sent more flowers when I was ill."

"Then why are you spreading stories about her?"

"Because they are not stories. They are the truth. And you should know. You've been miserable over her – for years, it seems. And – and I understand that better than I once did. But you need to know that she's not worth your devotion."

"I cannot credit such a story. That Randall hounds her I don't doubt. I've seen him do it. But to suggest that she ever encouraged his attentions – and worse – it's outrageous. And that Mr. Grant should speak to you of these things is despicable."

"Will," said Beryl, leaning close to her brother, "he told me because he knew I would tell you. That's why I came to see you. And he knows, Will, because she told him."

"Impossible."

"She wanted him to help her."

"A fine job of it he's done."

"He said she spoke of you."

Will froze. "What do you mean?"

Beryl rubbed her numb left hand with her right, playing on the wrist with anxious fingers. "I mean she told him she did not – " Beryl stopped, confused at how to word it. "She thinks you are a good man. When she got lonely, she did not turn to you, because – because she thought you were good, and she did not want you to be hurt. She respected you as a person of honor."

"And she did not respect Randall, so she gave her love to him? This story gets more bizarre all the time!"

Beryl leaned back in her chair. "Oh, William. Is it really so unbelievable? She's a beautiful woman, perhaps the most beautiful I've ever seen. The temptation must be so strong." Her voice was pitying.

Will was silent for several minutes. "Does Lydia know?"

"I don't know. I hope not. But Will, she's been unhappy. I could see it when she was at the farm, and it wasn't just my sickness that she was worried about, or even her miscarriage. Something's been wrong for ever so long. And she's never liked Mrs. Witley. I think maybe she has known – the way a woman does."

"And Mr. Witley?"

"I think not. He seems too shallow to observe much."

"Perhaps," said Will. But he remembered the effect of Avery's comment the day of the cricket match, the way that Mr. Witley had turned his monocle on Mr. Randall. And suddenly the story did not seem preposterous at all. He put his head in his hands.

"I'm so sorry."

Will stood up and put his hand on Beryl's shoulder, patting it. It was the first act of endearment he'd shown toward her since she'd regained consciousness. Then he went for his coat.

"Where are you going?" she asked.

"Out to walk off a hangover. A long hangover." He put on his hat. "You return to the villa?"

"Tomorrow morning. Marian and I will share a bed here for tonight."

He nodded and went out into the dark.

Arthur Witley found Jack Randall beaten unconscious behind the barn at Mount Halcyon the next morning. It was unclear who had beaten him, though many thought they knew why he'd been beaten. Lydia rushed to her husband and escorted him to the hospital in Hays City where she stayed at his bedside for two days and a night. But on the evening of the second night, she left and did not return. The surgeon received payment by post the next day and a letter asking that the man be cared for until he was well. The staff was mystified. Mr. Randall said nothing and seemed to expect nothing. Grant's secretary, Leslie Edwards, came to see him once after that, and then no one. On the sixth day, Jack Randall walked out of the hospital, limping and cradling a broken arm, but otherwise adequately recovered. Someone said they saw him go into Tommy Drumm's, but that was the last. No one remembered him coming out again.

When Beryl heard of the beating from Meg at luncheon, she grew very still. Mr. Grant said nothing at the head of the table. He merely pushed the newspaper flatter on the tablecloth. He kept reading and turning the pages. Then, after a couple of minutes, he glanced at Beryl. She lowered her eyes quickly and pushed away her uneaten meal. She took a silver spoon, filled it with sugar, and let it sift into her coffee. She stirred her coffee for a long, long time, almost until it was cold. At the end of her stirring she had no more answers than she had had at the beginning. And that, she decided at last, was all right. She didn't want to know.

Lydia Randall returned to England with her son on the first of December, 1877, in company with Robert and Marian Newland. No one threw furniture into the street, and no one shot guns off into the air. They left from Victoria rather than from Hays. Mr. Grant and Meg, Beryl and Will Newland, and Mr. Cabot and Mr. Avery stood in the cold dawn with the travelers waiting for the train. Marian fussed and fidgeted, admonishing Beryl to take care of herself, giving her advice on the cut of dresses and the style of hats, and telling her for the fortieth time anecdotes about her niece and nephew, all in effort to keep from crying. Robert stood with Will.

"It was quixotic to come and it's stupidity to stay. I wish you were coming back with us. But I will try to help out as much as possible. All I ask is that you take care of Beryl, that you be kind to her. And that you take care of yourself." Robert faced the north wind, feeling it blister his face. Then he added gruffly, "What's past doesn't matter, William. You're a good man. Be worthy of yourself."

Will burrowed his hands into his pockets.

Lydia stood near Mr. Grant, pale, thin, and still as stone. Her eyes were frosty, and her cheeks seemed to bleed rather than merely redden in the cold. She held her boy well wrapped in a buffalo robe and whispered to him. He was sleepy and seemed only partially aware of what was happening. When she heard the train's whistle, she shook as though something had struck her. She reached for Meg's hand. Meg clutched it, weeping. Lydia kissed her and then asked quietly, "Beryl?"

Beryl had been listening to Marian and watching the train push toward them, coughing black smoke into the white sky. She rose and embraced Marian, who brushed her with her lips and whispered, "My darling." Then Marian went to Lydia, took the boy in her arms, and handed him to Robert so that Lydia could make her goodbyes.

Beryl stood before Lydia. "How can I let you go?" she whispered.

"You don't let me go," said Lydia. "That is what is so hard." Tears hung on her lashes; the wind whipped them away before they could fall. She took Beryl's hands in her own and kissed them. "Be well, my dear," she said. "And do not be afraid."

"And you," said Beryl.

"Take care of each other, you and Meg."

"Yes," said Beryl, and Meg nodded.

James Avery lifted Lydia's luggage to the conductor. He and Mr. Cabot shook her hand, and, as she took the child back from Robert Newland, Avery chucked the child on the chin. "Little chap," he said.

Will came up to Lydia and after a long moment said, "You've done so much for me and Beryl. You are a wonderful woman." She shook her head no, but he kissed her cheek.

Mr. Grant took her arm and walked with her to the steps of the train. Then he stopped, as if unable to go forward. She looked up at him. He reached down and caressed the small cold face of the boy bundled in the robe. "We will miss you, Mrs. Randall. I will miss you. You brought this place grace and beauty." He bowed his head. Grief lined his mouth.

"God bless you, Mr. Grant," she said. She kissed him, and then she went into the car.

Marian followed her, shaking Mr. Grant's hand. Robert remained a moment with Beryl. "Come home, little sister," he said suddenly.

"I am home, big brother," she said. "Whatever you think of it." She smiled. "I love you and Marian. Thank you for the piano, you know." She threw her arms around him.

He held her a long time. The train whistle blew. He let her go, said an abrupt goodbye to Mr. Grant, and entered the train. The conductor shut the door.

Lydia's face appeared at one of the windows. She smiled down at the little group of people on the platform and then, as the train began to move, she raised her eyes to the Manor House – its yellow stones, its iron gables, its windows. Her smile faded, and one gloved hand touched the window, trying to hold the building in place. But it slowly passed behind and beyond her hand, and though she turned her head and looked for as long as she could, it escaped her, receding among the rooftops of Victoria until the whole small settlement was swallowed up in a sweeping plain that stretched endlessly to nowhere.

"He did not come," said Cabot to Avery later. He sipped his beer meditatively.

"He's gone," said Avery.

"Do you think she hoped he would come?"

"I don't know. I don't think so. She didn't seem to be looking for him."

They sat silent, the dark light of the tavern casting weird shadows. They stayed near the stove, but still the chill crept around them.

"You were right, then."

"About what?"

"About him. Randall."

"It's no pleasure. And it did her no good."

"I wonder where he is. Do you think Grant knows?"

"If he does, he isn't saying."

"No." Cabot rubbed his hand along his upper lip, where an infant mustache made a soft gold smudge. "He doesn't say much anymore. I don't think he's well."

"Not many of us are."

"No. You've gotten positively dull. I say, if you don't wear a scarlet waistcoat with peacocks embroidered on it for Christmas, I shall know that we've all been lost."

Avery smiled slightly, then shrugged. "Not much to dress for anymore."

There was a pause. "You've given up then?"

"She said no."

"You asked her?" Surprise sent Cabot's voice up the scale.

Avery nodded.

"When?"

"Last Sunday evening. I wanted to do it before her brother left in case — in case she agreed."

"And she did not."

"No."

"I say, Avery, if you'd waited a bit — it's too soon after the other chap. But perhaps if you wait — "

"No," said Avery abruptly. "There's no hope for that. She loves me — " he grinned wryly, "'like a brother.'"

"That little? Oh, I say, I am sorry, old man."

"She meant it well. And you know, I think she really does love me, in her way. That, after all, is something in life."

"Was she upset?"

"She was as she always is. Beautiful."

Cabot put his chin in his hand and studied his friend. "You take it better than I would have thought."

Avery shrugged and pushed his hair out of his eyes. "I went home and spent two hours with a loaded gun in my lap. Then I decided that would be poor payback for all she's meant to me — and she's had a dastardly year as it is. Besides, it made no sense. Killing yourself for a girl. It would ruin my shirt, my smoking jacket. So, I got drunk instead." He wrinkled his face. "And you know the really rum thing? It's been too long, Cabot. I hate liquor. Can't in the least stomach it anymore. Thought I'd vomit my brains out." He lifted his coffee cup as if to make a toast. "So you see – she has broken my heart and saved my liver. There's nothing left to do but sell up and go home."

Cabot had been laughing, but he stopped abruptly. "No, Avery."

"Yes."

"No. You can't do it."

"Of course I can. I've made a tentative arrangement with Neil Hunter. He's done well selling crackers and peaches. He'll buy at a generous price."

"You're overreacting. You may as well have shot yourself in the head."

Avery lifted his head and raised his eyebrows. "My mama would disagree with you, I think."

"Have you signed anything?"

"Heavens, no. He knows I'm not ready to leave until spring or summer anyway."

Cabot brooded. "You'll change your mind."

Avery swirled the coffee in his cup. "Perhaps."

Cabot finished his beer and slammed the glass down in frustration. "I've had enough. Let's go hunting, lad. Head to Denver for the holiday. What do you say?"

"But my good man, I've nothing suitable to wear."

"That's one of the things we'll hunt."

Avery considered. "We'll miss the Witleys' Christmas soiree."

"We'll hardly be the only ones now, will we? Forget the Witleys' French cook. I've heard that there are first rate chefs at the hotels in Denver."

Avery rubbed his arms and then shrugged. "Why not? Maybe Mason will come along. He'd enjoy seeing a bit of new country."

"Grand plan. It'll be a lark, eh, Avery?"

Avery put on his coat. He looked at his old friend with weary eyes, but he managed to smile as he headed for the door. "Of course, Cabot. Whatever you say. Of course."

Meg roamed the rooms of the villa, seeking a warm place. She couldn't find one. They all seemed cold. She wrapped a blanket around her shoulders and bundled through the drafty halls. She avoided the windows. The snow was still falling, and it made her shiver to see it. She would have joined Beryl and Mr. Grant in the library, but she had overheard a conversation that made her think she was better leaving them alone. She continued her wanderings. After a while she realized that if she kept walking fast enough, she would actually get warm. At least physically.

Mr. Grant and Beryl Newland sat before the huge fireplace watching the flames lick away the logs. It was, in truth, not much warmer where they were. And certainly the conversation was not calculated to produce a glow.

He had not meant to confide in this young woman. He almost never confided in anyone. His fears, his worries, all were locked away, carefully fortified against intruders. He had many investments in the world. After selling his part in the London business, he had erected buildings in Chicago and New York City, founded a small town in Colorado, and sold land along a stretch of railroad in Iowa and Illinois. Most of these ventures had done well. But none he cared for as he cared for Victoria. The stock farm was his pride and his passion; the town was his dream. He had thrown himself into it with all the fervor of a man who realizes that we are given but a few years, days, and hours in which to make our lives matter and then the hourglass runs out. The sands slipped fast, but they seemed to sparkle as they ran. Mr. Grant was able to convince himself that they ran for good. But as he watched the numbers on his ledger dwindle, the crops even in the best years prove disappointing, the lads he had hoped to make into men squandering their time partying, drinking, and hunting animals that had long since been shot into oblivion, he developed an uneasy feeling that the swiftly running sands were not filling a glass but were instead emptying into a dark vacuum that went nowhere and threatened to suck him up.

His physicians told him that the feeling was the result of overwork and warned him about the onset of his old illness. He had not rested, they protested, as he had been told. He had better stayed in sooty, dark London selling silk and satin behind a desk than push himself to death fighting the land, the animals, and the elements in this bright place, no matter how healthful the air. He sighed and shook his head. Bishop Vail told him he took too much upon his own soul; he could not be responsible for the mistakes of young men or the evils of a harsh land. He was the steward, not the master. And he could not always be the caretaker. He needed to allow himself to be cared for.

"I have Meg to care for me."

The bishop eyed him thoughtfully. "Perhaps, George, you need someone who can be closer than a Meg."

Mr. Grant had dismissed the thought. But as he sat before the fire, his troubles suddenly spilling from his mouth like the shades from Pandora's box, as he felt the pressure in his chest grow lighter from the sheer relief of not holding it all in, the thought recurred to him. This dark-eyed woman listened so calmly, so serenely. She had known enough of sorrow and unhappiness not to be shocked or dismayed. Better than him, she seemed to accept that evil came. Perhaps she accepted it too easily. She seemed, he thought, not to expect good at all anymore. But he did not chide her. He knew that she was still hurting, and that time would heal those wounds as it healed all wounds. It gave him a pang, however, to see those running sands and realize that time was what he did not have.

"They seemed such a promising lot of young men. I thought they would respond to the challenge of this place and give over their wild ways. I wanted their spirit, their joy in life, you understand. But they've not grown at all."

"Some have done very well, Mr. Grant. The Hunter brothers, and Mr. Cabot, Mr. Avery. And the Wyatt boys have made a show place of their farm."

"Don't talk to me about the Wyatt boys," growled Mr. Grant.

"He does not pursue Meg anymore," said Beryl quietly. "She told me – and she is glad."

"He's a creeping ghost, and for all the good in his older brothers, he has twice the devil in him. And a coward on top of it. You know why he does not come about anymore? Duncan threatened to thrash him."

Beryl shook her head.

"And the best of them are leaving along with the worst. You knew that James Avery thinks of going?"

Beryl gasped. "No, he didn't tell me."

"Aye. The Baldwins talk of heading east. And now Mrs. Randall gone, too. She was a light in this place." He paused. "It gets to feeling very lonely here these days."

Beryl looked into the fire. "Will and I are still here, Mr. Grant."

"That's a comfort." He looked at her, the light playing over her short hair, her bittersweet smile. He seemed to see the sands running before her, pushing her further and further from him – and suddenly he reached his hands into the falling mass to stop them. "You have been sad during your stay at the villa. But your presence has made me very happy. I'm loath to lose it."

"You'll not lose it, Mr. Grant. I'm happy to stay for as long as you want me."

He leaned forward and gently put his hand on the arm of her chair. She raised her eyes.

"You must heal in your heart as well as your body. But when you are strong again, when you feel whole and well – will you consider coming to stay with me? Never to leave again?"

She turned her face back to the fire. She was not startled at his words. They seemed natural, as if she had been waiting for them for a long time. She stared quietly into the flames, listening to their crackle and smelling the aroma of burnt pine. The wind pushed down the flue, and the cold outside seemed very close. For a fraction of an instant, she wondered if the wind froze this way in Russia, and she saw pale, silver-blue eyes, like those of a wolf, gazing into a driving snow. And then she was back before this fire, present to the distinguished man who leaned over, looking gently into her face.

"When I am well," she said, taking her good hand and laying it softly on his, "ask me again."

He knew she was his, and he went to bed that night dreaming the dreams of a young man. But when he awoke in the morning, the earth was covered with ice to the edge of the sunless sky, the pain in his chest was great, and he tasted the gall of truth. He closed his eyes, traced the curve of the woman's cheek in his mind, and then let it go. Just as surely as he knew that she was his, he knew that by the time she was healed, and well, and ready to answer him, he would be beyond asking. The sands he had clutched at fell away and, without fear, he leaned over the black pit to watch them spiral into a nothingness bigger than the world itself.

Lilacs, purple and white, bloomed outside the church door the morning of George Grant's funeral. Carriages and wagons rolled into Victoria from miles around, cluttering the streets and filling the churchyard. Like so many things in George Grant's life, the church had not gone according to plan. The chapel, which still missed a few stained-glass windows and shingles on the roof, was to have been dedicated in two weeks with an opulent and joyful celebration. Instead, crepe and bombazine filled it with black, and a requiem mass echoed from its buttresses and gables.

For two hours before the service began, the body lay in state. Flowers, many of them the wild, springtime blossoms of the prairie, were heaped around the coffin. People who had known Mr. Grant and those who had merely known of him streamed past. The Volga Germans came from Herzog and other towns, bringing their children to see the great man. Businessmen and politicians from Hays City came with their wives to pay their respects; farmers and cattlemen from as far away as Abilene and Wichita stopped by the coffin; and soldiers from Fort Hays – captains and majors, corporals and lieutenants – stood at attention before the body. The British colonists touched his hands, and some wept.

Everyone was quiet; they spoke in low tones both inside the church and out. Those who had only known him by reputation admired his handsome features, the silver hair that was combed over his head in distinguished waves, the expensive suit that testified to his success. Those who had known him better, who had followed him from England and Scotland, admired less. They mourned the grey lines that ravaged the once ruddy face and pulled at the mouth which had spoken so eloquently. Death did not make him beautiful. It did not erase the fatigue and the disappointment and the uncertainty. It merely made them still, so that their cancer could grow no more.

Despite grave illness and against his doctor's orders, Bishop Vail insisted on coming from Topeka for the funeral; he said that no one but he should consecrate his friend's body to the ground. He was still sick and trembling from a bout with malaria; he leaned heavily on Reverend Emerson. But when he spoke, his voice was magnificent. He made Mr. Grant come alive again as he had been in the early days of Victoria: glowing, invincibly sure of his purpose and destiny in this place. He spoke of Grant's hopes – for the land, the town, and the people – hopes realized and hopes unfulfilled. He spoke of cattle and farms and handsome homes. And he spoke of this church, the building which was to have been and surely still would be the crowning glory of his enterprise: the great tribute to his Queen, the final offering to his God.

"One thing I have desired of the Lord, which I will require," the Bishop read from the psalm, *"even that I may dwell in the house of the Lord all the days of my life, to behold the fair beauty of the Lord, and to visit his temple . . . I should have utterly fainted, but that I believe verily to see the goodness of the Lord in the land of the living. O tarry thou the Lord's leisure; be strong; and he shall comfort thine heart; and put thou thy trust in the Lord."*

Leslie Edwards and Douglas Keith, Ben Davis and Ian Duncan, Clay Grant and Neil Hunter carried the founder of Victoria out of the doors of that church and lowered him into the ground. Above them, the sky was blue and cloudless. Lilacs scented the air.

The Bishop raised his hand.

"Forasmuch as it hath pleased Almighty God, in his wise providence, to take out of this world the soul of our deceased brother, George Grant, we therefore commit his body to the ground; earth to earth, ashes to ashes, dust to dust; looking for the general Resurrection in the last day, and the life of the world to come, through our Lord Jesus Christ; at whose second coming in glorious majesty to judge the world, the earth and the sea shall give up their dead; and the corruptible bodies of those who sleep in him shall be changed, and made like unto his glorious body; according to the mighty working whereby he is able to subdue all things to himself."

There, in front of St. George's Chapel, Meg Grant stood beside her cousin and tossed dirt upon the coffin. Bagpipes played as they had for Major Tilson, who had rested in that earth for almost five years. The flags of Great Britain and the United States whipped in the wind. Then, after a moment of silence, the shovels began their work. The people turned to go.

Elizabeth Cavendar, standing near the back of the crowd with Cassandra Tyler and her husband, shook her head. "He was a fine man, he was," she said.

"I thought you didn't like him," said Cassandra mildly.

"He had all the arrogance of the Saxon," she replied. "But he had all the greatness, too. And – " she gestured to the two dogs that stood next to Meg Grant, whimpering as the dirt covered their master, "a man who can gain the love of an animal, he can't be all bad."

From her carriage Cynthia Witley, too, watched the burial of George Grant and the mourning of his niece at the grave. "'*Break not, O woman's-heart, but still endure . . . Remembering all the beauty of that star/ Which shone so close beside thee,*'" she murmured.

"I say, what?" said her husband.

"You'll call me a fool, Henry," she said after a minute, "but I sometimes feel I bear some blame for that man's death."

"What? Preposterous! Why, the fellow wouldn't even come to our parties anymore! Damned high and mighty of him."

"No," she said. "He would not come." Then, as an afterthought, "He was ill, Henry."

Witley kicked at the grass under the wheel where he stood. "Oh, he was a decent enough man, as men go."

"'*Ideal manhood closed in real man,*'" she whispered.

"Stuff and nonsense," he said, climbing into the seat beside her and putting on his hat. "Don't get carried away, my dear."

So, she did not. And, two weeks later, she broke a bottle of champagne over *The Jolly West*, a pleasure yacht of white and mahogany and brass that was lowered into the newly dammed Victoria Creek amid much clapping and laughter. Hared, the butler, costumed in the spanking duds of a riverboat pilot, stood at the helm. "Un-moor," he called out with great aplomb, "and strike for shore!"

For a moment the small steamer stood, belching smoke and shining on the waters. Then, unballasted, she suddenly tipped. The intrepid captain, Mr. Witley, Mrs. Witley, and fifteen of their guests plunged into brine.

"By God, Hared," sputtered Mr. Witley, "I told you to keep that quid in the middle of your mouth!"

"What, sir? Oh, yes, sir."

"And how dare you stand there dripping when Mrs. Witley is still in the water! Don't you know, fool, that the captain always goes down with the ship?"

Thus the maiden voyage of *The Jolly West*.

Chapter XVII

The *Jolly West* sent its smoke billowing into the sky above Victoria Creek all summer long. Its deck was the site of wild card parties with local soldiers and bets based on who could shoot the most jackrabbits from the water. There were excursions, and picnics, and even a theatrical starring, of course, Cynthia Witley. She became Queen of the Creek and enjoyed herself immensely. With the Randalls gone and Mr. Grant dead, she felt safe and breathed deeply for the first time in many months.

The Newlands did not take part in these festivities. Occasionally, from a distance, William watched the boat pushing its way up the dammed creek. But he said nothing about what he saw and spent most days in the fields with Red Thompson. His hair grew golden in the sunlight, his arms brown, and he sometimes laughed. He joined Neil Hunter at political meetings in Hays, where he was amused, if not impressed, by the fervor of American politics and the hatred between Republicans and Democrats. "The Liberals and the Tories are simply nothing to it," he said to Beryl. He retained the role of observer, however, and surprised himself by refusing to participate in party activity when asked. "It seems pointless," he said to Beryl.

"But this might be your chance to make a difference, to get involved."

"I don't know, Beryl. I'm just not interested." He did not explain that he was beginning to wish he had left Kansas with Robert and Marian.

For although Will worked and laughed, the unhappiness had not left his eyes. It had instead evolved into a bitterness that gave an unpleasant edge to his laughter, a certain triumph to his stories of others' trouble. At times fierce melancholy assailed him, and he rode to Hays City where he spent self-absorbed hours confiding to a brown-eyed barmaid named Emily, who actually believed that he was the tragic hero he portrayed himself as and who fell helplessly, hopelessly in love with him. When these confessions failed to purge him of his demons, he disappeared onto the prairie for days. Until the fit passed, he seemed rootless: lost, unable to focus on anything. He no longer drank, and he was no longer in love with Cynthia Witley, but part of him had been sliced away like a dead limb. When the ghost feelings came upon him, he seemed driven to seek what he'd lost along with his love – his idealism, his ambition, his belief in himself. These things eluded him. He came home hollow, as hollow as he had left it.

But wandering numbed him somehow, so that he was able to bury himself in farm work until he almost believed that he was whole again. Then the dead thing pricked and stung as if it still lived – and he was sent hunting once again. After several of these episodes, Will began to believe that perhaps the part of himself that he had lost could only be found at home, somewhere in England.

He missed George Grant. Mr. Grant had believed in him and encouraged him, had, in a distant way, been a father to him. The struggle and the fight to make things work had seemed worthwhile as long as Mr. Grant was there to see it, to cheer him on and to crown him with praise when he won the battle. But there was no one now whom Will Newland wanted to impress. The struggle to succeed seemed pointless. The land frustrated him as Cynthia Witley had frustrated him: seducing him with promises and then inscrutably withdrawing; impervious to his devotion, to the theories that should explain her and the methods that should win her. His failure as a gentleman farmer and his failure as a lover all seemed one to him. Had he lived, Mr. Grant might have been able to convince him otherwise. But Mr. Grant was dead, and Will Newland retained the egotism that made it difficult to convince him his conclusions about anything might be wrong.

Beryl was not heartbroken by Mr. Grant's death. She had been too shattered by her experience with Vonfeldt to have anything left to break. She felt the void where he had been, however; she felt that she could have loved him had he lived and had she been given time to heal. Not as she had loved Anton – that was a passion separate, irreplaceable, that she was certain could never come again. But she had revered Mr. Grant despite his flaws, and she had been gladdened by the idea that she could comfort him. She understood the way he felt about Kansas. The expansive horizon, the limitless sky, had begun to grip her as it had him. Further, and not least, this charismatic merchant and cattleman had also seemed to promise a protection from the world that appealed to her. She could, she had believed, hide in him.

When he died, she faced the fact that there are no hiding places on this earth; that life and pain and the power that we call God always find and uncover us. In the first few moments after Richard Cabot came with news of Grant's death, she had felt not grief but a white, blinding terror. She was unable to catch her breath; her heart pounded. She reached for Mr. Cabot's hand with the clutch of someone drowning. But the panic passed along with the hours of grief, replaced by a defiant anger that made her, at Mr. Grant's funeral, appear to those who did not know her (and to many who did) neither beautiful nor young, but strangely strong and stern. She did not cry. She stood tall next to her brother and James Avery, her chin high and her grey eyes hard and clear under the black veil. On her right hand, a red garnet shone like blood. She would cower no more.

She worked with Douglas Keith through the long hot days of June and July. She was scarcely hindered by her helpless left hand. She was present at the birthing of lambs and the shearing of sheep; she watched the branding and helped with the butchering of an ewe which had been wounded in a fall. She struggled to make sense of what she saw and experienced during those dusty days, struggled against the backdrop of all she had seen and suffered since coming to this place. Words came to her, hovering like a descant over the rhythm of the work, the smell and the cry of the creatures: *He was oppressed, and he was afflicted yet he opened not his mouth: he is brought as a lamb to the slaughter, and as a sheep before her shearers is dumb, so he openeth not his mouth.* She did not run from the blood and the suffering. She silently watched it, studied it, sought to understand it: the meaning for it, the necessity of it. *He was a man of sorrows and acquainted with grief: and we hid as it were our faces from him; he was despised, and we esteemed him not.* She tasted blood and sweat, watched the fear in a dying animal's eyes and the unbounded trust in those of an infant. *He shall feed his flock like a shepherd: he shall gather the lambs with his arm, and carry them in his bosom, and shall gently lead those that are with young.* She wandered among the bleating animals, Grant's collie by her side, and let the wind and sun burn her face and bare arms. She gazed into the glare of the midday sky until she was almost blind and stared into the distant reaches of clouds that piled themselves in glowing layers to the edge of sunset. *Who hath measured the waters in the hollow of his hand, and meted out heaven with the span, and comprehended the dust of the earth in a measure, and weighed the mountains in scales, and the hills in the balance?* Avery carved her a shepherd's crook and called her "Mary Had a Little Lamb," which made her laugh. But she took the crook out with her to watch the animals along with a gun. *He giveth power to the faint; and to them that have no might he increaseth strength. Even the youths shall faint and be weary, and the young men shall utterly fall. But they that wait upon the Lord shall renew their strength; they shall mount up with wings as eagles; they shall run and not be weary; they shall walk and not faint.*

She shot three rattlesnakes that summer, and one coyote.

When Vincent Spenser saw her again upon his return to America, he scarcely recognized her. "What happened to her?" he asked Mr. Keith.

Keith turned to him, puzzled. "What would you be meanin'? She's quite well – doesn't she seem so to you?"

"Well? She's brown as a milkmaid, walks like a boy, and dresses like a devotee of Oscar Wilde. She's positively splendid!"

Keith laughed. "Aye, that she is. I expect her to be taking up a pipe next."

Spenser raised his dark eyebrows, but Keith did not explain. After a moment, Spenser asked, "And underneath?"

Keith leaned against the door of the stable, took off his hat, and rubbed his neck with a weary hand. "She sits in the evening on the veranda and looks east, listening to the bells the man gave her. I don't think it's England that she looks toward."

There was a moment of silence. "I heard Grant wanted to marry her."

"It's been said. He never told me so."

"But she wears the ring?"

"You must ask her about it yourself, Mr. Spenser," said Keith shortly, putting on his hat. "It's none of my business."

"No, I s'pose not," said Spenser. "Good day then, Keith."

"Good day, sir," said Keith. He watched Lord Herries' son ride toward the hill where Beryl roamed with the sheep and then turned back to his work. The tall Scot spent a long time currying Beryl's pony that afternoon, so long that even his dog began giving him quizzical looks. The creature shone by the time Keith got on his own neglected-looking mount to help Beryl bring in the herd. As he rode toward her through the slanting light, he heard the singing bells follow him. He wondered at the beauty of the sound.

Ye Merry Cricketeers, their ladies, and their guests (assorted dignitaries from Hays City, Ellis, and Russell) all raised their glasses in a toast to Queen Victoria on July 1st, the anniversary of her coronation. They were assembled under a spacious tent, eighty of them all at one table, after a riveting cricket match where one man (Jason Mayes) was accidentally cracked on the arm with a mallet and where another (Thomas Carrigan) slid from his pony and only narrowly escaped being trampled. The excitement had died down; all were subdued now as Vincent Spenser stood, dark-haired and handsome, and lifted his sparkling goblet. "To the health of the Queen."

"To the health of the Queen," echoed the people, their glasses clinking. Then there followed a strange silence. The colonists were quiet, a few sipping from their glasses, one or two men clearing their throats. A hot wind pushed through the assembly; the edges of the great white tent flapped and snapped. Flies buzzed and circled, careening away from the busy fans of the ladies. The opulence of the feast (jewel-toned fruits, steaming vegetables, and succulent roasts that made a joke of the fresh peas and cornbread that had greeted Vincent Spenser when he first came to Victoria), the glitter of silver and crystal, gems and satin, none of it could fill that silence. The place, for a moment, seemed empty and abandoned: a ghost town where people have lived and loved and died leaving nothing but rusty tins, tattered curtains, and the swinging of knobless doors.

Leslie Edwards, Grant's secretary, was near tears — and that without having touched a glass of liquor. Meg Grant kept looking out toward the Manor House, as though any minute she expected someone to emerge; to come striding down across the tracks and over the blowing grasses; to join the party, to bring it back to life. It was, after all, his party, and his town, and his queen. But no one came. Just the wind – "And like a spook it was, sure," said Jane MacDonough to her husband that night after she tucked Victoria in to bed. "I've never thought to be so frightened in the middle of the day."

Daniel kicked away his boots. "Are you believing in ghosts now, Janie?"

"I've always believed in spirits, Daniel. And Mr. Grant – he was so big somehow. Dead though he is, I felt that he was more present this afternoon at the celebration than most of us who are alive."

"I wish you wouldn't talk that way."

She did not seem to hear him. She leaned against the pillow, her black hair spreading thickly over her shoulders, her eyes looking toward the dark window. "There are so many who are gone. I seem to hear them calling sometimes and feel I must answer. But, of course, I can't."

"Why not?" he asked uneasily.

"Because I am here, and they are there."

"They are where?"

"In the churchyard."

Daniel threw his suspenders against the dresser. The metal fastenings cracked into the mirror and knocked a hairbrush to the floor. The homestead was doing well. He was proving an astute stockman, and his share in Thomas Carrigan's meat market was bringing dividends. But damned if he was going to stay in this place and watch his wife lose her mind. After being well and strong for so long, she had, since spring, become thin and distant. Even Julia Hunter noticed it. And now this talk when another child was on the way. "We're going back to Scotland, Jane. You're growing morbid and sickly. I can't bear to hear you. You need to be home with your mother when the next bairn comes."

Jane looked at him and laughed lightly. "I'm quite all right. I just feel things sometimes, and you're the only one I can tell. I'm sorry they make you unhappy. You shouldn't worry so."

"Talk about churchyards and ghosts!" Daniel tore the covers back from the bed angrily.

Jane hugged her knees to her chin. "We can't go home, Danny. Home is here now. But I won't talk anymore if it's a bother to you. I just miss Mr. Grant, that's all. We all do. Probably that's what I felt this afternoon."

"Probably," he said, reaching for her and holding her thin body against his. He felt in a measure reassured. She knew this, so she did not tell him what else she had sensed that afternoon: that she would not be present at another celebration for Queen Victoria. That the reason she felt those who were gone so strongly was because they were coming for her; and that when the web of childbirth again wrapped itself around her, she would not escape. That other queen would weave her and her unborn child into the darkness, taking them to the black, dry ground where Mr. Grant lay, restless; and above them the winter winds would howl to the endless and unabating grief of her husband.

She kissed him and then rose to shut the window against the dark.

Autumn came. Anniversaries passed, some that Beryl treasured, others that she wished she could forget. Anton Vonfeldt was married now. She had heard this from Vincent Spenser. He was still in Russia, or so the Germans said. Consciously, she did not dwell on him. She kept busy during the day, working with the sheep, harvesting the garden, keeping up the house, and visiting back and forth with Meg Grant. Unconsciously, he seemed to be always with her. She closed her eyes at night and heard his music, saw his pale eyes through mists of snow, and felt his arms around her. These dreams always ended with a harsh cry that tore her awake and left her alone. She cradled her broken hand in the darkness and wondered why the voice which woke her was never her brother's, as it had been in life, but was always that of George Grant. Then she lay back down and prayed for George Grant and Anton Vonfeldt both, because her lover had once told her that when we dream of the living, and especially when we dream of the dead, they are appealing for our prayers. She did not worry over the theology of this; she merely observed to herself (rather wryly) that both men seemed voracious in their demand for heavenly aid.

One morning she woke early to find the wind whipping cold rain against the house, making the bells outside jangle furiously. When she went to her window and opened the shutter, she saw that the sky was grey like winter and that night still clung to the edges of the land. Abruptly, suddenly, a frantic desire such as she had not allowed herself to feel in months gripped her. She touched the glass with her dead hand, whispering Anton's name over and over, waiting for a sunrise that would not be coming that day. The uncanny light, the driving rain, the distant jangling of those too-sweet bells seemed to beat her stupid. Minutes passed, and then a quarter of an hour. She felt dizzy and desperate. She sobbed and began banging at the panes. Then — as though she were looking through a kaleidoscope that someone turned, shifting the pattern into weird, jagged prisms — the room went queer.

The pistol. The pistol she had used to kill snakes, to kill a coyote.

She ran in her nightdress from her bedroom to the kitchen. For a moment she saw Anton there, tearing open drawers and cupboards in a frenzied search for whiskey and sugar. Then all was grey and dark. She found the barn coat she had taken to wearing in the lean-to — a man's coat with deep pockets — and she reached into one of them, her right hand slipping into the blackness, feeling for oblivion.

Instead, she felt metal, cold as ice.

Involuntarily, she drew back her hand. She stood there, hearing the rain and the wind and that crazy jangling. "That way madness lies," she whispered. And above the wind and rain, she heard the scream of Mary Ramsay, the scream of the Wild Huntress of the Plains who raced with the buffalo, her blue robe flying, her mouth fallen open like the jaws of the dead.

Five minutes she stood there, listening and looking in the blackness, feeling her heart pound heavy and hard like an old, overwound clock. Then she pushed open the back door and went into the storm. Her unshod feet slipped on the mud; the rain hammered her bare head. She climbed up the cellar door and stopped, leaning against the house, realizing that she could not reach the bells and hold on at the same time. She had only one good hand. She swore and screamed. Then, determined, she reached out for the bracket where the bells hung with her right hand. The rain and the wind were blinding, her balance precarious, but she could feel where the nail had been driven in under the eaves, and she felt the edge of the chain by which the bells were suspended. She let her fingers run over the bracket, examining where the chain was attached. When she was sure, she grabbed and pulled. The bells fell to the muddy ground.

Carefully, she crept back down the cellar door. She clutched at the bells. Like the gun, they were icy to touch. She held them under her left arm, slogged her way back to the kitchen door, and pulled open the latch.

Then she was inside the lean-to, dripping, her teeth chattering, the collie barking at her, pushing his warm fur against her frozen hands. She let herself fall, resting on the dog for a moment. She was so cold. But she was also alone. Will had disappeared again for one of his "hunts."

After a few moments she went to the stove, teeth still chattering, and stoked the drowsy fire. She added more wood. As the room began to warm, she peeled away her soaking nightgown and threw it in a corner. She took a kitchen towel and rubbed herself as dry as she could, rubbed until her skin stung, the collie circling her and whining. Then she crouched, naked, before the red heat of the stove, winding her arms around the dog's neck. The storm continued, as did the wind and the rain. But the bells were silent, and she felt she could breathe.

After some time, she rose and went to the bedroom, where she dressed and wrapped herself in a shawl. She returned to the kitchen and put a kettle on the stove. She gave the collie a bit of dried bread and meat, and then she went to the lean-to and picked up the bells. She washed them in a basin and polished them until they shone. She sat down and looked at them shining in her lap. Then she kissed them, softly, sensuously, feeling not the cold metal but the warm lips of her lost lover. She cried, but without sobbing. After several minutes she carried the bells and a lamp to her bedroom, and there she opened the great trunk which she had brought from England. In it were some linens, some special items of her mother's, Vonfeldt's violin in its case, and a small volume of Elizabeth Barrett Browning with an orange pamphlet tucked into it. She pulled out the pamphlet. Five years in Kansas and she hadn't seen any grapes worth making wine from yet. It almost made her laugh. Then she opened the book of poems, seeking the page which, in a distant world, had given voice to another lonely soul. "*Go from me. But hence-forward I live in Thy Shadow . . .*"

She read through the poem, then put the book down. She took a long piece of fine white muslin from the trunk and unfolded it on the floor. Gently she raised the bells, listening to them sing and watching them glint in the lamplight. Then she muffled them on the muslin, laid the book on top of them, and folded the cloth carefully around it all. When she was done, she tied the bundle with a piece of blue string and placed it in a corner of the big trunk, next to the violin case.

She sat there, still for a moment, gazing at her hands while the collie nuzzled her. Then, using her mouth, she pulled the garnet ring from her right forefinger. It fell to her lap. The stone glowed in the lamplight; something of the life of its original owner seemed to flame in its depths. She lifted it in her hand, kissed it (with reverence rather than passion), reached into the trunk and tucked it into one of the folds of the newly made bundle. Then she stood, closed the trunk, called the dog to follow her, and returned to the kitchen.

There she had a cup of tea and made three loaves of bread, taking pleasure in the living warmth of the dough against both hands, the one that kneaded as well as the one that rested maimed. She baked the loaves, and their fragrance filled the little house. After the rain stopped, she took two of them, carefully stowing them into a bag on her saddle, and rode to the Villa, where she presented them to Meg.

"For your wedding breakfast," she said.

Meg Grant married Ian Duncan in St. George's chapel on October 18, 1878. Had her uncle been alive, the wedding would have been celebrated with pageantry and pomp; instead, it was a quiet ceremony. The tangle of George Grant's estate was just beginning to come undone, but it was already clear that, appearances to the contrary, he had not prospered in his livestock operations. The debts were many and massive; much would have to be sold to clear the board. Meg had the villa and £5,000 as her dowry. Her husband cared little about such things, but he was a sensible man who knew to be glad that she had something to her name. There were no displays of jewels and silver for the wedding, no grand spectacle with court-length trains and dozens of bridesmaids. Meg wore a simple cream-colored gown, her husband a dark suit. Beryl Newland and Douglas Keith stood up for the couple; Clay Grant, Leslie Edwards, and Ben Davis were sole guests at the ceremony. Neil and Julia Hunter, the Spenser Brothers, and Will Newland came along to the wedding breakfast at the Alma House. Then everyone went home to work. There was no dance and no party. Meg put her mourning back on a few hours after the wedding and accompanied her husband to one of Grant's large stables, where he presented her with his wedding gift: a jersey cow and calf, and a new spaniel pup. She was delighted. They had a cold supper of ham and bread, then shyly retired to her room, where they made love.

At 4:30 a.m. they were disturbed by the drunken cheers and cat-calls of the Spenser brothers and Ben Davis. Duncan tore open the window, shoved out his great curly head, and told the revelers that they made a sorry excuse for a shivaree; that when they married, he'd show them how the thing should be done proper; and that if they didn't shut their damn mouths, he'd set the dogs on them. On the other hand, if they'd come into the house peaceably, like gentlemen, he and his bride could offer them a hot breakfast and coffee so strong it was guaranteed to sober them up in five minutes flat. Vincent needed some persuading, not being quite sure that he was ready to get sober. But reason prevailed, and the three men joined the bride and groom for eggs, tomatoes, and ham just as the sun came over the horizon.

It was a testimony to her good nature that Meg considered this all great fun. Duncan recognized his fortune in such a wife, and he prized her accordingly.

The subdued wedding of Meg Grant to Ian Duncan was largely the result of their own wish for privacy and no fuss, but it was also symptomatic of a certain fracturing of community that occurred with Grant's death. Ye Merry Cricketeers continued their matches; dances were held weekly at the schoolhouse as they had been for the last two years; the Victoria Hunt Club went on excursions that demanded elaborate costuming and much baying of hounds and men; but the group spirit of the colony, perhaps tenuous in the best of times, was disintegrating. The colonists quarreled over water rights and property lines and bickered about the governance of the town. They complained about the weather, about the Russian immigrants and the American settlers, and about the ever-dwindling financial support from home. Many grumbled that there was nothing interesting to do; they had hunted and built their fancy houses and lived the wild west life, and now they were bored. People talked of returning to England or migrating elsewhere. A number did more than talk. The Baldwin family was moving east to Lawrence; Ben Davis had plans to go to South Africa; the Petries intended to sail for Australia; and James Avery had determined upon returning to England in the spring along with Jason Mayes and Gerard Staples. Pettimore was considering transferring his lumber operations to Hays City, and Garth Mason thought he might take his livery stable there as well. Discontent and discombobulation grew as people argued over whether to go or stay. The ground beneath the town seemed to shift and heave, making the inhabitants unsteady and uncertain in their course.

The mood grew darker as the rowdier elements of Victoria that Grant had contended against began to break free from his restraining influence. Drinking in the streets became common once dusk fell. There were fist fights over card games and loud arguments about racing bets. Windows were broken by drunken rowdies, causing an uproar among the families living in town. And if the behavior of the sons of England was such in the streets of Victoria, it was far worse in Hays City. Tommy Drumm wrung his hands and wept; when the English got out of control, he no longer had George Grant to go to for reparation. His only recourse was the law, which of course heightened tensions another notch.

Already in September the sense that Victoria was not quite safe anymore, that those who masqueraded as gentlemen might be something less than that, began to pervade the town. In the middle of the month, on a warm windy night when the moon was full, Alec Hunter was riding back from a political meeting in Hays City when he discovered the body of a colonist named John Conlyn in the grassy stretch just west of Victoria. The cause of death could not be determined; it was perhaps aneurysm or heart failure, though that was striking in such a relatively young man. Unsubstantiated rumors of foul play began to spread. Indians could not be blamed; they'd been banished from the area. A renegade soldier from the fort might be responsible. The veterans of the American war were so wild, said some people, that they couldn't get out of the habit of killing. Someone raised the possibility of supernatural agency. When he heard this theory while sitting in his brother's store, Alec, who had been plenty unnerved by the discovery of the dead man, nonetheless burst into whoops of laughter that had people turning their heads all down Main Street.

To prove what he thought of the idea, Alec rode home from the next meeting at Hays by himself, in the deep of night. No ghosts and bogeymen that he could see, he insisted the next day. The most frightening thing he ran into was his new wife who, with every bit as much temper as her sister, lit into him for worrying her just so he could prove he wasn't afraid of monsters. It wasn't the supernatural monsters one had to fear anyway, she said, almost crying. It was the real ones.

"There are no real ones either," Alec told her mildly. "Conlyn died of natural causes, as the good Lord knows. It's all decent folks living in Victoria."

But that assumption was destroyed two weeks after the wedding of Meg Grant.

Cabot and Avery rode to the Newland farm with the news. Will and Beryl were sitting on the porch, resting after the midday meal and enjoying the warmth of a late October sun. She was rubbing tallow into her chapped hands while he read to her from *Harper's Bazaar*. The collie perked up its head at the sound of galloping horses, and the dogs in the yard set up a ruckus of welcome. Will and Beryl stood to greet them.

"Newland, have you heard?"

"What?"

"Murder! In Victoria!"

Beryl sank to her seat.

"Who?"

"Now don't blurt it out all at once, Avery. Let's tell the story straight. We have a captive audience and may as well let them enjoy the suspense."

Avery ignored Cabot. "Oscar Jones. He was playing cards last night in the Manor station room with Nigel Wyatt. They got into an argument; one of them claimed the other was cheating. They were fighting, ripping things up. Neil Hunter and Garth Mason had to pull them apart. Neil thought they were under control; had them shake hands like gentlemen. But then this morning, near the old railroad cemetery, Keith found Jones unconscious."

"The lad hadn't a chance," said Cabot. "Forgive the ugly details, but you'll hear it from others if you don't hear it from us. The boy was stabbed more than once, and his belly was sliced across. Entrails spilled onto the grass like dog food."

"My God," whispered Will.

"He died about an hour ago. The sheriff from Hays is coming in. They're gathering a posse to go after Wyatt. Wanted to know if you'd come, Will."

"A posse! Are they sure it is Wyatt?"

"Quite. Weapon was found in the brush. One of his brothers identified it."

Beryl pulled her shawl close around her shoulders. "The Duncans – do they know?" She had felt vague fears on behalf of Ian and Meg even before the couple were engaged; she knew that Wyatt had threatened Duncan after the latter thwarted his courtship.

"Duncan's already with Keith and the sheriff. Meg is staying with the Hunters. Not likely he'd head for the Villa, but then you never know."

"Let me talk to Thompson, so he can keep an eye out here. I'll come along; I'd like Beryl to come to Victoria. I'd feel better, knowing she's in town."

"How soon can you be ready?"

"Red's in the barn. Couple of minutes to get the horses and some ammunition. They're not waiting for us?"

"Keith, the Hunter brothers, and the sheriff were setting out right away. Mason, Spenser, and a couple of the Russians will meet us. Carrigan and MacDonough have gone with the Wyatt boys, just in case he goes back home. He won't get a brotherly welcome, that's sure."

Beryl spent an anxious afternoon waiting with Meg Grant, the two Mrs. Hunters, and Jane MacDonough in Victoria. To keep busy, they helped Julia dust and take inventory in the store. Beryl counted buttons and spools of thread, wiped jars, and sorted mail. She regretted being indoors away from the blue sky, the falling leaves, the bright air.

Anxiety hung over the town like a cloud of dust. The yellow-gold stones of Victoria's major buildings – the Manor House, the store and stable, St. George's Chapel, the Hunters' home – seemed dulled and dirty, grimly aware of their locked doors, their latched windows, and the bloody corpse that lay stiff and staring in their midst. Not that anyone really expected Wyatt to be lurking in a corner of Victoria. Yet the knowledge that a killer had lodged among them – had walked their streets and eaten at their feasts and danced at their parties and had, like a specter present but unseen, blended easily into the backdrop of their everyday lives – left them unnerved. The brutality of life on the frontier had always been present, but it had seemed outside them. Yankee desperadoes, rogue Arapaho or Comanche, fires, diseases, accidents – all had been threats from beyond the boundaries of their civilized British selfhood. Now they discovered that the savagery and the brutality was with them and in them – and, worse yet, had been so all along. Nigel Wyatt, with his pink rabbity eyes, his white-yellow hair and his painfully pale skin was merely the underbelly of the community exposed. Thrown on its back, Victoria was forced to look at its own ugliness and vulnerability. The disemboweled Oscar Jones, eyes frozen in horror, testified to its weakness, its delusion. Beryl watched Meg stand staring out the window of the store and thanked God that George Grant had not lived to see this day.

They did not find Nigel Wyatt. Like Jack Randall, he disappeared into that expanse of dry, blowing grass without a trace. America is such an easy place, Beryl thought, in which to be swallowed up. To die to your old self and be resurrected as something new, all it took was a new territory, a new town, a new name. And Nigel Wyatt was so much a ghost. One did not see him unless he chose to strike. Even then, he seemed to leave visible only the stain of blood.

The stain would not wash out. Victoria saw her dirty linen hung before the Americans she had felt superior to in the country she had intended to "civilize." The Victoria correspondent for the *Hays City Star* wrote, "Business is at a standstill here except for the coroner."

The Britons cringed and scowled, and those who could not bear the face of Caliban in the mirror began to dust off their trunks and pack their bags. George Grant was dead; the land could not be profitably cultivated with plant or animal; it was time to go home.

"I am not going," said Beryl.

"But you must," said Will. "You can't run the farm by yourself, and you cannot stay out here alone."

"Will, I have been running this farm by myself. You know that. You've been so unhappy that I've had to make decisions and sign documents when I didn't even know where you were. When you go back to England with Mr. Avery, I'll merely be as I have often been during the last couple years." She sighed and looked out at the spring snow melting on the ground. The view from the window was dreary: brown and grey and some trepidatious stalks of infant green under the soggy white. "What's more, I have made money on the sheep venture. Mr. Keith has proven an excellent advisor, and I expect him to remain so. And Red Thompson will stay on. He's loyal and a hard worker. I can depend on them both."

The implied comment on Will's character bit hard. His jaw stiffened, but he felt he could say nothing in response. She went on:

"It's ridiculous for you to decide to go home and just assume that I will come along."

"Robert will be furious with me for leaving you."

"Then don't leave."

"Why should I stay? There's no future! Grubbing in the dirt the rest of my life. Surely a gentleman can do better than that."

Beryl lowered the wick in the lamp. "So you will go home and finish your degree?"

"What, and become a clergyman? I didn't want to do that when I still believed in God; I'm not likely to commit myself to spreading lies now. If I did, I'd turn into an Epis Emerson – doping myself to keep from facing reality. Why you cling to superstition after all you've seen and been through is beyond me. It's a lie."

"Perhaps," said Beryl, playing a scale on the table with her right hand. "I would have agreed with you once. Not so long ago. But as far as I can tell, we all choose our own lie to live by. And unless your lie makes you a better person than mine does me, you'd best leave off assuming your answers are better than mine. Disagree if you must. But don't call me a liar."

Will shifted and stretched his long legs irritably. "At least come home for a visit. I already have the tickets. You must want to see Marian and the children. If you insist on returning here, I'm sure that Robert will allow you to."

Beryl burst into laughter. "As though he – or you – can allow or disallow me anything! I'm twenty-eight years old: no child, and no spinster sister in need of support. But of course if I go home, that is exactly how he – and Marian, and you too – will treat me. When I go home – if I ever go home again – I will decide when. I will buy the ticket. And I will not wait for anyone's permission to return."

"I can't believe you don't care about seeing your niece and nephew."

"Don't play the sentimental uncle to me, Will. For years you haven't even asked about them. I've been writing them regularly, and they've been writing back. And both of them intend to come see me in the United States when they are old enough. Indeed, I shouldn't be surprised if they stay here. Charlie has read enough Mayne Reid books to convince him that there's no better life than life on the frontier." She laughed, a bit sadly.

"Charlie has duties to take up at Lindenhurst. I wouldn't count on him coming to keep his old auntie company in Kansas."

"No, neither would I. On the other hand, when the day comes that he must assume the duties from his father, I'm sure if he chooses to abdicate in favor of his dear Uncle William, Uncle William will not reject becoming Lindenhurst's master."

"I still don't see why you don't come. Victoria is no place to be any more. Nothing happening, nothing growing, nobody coming – and in five years the Russians will have taken over. You'll see. They might be good people, but they're not our people."

This was dangerous territory, and Will knew it. But Beryl only gave a slight shake of her head. She depended very little on others' opinions now. She had fallen in love with a Volga-German immigrant who barely spoke English, and with that love she had learned regard for his people. Anything Will might have to say was unimportant, because he could touch neither her feeling for Anton Vonfeldt nor her gratitude to the woman from Herzog who had saved her hand. They were not her people, but they could have been in a differently ordered world.

"Many are staying on. The Hunters, the Duncans, the Spensers, Mr. Cabot."

"Cabot is not. He's going home with me and Avery."

Beryl smiled and raised her eyebrows. "He's going home to bring back his bride. He's marrying his cousin, Elinor Standish. She's agreed to come out and ranch with him. He's not going home to stay."

"No," said Will in amazement. "He didn't tell me."

"You didn't seem interested. But he told me. I think he thinks it will redeem him somehow."

"Redeem him? It'll be his damnation. A man like him shouldn't marry."

"Not if he has been leading the life he's led us all to believe. But Meg suspects – don't ask me on what basis – and Jane Mac-Donough has maintained for years that he's not quite the devil he pretends to be."

Will shook his head. "I wouldn't want you marrying him."

"I'm not. But if he is a good husband, and I rather think he might be, then I'm hopeful for their happiness. And I shall be glad that they are here."

Will was silent. It galled him to think that Cabot had not only done fairly well in Kansas, but that he was sticking it out when Will had determined on moving back to England. He leaned back in his chair, his right leg bouncing up and down. After a moment he said, "Forget Cabot. Come home, Beryl."

Beryl walked from the table and put her cloak on. Then she went toward the back door. "Will, I'm staying. There is nothing more to be said. Now I must go see after the livestock."

"You don't care about me at all, do you?" said Will, something between anger and anguish rising in his voice. "All you care for is yourself. You wouldn't even be here if it weren't for me."

She stopped and turned, her face somber in the brown hood of the cloak. "Of course I care about you. I have always cared about you, ever since you were little. After father died, when I was alone in London, I longed for your visits from Oxford. I sat in the parlor listening to the rain, listening to the carriages passing, listening for your footstep, and praying you would come, so there would be life in the house again. But I cannot keep waiting for you to come home, for you to pay attention, for you to approve. I can be apart from you and still love you. But I cannot be dependent on you and live."

She went out and shut the door behind her, leaving him alone in the shadows with the guttering fire and the quiet ticking of a clock.

"You didn't tell him then?" Keith was incredulous.

"I wrote a letter to him and Robert; he'll find it when he gets home. But there was no reason to tell him while he was here. I wasn't totally sure I would sell, and it would just have made for more arguing."

The goodbye had been hard enough as it was. Will left much in the cottage he had built for them, but his trunk was packed, his books removed from the shelves, his papers gone from his room, and the bureau empty except for an old hat and pair of Levis. He left worn but still sturdy boots in the corner for Beryl to use on the farm. When he walked into the parlor and saw her, standing quiet and stern in her grey dress and brown cloak, he was angry at how implacable she seemed. But when she turned and looked at him, her good hand resting on the piano, her clear eyes clouded by tears, he broke down. He remembered when he was little, and she used to bundle him in a nursery blanket and make up stories in which he was always the hero. As he silently drove the wagon carrying his sister, James Avery, and Richard Cabot to Victoria Station, he wondered whether without her to make him the hero he could ever believe in happy endings again.

James Avery almost never looked at Beryl while they waited for the train. He complained that the drizzle would ruin the plush of his buffalo skin coat, which he had purchased specially to impress his mama and his turnip-faced cousin. He intended to tell them that he had shot the buffalo himself and hoped against hope that the odious girl (his cousin, not his mother) would not notice the insect holes suggesting a vintage significantly prior to his gun-toting days. He munched a bag of biscuits and shared several with the dog who always haunted the platform. He bewailed the fact that on the return trip they would not be going through New Orleans (he still regretted the basket of crabs he had been dissuaded from bringing on the way out) and wondered if they would have time to see George Grant's buildings in Chicago. In short, he chattered as he hadn't chattered in years. Cabot smoked and made sardonic comments every now and then. He avoided looking at Avery; he didn't want to see the pain in his eyes.

Newland stood with his hands buried deep in his pockets, staring to the west where the Kansas Pacific train was coming. When it screeched into the station, loud and noisy, he clasped Beryl convulsively and then rushed into the car, his eyes wet. He could hardly bear leaving his sister behind. He could bear even less the expression on Cynthia Witley's face, which had appeared for an instant, framed by soft fur, in the window of the station house. The scorching love he had felt for her flared up, singing him with the realization that she hated to see him go not because she had loved him, but because sacrificing his devotion had been the one good thing she had done since coming to this place.

Cabot shook hands gravely with Beryl; he was confident of seeing her again. Then Avery was left with her, the dust and smoke swirling over the platform. He struck a manly pose before her, his handsomely booted foot sticking from beneath the long coat like a dancer's, the rifle in his left hand poised at the sky in a menacing manner. He made an elaborate bow, his brown hair flying into his eyes and his hat – which he had decorated with three "Indian" feathers – threatening to fall to the ground. But when he dared at last to look at Beryl's face, all pretenses fell away. He threw his arms around her and whispered a desperate, "I say, God bless you, dearest Beryl."

That should have been a highly affecting moment. But when Avery threw his arms around her, he dropped the rifle and it went off, sending crows screaming from the gables of the manor house; dogs (and several would-be passengers) scurrying for cover; and the station master's wrathful oaths upon his own head. Thus, Beryl's last view of James Avery was not that of the tender and broken-hearted fellow he was. Bowing and apologizing, he stumbled into the car, threatening to set the gun off again (several people, including Cabot, dove behind their seats), and letting out a volley of expletives when the scones Beryl had made for him got crushed beneath one of his very handsome – and rather too tight – cowboy boots.

But Cabot was no more likely to see Beryl Newland again than James Avery, or even William Newland. Before leaving Victoria, Will transferred complete ownership of the farm to Beryl. Two weeks after he had left, Beryl Newland sold it, including the buildings, the chickens, a cow, and all but fifty of the sheep, to Jacob Hoffman, a Volga German who had done well since coming to Kansas and hoped to do even better.

Hoffman was driving away with Vincent Spenser after inspecting the property when Douglas Keith spoke to Beryl about the sale. "I'm still surprised at you, not telling your brother. 'Twas a bold thing to do."

"I've gotten rather bold, I suppose. But I wasn't sure I would sell," said Beryl, walking down the road to watch the wagon with Spenser and Hoffman in it drive away.

The morning was bright, much like the day when Keith had first brought the Newlands to their land. To the east, he could see the plain where the antelope had grazed. Mr. Grant's rage at the abandonment of Beryl Newland still rang in Keith's ears. Well, never again, he thought. It was a pity, her selling this farm. She and Will – mostly she – had made it into a valuable piece of property. He would not have thought it possible of the girl who, wearing a ridiculously fashionable riding habit, had almost fallen from her pony not once but three times on her way to the place she would call home.

"I wonder how bold you've really become."

Beryl stopped and looked at him, shading her eyes from the sun with her hand.

He leaned against a fence under the lonely cottonwood and folded his arms. "Many folks are leaving."

She joined him in the shade. "Yes, that's true."

"Mr. Grant would take it hard, could he know."

She shook her head a little. "I'm not so sure. He was a man who believed in dreams. His dream couldn't be everyone's."

"Ben Davis goes to South Africa. You knew that?"

"Yes, I heard. Is he going for diamonds?"

"Maybe. Or he talks about starting an ostrich farm on the veldt."

"An ostrich farm! How exotic." She laughed.

A breeze blew from the south. The greening trees opened their branches to it.

"He's asked me to go along."

"He has? What an adventure! Though – I was rather counting on your help."

"What help would you need with the ranch gone?"

She didn't answer, just shrugged, gazing toward the shadows of the Smoky Hills with a vexed expression. He watched her, unfolding his arms and putting them against the fence. After a moment he turned his eyes to the faraway hills as well.

"What would you think of such an adventure?"

"You mean Africa?"

He nodded, keeping his gaze on the horizon. "I wonder if you'd like to accompany us. Accompany me."

"Africa?" she said again.

He laughed and at last turned to face her. "Yes, Africa." He paused a moment, took off his hat, and then said. "I was wondering if you'd like to come as my wife."

Her silence felt long. A meadowlark trilled. The collie, who had been lying on the porch, stretched and sauntered down the road to join the people under the tree. He sniffed at the grass. Keith reached down and petted him. The man's long, lean face was calm. He waited.

"I'm going west, Mr. Keith. To a place called South Park. In the Rockies. It's good ranching country, I've heard. I like ranching. I like sheep. And I want to see the mountains. Mr. Cabot and Mr. Avery say they are very beautiful."

"You got this idea from them? You can ranch here."

"I love it here. But I can't stay anymore."

"Why not?"

She didn't say anything. She just shook her head.

"Then why not come to Africa with me?"

She folded her arms tight against her shawl. The black hair blew across her face; she pushed it back with her good hand. "Because I can't, Mr. Keith. Just – something in the wind is calling me. I can't say more than that. Even to myself. I'm sorry."

The tall, quiet Scot said little at this rejection. His face merely grew grave, and some of the light faded in his brown eyes. He stroked the collie gently. "I'm sorry too," he said at last. "You've become a fine figure of a woman. None finer." He almost smiled but couldn't quite. "But I'll not bother you with it, lass. And you just let me know how I can help you get ready for your leaving."

He walked away, the collie looking after him with a cocked head.

Beryl put her hand on the fence where his had been and stared into the sky. She saw the clouds drifting along with the wind. Far away they cast great shadows that paced over the land slowly, the sure and unceasing footsteps of time. Where they passed, they left no mark. The greening land moved from grey to gold with no other comment than that of a lark which raised its voice in joy at the resurgent sunlight.

"Mr. Keith!"

He turned.

"Come with me."

He stood still. The breeze ruffled his russet hair. "What do you mean?"

"I'm asking you to come with me. West. If you like." She faltered a bit.

He gripped his hat hard in his hand. "But I'm bound for Africa."

"Come to Colorado."

He took a step toward her. He did not speak for a moment and then asked, "But what is there for me in Colorado, Miss Newland?"

"Oh, Mr. Keith! Douglas!" She reached out to him, her face shining like the morning. "Everything, everything! And you know – they say that the very air is like champagne!"

The End

George Grant, 1871
Photo courtesy of the Kansas State Historical Society

*The Victoria Colony -
Cast of Characters*

The Newland Family & Friends

Beryl Newland – only daughter of Warren and Eleanor Newland

William (Will) Newland - youngest son of Warren and Eleanor Newland; Oxford student

Robert Newland – eldest son of Warren and Eleanor Newland; member of Parliament; heir of Lindenhurst

Marian Newland – his pretty; well-dressed wife

Charlie Newland – their 8-year-old son

Beatrice Newland – their daughter

Warren Newland – master of Lindenhurst; an avid amateur paleontologist

Eleanor Newland – his devoted, commonsense wife

Rev. Sealey – rector of the Lindenhurst chapel

Mrs. Sealey – his loquacious, gossip-loving wife

Captain Bradley Denton – friend of Robert; admirer of Beryl

Original Colonists

George Grant – Scottish silk merchant; investor in western American railroads and settlements

Leslie Edwards - Grant's bespectacled secretary

Douglas Keith – one of Grant's three Scottish foremen; agricultural manager and friend of the young Newlands

Ian Duncan – Grant's burly foreman in charge of livestock

Ben Davis – Grant's practical, good-humored youngest foreman

Meg Grant – Grant's teenage niece; close friend of Beryl

Clay Grant - Grant's teenage nephew

Lydia Randall – daughter of Lord Stannard; pale and self-deprecating

Jack Randall – her truculent husband

Christopher Randall – their only child

James Avery – comical dandy, friend of Will Newland

Richard Cabot – wealthy friend of Will Newland; reputation of a roué

Garth Mason – a genial naturalist in charge of Victoria stables

Daniel MacDonough – young Scot, devoted to his wife

Jane MacDonough – a woman haunted

Victoria MacDonough – their first child

Neil Hunter – owner and manager of Victoria's first general store

John Baldwin – father of a big family; committed homesteader

Sarah Baldwin – John's wife; mother of three boys & two girls

Neville Baldwin – eldest son of John and Sarah

Thomas Baldwin – Neville's preschool-aged brother

Elijah Baldwin – youngest of the Baldwin children

Gerard Staples – an Englishman who makes the wagon journey to Victoria with Ben Davis

Jason Mayes – towheaded heir to a Derbyshire estate; frequently inebriated

Nigel Wyatt – a rabbit-faced man with violent tendencies

Frederic Wyatt and Stanley Wyatt – Nigel's more amiable older brothers

Mr. Pettimore – sawmill and lumber merchant

Oscar Jones – a Londoner with relatives in New York state

Andrew Miles – Oscar's fellow-Londoner and comrade

Michael Fletcher – a man of ill luck with horses

Later Arrivals

The Seth Family – parents with 6 children from Elgin, Scotland

Captain Charles Prescott – son of the late Sir George Prescott of Kent; raises Lincoln sheep

Major Tilson – friendly bagpiper from Her Majesty's 42nd Highlanders

Julia Hunter – Neil's pretty, opinionated wife

Alec Hunter – Neil's younger, consumptive brother

Vincent Spenser – wealthy, Catholic Briton of high ideals; hounded by personal demons

Richard Manley – manservant to Vincent Spenser

Oscar Tabermann – Spenser's French chef

Bernard Spenser – Vincent's brother; a steadying influence

Lord Petrie – British aristocrat from Argentina, raising cashmere goats

Angelina Petrie – Lord Petrie's titled wife

Michael & John Gunther – prospective colonists; sons of the New York City mayor

Rev. Epis Emerson – Episcopal priest sent by the bishop to serve the Victoria colonists

The Volga Germans

Franz & Henry Geist, Andreas Herman, Franz Krause, Peter Hoffmeister, Johannes Storm, and **Joseph Braun** – farmers who greet the Spenser brothers when they first ride to Herzog

Nicholas Hammerschmidt – first of the immigrants from Russia to welcome Britons into his home

Anton Vonfeldt – young violinist and hired hand

Peter Dreiling & Martina Brungardt – the first couple to wed in Herzog

Anna Maria Riedel – healer and bonesetter

Hays City and Fort Hays

Tommy Drumm – proprietor of Hays' only "high-class" saloon

Elizabeth Cavendar – Irish American midwife

Rachel Cavendar – Elizabeth's teenage daughter

Dr. Lewis Watson – physician and farmer near town of Ellis

Captain Gerald Walker – respected leader of a regiment of Black soldiers at Fort Hays

Elizabeth "Betsy" Walker – Captain Walker's do-good wife

Arthur Witley – Oldest son of a prominent wine merchant; founder of Mount Halcyon Ranch; great horse lover

Henry Witley – Arthur's younger brother; a man of polished predilections and questionable manners

Cynthia Witley – Henry's seductive wife; daughter of a famous English stage actor

Sheriff Alan Ramsay – young sheriff of Hays

Mary Suzannah Ramsay – the sheriff's wife

Sergeant John Tyler – career Union officer in the American west

Cassandra Tyler – Virginia-born wife of Sergeant Tyler

Dr. Silas Hanson – a Hays physician

Mr. Jameson – a Hays undertaker

ACKNOWLEDGEMENTS

This book grew at the intersection of my scholarly work in Victorian literature and my wonderment that so many of my German forebears called "home" a Kansas town named for an English queen.

For information on its founding, I am particularly indebted to the following histories: *Victoria: The History of a Western Kansas Town* by Marjorie Raish; *At Home in Ellis County, Kansas*, Vol. I, published by the Ellis County Historical Society; *Conquering the Wind* by Amy Toepfer and Agnes Dreiling; and *West of Wichita* by Craig Miner. Special thanks are also due to the Mikkelson Library & Center for Western Studies at Augustana University in Sioux Falls, SD for its financial support and to the Kansas State Historical Society in Topeka, KS for the use of its archives. I wish to acknowledge the intellectual influence of both the late Nina Baym, who directed my Anglo-American dissertation at the University of Illinois, and Martha Vicinus, whose 1996 National Endowment for the Humanities Research Seminar at the University of Michigan encouraged my study of British immigrants in America.

I owe personal and professional thanks to Dr. Laura Bird for her editing help and – most of all – for her abiding friendship. I am grateful to my parents Eveleen and Walter Windholz for teaching me to be proud of our heritage; to my children Nathaniel, Miranda, and Benjamin for showing me what real courage is; and to my husband Mark Van Wienen for tutoring me every day in the wonder of lifelong love.